The Duke of Dubai

Luigi Falconi

The Duke of Dubai
by Luigi Falconi

To order additional copies of this book:

Publisher Page
P.O. Box 52
Terra Alta, WV 26764

Tel/Fax: 800-570-5951
Email: mybook@headlinebooks.com
www.publisherpage.com
www.TheDukeofDubai.com

Publisher Page is an imprint of Headline Books

ISBN: 0-929915-76-3
ISBN 13: 978-0-929915-76-0

Library of Congress Control Number: 2007942535

PRINTED IN THE UNITED STATES OF AMERICA

This Is Dedicated to the Ones We Love

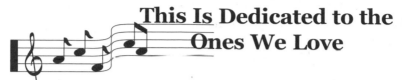

The Shirelles, 1959

Writing is hard work. After struggling for years with this project I have developed a great respect for those not-so-prolific writers who toil much longer than I have on each novel, yet produce a masterpiece every time. It has also changed my opinion of those gifted writers who produce one good book after another. They have the literary gift, but they still work hard to produce the product. Most of all, it has given me the utmost respect for the people who live and work with these writers, putting up with their obsession and acting as enablers, helping them to achieve their goals.

My wife's support has been paramount in helping me through this eight-year odyssey. For over forty years she has been by my side as my friend and traveling companion, giving me the support and love necessary to make it through this journey of life. Thank you.

Family is an intricate part of my life, and my children have proven to be the greatest investment that my wife and I ever could have made. Not only have they put up with my parenting flaws and personal inadequacies to become wonderful adults with wonderful spouses, they have paid me the best dividends possible on our investments, my grandchildren.

Amateur writers rely on professionals to guide them through the intricacies of the written word. Without the editing skills and critical analysis of Sandy Tritt and the many motivational tools made available through her personally and her "Inspiration for Writers" website, I never would have completed my task. After seven years working with Sandy, the final product is so much different than the original, much better and more fun, because of her help.

And my friends, Dubai friends who have come and gone, who have been an inspiration for my characters, let me thank you for being my friends. Being the last of us to still hold down the Dubai fort, I know *The Duke of Dubai* is not what you expected of me and not what you would have liked to see in print, but it is a start. Maybe we can continue. And if I have offended anyone who thinks that he/she was a model for any of my characters, my apologies, but as stated in my novel, my book-people are not real. Remember—this is fiction.

I also thank the Royal family and the Nationals of Dubai, a benevolent and dedicated people who have done marvelous things for their country. Thank you for allowing me to be a guest in your dynamic Emirate. If I have offended any of you great tribesmen, please forgive me and accept this in the spirit of fun, as is the intention of this book.

Luigi Falconi

Table of Contents

Part One
Life in Camel-lot

I Dubai —The Early Daze

II Earning My MABA Degree

III Teaching Is Learning

IV You Play the Hand You're Dealt

V Sam and Abdul

Part Two
Dubai Delight

1974

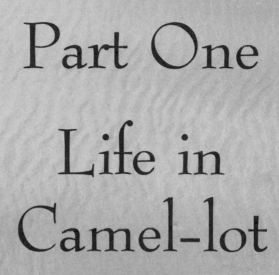

Part One

Life in
Camel-lot

I
Dubai —
The Early Daze

Diving with Medusa

It was just after lunch when Frankie, Josh and I arrived at the Umm Saqueem jetty and unloaded our gear from Josh's yellow Suzuki jeep. There were few large powerboats in Dubai in 1974, so it wasn't hard to spot Tim Johnson, or "the Duke," as most people called him, waving from the back of a 35-foot Bertram.

With the help of several seamen we lugged our tanks and other diving equipment to the boat and loaded everything onboard. After arranging the gear for easy identification when suiting up, we sat down on the blue Naugahyde cushions for what we thought was a brief trip a few miles offshore.

It was pushing 5:00 PM when the Duke slowed the engines to a drift. He walked back from the cockpit and instructed the boatmen to set up the outriggers and bait the fishing poles that were stored on deck.

"What're you doing?" I asked in an uneasy tone. "It'll be dark soon."

"Just thought we may as well take advantage of the calm seas for a little fishin'. We got plenty of time."

As we trawled in an expanding circular pattern my apprehension concerning our underwater task was soon gone. The breezy sea air and rocking motion of the boat relaxed me into a tranquil state of confidence. The elements of humidity, heat and sand particles suspended in the atmosphere provided the perfect ingredients for brewing a soupy brown haze that covered the Arabian Gulf sky. The dreary mixture sheltered the descending sun so that only the lightened sky above the horizon indicated that the day would soon be over.

Before long it would be dark. I moved forward to the cockpit and confronted the Duke. "We're not rigged up for night diving. Do you plan to bunk down here and start in the morning?"

He cut the engines and yelled, "*Hubba hubba*! Veloo, get the car batteries and those underwater lights, and put them on deck. Saleem, bring up those lift bags and assemble that portable winch."

It looked like it was going to be a night dive after all, and what a night, not even a sliver of moon. I didn't mind diving after dark and had made several nocturnal excursions into the deep to photograph sea life, but not to lift heavy objects. I was concerned, but I wasn't going to let my diving buddies know it, especially not the Duke.

This excursion was my baby. Mr. Tandoody had asked me to arrange this salvage job, and I recruited Josh and Frankie to assist, but I was smart enough to know my limitations as a diver. Because of his experience as a professional diver Frankie would be the dive leader and direct Josh and me underwater.

We gathered around the small table in the cabin, and Frankie gave the pre-dive briefing. "We've anchored close to where we believe the lost cargo should be located. There are four crates; the biggest is about eight-by-eight feet. We'll lift the two largest with the portable winch. The others we'll raise with lift bags. Once we bring them to the surface the crew will slip the cargo net around 'em and lift them on deck."

"How deep is the water here?" I asked.

"Sixty-three feet," Veloo responded.

Veloo and Saleem rigged up the lights and dropped them into the water while Josh, Frankie and I put on our scuba gear and went through a checkout of one another's diving equipment. Veloo secured the lift bags, extra lines and hardware in a heavy rope-net bag. Weighting the net with a couple of extra tanks, he dropped it over the side and watched it descend beneath the smooth surface of the Arabian Gulf waters.

The Duke paced back and forth across the deck like an expectant father. Turning abruptly toward his three-man dive team, a beaming smile broke across his face and his bare feet began tapping out a silent jig to accompany his choreographed vocals.

And the three little fishes they swam and they swam right over the dam   Boop Boop Diddim Daddum Waddum Choo!

Shaking my head in amazement I watched the Duke wiggle his fingers in the air as he sang the second chorus, "*and they swam and they swam right over the dam,*" slapped his knee on the "*Boop Boop,*" and snapped his fingers on the "*Diddim Daddum.*" Then rolling hand over hand like a basketball coach calling a traveling violation, he sang the "*Waddum Choo!*"

Tim abruptly ended his little vaudeville exhibition. "Now you three little fishes don't swim over the dam," he cautioned.

Returning to our task, Josh, Frankie, and I partially inflated our horse collar buoyancy device, known as a "Fenzy," grabbed our masks securely in one hand and our regulators in the other and, one by one, like synchronized swimmers, flipped backwards into the water from our perch on the side of the boat. Gathering on the surface and holding onto the anchor line we made one final safety check, turned on our waterproof flashlights, and descended down the line into the black abyss. Once we reached bottom, Frankie secured a thirty-foot rope to the anchor, using it as our pivot point. I positioned myself about ten feet from the anchor while Josh went out another ten. With Frankie on the end we began a circular search. After just a few minutes, Frankie tugged three times on the line, indicating that he had found the goods. Josh followed the line out towards Frankie and tied an inflatable surface float to one of the discovered crates so the topside team could move the boat and tether lights overhead.

Frankie selected the largest crate. Using sign language, he instructed Josh and me to tip the crate and dig the sand out from under, allowing us to pass the lift-belt beneath. We repeated the process on the opposite side of the crate so that the steel rings on all four ends of the two belts met at the center of the square crate.

Working patiently to secure the shackles to the rings and then to the commercial lift-belts, I concentrated on watching Frankie guide me from the other side of the sunken box. The underwater lights cast a dim glow on the area where we worked. A chill shot though my wet body. A cold thermal current passing, I thought, or was it Frankie's grotesquely glowing eyes, magnified by the glass of his mask and distorted by the bubbles rising from his regulator that caused me to shudder? Beyond the formless face of this aquatic life form was total darkness.

Just as I recovered from my imagined encounter with a creature of the deep, I felt a strange tingling sensation on the back of my bare neck. Shit, a poisonous sea snake, or maybe that not so surreal creature I just saw, was objecting to my nocturnal foray into their domain. My pulse raced, causing my blood pressure to rise, along with a few noxious flatulent bubbles that worked their way through my bathing suit up the back of my diving coveralls and out the opening of the cuff of my long sleeves. I threw up my right hand toward the back of my neck to shoo away the undersea predator that was trying to nibble on my exposed body, and carelessly knocked my regulator from my mouth.

Think, think, think what do I do? My mind reverted to my training. Just as I was about to enter the "passive panic" stage, all was revealed.

Ahh, Section I, PADI DIVER MANUAL, circa 1974, I got it!

I was getting a bit frantic now, but hell, I'm a PADI trained diver. Like an underwater Boy Scout, I was prepared. I reached back over my right shoulder to my air tank, which was secured on my back. The task was to feel my way from the first stage of the regulator, where it connects to the tank, to the breathing hose. Then I needed to follow the hose until my hand reached the second stage of the regulator, the breathing apparatus, grab it and bring it back to my air-starved mouth.

Hell, no problem, I thought. I did this in training. As my lungs screamed for air I started the retrieval procedure. "You can do it," I kept telling myself. Tilting my head back so I could reach the hose, I looked directly at the lights hanging from the boat near the surface, where I knew there was fresh clean oxygen. I'm outta here!

Just as I was starting my emergency ascent, a hand materialized from out of the darkness and shoved my regulator back into my mouth.

I looked my savior in his mask-covered eyes and saw the smiling Josh shaking a sea cucumber in my face, the same turd-looking sea animal that he had used to "tickle my neck."

Having recovered both my dignity and my regulator, I returned to the task of securing the crate. Frankie checked my work and made sure that Josh and I moved away from the box before tugging three times on the lift rope, the pre-arranged signal to haul up the crate with the deck winch. We repeated the process on the second crate, which was just a bit smaller, and then swam over to the two small boxes. Instead of hauling these up by the winch, Frankie decided to use the lift bags. Positioning Josh and me on opposite sides of the first crate, Frankie attached the bag and then slowly inflated it with air from his regulator. As the bag filled it began a leisurely graceful ascent to the surface, lifting the small crate like a hot air balloon rising into the sky. Josh and I swam upwards, guiding it toward the waiting arms of the crew who netted the box and pulled it aboard.

Frankie connected the airbag to the second small crate and slowly inflated it. The bag rose, pulling tight the belts that connected it to the box, and then stopped. Frankie took hold of the writing slate that was connected to his weight belt. TOO HEAVY USE WINCH, he scribbled. Giving Frankie the thumb-touching-forefinger diver's okay sign, Josh and I began the sand clearing process and connected the rings of the lift-belts to the shackles, while Frankie surfaced to advise the crew to drop the winch cable.

When the cable broke the surface above, Frankie grasped it with both hands and swam downwards, guiding the steel, snakelike rope-wire towards the crate, where he connected it to the rings. Before Frankie could give the normal three-tug lift signal, the cable prematurely slithered upward, pulling taunt on the belts. Strange sonar sounds emanated from the now obviously straining umbilical. Sensing danger, the three of us back-paddled like frenzied fish to distance ourselves from the erratic shifting of the wooden chest. The eerie underwater symphony continued until a loud twang, the resonance of an enormous popping guitar string pierced the dense water causing a sharp pressure squeeze on my eardrums. I looked upward through the lurid lights to the bottom of the boat, trying to trace the source of the sonic vibrations. Gracefully slithering toward us was the spiraling serpentine coil from the winch, Medusa in a free dive.

Taking advantage of the extra milliseconds that the physics of undersea sound waves gave us, Josh and I put our power fins into motion. Legs kicking and arms wildly cutting through water, we navigated away from the falling line. Frankie must have misjudged the refracted light from the underwater object coming down on us and moved in the wrong direction, allowing the lengthy cable to encompass his head and tanks in a snarl, like a large Slinky gone wild.

The weight of the coil-wrapped tanks pushed into the seabed pinning Frankie on his back, legs floating upward to seek their level of buoyancy. A plethora of bubbles exited from the wildly lashing air-hose that was once connected to Frankie's regulator. Josh and I raced toward him. Before we could reach Frankie, he calmly pulled the large knife from the black rubber scabbard attached to his right calf. Without a second thought he reached over with his right hand and slashed the left shoulder belt of the Fenzy and then calmly cut the waist belt. Pulling the orange-colored artificial lung over his head, he allowed it to float slowly to the surface. In simultaneous motions, his left hand released the waist belt of the dive tank harness while his right sliced through the left shoulder harness attached to the dive tank. Reversing the technique, Frankie transferred the knife to his left hand and sliced through the right dive tank shoulder harness, while reaching with his right hand to release the weight belt buckle and letting it fall to the seabed. Completely unencumbered, Frankie righted himself. Only when Josh thrust his regulator towards him did Frankie finally let his own airless mouthpiece fall toward the ocean floor. After taking a big suck from the offered lifeline, he guided it back to Josh's mouth. Slowly following them to the surface I studied their motions as they calmly swam, face-to-face, taking turns breathing from the one regulator, as if the natural thing to do.

Reaching the surface, the crew helped us onboard and took our gear. Still shaking from watching Frankie's great escape, I looked at Josh, who was lying on deck, chest heaving and deep breathing sounds escaping from his diaphragm. I thought of how calm he was during the ordeal, but looking at him now I could see the tension leaving his body. What was it about guys like Frankie and Josh? Sure, the training taught them the mechanics of what to do, but it was just plain guts and discipline that allowed them to overcome stress in such a situation. I wanted to be just like these guys, but rich, like the Duke.

All too soon for me, Veloo and Saleem returned with fresh air tanks and another Fenzy and regulator for Frankie.

Laughing loudly, Frankie and the Duke slowly walked toward us. Tim stopped directly in front of me and eyed me up and down. "Hey, hooky hooky, you ready to finish the job with the men, or you want to stay onboard with the pussies?"

I still hadn't fully composed myself, but after seeing Josh and Frankie in action there was no way I was backing out now. If I wanted to be like them I had to act like them. "Fuck no. I'm ready to go. You stay here with the pussies."

The Duke bellowed out his deep laugh, *Haw Haw Haw*! "We got your ass now, don't we, Falcon?"

Ignoring the Duke and me, Frankie again took charge. "Looks like we have to adjust our plan," he said. "Not enough time to recover and rig the cable; probably not strong enough anyway. We'll have to open the big crate underwater. Tim says that there should be some metal boxes inside. The lift bags will be able to handle them. If we hurry we should have plenty of air to finish the job."

"Plenty of air up here, Falcon. Sure you don't want to stay here and enjoy it?"

"Fuck you, Tim."

After gearing up we repeated our back flip water entry, but this time we each held onto a prying bar. Reaching the bottom, we gathered around the stubborn crate and Frankie levered open the top. On cue, Josh and I worked on the sides. First the top, then side after side fell onto the sandy bottom revealing twelve metal boxes.

Josh and I attached a lift bag to the first box while Frankie worked alone. The boxes were heavy but easy to manage underwater. One chest ascended, the bag returned and another followed. After about half an hour we followed the last bag to the surface, stopping at the ten-foot level for a ten-minute decompression hang off. Frankie and Josh were fearless but they were also safe divers. Enough close calls; we didn't need a case of the bends to top off the evening.

By the time we were back onboard, the crew had stowed the gear and removed the portable winch. Using a large crowbar, the Duke pried the lid off the largest of the crates. He removed the top and cut into the waterproof fabric that enclosed numerous cardboard cartons, and then opened one of the cartons. Hundreds of "Citizen" watches in all shapes and sizes sparkled within.

"Shit," I said just as the top of another package was opened to reveal even more watches, this time Seiko's. "There must be ten thousand watches here," I said to no one in particular.

The Duke looked at me. "How about a thousand dozen?" he said. "These are the cheap ones. Wait until you see some of the others."

The next two crates, about half the size of the largest, contained gold Rolex, Cartier and Patek Phillipe watches.

Using his California cowboy strut, the Duke slowly and deliberately moved toward the twelve metal boxes neatly piled, four by three, at the side of the deck. Each sheet-metal rectangle looked to be about two feet long, two feet wide and two feet deep, secured by a metal clasp with a small brass padlock.

Inserting the bar between the lock and the clasp, the Duke

twisted his wrist in a quick, smooth motion and popped the brass ring from the bottom of the lock. "Takes me back to my teenage days in California," he said. He lifted the top of the chest a sliver, peeked inside, and with a slap of his right hand against his raised right knee, let out an "Ooo Eeee, we found the right boxes."

"Come here Falcon," ordered the Duke. "What do you think of this?"

Dazzling rays, reflected from the boat's lights, bounced from the shiny metal bars, ten-tola gold bars. My heart pumped wildly as I gently took one of the smooth bars, felt the weight, rubbed the cool bright metal on my cheek and even kissed it. As if in a trance, I continued to sensually stroke the gold bar.

Enough foreplay; I wanted to know how much gold there was, and counted the visible gold bricks, eight across, four long, thirty-two per row. Stacking them on the deck as if I were a child playing with building blocks, I reached row thirteen, a portentous number I thought, as I tallied a total of four hundred and sixteen ten-tola bars per metal container. The Indian tola measurement was commonly used in the Arabian Gulf, so I knew that each of the almost five thousand bars of gold weighed three and three quarter ounces. At the current rate of $35 per ounce it was worth over $600,000 on the local market. Once smuggled into India it would be worth more than 2.5 million dollars.

I pulled my camera from my dive bag and took a few shots of the bars before replacing them in their treasure chest.

With a shit-eating grin the Duke looked at us. "Why don't you guys have a beer and get some rest while the boys and I get underway?"

The Bertram built up speed, and with beers in hand, we lay back on the cushioned bench seats and talked about our dive.

"Damn, Falcon," Josh said, picking up on the moniker the Duke used. "I wish I had a movie camera so you could see the look on your face. It was like you were doing an underwater sea ballet, flaying arms, twisting legs and so on. It was just a little sea cucumber tickling you."

"Fuck you, Josh," I mumbled and closed my eyes, trying to will him out of my presence. Just as I started to doze off a jolt from the thrust of the engines knocked me backward into the rear of the bench seat. My slumber aborted, I watched Josh and Frankie as they tried to keep their balance. Holding on to the side of the boat they sidestepped toward the bow until they finally reached the cockpit. As the boat gained speed and the bow bumped madly on the sea, lifting higher and higher, I took my chance and crawled on hands and knees to join them.

"Yaaa Hooo!" cried the Duke, bucking up and down like a rider on a bull in a rodeo. Just then he pushed the throttles forward and we shot onward at breakneck speed.

"What's the hurry?" Frankie asked. "Got a couple of those Indian beauties waiting at home?"

"Fuck, no; we got an I-ranian customs gunboat on our ass. See that little speck of light over there? That's them. Word just came in over the radio from some nearby fishermen friends."

"So what? We're just picking up lost cargo, salvage rights, law of the sea and all that," I said.

Frankie, Josh, and Tim looked at me like I had just said the dumbest thing they'd ever heard.

"Shit, Falcon," said the Duke, "for being smart enough to run a school, you sure are thick when it comes to real life. This here ain't no lost cargo and we ain't in Dubai waters. One of Bin Jabir's dhows was sneaking it into I-ran. They was gonna be boarded and inspected, so over it went."

Josh and Frankie stood on the side laughing.

"You sons of bitches knew all along, didn't you?" I said, looking at them.

"Fuck, Falc," Frankie said, "no one had to tell us. Anyone wet under the collar could have figured it out."

Josh just stood there shaking his head and smiling at me.

An abrupt "CRACK" and then another came from the side of the boat while fiberglass splinters sprayed our faces.

"Motherfucker, them bastards are shootin' at us. Let's get our butts moving," yelled the Duke. "They ain't supposed to do that— that ain't playing by the rules. Hold on, boys," ordered our crazy leader as he pulled a knob on the instrument panel and kicked in the supercharger, sending the boat flying.

Josh laughed like a kid on a trampoline, bouncing up and down as the boat pounded the waves

Frankie moved to the cockpit. "Go for it, Duke. Let's show those fuckers who not to mess with."

The Duke yelled over the noise of the engines, "Well, if them mothers want to fight, this will be the 'Mother of all Battles'."

"Battle?" What had I gotten myself into? These two assholes, Josh and Frankie, were just as certifiable as "ole Bimbo Timbo" over there.

It seemed like hours, but it was only a few minutes later when the Duke suddenly pulled down on the throttles. Just as rapidly as we had picked up speed, we dropped to a smooth, brisk pace.

The adrenaline rush didn't take away the fear. I was scared. "You're not giving up, are you? If you are, I'm over the side 'cause I am not gonna spend my best years in some Persian jail."

The Duke looked at me with his piercing blue eyes. "Hold on to your dick, Falc, we're back in Dubai waters. Those customs creeps can't touch us. We're home free, baby." Reducing our speed even more, the Duke set the throttles on autopilot, and then walked towards the ice chest on the stern. "Come on, the captain here will buy you a cold one."

I grabbed the beer from Tim's extended hand. "Damn you, Tim. I thought I was gonna be the bum boy for some Iranian prison guard. Your buddy Iskar told me that he just needed a couple of amateur divers to salvage some worthless equipment for a friend." Walking away from Tim I took a swig of the Heineken and let the cool liquid run down my parched throat. I felt like an imbecile. Brought here under false pretenses and having my naiveté ridiculed was one thing, but being shot at by Iranians was another. I was really pissed off.

During the half-hour it took to reach the dock I barraged the Duke with all of the new cuss words I had learned from him.

"Calm down, Falcon," he said with a smile. "No one was hurt, you had a nice dive and we had a little excitement. What's the big deal?"

I could see that I was wasting my time. As the boat glided into the slip I turned and addressed my mates. "You fuckers are crazy. This is like living in a sci-fi movie. You're all being cloned into little Dukes. I'm outta here, assholes." I hit the deck, loaded my gear and took off with Josh's yellow Suzuki, leaving him and Frankie on the boat still laughing and shooting the shit with Tim.

Marie and the kids were fast asleep when I crept in at dawn. I showered and climbed in bed, snuggling to the security of Marie's warm body. Lying there waiting for my heart rate to drop back to normal, I replayed the evening's events in my mind. Tim's strange comment about the "Mother of all Battles" seemed to repeat itself in my brain like a broken record. What a curious thing to say. Only someone a little eccentric like Tim would use such an expression.

How could I let myself get into a situation like that? Less than a year ago I was Luigi Falconi, mild-mannered school administrator, hired to come to Dubai to run an oil company school, and today I'm "The Falcon," leading a team of divers recovering smuggled goods.

This is one helluva way to spend my Christmas holidays, I thought. The adrenalin rush, the gold, and the machismo—I had to admit I loved it.

Some of the gold salvaged by the Duke and his dive team

Meeting the Duke

After tossing and turning for a couple of hours, I got up and headed to school. The quiet weekend morning would allow me to catch up on paperwork before I left for the Christmas holidays. A cool December breeze passed through the open window of my ragtop Daihatsu as I drove down the dirt track. Passing several camels foraging for breakfast in the garbage bins outside of the houses, the gurgling of my empty stomach reminded me I hadn't eaten since yesterday afternoon. I decided to make a detour to Pinky's to grab some pastries. Through the crackling reception of Dubai's only English radio station, the voice of Frank Sinatra crooned out the final chorus of "My Way." As if programmed by the song, my mind drifted back five months to an earlier visit to Pinky's and my first encounter with the Duke.

Pinky's was the "in" place to do grocery shopping for expatriates living in Dubai. On a lucky day you could get real Jif peanut butter, Kraft mayonnaise and even Fritos. As soon as any honest-to-goodness American product arrived at Pinky's, the word spread like wildfire, and the entire Yankee community rushed to get whatever the ship had brought in that month. It didn't matter what it was, as long as it was from the U.S.A. As I waited in the checkout line with my stuffed grocery cart the bellowing voice of an angry shopper flowed forward from the back of the store.

"BUSY! What the fuck you mean, you're busy? Look, motherfucker! I'm busy, your boss is busy, the Pope is busy, the Ruler of Dubai is busy, and God is busy. They're busy doing their jobs. Now, do your fuckin' job and get your ass in back and find me my cake mix."

Now that's what I call one unhappy customer, I thought. Even with the air-conditioning blowing, it was hot. The small a/c units in Pinky's supermarket were ineffective against the 120-degree midday sun. This guy had definite signs of "desert burnout." I was told when I first arrived not to stay too long in Dubai; after a few years the hot sun boils a good brain into mush "desert burnout." I thought it was just a joke, but now I wasn't so sure.

Just standing in the checkout line was enough physical activity for the August heat and humidity to drain all of the energy from my body. I crossed my arms on the cart's push-handle and cushioned my sweaty forehead on my biceps as I waited my turn. Hearing a shuffling of feet and sensing motion nearby, I raised my head and caught a glimpse of an unusual looking gentlemen whom I had never seen before in our small expatriate community. Watching the stranger walk up to the "ten item or less" lane, I realized that he was the only other male patron in the store and must have been the one who hurled the verbal abuse at the stockboy.

It wasn't hard to understand why he caught my eye; this was 1974, the early days of oil production, well before the bankers, lawyers and other big shot executives hit town. Dubai was an oilfield boomtown, and just about everyone here was considered a "redneck," "Okie," "coon ass" or some other brand of high-octane petroleum worker. They all seemed to fit the oil worker stereotype—Southern drawl, blue jeans or coveralls, and the permanent halo around their skulls caused by the headbands of baseball caps or hardhats.

This guy was different from anyone I had met in the two months I had lived in this Middle Eastern desert town. Judging not only by his looks, but also by his behavior, this man wasn't typical "oilfield trash." The only ring on this self-shopping expatriate was the large gold and diamond band on the third finger of his right hand. His long white locks reached well past the collar of his shirt, giving him the appearance of one of those drug-guru hippies protesting the Vietnam War back in the States. The hair on this aged flower child was a bit sweaty and kept falling down into his eyes, landing on the bridge of his nose. Using his long, thin fingers, the kind of fingers I always thought a piano player would have, he raked the hair back in line with the rest of his white fleece. As he raised his arm, his shirtsleeve pulled the cuff away from his wrist, revealing a large gold Rolex. Judging from its flash and sparkle, the bezel had to be surrounded with diamonds.

Just as he was ready to take the last step to the quick-check counter, a local Arab woman in traditional clothing and mask-covered face shot in front of the stranger and rolled her full trolley of groceries over his right foot.

"What the fuck!" Red blood cells brought color to his face and the tightening muscles of his jaw pushed out the skin covering the mandible joint. He was definitely pissed. Lifting his right hand to his sun-hardened face, he rubbed the two-day growth of gray/black beard. Even with his angry expression, he was handsome in that "Marlboro Cowboy" sort of way. Gazing in my direction, yet talking to no one, he continued his muffled-toned diatribe. "Fuckin' local lady. Just because she's dressed like the fuckin' Lone Ranger she thinks she can do whatever the fuck she wants."

Few local women spoke English, so I was sure that she didn't understand a word he said, but I looked away, not wanting anyone to think that I knew the foul-mouthed man.

The "ten items or less" sign above the cash register was printed in both Arabic and English, but as a foreigner in an Arab country you soon learn that signs and rules are not made for the local citizens, as my fellow foreigner so rudely experienced.

I turned my attention back to the Arab lady, who was now hovering at the front of the checkout stand while the store manager personally unloaded her cart and two employees bagged the goods. With all of the attention she received from management and staff, I had to assume that she was a VIP, her husband one of the wealthy Dubai Nationals, or else she was a *Shaikha*, the wife of one of the local royalty who held the title of *Shaikh*.

Shaikha Ranger and her silver cart—the fastest cart in the Middle East

The clothing-confined lady must have been stifling hot under her black garb. She reminded me of Sister Flora, my favorite nun in high school.

I had to admit that the annoyed customer was right about the Lone Ranger analogy. Besides dressing in what looked like a nun's habit, the woman wore a mask called a *burka*, which covered the top half of her face and nose. It was exactly like the type that I remembered the Lone Ranger wearing. Not only did the mask remind me of the man with the silver bullet, Shaikha Ranger even had a faithful Indian companion by her side. In this case, however, I heard her refer to him as Baboo, not Tonto. In Dubai, it was common for families to hire Indians to take care of household chores, cooking, shopping and driving. These Indians weren't Apache, Sioux or Iroquois; they were Goan or Tamil or Karalites from the Indian subcontinent, brought to Dubai to work as servants and laborers. You can bet Baboo wasn't gonna lay down his life for "Kimosabi Shaikha Ranger," not for the $100 a month that he was paid. It was enough sacrifice just to carry the groceries.

As the white-haired man continued his grumpy sermon, I camouflaged myself behind the pages of a magazine taken from my cart, stealthily observing his appearance and behavior. His long, thin Romanesque nose seemed in contradiction to his sunken cheeks, which gave him the gaunt look of a long distance runner. He sure didn't have the body type of the oil field workers I knew. There was no beer gut, he had a full set of teeth and sported remarkably long hair. Who was this character?

He looked up at me with mysterious, mesmerizing pale blue eyes that radiated puerile innocence, but with an impish sparkle. I gazed away, embarrassed, like I'd been caught picking my nose. I wanted to keep looking, but instead I turned my head abruptly and stood rigid like a mannequin, as if his frigid blue eyes froze me.

My embarrassment must have been apparent to him. When I finally had the courage to take my finger from my nose, metaphorically speaking, I glanced back to see a small smile on his face, like he was saying "gotcha" to himself.

Forcing myself to redirect my attention away from the man, I watched "The Lone Shaikha" being escorted out of Pinky's by almost the entire staff, while her faithful Indian companion paid her bill.

The white-haired hippie slowly moved toward the vacated checkout and tossed his entire hand-basket on the moving belt, not bothering to empty it. Strange eating habits, I thought. Fifteen small jars of dried beef and half a dozen boxes of angel food cake mix.

While he watched his beefcake ingredients being tallied, I unashamedly scrutinized the rest of his appearance. A designer quality, cream-colored shirt unbuttoned to his waist exposed a sweaty sunken chest and some unruly body hair. I'm sure his shirt was opened to better deal with the heat, but the thick gold chain around his neck supporting several pendants made me wonder if it wasn't just for show.

He wore stylish pleated pants held up by a belt made of brilliant black skin from some unfortunate reptile. According to the name on the buckle, the skin belonged to Pierre Cardin. His shoes were dusty but I could tell they were Italian, probably Bruno Magli's. The thin delicate soles were not very practical in a city where most of the roads were still dirt tracks, but they were fashionable. This guy had class when it came to clothes, an Arabian Armani shopper, no *souk* or market shopping for him.

Deepali, the young woman at the register, had obviously dealt with him before. She simultaneously emptied the basket and rang up the sale. As the total "clanged" out on the dated NCR machine, he put his right hand in his pocket and removed a large wad of bills bound in a gold money clip. Without saying a word, he tossed the gilded bundle on the counter toward the cashier and held out his hand, palm downward and waving rapidly as if saying goodbye to the floor. I watched intently—after all, I was fresh from the U.S.A. and wanted to learn all I could about the new culture I was living in. This must be some Arab gesture meaning "take the money," because that's exactly what the cashier did.

Deepali removed a couple of one hundred dirham notes, each worth about twenty-five dollars, arranged the currency in the cash drawer and then withdrew several smaller notes. Just as she was starting to place the change in the gold clasp, the customer again waved at the ground and took the clip, leaving the small bills in the cashier's hand. Lifting his gold-banded wad of bills high in the air he swayed it back and forth and yelled, "Ho Bubba! Let's go."

A short stocky man in a white cook's uniform appeared from behind the newsstand and rushed up to take the bags. The lanky stranger brushed his hair back once more and, as if in a trance, glided toward the door.

When it was my turn to check out, I dutifully unloaded my groceries and chatted with Gopal, the young Indian clerk, while he keyed in my items. Being a regular customer since my arrival in Dubai, I was familiar with the staff. When he finished, I threw my billfold on the counter, and with my hand palm down, waved just like the stranger. Gopal looked at me with that "crazy foreigner" smirk. Obviously I had done something wrong.

"Gopal," I asked, "When that man at the next counter did this," I said and repeated the motion of waving at the floor, "Deepali took his money and gave him change. Yet when I did it, you just look at me strangely. Why?"

Gopal stared at me with a blank smile and bobbed his head back and forth in a jumble between a "yes" and a "no" and a "duh" just like one of those dolls with the shaking head that you see in the rear window of automobiles in the States. Hearing a giggle, I turned toward Deepali, who stood at her register with her hands in front of her mouth as if embarrassed. The big smile that crossed her face finally broke into a full laugh.

"Oh, Saahib," she said, addressing me with the Urdu term for "master." "This man has been coming here for many years. Sometimes he talks and behaves in peculiar ways. We have just learned how to deal with his unusual manners. And, he is a big tipper. Dubai is a small city. I'm sure that you will get to know him while you are living here."

"Thanks, Deepali," I said, although I doubted I'd ever see him again. He wasn't the type of person I would socialize with. I picked up my blue plastic bag of groceries and left, completely forgetting about the stranger.

CIA—Caught In the Act

The following Thursday evening, my wife Marie and I attended a dinner party at the home of Pat and Nan Riley. Pat was the public relations man for Continent Oil Company (COC). He was a fluent Arabist and dealt with the Ruler of Dubai and the Government Energy Office on behalf of COC.

Because of his language skills, association with the US Embassy staff and the fact that he dealt with high-level UAE government officials, it was reputed that Pat was the local CIA agent. Behind his back everyone called him "Rat Riley." It was the joke in Dubai that if you wanted to get any gossip back to the oil company management or US Government, just tell Pat and he'd rat. Pat was really a good guy, a bit of an intellectual, but easy to talk to, unlike the other COC managers, hard-ass oilmen who had worked their way to the top. This included the president of Continent Oil, Earl "Good ol' Boy" Scrudds. Earl was a Texas wild-catter who was sent to Dubai for pre-retirement. Earl was known to be incontinent in the top floor office of Continent. Poor Earl had seen his last gusher years ago. He was happy just to get a steady stream flowing once in awhile.

It was at this affair that a conversation about Vietnam protests and the US West Coast drug scene made me think about my encounter at Pinky's, and I mentioned the man with the long white hair. Describing him to the guests around me, I made the unfortunate comment that, "with the two-day beard and unkempt hair, he looked like an alcoholic hippie." Two of the group immediately identified him as Tim Johnson, known locally as "The Duke." He was a business partner of Iskar Tandoody, an Indian who was the personal assistant to Majid Bin Jabir, Director of the Energy Office, and the most powerful person in Dubai next to the Ruler. No one knew much about the Duke's background except that he was once an oilman and was known to have come to Dubai with the first drilling rig in 1965. The only other thing anyone could say was that he was making big money.

The party ended up like the others I had attended: a few of the boys and girls overindulging in the refreshments, some rank stories, a husband catching his wife in the bathroom with a friend, a fight, a couple of people nude in the pool. It was the typical oilfield house party. *Geeze,* I miss those days.

Gulf Rig Is Not a Drilling Platform

Because the Muslim holy day was on Friday, the Dubai Oil Company School (DOCS) had a Friday/Saturday weekend. The business community only had Friday as a day of rest. I was back in my office on Sunday preparing for the coming school year. Opening my mail, I was pleased to see invitations for the coming week's social events. One in particular caught my eye. It was for a "Back to School" reception on Thursday evening at the Bustan Hotel, hosted by J. R. Dumont, a big oilfield construction company.

Dubai was a social town, and the major entertainers were the managers of the service companies who fawned over the Continent Oil Company masters for the millions of dollars of material and service contracts they handed out. Expense accounts were big during the oil boom days and wining and dining the big boys was just part of the cost of doing business for them.

Marie and I were still a couple of impressionable kids, and each invitation was a new adventure. Our social status was well beyond our level of income, and although I would have liked to believe that it was my personality, I knew that it was my status as headmaster and Marie's good looks and waist length hair that made us regulars on the party and dinner circuit.

What drew my attention to this particular card were the words "Gulf Rig" written under "Dress" for the evening. Although I was a novice and not very socially educated, I did know what the terms "formal," "informal," "National Dress" and "casual" meant when they were listed on the invitation, but "Gulf Rig" was new to me. Perhaps it was hardhat and coveralls like they wore offshore on the drilling rigs and barges; one never could tell with the type of people here.

This was a job for my "Super Secretary" Maggie Straight. Maggie was a Texas girl who had been at the school several years before I arrived. She was kind-hearted, well-intentioned and full of information not only about the school, but the community, the oil company and the royal family. Anything I needed to know, I could get the answer from Maggie, like having my own oracle.

"Maggie, what's 'Gulf Rig'? Isn't it one of those big steel platforms with a big derrick that they use to drill offshore oil wells?"

A dumbfounded look crossed Maggie's face. Using an Arab expression of frustration she'd adopted from her host countrymen, she threw her head back, clicked her tongue on the roof of her mouth and sympathetically shook her head back and forth. "You Yanks just don't know nothin' about the Middle East. 'Gulf Rig' is formal attire for gentlemen in these here places. You wear tuxedo pants, a tuxedo shirt, but short sleeve, so you have to buy a long sleeve one and cut them off, and a cummerbund. Now you don't wear a tie and you leave the neck unbuttoned just like a sport shirt. Our colonial British friends came up with the idea, formal yet comfortable in the heat of the Middle East."

"I guess ideas like that is why their empire collapsed," I said. "The only good thing to come from the British Empire was gin and tonics—all of that quinine in the tonic to keep away malaria and all that gin to keep away the French."

I liked the idea of coveralls and hardhats, but being an expatriate means learning to adapt to the environment and situation, so I went out and bought Gulf Rig.

He Did It His Way

The following Thursday evening, dressed in my new outfit, I escorted my stunning wife into the barely air-conditioned ballroom of the Bustan Hotel, the only decent hotel in Dubai. Dubai was a small town and at least half of the guests were parents of the kids from school, and all of the moms wanted to talk to me about their little Janie or Johnny. Many of the moms were quite attractive so I suffered through the kiddie-chat just to be the center of their attention. Surrounded by several of these young mothers, I looked across the room for Marie when my eye caught a blur of black and white moving swiftly toward me, and not in a friendly manner. When my vision focused I realized that it was the Duke, the mysterious grocery shopper, Tim Johnson.

Barging through the group with a loud "excuse me, ladies," Tim placed his face inches from mine.

"Are you Lou Falconi?"

"Yes sir, that's me."

"Falconi, you asshole, you miserable mother fucker, fuck you, you fucking fucker you, fuckin' silly bastard, who the fuck do you think you are, what the fuck are you, you miserable piece of shit, you fuck camels, camels fuck you, who the fuck are you to say I look like an alcoholic hippie, you fuckaholic, you don't know me, you don't know a fuckin' thing about me!"

Oh shit, I thought as I remembered my comments last week at Pat and Nan Riley's dinner party.

For an English teacher with a Master's degree, I'd just received one hell of an education. In one sentence Tim Johnson used the word "fuck" as a verb, an adjective, a noun, a transitive verb, an intransitive verb and even added a few new "F" words to the English language.

What could I say with all those lovely moms looking at me, not at Tim, but at me? I just wanted to run into the desert, climb a big sand dune, find a camel, crawl up his butt and dry up into one of those little brown balls they shit out. I really felt like camel crap. Red-faced, yet still trying to be "smooth" in front of the ladies, I did what anyone proven to be guilty as an asshole would do. I apologized.

"Mr. Johnson, please accept my sincere apologies. There was never any malice intended; I just used the term to describe an appearance."

"What the fuck you mean, 'term to describe an appearance'? Do I visually appear to be an alcoholic?"

"No sir, you look very non-alcoholic to me. I'm really sorry."

Tim's face erupted with the biggest grin I'd ever seen. His right knee rose up to his waist and with a resounding slap he hit it with his right hand and began a deep, full laugh like that of a school kid who just pulled off a big joke on the teacher. *Haw Haw Haw!*

Soon I was surrounded by a group of laughing moms. Still stunned by the verbal introduction and what appeared to be acceptable humor, I couldn't quite bring myself to join in the joviality.

Slowly coming toward us from behind Tim was a diminutive, yet dignified looking gentleman, light brown in complexion. Between two fingers he delicately held a long, slim, black tube with a band of gold where it met the French Gauloise cigarette. Laughing like hell, he placed his hand on Tim's back and looked directly in my eyes. Without a blink and with English even the Queen would have appreciated, he said, "I understand that this is the gossipy new headmaster. Perhaps you would introduce me, Tim."

"Falconi, this is Iskar Tandoody," Tim said.

I really wanted to break the ice and say, "Howdy, Tandoody," but I fought the urge to resort to the humor of '50s U.S. television. Instead, I extended my hand and phrased the traditional, "How do you do, Mr. Tandoody? I'm pleased to meet you."

Tandoody grudgingly extended his hand. When I grasped for the handshake it was like shaking the hand of a dead man or a limp penis, or a dead man's limp penis. I had the impression that this man, the shaker, felt that he was well above the status of the shakee and would just let me do all of the work. Without paying much attention to my handshake, or me, Iskar turned to the moms.

"Good evening, ladies," he said. "My, you all look lovely and devilish."

While giving the salutation, he gracefully, and almost unnoticed, slipped a gold Cartier lighter out of his pocket, and in one smooth motion flicked and lit the cigarette entering the mouth of May Jamieson, one of my favorite moms.

This guy was suave. I could see each of these ladies knew him and were obviously enthralled, if not enamored. And me, well, what could a kid who spent his whole life in a small town in Southern Michigan think? This was real class. Here was a man who knew how to act around women. I could really learn something from this person.

May responded in a silky tone, "Why, thank you, kind sir."

I was so accustomed to the hard-core oilfield drawl emanating from the Texas oilmen that it was hard to believe her Southern English could be so sensuous. It was like listening to Scarlet talking to Rhett. Iskar had nothing on May; she was as smooth as he.

Tim placed an arm around my shoulder and said, "Come on, Falconi, let's take a stroll over to the Gold Tola Bar and I'll buy you a drink."

As I followed Tim and the very important and very limp-handed Iskar, I noticed Iskar's palm sweep across the slim curve of Darlene Thompson's derriere and the resulting subtle smile that parted her lips. Damn, another of my favorite moms being entrapped by this bewitching Indian Casanova.

We left the reception and walked across the Bustan's lobby to the lounge. At the door to the saloon a small marquee informed patrons that Sal Kumoyu, the Kenyan Frank Sinatra, would be at the piano tonight. As we entered the dimly-lit, smoke-filled bar, customers sitting in the circular booths along the wall shouted greetings to Tim and Iskar. We walked up to the bar. Tim raised a foot onto the brass rail and rested his arms on the polished teak.

"Hey, Bubba, give me a Saudi soda and wine for my friends here," he commanded. Tim turned toward me and with his right hand made a flowing circular gesture toward the center of the lounge. "This is the only real bar in Dubai. Even got women waitresses here. You won't find that nowhere else in the Gulf. Shit, more deals are made in the Gold Tola than in the Ruler's palace. Iskar owns the place. The previous owner was a cashiered U.S. Army Colonel, a good friend. That sumbitch seemed to know everything that was going on in town." Tim laughed. "After he left Dubai we found out that he had the whole place bugged."

Above the hum of Tim talking and the soft piano tones of "My Way" played by the black Sinatra, I heard a commotion in the back of the lounge. Looking toward the rumpus, I saw a large man being coaxed back into his chair by his tablemates. By the slur in his speech and lack of motor skills, it appeared he had been imbibing the imported liquor a good part of the evening. With a loud crash, he broke free from his friendly captors and like a determined fullback on a touchdown drive, headed straight toward Iskar. Just as the alcohol-impaired customer zigged and zagged around obstacles in his path, ol' dark eyes, Kumoyu Sinatra, began singing a well timed and appropriate:

> *And now, the end is near;*
> *And so I face the final curtain.*

The inebriated expat stumbled, falling to his knees. He was now almost face-to-face with the altitude-disabled Iskar, who calmly stood his ground and continued to smoke his cigarette. The angry man stood and regained his height advantage over the seemingly unfazed Indian. A spray of spit accompanied the words aimed at Iskar. "Tandoody, you curry-breath, greasy-haired, Harijan bastard."

The fullback began to falter. Placing his right hand on the bar to steady himself, he continued his attack. "I worked two years on that fuckin' project. You know I had the best product and the best price. You fucked me."

Slowly he lifted his hand from the bar and tried to point his finger at Iskar. The combination of booze and emotion held sway over his body and the attempted gesture morphed into a vibrating fist. "You can pull my visa and get me deported, but you better not ever set foot in the U.S.A. or I'll cut you into pieces too small to make barbeque Tikka."

As Kumoyu continued singing the Sinatra tune in his Swahili-British accent, the bartender hurdled over the teak barrier with a Louisville Slugger in one hand and what looked like a small caliber revolver in the other.

"Are you okay, Mr. Tandoody?" he asked.

Iskar's eyebrows lifted roguishly and his lips parted in an arrogant smile. "Why wouldn't I be?"

As the "oh shits" were still being muttered throughout the bar, Tim stepped between the boozy businessman and the bartender. "Put that fuckin' bat and toy gun away, Omar," he said to the bartender. "Someday you're gonna get called down by someone smarter and braver than you, and if you miss with the bat you'll end up floating in the Creek with that plastic gun up your ass."

Turning toward the dispirited fullback, Tim lifted his clenched fist and flipped out his long forefinger. Holding his right hand as if it were a pistol, he touched the nose of the large lush. "You oversized drunken dromedary. Hump your ass back to the desert and don't ever stick your camel dick in the Gold Tola again."

The three friends of the drunken antagonist swiftly moved into the cluster and escorted him from the premises.

"Omar," Tim said, "call our friend Colonel Harcross at police headquarters and tell him Iskar wants that tequila-breath bozo escorted to the airport and put on the next plane outta here."

I reached for the drinks and gave Tim his Saudi soda, which turned out to be Perrier water. As I handed Iskar his Chardonnay, I noticed how calm he still appeared. During the entire confrontation not a bead of sweat broke out on his brow. He just kept slowly puffing on that long cigarette holder which still dangled from his lips. He was either the coolest dude I had ever met or the stupidest. I took a big gulp from my drink. Tim held up his glass and with a "cheers," clinked Iskar's and my glasses. Before putting the drink to his lips, Iskar reached toward the cigarette holder in his mouth and removed it—both halves. During the face-off he had bitten the expensive black coral holder into two pieces. Undaunted, he coolly put one, then the other section on the counter, saluted us and tipped his glass.

Almost as if choreographed, Sal was right on queue with:

Yes, there were times, I'm sure you knew,
When I bit off more than I could chew,
But through it all, when there was doubt, I ate it up and spit it out.
I faced it all and I stood tall . . .

At the "*. . . did it my way,*" Tim Johnson broke my concentration away from the background music.

"Falconi, I haven't had a real drink in over fifteen years. Sometime I'll tell you about my drinking days. Shit, if you wanted to see what a real alcoholic looked like, you should have seen me then."

"Talk about drinking," I said, "that man who caused the scene was really under the influence. Just what was that ruckus all about, Mr. Johnson?"

"Nothing, really. That fella didn't know how to take care of his business and got caught on the short end. He thought he could operate out here like he was still back in the States. Everyone tried to tell him things were different in Dubai. He could have been a friend, but he was just too stubborn to learn the rules, and now he blames Iskar for his failure. Out here, Falconi, anyone, even you, can be a friend as long as you play by the rules."

Tim turned toward Iskar. "Come on, Iskar, let's get the fuck out of here and go get some pussy."

Without a word or a goodbye gesture, Tim placed his arm around Iskar's shoulder, and they walked away, leaving me standing alone at the bar.

My eyes followed their departure as Sal Kumoyu belted out his finale:

"The record shows I took the blows -
And did it my way!"

Thank God the timely tenor wasn't so timely after all. No one met with any blows, but I'd finally made the acquaintance of Tim Johnson, the Duke. The mysterious shopper who mesmerized me in the supermarket was even more of an enigma now. In front of all of the people at the reception and in the lounge, not a sign of embarrassment, self-consciousness, fear or whatever; Tim just did his thing, when and where he pleased, and didn't seem to care what people thought. I wished I could be like that.

II
Earning My
M.A.B.A. Degree

The Arabian Clipper

The weeks before a new school year starts are the most hectic: orientating teachers, distributing material, and registering new students, and the August of '74 was no different. This was my first year as headmaster, and I wanted everything to be in perfect order before the first bell rang. Right now I needed to be back at school, not sitting on a grubby, sponge-leaking couch in Iskar Tandoody's office. When the summons arrived that Iskar wanted to see me at 10:00 a.m. on Sunday, I told Maggie to call and apologize, explaining that I had a parent interview at that time, and to ask if we could reschedule the meeting.

"When Iskar calls, you go," Maggie ordered as if I were an impertinent student. "Mr. Tandoody is one of the most important people in this community. You just go to your meeting, and I'll handle things around here."

Not that I wasn't curious about why Iskar wanted to see me, but hell, what was the big deal about rescheduling a meeting? I finally deferred to Maggie's wisdom and now, here I was, still sitting on this cracked, dirty, fake leather couch at 11:00 a.m. on Sunday morning.

High noon, still no Iskar.

By now I was surrounded by Arabs in their national dress, a white tailored sheet with a tablecloth on their head. I'd soon learn the proper name for the white robe, *dishdashah,* and the long cloth headdress, *ghutra.* The tablecloth headscarf was held in place by a piece of black rope, which was called the *hegaal.* After a summer in the desert heat you understood why it was worn. Having air blowing up your crotch kept those Arabian jewels cool, and the white sack dress reflected the heat from the sun. However, at this early stage of my acculturation, it was still a sheet.

After two hours my once comfortable, three-seat sofa held two hefty Arabs, one medium size Arab, and me. A dozen mismatched chairs around the office perimeter had also filled with visitors, while other guests stood in the open doorway, allowing the outside desert atmosphere to dissipate what little cool air there was in the office. Adding to the discomfort caused by the heat and humidity, the hodgepodge of multinational bodies created a stew of pungent odors that permeated my breathing space. But the ultimate affront to my Western sense of social courtesy was exhibited by my Arab seatmates who had their sandals off and were either picking skin from the leathery calluses on their feet or shoveling goop out from between toes.

From the corner of my left eye, I saw the heavier of the two stout Arabs raising his leg in an uncouth and undignified fashion, exposing the dark and dirty sole of an authentic "Arabian Bigfoot." As the paw lifted higher and higher it came closer to my face. This monster with its five little appendages protruding from the end couldn't have been twelve inches from my nose, but it was heading toward the mouth of its owner. With a movement almost as quick as the flick of Iskar's Bic, the corner of the big toe, now being held in a two-handed death grip, was shoved into the opening beneath the untamed mustache of its Arab owner. The man's right incisors crunched into the left corner of the nail and tore off a chunk of the cartilage. With a "PHOOOP," it was promptly discarded from his mouth towards the floor, landing on the tassel of my right shoe in an egg-shaped glob of lugey with a toenail nucleus. In a matter of seconds the big foot returned to its normal size and proper location on the floor in front of the human nail clipper.

Looking around the room, I expected to see a look of disgust on the faces of my seatmates, but not one person seemed offended. Except me, the grossed-out Westerner.

Just then the door opened and Iskar casually strolled through the portal. Immediately the entire group stood. Without acknowledging the presence of his visitors, he took a seat at the only desk in the room, which I earlier presumed belonged to the secretary. Continuing to ignore us, he read documents on his desk, scribbling on the occasional paper, and pausing to drag on his fag, still paying no attention to the crowd of humanity surrounding him. Finally, Iskar apathetically motioned to one of the older Arab visitors, who promptly rose and walked toward him. As the Arab arrived at the desk, Iskar stood and stepped toward the elderly man. Each of them placed their hands on the outside shoulders of the other, and then touched right cheek to right cheek, left cheek to left cheek and then right cheeks again.

The physical contact between the two men displayed in the traditional greeting fascinated me. Smiling to myself, I envisioned doing this triple kiss with my peers and staff back in my old school. Not quite an acceptable cultural norm in the good ol' U.S.A.

The Arab gentleman was invited to take the seat next to the desk as Iskar proceeded to again sit in the chair that I had mentally reserved for a secretary. Dumbfounded, I realized that this was not a reception room where a secretary would preside; this was Iskar's office and that was his desk.

Just then a young Indian man with a plaid cloth skirt wrapped around his waist and a white loose-fitting blouse-like shirt entered the room. He was one of those "faithful" Indian companions hired to serve their Arab masters. This one had the job of preparing coffee and tea for the workers in the Government Energy Office and their visitors. In an Arab office, it's the custom to offer guests Arabic coffee, which is a refreshing java mixed with cardamom, after which the guest is offered tea or Sanka.

When serving the traditional Arabic coffee, the attendant held a copper Arab coffeepot, which had the contours of a penguin but with a pelican beak-shaped spout. He clutched the flask of the brew in one hand while balancing several small demitasse cups in the other. In this case the coffee server held three cups. After first serving Iskar and retrieving the cup, he then moved to the right, pouring the coffee and distributing the three drinking vessels. Returning to the first one served, he waited until he was finished, collected the cup and moved over to stand in front of the second visitor, repeating the process for him and then the next guest. Having completed the procedure for the first three, he moved on and replicated the operation with the next three people, using the same cups. Occasionally some guests requested a second serving by holding out their cup like Oliver Twist asking for more porridge. Those declining seconds held the cup, face up, and rapidly waggled it several times, right to left, as an indication that they had finished and wanted no more.

By the time the coffee server reached me, I calculated that no fewer than three other mouths had touched the rims and left their signature bit of backwash with the dregs in the bottom of the cups.

The last cycle of this three-cup shuffle ended with Bigfoot. Then it was my turn. Calculating the cup movement as if counting cards in Black Jack, I was suddenly struck with a nauseating terror. If the coffee boy handed out the cups, one, two and three, he would then have to return to number one first. This meant cup number one would be collected and then cup two would be placed on top of number one, and cup number three would be placed on top of cup number two. Therefore, starting the next cycle, cup number three would now become cup number one, which was the one I would be offered.

Oh my God, Bigfoot had cup number three, which would soon be given to me as cup number one. This mini-goblet would have been kissed by Bigfoot's nail clipping mouth. Gag me, I couldn't do it.

Just as a hand extended in front of me bearing the mini-chalice brimming with the fragrant brew, my mind flashed back to the anti-war protests of my college days. Except the "Hell, no, I won't go," was replaced by a new chant, "Hell, no, I won't gulp!"

Hesitating long enough for big wet circles to form under my armpits, I searched the room hoping someone would come to my rescue, but I only locked eyes with Iskar, who peered at me intensely. There was no getting out of it. I couldn't refuse. It would be rude and possibly considered a sign of disrespect. Taking a deep breath, I grabbed the cup and chugged it down, my lips not even touching the rim. The expected scratching on my gullet, caused by horny epidermal tissue being flushed down into my gut didn't occur. I actually found the nail-free coffee to be quite refreshing. Only time would tell if I'd pick up a parasite or an Arabian form of camel hoof and mouth disease.

Once the ritual was over, I received a proper serving of Sanka in a mug that appeared to be clean.

The First Episode of Friends

I became fascinated during the next half-hour as Iskar conducted business with the individuals in the room. He would invite a specific person to sit at one of two chairs near the desk. In the presence of everyone, the two discussed their affairs. Sometimes both seats were occupied and he carried on dual discussions. The observers, of course, strained to hear what was being said, especially the local Arabs. Iskar apparently felt no need for confidentiality and made no attempt to keep his voice down. He skipped from English to Arabic to Farsi and Hindi as if it were one language.

Some of the discussions between Iskar and a visitor were business matters, others were pleas for government assistance for an airline ticket for a holiday, or for medical attention, or for a scholarship to study abroad, or just a handout. It seemed that Iskar not only handled Mr. Bin Jabir's business, he was also the one who carried out Mr. Bin Jabir's decisions on which of these petitioners were deserving of their request. Since Iskar was the one who distributed these favors, he was a powerful man in the eyes of the local Arab supplicants. As keeper of the appointment book for Bin Jabir, Iskar was even more powerful to the Western businessmen seeking an audience with his boss. Access to the most important man in Dubai was via the most important secretary in Dubai.

Finally, two and one-half hours after my scheduled appointment, I was summoned to the bench.

"Lou, how good of you to come," greeted Iskar. "Please forgive my late arrival and for keeping you waiting, but His Highness required my assistance on an extremely important matter."

Wow! I was impressed. He'd been dealing with the Ruler on important matters. Of course I didn't mind waiting for such a VIP.

"No problem, Iskar, it's always nice to see you," I said.

"Mr. Tandoody, if you don't mind," he rebutted.

"Yes, of course, Mr. Tandoody," I said. "Please excuse me for being too familiar."

"No, no. It's quite all right, my dear boy. I consider you a *friend*. I just feel that in a place of business it is best to be a bit more formal."

I was really coming up in the world. I was a *friend* of Iskar Tandoody. I had moved from being a school headmaster to being a *friend* of powerful people. I was flying with the jet set now.

"Lou, I asked you here for a very special reason. You know Tim Johnson? I believe you met him several evenings ago. Well, Tim has a small contracting and maintenance company and I understand that the American school requires cleaners, maintenance personnel, and other services. Lou, Tim is a *friend* and I would like you to see that Tim's company gets the contract for these services."

"Mr. Tandoody, the school already has a company contracted to do these services, and they do an excellent job. It would be hard to justify removing them."

"Lou, as I said, Tim is a *friend*. I'd like you to be a *friend* also. In Dubai, *friends* help *friends*. I'm sure that you understand. Please see what you can do. Tim will call on you at the school later this afternoon. Thank you."

With an abrupt "thank you," my new friend Iskar Tandoody dismissed me, with what sounded like an order to change maintenance services at the school. Walking from Iskar's office, I was a bit perplexed. I wanted to be his *friend*, I wanted to mix with the important people, but I had some really good men working at the school, and they had been there since the school was built. No, I decided, I wouldn't do it.

When I returned to school, Maggie could tell I was upset and had the tactfulness not to confront me about my meeting with Iskar.

Tim didn't show up that afternoon, but I had another visitor, Mr. Earl Scrudds. As the President of Continent Oil Company (COC), he also served as the chairman of the school board. With his right hand yanking my right hand, and his left hand gripping my right bicep, Earl bellowed "Hell, Louie, how y'awl doing today?"

By his tone and casual, overly-friendly greeting, I knew that this wasn't a social visit.

"Ya know this here school building, which was built by and is owned by COC, doesn't look like it's being kept in good shape. Ya know now, during the summer, I've had a couple of parents complaining to me about them toi-lets not being kept clean enough for their little kiddies' butts to sit on. Y'awl are doing a great job with this here educatin', which, as we know, is the main reason y'awl are here, and since you have only been here a few months, the board and I decided to help you out and get a better contractor to take care of the place."

Mr. Scrudds pompously led us into my office, seated himself in my big leather chair, behind my big desk, while I sheepishly plopped into the cheaply upholstered guest seat in front.

"Look, Earl," I said. After all of those ya know's and y'awls, I figured I could be casual too. "This building is spotless and the maintenance is A-1. I can't cancel a contract and put people out of work just like that. Some of these workers have been here for years, and they have families to support. If they were doing a poor job, fine, they'd go, but they do a good job."

"Look here, Falconi!" Scrudds' face turned as red as his bulbous, vein-mapped nose, and his voice climbed into the 10,000-decibel range. "I run the major oil company in this here Emirate and this here oil company owns the school. And I am the chairman of this here school board. Now that to me looks like I am the boss, and as your boss, you do as I say."

He was the big oil derrick in this oil field, and he was having a blow-out while sitting in my big chair behind my big desk. As suddenly as he ignited, he defused and all was quiet.

In a relaxed tone of voice, he continued. "Lou, business here just ain't like it is back home. You do things the way you have to in order to get the job done. Mr. Tandoody called me this afternoon, and he highly recommended Tim Johnson's company to take on the school contract. Mr. Tandoody is a *friend* and Tim Johnson is Mr. Tandoody's *friend*; therefore, he is our *friend*. You *will* give him the contract. Good Day."

Our *friend*! It didn't take a rocket scientist to see what was going on here. Earl was a *friend*, Iskar was a *friend*, Tim Johnson was a *friend*, and I could be a *friend*. I bet Dubai had more *friends* than a Quaker congregation.

T&J Maintenance and Contracting Company got the contract to do the school cleaning and maintenance. When I presented their bid to the school board for approval, there was not one dissenting vote, even though the price was more than twice as much as the old contract. I was truly a *FRIEND* now.

It took many years to learn the real meaning behind what Earl was trying to tell me. Business in Dubai—and business in general throughout the Middle East—ain't like it is back home. The Arabs are masters at conducting business. After all, they had been traders and merchants for thousands of years. Arrogant and self-assured, we Yanks thought we were going to come to the Middle East and teach these guys how to put a deal together. My ass, we were! It was a totally different camel race with a different set of rules. And it was their rules and their camels.

This experience with the maintenance contract gave meaning to the incident with Iskar and the drunken businessman in the Gold Tola Bar. When you enter their camel race, you follow their rules or you eventually get humped out of town.

Pool Picassos and Magic Carpets

Handover Day had arrived at the American School. The T&J work crews were coming that Saturday morning to take over the cleaning and repairing. The last thirty days of the former contractor were tough for me. I couldn't look the cleaning staff members in the eye. I had let their livelihood be taken away just so I could be a *friend*.

Promptly at 8:00 a.m., five open pickup trucks jammed with a blue mass of human cargo, pulled up in front of the school. The procession of pick-up trucks was led by a big black Cadillac that ignored the lined parking spaces and drove to within three feet of the front door.

With the enthusiasm of a second grader, Tim Johnson, white hair flying like a wild Andy Warhol, sprung from the Caddy, skipped the three steps and spun around on the landing facing his trucks.

"Hubba hubba hubba. Let's go, motherfuckers, get your asses moving," he yelled.

A couple of kids shooting hoops at the basket on the far end of the parking lot turned their heads toward us. Christ, just what I needed was a bunch of parents calling to complain about some wild man using profanity on school grounds in front of their kids.

On Tim's command, a herd of blue coverall-clad, flip-flop wearing, curry-odored, big-smiling Indian laborers jumped out of the trucks. A young Indian man dressed in slacks and white shirt joined Tim on the steps.

"Falconi, this here's Alex the foreman. Anything you need or any problem you have, you call Alex here, night or day."

As they sprung from the trucks, Tim counted aloud in a singsong manner: "One little, two little, three little Indians, four little, five little, six little Indians," until he counted fifty little Indian laborers exiting their transport.

Considering that the last contractor had ten men at the school, I was aghast to see so many workers. Doing a quick head calculation of five hundred students and staff, this meant that we now had one cleaner or maintenance person for every ten students.

"Tim, I see people, lots of people, but where are your cleaning machines? Where are the electric floor buffers, and where are the cleaning equipment and supplies?" I asked.

"Shit, who the fuck needs floor buffers? Each one of those guys has a broom and mop. They'll keep this place spotless." Tim stared directly into my eyes. Manpower, Falconi, manpower," he said, overly emphasizing the syllable "man." "Putting people to work, keeping the unemployment in India down and people fed. Fuck, who the fuck you think built the fucking pyramids? Fuckin' people, that's who. Machines cost money. These guys are cheap. If they're lazy or break down, you ship 'em home and bring in another one."

All the while that Tim stood cursing, giving orders to the crew, and cursing some more, the boys on the basketball court watched and listened to every word.

While Alex took the team into the building to assign jobs and locations, Tim motioned toward the Caddie.

"Let's go, Falconi. I wanna take you to see something you've never seen before."

"I need to stay here and get these guys organized," I said.

"Fuck those guys, that's what ya got Alex for. Get in, motherfucker."

For the first time since meeting Tim and listening to his unlimited vocabulary of "F" words, I wondered why he talked like that. I knew that it was common speech on the male dominated oilrigs and barges, but Tim had been away from that for several years. I had done some checking with some of his other customers and was told that he treated his employees extremely well, much better than many of the Arab bosses, and that his workers respected and worked hard for him. I even sensed a feeling of camaraderie when he called me "motherfucker." It wasn't quite a term of endearment, but coming from Tim it had a friendly tone. I can't say why he chose to use these words. Maybe his years as an oilman working offshore resulted in the imprinting of that macho vocabulary into his normal speech, but I don't believe he ever meant anything in a derogatory manner.

Driving off in Tim's big black Yank tank, I kept thinking of the chaos going on at the school and the phone calls I would receive from the parents of the boys who were exposed to Tim's colorful vocabulary.

It was a short drive from the school to the beach road, where Tim turned into a great compound consisting of one enormous house surrounded by four smaller ones.

At the entrance, Tim sounded the Caddie's horn until a large man wearing a Turkish style turban, a beautifully decorated vest over a bare, muscle rippled chest, and a magnificent handlebar mustache opened the elaborate metal gates just the width of his body. He peeked out at us and squinted toward the driver's side of the car. When he spotted Tim, a smile spread across his face and the gates hastily swung open to allow the car to proceed into the drive.

The big Turk closed the steel doors and ran up to Tim as he stepped from the car. Still smiling broadly, the big man grasped Tim's right hand between his two huge ones. Rather than shaking as I expected, he kept Tim's hand at waist level, still in his grip, and lowered his forehead to touch the back of Tim's hand. He raised his head, released Tim's hand and stepped back two paces.

"Hi, Abdul, you asshole!" Tim said, stressing the Ab, like Aaabdul. He smiled and grabbed the Turk in a big bear hug. Abdul reciprocated and wrapped his massive arms around Tim's beanpole body, lifted him off the ground and carried him ten feet to the entrance of the garden. All the while, both Tim and Abdul laughed like a couple of young brothers horsing around.

With both feet back on terra firma, Tim turned toward me and pointed to his greeter. "That's Abdul. He's the chief guard here. Used to fight in the Turkish army. Someday I'll have him show you his knife and bullet scars. You don't want to fuck with that one."

We stood at the entrance to one of the most elaborate gardens I had ever seen, and certainly the most beautiful garden in Dubai. I couldn't imagine such an array of vegetation growing in Dubai's arid climate. Several types of palm trees lined the labyrinth of walkways that zigzagged through the oasis. Acacia and ficus trees, intermixed with smaller bushes I didn't recognize, leafed out all the way through the interior gardens. The walls surrounding the garden were covered in yellow, red and pink bougainvillea. Oleander, hibiscus, jasmine and gardenias flourished in sporadic locations.

Following Tim, Abdul and I meandered toward what appeared to be a large garage with a fifteen-foot roll-up aluminum door in the center and a normal size wooden door on the side. Tim opened the small door and led me in. I took off my sunglasses to allow my eyes to adjust from the bright sunlight to the subdued illumination inside. Looking around I saw six heaps of Persian carpets, each pile a different size, ranging from about five by eight feet to at least twelve by twenty-four feet. Each stack of carpets was four to five feet high. Without saying a word, Tim approached the mound with the largest size carpets and began flipping them back one by one for me to view. This had to be the most stunning array of Nains, Isphani, Ardabil and Tabriz woven treasures ever collected.

"Fuck, Falconi, if you think this is something, there are two more store rooms bigger than this with a hell of a lot more of this shit."

"My God, Tim, whose villa are we invading? It must be one of the Shaikh's."

"Hell no, this is Majid Bin Jabir's house. Pretty nice, huh? Come on, I'll show you the pool."

Leaving the treasure chest of knotted artistry, we exited by a back door and walked toward a red brick wall, about six feet high and covered in climbing bougainvillea. Standing on tiptoe, we were able to look over the top of the masonry partition to view an Olympic-size swimming pool surrounded by an ornate patio scattered with blue and white cushioned sun lounges and chairs.

"See that chair over there with its back toward us?" Tim said, pointing. "I came over here one day just to check on the gardeners and household staff. I looked over the wall, right here, just like we're doing now. I could see the back of the chair and two fuckin' hairy legs spread one on each side of the chair with the feet planted on the ground. On the other side of the pool was this red-haired bitch. Shit, I know her, I thought, that's ol' Bill Steven's Irish wife, Maureen. Bill was the Manager of Oilfield Services Company. She's one helluva woman. What a fuckin' body! Red hair down to her waist, a tiny blue string bikini and a pair of high heels, she was really hot lookin'. Perfect legs, feet at one end and pussy at the other."

Tim paused to laugh at his own joke and then continued his tale. "I know this is gonna be good, so I sneak around to the gate where I could peek through the iron slats and took my seat for the show."

Role-playing his own character, Tim bent over at the waist, and dangling his arms toward the ground like a gorilla, led me toward the gate. Standing erect, he smiled and asked, "Know who was sittin' in that chair with his white Arab dress pulled up to his crotch?"

"Mr. Bin Jabir," I replied.

"Hell no! It wasn't even an A-rab. It was Earl Scrudds wearing one of those white robes. Earl says something, and Maureen starts to giggle and struts over toward him. Now I'm lookin' at Earl sittin' on this chair with his legs extended in a 90 degree, welcoming vee, *dishdashah* pulled up, and his big willy standing at attention. Hell, I have to give the old man credit. I thought he was past the days of raising the flag. Anyway, while he's talking to her he grabs his prick and starts shakin' it like he's waving Old Glory, like this."

Tim shook his hand back and forth in front of his crotch, mimicking the oil company president. "Well, Maureen strolls over to him, drops to her knees, and puts the lip on 'em. This bitch doesn't mind sucking on the bastard's sand slurpy 'cause she knows that he's gonna give her husband's company lots of business. Earl's laughing and groaning. Shit, I couldn't tell if he was enjoying it or she was biting his dick. Finally he lets out a yelp and her head pops up, face drippin' with the thickest sweat I ever seen. Power and money can get you anything, Falconi."

Tim scanned the pool area to see if anyone else was around to hear us, then continued. "So here I am, playing peeping pervert when Abdul sneaks up behind me and grabs me around the chest in one of his barrel hugs and carries me away from the gate. By this time both me and Abdul are laughing like banshees when Abdul trips on the sidewalk curb, and we both plop down in that manure pile over there. We smelled like shit for three days and laughed for four."

After acting out the story of Earl, the redhead and Abdul, Tim was chuckling so hard that tears dribbled down his cheeks. His actions and infectious laugh soon had me doubling up and laughing right along with him.

Pulling ourselves together, Tim led us through the gate to the edge of the pool. As we drew closer I realized that it was empty of water, but the deep pit contained two men wearing only shorts, tennis shoes and baseball hats. Their bodies were already soggy with sweat from the mid-morning, 100 degree temperature and ninety-percent humidity. The shorter of the two men yelled to us.

"Hi ya, Tim. How ya doin'?"

"Hi, Tim," followed the second sweat-sodden pit-dweller.

"Hey, Lenz, yo, Raymundo. What are you fuckers doing? If you're taking a swim, you're fucked cause there ain't no fuckin' water in there." Tim clapped his hands together and laughed. Still smiling, he turned to me. "Falconi, this here is Raymundo Raymund and Matt Lenz, a couple of snake oil peddlers."

"Pleased to meet you," I said.

Surrounding the two men were two dozen one-gallon paint cans, along with brushes, scrapers, sandpaper, sanding machines and other paraphernalia.

"Tim," Matt said. "See this great looking aqua coating Raymundo and I are putting on Mr. Bin Jabir's pool? It will look better than new when we're finished. This product is the most durable coating ever developed. The possible uses offshore on the oil platforms are endless."

"Why the fuck you two doing this coolie work?" Tim said. "Why don't ya get a couple of indjins to do it for ya?"

"Oh, no, Tim, this is a really big break for me, having the honor of doing the Bin Jabir pool," Matt said, his big brown eyes glistening with sincerity. "I couldn't trust just anyone to do it. That's why I recruited my friend Raymundo here to help me so we could do the best job possible. I don't want to disappoint my company sponsor, Mr. Tandoody, since he is the one that got me this first big assignment using this new coating."

Matt turned in a circle, his arm extended to display his work. "No, sir, it's a job I can't trust to anyone. This is $20,000 worth of coating. I'm doing this at my cost but the payout in the long term will easily be worth it. When Mr. Bin Jabir sees his pool, he'll make sure that Continent Oil Company uses this paint on their offshore facilities. Come on down and let me show you how it works,"

"Fuck, no. You go on painty painty. I don't have time to watch. Come on, Falconi."

When we were out of earshot of the boys painting in their blue burrow, Tim stopped and turned to me with a big smile. Slapping the right side of his thigh with his open hand, he threw back his head of white locks and roared in laughter. "Those silly motherfuckers! Shit, Iskar got them to re-do Bin Jabir's pool with this expensive oilfield paint. Shit, $20,000 worth of it. That poor fuckin' paint peddler Lenz is getting his first lesson in Dubai Business 101. He ain't never gonna get paid for that job! Iskar is sitting in his office laughing his ass off." Tim swiped at the tears forming and shook his head. "That little Indian fucker Iskar has got two high-paid, white-faced, college educated executives in the bottom of a hole, dehydrating in the Arabian sun, working as laborers for him." He paused to allow an eruption of "haws" to escape, then continued. "Iskar loves to play these fuckin' games with the Western expats. And you think Bin Jabir is gonna give a shit about how great his pool looks? Fuck, he's never been swimming in it since he built the fucker."

As he laughed at the painters, Tim grabbed my arm. "Come on, follow me."

Circling around the pool we passed through a doorway, which led us down six or seven steps into what appeared to be a basement. Entering the air-conditioned room, a wonderful respite from the outdoor heat, I looked around to see beautiful rock walls constructed of natural rough blocks of granite. Mounted on the walls were a sailfish, a marlin and a large sea bass or grouper. A grand teak bar with brown leather stools made from camel saddles fronted the room. Above the back of the bar and extending the length of it, a large window about twenty feet long and five feet high emanated the only light in the room. The large glass was a motion picture screen with Lenz and Raymundo the stars of the movie.

Tim slid behind the bar, opened a cooler and grabbed two soft drinks. Handing one to me, he said, "Hell, we may as well take a break and laugh at these dumb assholes."

"Can't they see us?"

"Na, this here is that one-way glass. It looks like a big shiny wall from inside the pool and you can't even tell it's one-way glass. When Bin Jabir isn't around, Iskar gets a bunch of them Gulf Air stewardesses over here for fuck parties. Iskar and his parties are famous throughout the Middle East. These bitches just love to get invited. They know the food will be great, the booze plentiful, and the young Shaikhs horny and loaded with gifts. After a few really stiff drinks, and maybe something else up their nose, they're ready to fly without their airplanes. Iskar gets one or two of the best ones down here and watches Ahmed, Abdulla, Hooky Pooky and whoever, skinny dippin' with the ladies. Eventually they're playing hump the whale, hide the trout and suck the eel. Meanwhile Iskar is havin' a good time down here with his babes, who by now are drunk, naked and randy. Every once in a while he'll take a break and take a few photos of the boys through the glass for later enjoyment and future insurance."

Sitting at the bar and watching Matt and Raymundo, I lifted my drink and took a long swig. In my mind I tried to comprehend the extent of the material wealth I had just seen manifested in rectangles of colorful wool and silk designs. "Bin Jabir must be one of the richest Dubai nationals next to the Ruler."

Tim laughed. "Hell, he ain't even a Dubain. He came here from Qatar, Bahrain, Iran or one of those countries nearby. And rich, shit, he's on his way to becoming the richest man in the world. And he'll get there too."

The Duke had my attention. "How do you do it? How do you get yourself into a position where you can make that kind of money? I'm sure that you have to be smart, but it has to be more than that." I know my eyes pleaded as I looked at Tim, hoping that he would reveal the secrets I so desperately sought.

Oil Field Professor

"Falconi," Tim said, raking his long fingers through his white hair. "In the States ya got to have two things: timing and luck. Here you also need *wastah*. I always said I would rather be lucky than smart, and Bin Jabir's lucky. He's also in the right place at the right time. But he's smart too." Tim bowed his head and nodded in respect, as if he were talking about God. "Ole Bin Jabir is the master of the ten percent fee. He's even known as Mr. Ten Percent. Now, don't let his looks fool you. He may appear to be just another Arab when he wears his *dishdashah*, but put him in one of his tailor-made two-thousand dollar Savile Row suits and he becomes the millionaire businessman that he is."

Tim was talking about big money. The ability to generate this type of wealth fascinated me. "Tell me about him, Tim. I need to know how he did it."

Tim flicked his head back, throwing his hair in place, took a big gulp of Pepsi, and walked out from behind the bar. Pulling up the stool next to me he began to spin the yarn about the rich man who owned all of these luxurious surroundings. "OK, I'll tell you what I know, but this is just between me and you. Got that, Falconi?"

"You bet."

"Majid Bin Jabir came from Bahrain, but his heritage was I-ranian, like many of the local businessmen in Dubai. When he was young he came to work in Dubai. He was a charming sonofabitch, but he knew business. Charmed his way into the confidence of the Ruler of Dubai.

"The Ruler made Bin Jabir head of customs for the port of Dubai. Now ya have to remember that this was before oil, and the only money Dubai made was from trading goods and smuggling gold, oops— transshipping gold. Bin Jabir was good at his job. He personally went out to each dhow to collect customs duties. He increased customs fees, streamlined operations to make it efficient and made a good profit for the government.

"Not long after his appointment, oil was discovered. Oil revenues would mean a boom to Dubai's economy. But it took about two to three years before the oil and the river of greenbacks it brings started flowing into Dubai. The Ruler needed funds to tide him over and to carry out infrastructure developments to prepare Dubai for the coming oil bonanza. So who did he turn to for help but Bin Jabir, the man who was making money for the government. Bin Jabir tried the banks, but until oil was flowing, they wouldn't help. He couldn't ask the local merchants. They paid a lot to the government in the past for turning its head while they . . ." Tim paused, then continued, "um hum, re-exported, yeah that's it, re-exported, tons of gold to India and watches and electronics to Iran and Pakistan. But they were suffering from a business recession. Indian naval vessels had stopped several local cargo ships called dhows, and rather than have the ships confiscated, the *Nakhuda,* or captain, dumped their contraband cargo overboard for later recovery."

Tim looked toward the ceiling as if in deep thought and a soft smile crossed his face. "Ya know there is an ol' saying here. 'Your neighbor is your enemy, and your neighbor's neighbor is your friend.' The individual Emirates didn't help each other, they worked against each other. Pirates from other Emirates worked with the Iranian or Indian Navy and retrieved the cargoes before the Dubai merchants could get back to recover them. Many of the merchants lost everything. Besides the smuggling, the honest trade in rice, sugar and other staples that was carried out throughout the region and East Africa was affected. Tax-paid goods that had been brought into Dubai for re-export were piling up in the government-owned customs warehouses."

Tim turned, carried the now empty bottle to the end of the bar and set it in the case. "So here's Bin Jabir, thinking how in the fuck do I get some money for the Ruler. Like I said, he's smart. When he reorganized the Dubai Ports & Customs operation, he copied what he had learned in Bahrain where the British trained the bureaucrats. One thing them Brits taught the civil servants was about insurance. Well, Majid Bin Jabir decided that the government should offer protection for itself and the clients of the port who rented warehouse space by taking out storm and fire insurance from Lloyds of London. Shit, nobody in Dubai knew what this insurance crap was. As far as they knew, Lloyds was the name of some salesman from London rather than a big London insurance company. Hell, the merchants of Dubai had actually been insuring their commodities for years by informally sharing the risk on honest, as well as smuggled, goods. But, formal insurance was a new concept to them."

Looking back toward the glass to check out the Matt and Raymundo daytime paint opera, Tim continued his story. "A couple of weeks after Bin Jabir was given the fundraising assignment by the boss, there was a major fire in the port. All of the warehouses and everything in them were destroyed." Tim slapped his thigh and broke out in his donkey laugh. "Some fucker burnt down the fuckin' port."

Tim continued slapping and laughing. "Can't ya see it now? Here's the poor Ruler, in the middle of the night, standing at the port watching it burn, tears dripping from his eyes. Next to him ol' Bin Jabir is smiling, or maybe he's laughing. I would be. Can't ya just see him," Tim held his hands up in front of his face, thumbs rapidly clapping index and middle fingers, mimicking the conversation. He turned toward me as if he were Bin Jabir talking to the Ruler through his hands. "Can't ya just see him as he turns to the Ruler and chatters in that gobbly gook language of theirs and explains about insurance? The Ruler now sees dollar signs coming up with the smoke and is more excited than a kid watching a Halloween bonfire. Bin Jabir's happy, the Ruler's happy and the merchants are happy. Shit, the fire turns out to be a windfall because of this insurance thing. The local merchants were paid for all of their lost goods and the government built nice new modern warehouses to replace the old rickety firetraps. It wasn't long before new cranes, bigger than any ever seen in these parts, and fancy loading equipment was bought for the port to handle the oilfield machinery and supplies that would soon begin arriving. The best part is that Mr. Lloyd, that generous salesman in London, paid for all of it. Every tablecloth-head up and down the Gulf is praising ol' Bin Jabir for being so fuckin' smart to have everything insured."

Tim looked me up and down as if to judge my character from my appearance. "I like you, Falcon," he said, initiating the nickname that eventually became my trademark in Dubai. "And I'm gonna tell you something that few of us fer-a-ners know. But even though I like you, ya ever tell anyone about this, your ass is mine."

I put on my cherubic face of innocence and looked at Tim. "Shit, do you think I'm gonna write a book or something? Trust me," I said.

"People who know, say that for several nights before the fire, a continuous caravan of large trucks was seen loading goods from the warehouse and heading into the desert. A few months later, goods and equipment similar to those listed on the claim affidavits submitted to the insurance company began to surface in the local market." The slapping and laughing started again. "What a fuckin' surprise. Now how in the fuck could that happen. Who do you think would have done that?" Tim blurted out while still laughing.

"Ever since then, Bin Jabir was the Ruler's main man. He was at the right place, at the right time, and he was smart enough to ignite the match of friendship."

From the allegations made in Tim's story, it sounded like Bin Jabir learned well from his ancient Semite cousins. They parted the waters of the Red Sea, drowning thousands of pursuing soldiers in the closing floodwaters, determined to get to where they were going. Bin Jabir couldn't start a flood, but a fire was easy, and he was determined to get to the top.

Having finished our drinks and the story, which I believed was probably a Johnson fable, we left the underground pool bar. As we started up the stairs, I paused to look at the mounted grouper. "Man wouldn't I love to see one of these babies the next time I'm scuba diving."

"So you're a diver," Tim said.

"Sure am. It's a great sport and Dubai is a great place to dive."

Back outside we headed for Bin Jabir's main house. From the outside it looked enormous but not exceedingly elaborate. The structure appeared to be a simply designed two-story house with brown stucco walls. The external entrance facade and flooring were marble covered, but with the local Ras Al Khaimah marble, not the expensive Italian variety.

We climbed up the marble steps, and Tim opened the large, intricately-carved rosewood door and allowed me to look into the foyer. From this position I could peer into five large rooms that fingered off from the anteroom like wagon spokes. Beautiful Persian carpets covered every inch of floor, and ornate chandeliers hung from the ceilings. Vibrant oil paintings decorated the richly papered and fabric-covered walls. I'm sure some of the paintings were expensive originals, but being art ignorant, I couldn't really say. The furnishings varied from room to room; some gold-gilted, some red satin in the style of Louie XV, some solid silver chairs with blue cushions, and some modern-style sofas. He wasn't a very good decorator, rather tasteless, actually, but everything looked extremely expensive, which may have been what really mattered to him anyway. Tim didn't take me inside. He didn't explain why, but I believe that he felt that it would be an invasion of privacy to take a stranger into Bin Jabir's home, if you could call it a home.

As Tim and I stood on the steps, a million questions cluttered my mind. The inquisition wasn't over. There was much more I needed to know. "Mr. Bin Jabir must get paid a lot of money from the Ruler."

"Pay, fuck, he's a civil servant. As Director of the Energy Office he probably makes a grand a month."

"But all of this wealth, how—"

"Power, Falcon. Power brings side benefits that makes Bin Jabir the most envied man in Dubai. He's no longer a fire starter, but the chief advisor to the Ruler of Dubai. Almost every bit of business in the area is focused on oil, and Bin Jabir makes all of the major decisions on behalf of the government. Even Earl Scrudds had to ask Bin Jabir's permission to drill wells, lay pipelines and buy toilet paper.

"The Ruler is a smart man. He understands the value of having a sage of Bin Jabir's caliber working for him. He knows he can't pay him a Wall Street salary in a fuckin' desert town. Do you think he gives a shit if a little bit of the cost of every project and every barrel of oil sold found its way into Bin Jabir's personal account? It's his way of paying a bonus. Hell, Dubai is making over $10 million per day. They ain't gonna miss a little bit. It's okay for civil servants to take a little, as long as you followed the rules."

I couldn't believe what I had just heard. "Rules? That's corruption. What kind of rules can you have for corruption?"

"You don't know jack shit, Falcon. This is the Middle East, not Podunk U.S.A. This is just doing business. And yes, there are rules. First and foremost is never flaunt your wealth. Ya don't shit where you eat. The Ruler of Dubai is a simple man of few material needs. He doesn't care if his employees drive nice cars and have nice homes, but building a huge palace and driving a Rolls Royce down the streets of Dubai is a no-no.

"Keep your head down. A low public profile, another rule. Locals who like to see their name in the press and mugs on television soon have their hands slapped. If a second slapping is necessary, they lose their government job and its benefits. Never go public. There are courtiers such as 'Rent-a-Shaikh' who are unofficial spokesmen for the government."

"Rent-a-Shaikh." I laughed.

"Yep. Every time a new government building or hospital was inaugurated, Rent-a-Shaikh was there taking just enough time to cut the red ribbon and collect his gifts from the owners. Afterwards he would rush home and watch the replay on the evening news. He knew what to say and how the Ruler wanted it said. It's real prestige for the local Indian and Paki businessmen to have a member of the Royal family, even one on a low rung of the importance ladder, attend a grand opening. These local merchants have the poor guy cutting ribbons at third class venues such as the opening of Ravi's Restaurant, Abdul's grocery, and Vinod's Department Store."

The Duke thrust his right hand in front of my face, forming a "V" sign with his index and middle fingers. The two tentacles began moving rapidly; together, apart, together, apart, closer and closer to my nose. As if toying with a small child, Duke Scissorshands mimed Rent-a-Shaikh, cutting a ribbon, or rather my nose. Abruptly he stopped, dropped his scissor hand, and peered fanatically into my eyes.

"Now, Falcon, this here is the most important rule of all. Don't be greedy. Take a ten percent commission, or even less, but never take more and don't try to take every project. Spread the wealth.

"Now you figure out the answer to your own question, Falcon. Bin Jabir has control of the biggest projects and the petrol dollars. Can you work it out in your over-educated Eye-tallion head why's he so rich?"

"So the story around town is true. The offshore oilfield fabrication company, J. R. Dumont International, pays off Bin Jabir." I looked in Tim's eyes, wanting to see their reaction.

"No, no, no. Companies don't pay Bin Jabir. Now that would be corruption. He's too smart to be caught up in that. Some of the top executives of Dumont and a few of Bin Jabir's local friends formed a company conveniently named Dumont Middle East. Continent Oil

Company would put out a tender for $300 million dollars for construction of offshore oil platforms or a $100 million pipeline, and Dumont Middle East usually won the contract. Not always. Remember the rule, spread the wealth. Dumont Middle East would then subcontract the work to Dumont International, or one of the other fabrication companies. The value of the subcontract was considerably less than the value of the contract that Dumont Middle East was awarded. A profit of twenty-five or thirty million dollars on each job was not exceptional. It only took a few of those to make Bin Jabir a rich man."

"What about this *wastah* thing you mentioned?"

Tim's eyes grew bright. "Ah good, you've been listening. What I been tryin' to tell you is that the A-rabs have a sense of professional values that are completely different than us guys from the U.S.A. It doesn't mean that the way they do business is wrong. What we may think as unethical is accepted commercial practice in the Middle East. If you want a certain contract, it is expected that the people in the decision-making positions will be rewarded. This is always done through a person or a company that becomes your agent. An agent is usually the front man for one of the top Shaikhs, or someone in a decision-making position in the government, such as Bin Jabir.

"Remember, Lenz just told us Iskar was his agent. Well, Iskar is probably fronting businesses for Bin Jabir. The people at the top are invisible and never directly involved in the payment of commissions. The agent handles all of these transactions for a fee, which is usually five to ten percent of the value of the deal you're after. It's not considered a pay-off. You receive support as well as information for your money, and most importantly, you receive influence. Hell, your agent can find out what your competitor's price is for the project you both are bidding on. He can even get the complete copy of their bid, as well as copies of all of their correspondence, anything you want. But remember, your competitor has an agent too and is getting copies of your bids and correspondence.

"This assistance and influence is known as *wastah*, or mediation. Business can't be done without *wastah* because that's the way the tribal and vertical patronage network has worked for hundreds of years, and we blue-eyed Westerners aren't gonna change it. If you want to be a successful businessman here you go with the flow and use all the *wastah* you can get. It's not only the big things. Sometimes it's the little things your agent can do that can help make life a bit easier for us infidels."

"Oh, you mean like when I went to get my driving license? I was guided to a comfortable office and drank tea with the police captain while my license was being processed. When I got back to the office and told Maggie that everyone else was waiting in long lines, she just shrugged and said that being a COC company school gave us certain benefits."

"Yep, that's a kind of *wastah;* you got it," the Duke said, like a teacher having a student finally understand a math problem. He led the way down the steps without looking back. "Come on, I'll drive ya back to your school."

The professor was dismissing his student.

Emmanuelle

Not a word was exchanged as Tim chauffeured me back to school in the big Caddie. I thought of the events that led to the changing of the cleaning contract and how I dealt with them. By submitting to the local system and becoming a friend, I had just earned my first credits toward my Masters of Arab Business Administration (MABA), Business in the Arab World 101.

The Duke's lecture was just the beginning of my education. This was to be a work/study program and I was the only student. I felt like a character in a soft-core skin film I had just seen, "Emmanuelle," except I wasn't a young, beautiful, vulnerable woman being introduced to an uninhibited world of eroticism and sensuality. And the Duke wasn't a dirty old Frenchman, although I bet he could play the role well. I was still an eager student and could only hope that my education would at least include a few courses on sex.

III
Teaching Is Learning

The Italian Job

The first semester of the school year seemed to zip by. Organizing the first little league baseball teams, the first Boy Scout program sanctioned by the Boy Scouts of America, and a multitude of after school programs and adult education classes kept my staff and me so busy there was no time to think of Iskar, the Duke and how to make my fortune.

One thing I didn't have to worry about was keeping the school clean. The Duke was true to his promise; his men kept the place spotless. The minute a student tracked in sand or trash from the field, a little blue body was right behind him with a broom, and right behind him was another little blue body with a mop. If you ran out of toilet paper in the john, you just called out "paper," and a blue arm with a little brown hand at the end of it reached under the bottom of the cubicle door and up popped the Charmin. If something needed to be fixed, a carpenter or plumber was there in a jiffy with his box of tools. God knows what they did for supplies; they just seemed to use whatever was handy. Cotton thread around leaky faucets for washers, Vaseline for grease to silence a squeaky hinge, and a garden hose shoved down a clogged toilet and turned on full pressure did a great job for blowing out all the toilet paper, science papers and other goodies kids liked to flush away. Growing up in the Third World, you learned to improvise.

During the coming Christmas holidays, they were scheduled to polish floors and clean windows. I was thankful that my family and I would be traveling during some of that period. I didn't want to be around to watch them polishing floors on hands and knees and cleaning windows without a ladder.

How would they do the second floor windows, I thought? I turned my chair toward the window. Gazing into my reflection in the glass I could envisage three men standing on each other's shoulders like high school cheerleaders in their blue coverall cheering outfits. Instead of a pom pom, the cheerleader on top was shaking a rag in one hand and a squeegee in the other. As a part of his cheering routine, he washed the window from his precarious perch while the two men below chanted a Hindu prayer. Or maybe it was a pyramid, much more stable.

"Mr. Falconi!"

I swiveled my chair around and saw Maggie standing at my desk.

"Iskar just called and wants to see you. You better go right away."

The three-week vacation was to start next week, and I had arranged to use ten of those days for a trip to Bangkok, my present to the family. I just hoped that whatever Iskar wanted wasn't going to screw up my plans.

When I arrived at his office it was déjà vu. The office was again filled with *dishdashah*-clothed men, and Iskar was conferring with them one by one. I took a seat on the same dirty couch and prepared for the long wait to be summoned to pay homage. After only a few minutes I heard, "Mr. Falconi, please come here."

I jerked to attention from my half slumber, leaped the few paces to the front of Iskar's desk and was motioned by the master to take the empty chair at his left. All the while Iskar continued his Arabic conversation with a small Arab sitting at his right. When that discussion was terminated another motion drew me to the vacated chair beside Iskar, and I took the position of honor. I was seated at the right hand of a man who thought he was a god. Immediately Iskar began the small talk that always took place before coming to the main subject in any meeting in the Middle East.

"Lou, how are you? How is your beautiful wife and how are your children? "

I replied and then asked some similar questions of Iskar, but he interrupted.

"I understand from Tim that you're a scuba diver," he said.

"Yes, as a matter of fact I'm a taking my advanced diver course. Would you like to learn to sport dive?"

"My goodness, no, I never swim in the sea. It's full of snakes and other eerie creatures. No, no. I'm not in the least interested in learning to dive. There is only one type of diving that I do." He moved closer to me. "Lou, I have a small favor to ask of you. It seems one of our good friends has lost a few boxes overboard when one of his dhows ran into rough weather. They've marked the position where the cargo went over. We need to retrieve it, and I'd like your help."

"Why sure, but why don't you just get one of the diving companies to do it for you? I don't think they'd charge much."

"I had thought of that, but they're so busy with the oilfield work, and it's such a small job that it seems quicker and easier for Tim Johnson to take you out in one of my small craft to pick it up. You may need one or two other divers to help. Do you have anyone that you could get to go with you?"

I should have realized immediately that this was not a request, but an order, and in my youthful eagerness to use my scuba skills, my mind didn't register the command, only the enthralling and ego-inflating petition for a favor by Iskar Tandoody. "Of course I'll do it. I have a couple of dive buddies who would be happy to help. Just let me know when. Preferably before I leave for the Christmas break."

"I'll have Tim contact you later to fill you in." And with that Iskar stood up and offered me his hand.

I had just entered into my first Middle East barter contract exchanging my services for a future favor. One thing I had already learned from the Duke was that a favor owed was better than money in the bank. Repayment of this type of debt was a matter of honor, and the trick was not to call on that debt until you could get the most out of it. One, two, or many years down the line, if the original debtor died, then his sons were obligated to repay you. I was starting an IRA in favors.

During the following few days at school, I immersed myself in getting ready for a well- deserved Christmas holiday, my first break away from the desert since the previous July.

It was the last hour of my last Thursday in the office, just a few days from my Bangkok trip, when Maggie's voice echoed from the outer office. "Mr. Falconi, line two."

"Good day, this is Mr. Falconi," I said, using my formal headmaster diction.

"*Ha ha*, what's this mister shit, *haha*." It was the unmistakable voice of Tim Johnson. "Hey, Falconi, we're gonna swim with the fishes tomorrow. Get your team ready and meet me at the Umm Saqueem jetty at 2:00 p.m. I'll have all the gear we'll need."

When Iskar first discussed the dive trip, my memory registered the names of two friends whom I knew I could call on for help. Frankie Focaccia was a young man I'd met at the Petroleum Wives Club's '50s-'60s dance a few months before. Frankie was a big dude, about four inches over six feet. His two-hundred twenty pounds wasn't rippling muscle, but he was well-proportioned and brick shithouse solid. When he walked, it was with vigorous strides exhibiting a confidence well beyond his twenty-two years. People noticed Frankie when he entered a room, especially at the dance, with his plaid polyester bellbottoms, white belt, white shoes and red polyester sport coat covering a baby blue silk shirt, chest naked to the third button.

The night of that dance, Frankie's Bryn Mawr-educated wife Joanne, wore one of those 1950s' felt skirts with the big wide belts. I remember the skirt was turquoise blue with a big black and white poodle outlined in sequins on the front. The thick red belt surrounded a waist that was so small I could fit my two medium-size hands around it. Her blond hair fell over her white blouse to the middle of her back. She was the epitome of an Eastern-bred lady, and he was a teddy bear who tried to be a good ol' New Orleans homeboy. Her small stature in relation to Frankie's bulk and height and the difference in their personalities and backgrounds made them an intriguing couple to get to know.

Marie and I hit it off with Frankie and Joanne, and we soon began doing the social scene together. My relationship with Frankie was a bit unusual. I was eight years older, with a family and limited worldly experience. We were friends but sometimes I felt like his father. Though young, Frankie had attended university in Beirut, became a certified oilfield diver and worked the shores of the Arabian Gulf and India. He was vice president of an oilfield construction and service boat company, Marine Offshore Maintenance Services (MOMS).

MOMS was owned by Frankie's godfather and some of the locals, Bin Jabir and Iskar included. The story was told that Frankie's uncle was the reputed mobster Flatface Focaccia, kingpin of the U.S. Gulf Coast. Flatface's brother Salvatore sent his son Frankie out of the country to get him away from the family business, hoping that by his absence he would be passed over and have a chance to follow his own destiny. Recent investigations into the assassination of President John Kennedy fourteen years earlier still pointed a finger at an organized crime conspiracy. And Uncle Flatface was reputed to be the main conspirator. Nothing was ever proven, but the books, articles and television coverage created a fishbowl existence for the Focaccia family.

Cio Fabio, as Flatface was known before the accident that flattened his mug, was a successful restaurateur and may not have become a racketeer and leader of organized crime if it hadn't been for his wife Rosa. When she left the old country, Rosa brought her mamma's entire collection of cooking secrets. She cajoled Fabio into opening "Fabio's and Rosa's Casa de Pasta" in a little storefront just off Bourbon Street in 1921. Rosa, the culinary expert, prepared the menus and acted as the hostess and cashier, while Fabio did the cooking.

According to the legend, Fabio was a young, handsome and virile Italian who loved women. And the women, especially waitresses, seemed to love Fabio. One evening Frankie's mom Sophia was in the restaurant visiting Rosa when, through the two-way swinging door separating the kitchen and dining room, she caught a glimpse of Fabio playing "slip the salami" to the new waitress on the stainless steel food preparation table.

Sophia told Rosa about the appalling spectacle. Rosa never said a word to Fabio.

One evening about two weeks later, Fabio was assisting the same waitress by helping to carry a large tray piled with plates full of spaghetti to the dining room. Rosa must have had the mind of a physicist because she calculated the sway of that kitchen door perfectly. At the precise moment that Fabio approached the door from the kitchen side, Rosa ran up to it from the dining room side, and with the force only a wronged Italian women could produce, pushed inward toward the tray-carrying Fabio.

The resulting cacophony of crunching bone, smashing plates, and plopping pasta could be heard two blocks away. When the ambulance arrived, they discovered that red tomato sauce covering his face and imbedded in his hair made Fabio's injuries appear much worse than they actually were. Removing the sauce and spaghetti from his ears, nostrils and top of his head, they found that the damage was concentrated to the long straight protrusion that once gave Fabio his Romanesque profile. He now had the look of a pathetic pugilist. Cio Fabio, or Flatface, as he since became known, never worked in that restaurant again, nor has he spoken to Rosa since, even though they stayed married and had five children. He obviously was all action and no talk. Fabio's children still own the restaurant and it remains a popular eating spot in the French Quarter featuring Rosa's mamma's special bread recipes.

If only Rosa and Fabio had patented the ingredients or at least copyrighted the name they gave her mamma's bread, "Focaccia Bread," they might have become rich, and Fabio might have avoided his less seemly career path to fame and fortune.

Unfortunately for Frankie's father, he didn't realize that by sending his son overseas to his godfather, Nicholas Nicandro, the Chairman of MOMS, he was sending him from the frying pan into the fire. NN, as Nicolas was called, made Flatface look tame when it came to organized business. Frankie was getting a more intense mob education in Dubai with NN than he would ever have received in New Orleans.

I was glad Frankie agreed to help. Since my knowledge of raising sunken objects was limited to a PADI course on underwater salvage, having his professional diving skills along on the trip gave me a feeling of comfort.

The second diver I recruited was Josh Sampson. Josh looked the part of a salty sea captain with his fire red hair and matching bushy beard, except that until he came to Dubai, Josh hadn't lived anywhere near the sea. He was from Big Sky country, a Butte, Montana boy. Josh and his wife Nellie were close friends. They had three kids and so did Marie and I, each group about the same age as the other. Josh was an experienced sport diver and was usually my partner on our frequent diving excursions. He was not a good diving partner in that he liked his underwater independence and periodically swam off without me. He was fearless and overly comfortable underwater.

Once, while wreck-diving in about sixty feet of water near the port of Dubai, I watched in fascination as Josh removed his diving tank from his back and deflated his buoyancy device so he could stand comfortably on the sandy bottom. Then he stepped first one leg, then the other, out from the coveralls that we all wore while diving. Sidestepping to the right, he dragged his tanks by the umbilical protruding from his mouth and took cover behind a rock. Now I could only see him from chest up, but all the time he had this big smile on his face. What the fuck was he doing, I thought?

I soon found out as the black Baby Ruth-like clumps rose slowly from behind the waving burning bush that covered his head. Shit floats! There was no doubt in my mind that this physical law of nature was true. Josh just took the first sub-sea shit I had ever seen. Josh was just as crazy above water as he was under, but he was a good diver. I was pleased he was coming on our excursion.

I would be glad to get this obligation over so I could relax on the beach in Thailand, knowing Iskar owed me one. With the team I had assembled I felt assured that everything would go on without a hitch.

The Golden Rule

Even the ten days of vacation in Bangkok with my family couldn't get my adrenaline level back to normal. I kept thinking about the foray into the deep, the close calls with Neptune, the gunboats, Iskar and the Duke. The excitement of my experiences during the past few weeks had made me antsy.

Back at school after the holidays I immersed myself into the routine of ordering next year's books and supplies, and preparing the budget and getting ready for classes, which were to begin in a couple of days. In the evenings I drank a little and even smoked some pot, hoping to recapture the excitement and exhilaration of the salvage operation. I was feeling what it must be like to be dependent on a substance to keep you high. I was becoming an adrenaline addict, craving excitement.

When Iskar called the day before school was to begin, asking me to come see him, it was like getting a fix. Maybe he had another adventure for me.

I arrived at his office and went through the normal ritual of coffee and waiting. Summoned forward, I sensed something different in the tone of his voice and in his body language when he spoke to me. He even stood up as I approached. Positioned in front of his desk, Iskar reached over and held out his hand to greet me. Taking it, I was prepared for the limp squeeze I'd received previously, but to my surprise he grasped my hand tightly and shook, just like you'd expect from a real friend. Iskar invited me to take a seat and waited until I did before he sat down.

"Lou, you don't know how grateful all of our friends are for what you and your companions did for us." Then, taking an envelope from his inside pocket, he handed it to me and said, "This is just a little gift to show our appreciation. We always take care of our friends."

With that, he stood and shook my hand again and bowed his head in a farewell gesture.

I left the office and jogged to the parking lot, eager to reach my car and inspect my package. I opened the car door, sat down, started the engine and turned on the air conditioner. Leaving the door open while the a/c blew out the desert heat, I tore the end from the small white packet to find a wad of local currency in denominations of one thousand dirhams each. Calculating that each one thousand dirham note was worth about two hundred and fifty dollars, I estimated that our little excursion had earned us an unexpected windfall of $10,000. Not bad for an evening's work and a few bruises from a bouncing boat. Divided by three that came to $3,333.00 each. Wait a minute, I thought. This is the Middle East. After all the lessons that the Duke taught me, BULLSHIT! I could be dumb sometimes in the real world, but I was a quick learner when it came to learning the rules of doing business in the Arab world. He who has the gold rules.

I divided the money, $2,500 for Frankie, $2,500 for Josh and $5,000 for me. Not bad math, just good business. I was in Arabia and this was just another course toward my MABA.

The Little Things in Life are Free

School had been in session for a few weeks after the Christmas break when the boredom really set in. Getting back into the routine of academia was tougher than I thought, especially after the nautical rush during my vacation. What little diversion there was in meeting new students and moms, and getting the staff and students back in the swing, was over within the first few days. The little blue men had the Christmas decorations cleared and packed, and Maggie had the front office running as slick as a well-oiled wheel. With little to do, I relegated myself to my office. Curling up in my big leather administrator's chair behind my big administrator's desk, with my administrator's mug of coffee, I began my Walter Mitty daydreaming exercise.

The 9:00 a.m. bell had just rung as I sat back and let the warmth of the coffee mug disperse through my hands to the rest of my air-condition-chilled body. The cup had just touched my bottom lip when I looked up and saw the face of Alma Fahad, one of the kindergarten teachers, peeking around the doorjamb at me with a shy grin on her face. Slowly the rest of her head and then her petite body sashayed to the left, until she framed herself in the portal. Alma was one of the best teachers I'd ever worked with. She could weave that magic with her students as only a gifted educator can do.

"Hi, Alma, come on in."

With her head bowed and her hands grasped together and hanging down in front of her long skirt, she moved a few steps toward my desk. Looking up at me with a sly smile, she said, "You'd better come with me to my room. I need a man's help—and a witness."

Without another word she turned and headed down the hall. Not knowing what this was all about, but knowing Alma seldom needed my assistance, I figured that it must be important. I jumped from my warm cradle and chased after her.

After a short jog I caught up with Alma halfway down the hall and slowed to her pace, continuing toward her room. "What's the problem?" I asked.

"Oh, Mr. Falconi, in all of my years of teaching this has never happened. What will the parents think of me?"

Taking one of her hands, I stopped her forward thrust. Then taking the other hand I turned her to face me. "Alma, now calm down and tell me what happened. Nothing can be as bad as you think."

Alma looked at me skittishly. "Today is art day. As always I pick two children to clean paintbrushes and trays in the bathroom at the back of the kindergarten room. Well, today I picked two boys who are close friends, and I know from past experience, can be quite mischievous when they team up. But today they were so good in class and worked so well together, I thought they needed to be rewarded, so I chose them as clean up monitors." Alma took a deep breath. "I collected the children's art papers while the boys entered the bathroom with the brushes and paint trays. I continued class by reading to the students and completely forgot about the little guys in the bathroom until, quite some time later, I heard giggling coming from the back of the room. It was then that I remembered. I stopped reading and walked back to hurry them up. When I opened the bathroom door, oh! oh! I can't explain it; you just have to come and see for yourself."

Turning the corner to the kindergarten hall I could see Ms. Smith pacing between her room and Alma's room, keeping an eye on both during her partner's journey to fetch me.

Entering the kindergarten class I was greeted by the smiling faces of the cutest group of five-year-old munchkins. "Good morning, boys and girls," I said.

They responded with a "Good Morning, Mr. Falcaroni," or something closely sounding like that.

I walked to the back of the room and opened the bathroom door to confront Alma's worst nightmare. Standing there in front of me were two little urchins, Tommy Venter and Bobby Joe Boudroux. Both boys had their shirts and shorts removed and their little jockeys draped around their ankles.

Staring at me from Tommy's undersized torso were several black rings painted around both little nipples, forming concentric targets. From the bulls-eye nipple of each target was a blue arrow that extended toward, and pointed to, the reddest little pecker I have ever seen.

On Bobby Joe's little chest was a large green head with immense yellow ears. Thick, eyebrows, fashioned in dripping black paint, drooped over each of the itti-bitti titti-eyes. Underneath sprang wild lines of black eyelash. Protruding from the red mouth, which was drawn around his belly button, was a big brown cigar. Further down was another, smaller cigar, which upon closer inspection, revealed itself to be his pint-sized penis.

I hated to think what the future held for these two little hellions: paint and high rider bicycles today; tattoos and Harleys tomorrow.

Tommy looked up at me with a smile as big as his bulls-eyes. "Hi, Mr. Fal-con-nonni!"

"Hi!" said Bobby Joe in a soft, sheepish tone.

Mustering courage not to laugh and trying to sound stern, I put my hands on my hips, looked them in the eye and greeted them with, "You boys wash that paint off NOW, and get out there with the other kids." Well, they were still little boys, so Alma and I helped them wash and dress, and guided them back into the mainstream.

How do you discipline something like that? I really don't remember what I did, but I know all of the parents involved, as well as Alma, had a good laugh. Knowing Tommy and Bobby Joe's parents as I did, I'm sure there was some type of penalty inflicted at home.

At least this time it wasn't my own son that was the cause of Alma's distress. The week before, I was called out to the playground by Alma. When I arrived, she was standing by the little merry-go-round, one of those small centrifugal discs with bars on top that kids push and then hop on to ride. Standing next to her was my son, a first grader. It seems that while riding the merry-go-round he decided that he had to pee. And he did; right where he was. According to Alma he just flipped it out and proceeded to mark his territory. The steady stream that flowed in a circular pattern with the movement of the merry-go-round left a wet line in the sand around the perimeter. While the hot sun evaporated the evidence, I had to keep from laughing as I explained to my son why that was not acceptable behavior. No real need for punishment in this case, just having your dad run the school was enough punishment for any little kid. If you think it was hard for me to discipline my kids in school, you need to ask them how hard it was to have their dad as the headmaster.

Little occurrences like these made me realize that education did have its exciting days—days when the adrenaline flowed and you remembered why you got into the business in the first place. I joke about them being little shits, but most of the time they were great. Being a headmaster has its positives, but the thrill in education is in the classroom.

These episodes placated me for awhile, but by the next day I again craved excitement. That damn diving excursion seemed to have ruined my ability to lead a normal life.

And Gladly Would He Learn and Gladly Teach
(Chaucer, *Canterbury Tales,* Prologue)

The following morning I did a bit of work then closed the door to my office. With my faithful coffee mug in hand I settled into the leather security saddle behind my desk. I was just starting to meditate on the meaning of life when my door flew open with a bang and a flustered Maggie burst in, disturbing my tranquil life.

"Mrs. Paltree's sick and will be out for a week, and I can't get a substitute. We got fifteen ninth graders with high hormone levels tearing up a classroom in the junior high building, and unless we get a warm body in there soon, we're gonna have more arms and legs twisting around each other than a group of Indian fakirs. It looks like your days of administratin' are over, Mr. Falconi, y'awl is now an Arab Culture and Arab History teacher."

Maggie thought she was a bearer of bad tidings, but after the underwater salvage excursion and yesterday's kindergarten paint removal operations, I couldn't handle the boredom of the office. This sounded like another chance to get a teaching high.

"Where are Mrs. Paltree's lesson plans?" I asked.

"Got none," said Maggie. "She didn't have anything prepared."

"Well, what do I teach? I've learned a bit about Arab Culture and the history of Dubai in my Arabic classes, but not much."

"Hey, whatever you know is more than they do. Just wing it and teach them whatever you have stored in that gray matter on top. Here's a bunch of books for you to do some research with tonight. Until then, you're on your own."

With that unsage advice from the woman who was supposed to be my oracle, I headed to the junior high building to calm hormones and teach Arab Culture.

Entering the dim hall from the bright courtyard, I saw five teachers from the other classrooms had joined forces and were ready to make an assault on the unattended class. I, their Commander in Chief, rushed to the site of the mutiny and took control of the situation.

"Good morning," I addressed my troops. "You can all head back to your classes. I have everything under control."

The statement was just leaving my mouth as a book came flying through the open door toward my head, along with fifteen obnoxiously loud teenage voices. I picked up the thin book and looked at the students with one of those stern scowls that only schoolteachers and mothers can make.

Using another teacher technique, manners and authority, I addressed my new charges with a commanding "Good morning, ladies and gentlemen." This seemed to shock the teens into submission.

SILENCE————

"Mrs. Paltree won't be here today, so I volunteered to take her classes. Now, will the person who threw the book please step forward and sit out the class in my office?"

A brazen, handsome young man rose from his desk, and with bold confidence walked up to me.

"I guess it be me—only, Mr. Falconi," Nick Nicandro said in a rhyming singsong. Nick or Nicky, as he was called, smiled at me, and with an "I'm outta here," headed for the office.

Looks like little Nicky was a chip off the ol' block. If this was any indication of the type of training NN gave to his protégés, I needed to get my buddy Frankie away from that man's influence and back into the loving and safe arms of his Sicilian Mafia family.

With Nicky out of the room, I did something that can get you higher than grass, and can be more exciting than any adventure. I was teaching.

IV
You Play the Hand
You're Dealt

Urine Therapy

After an energizing week teaching fifteen teenagers about Dubai, I found myself back in my inner sanctum. Just as my mind trip to Mittyland was beginning I heard a loud clanging noise, kind of like cymbals, coming from the hall, and then someone yelling.

"Veejay, you stupid f-aaa!"

I knew that voice. Like a shot I made a beeline for the front door, "Whooo, Tim. Cool it and come to my office where the kids can't hear you."

Tim laughed. "Being sent to the principal's office," he said. "Hope he'll give me a cup of coffee." He rubbed his shin. "Damn, Falc, that silly little brown shit left a mop and pail right in front of the door. Bang, as soon as I opened the fuckin' door. I could have broken my leg. Christ, you got to watch them all the time." He shoved his long white locks out of his face. "Shit, just what I need, riding in one of those government ambulances to the hospital. Ever seen the way they drive them crazy vehicles?"

"Come on, Tim. I'll get you that coffee."

His right pant leg wet with soapy water, Tim shuffled into my office with a gimpy gait, like he was trying to keep the wet pants from touching his leg. He plopped on the green velvet couch and raised his wet shank on the cushions.

As I walked to the office bathroom to get a towel, I thanked God for the Duke. My day wouldn't be entirely boring. Ever since T&J got the contract for cleaning the school, Tim visited my office almost daily, checking to see if things were going OK. When Tim first visited I tried to avoid him. Maybe I was concerned about being seen with him, or maybe I knew he was like smoking dope, addictive. I'd tell Maggie to make up some excuse; tell him that I was in a meeting or teaching a class. When he did corner me I would be polite and tried to rush through the encounter, but Tim never took the hint. He kept coming. I assumed that he did this for all of his clients, that his job was public relations, but with the techniques Tandoody used, Tim certainly didn't have to make sales calls. I really think he just liked to check out the young teachers, shoot the shit, and get a free cup of coffee.

This man could finesse people: an artful mind-master. I don't know when it happened and how he did it, but I began to anticipate his visits. Each encounter became a lesson in history, sex, humor or philosophy. Yes, maybe that's it; Tim was a philosopher of sorts. He was my guru and I was his disciple.

I took the towel and a cup of black coffee to Tim, who was now lying prone on the sofa with a big smirk on his face.

"Remember me telling you about those crazy Dubai ambulance drivers, Falcon? Did I ever tell you that I used to drive an ambulance?"

"No, you never told me much about what you did before the oil business."

"Arthur Murray dance instructor and am-bu-lance driver, that's all. Fuck, I was the most sought after dance instructor in Hollywood. I had more requests for my services than ol' Arthur himself, and it didn't make him too fond of me. Every widow, lonely wife and spinster in Los Angeles wanted me to come to her house to teach the tango, the lindy, the cha cha."

Forgetting completely about the damaged and wet leg, Tim stood, left arm up, right arm held out and curled at waist level, and began a sham cha cha. He moved about my office floor, smooth, graceful and funny. He stopped, sat down, and continued his story.

"I preferred the widows and vestal virgins cause you never had to worry about their husbands walking in on you. Sometimes, though, I'd swear those big old Hollywood mansions were haunted. Once I spent the night with one of my students and went down to the kitchen for a glass of water. Thought I saw the specter of Fatty Arbuckle looking in the refrigerator." Tim laughed nervously, as if he still feared the vision that was in his memory. "The next day the instructee told me that Fatty had built the house when he was a star, and her husband bought it when Fatty went to prison for rape. You can bet your ass I never went back there, even if she was a good tipper."

Tim leaned his head back and rested his neck on the back of the couch. He stared at the ceiling in deep thought. Jumping back into a formal sitting position, he lifted his jewel laden watch and glanced at the dial. As if deciding that he had more time to spend with me, he said, "Lora, one of my students, was a silent movie star who retired when the talkies started. Once she started vocalizing, you knew why she went into seclusion. Had a voice like a castrati who tried to sew his balls back on. Probably couldn't mend straight." Tim laughed. "Get it, menstruate. Terrible voice but good blow job, especially when she took her teeth out." This time he slapped his thigh and broke into his donkey laugh.

"All of the Hollywood homes I worked in had thick white carpeting in the living room and satin sheets on the beds. Guess it was a status symbol in the '50s. It was a way to let people know they were Hollywood money. Shit, I thought, when I get that kind of dough I'm gonna have white carpeting and satin sheets. Got 'em too. Come over some time and see my place. Man, I could dance—still can."

"I could see from your demonstration that you have the moves," I said.

Again Tim stood and sailed around the office. "One, two, cha-cha-cha, three-four, on the floor, five six, stick in dicks. That was my line when I was teaching other male instructors how to handle students."

I had to ask the question. "Were you what they call a gigolo?"

"Gigolo, naw. I had class. I only slept with the ones who recognized my talent and ability and remunerated me commensurately. Some, I didn't even sleep with, just cuddled or talked. I like to think of myself as a comforter of lonely women." Tim paused to give time for his euphemism to settle. "Widows were lonely; married women whose husbands were always working were lonely; women whose husbands lost their desire were lonely. I was their knight in shining armor, their Sheik of Arabi, the stain on their sheet. I could be washed out of their mind and out of their linen, but I helped them—for a short while, at least. Hell, I was a married man, Falcon!"

"You still married?"

Tim's face clouded; his pale blue eyes turned dark. "Shit, no; not to that bitch. She went with the furniture and the am-bu-lance job." Tim's face brightened, his wife forgotten. "I drove a cadaver car to earn extra money. It was usually a night job. Not a bad fuckin' job, driving around Hollywood and the canyon roads." He smiled and I knew the knee slapping wasn't far behind. "We didn't have trainin' like the rescue squads today. Our job was to scoop 'em up and drop 'em off; the hospital or morgue, whatever the case. Sometimes we mixed 'em up."

"GEESUS, Tim." I stared at him, waiting for some kind of hint that this was another of his "gotcha" jokes. But Tim just shrugged and continued.

"Hell, I told you we weren't trained. BREATHING—HOSPITAL. NOT BREATHING—MORGUE." He looked at me as though I should understand the simplicity of the plan. "When we had no calls we would just ride around or make a quick stop at a roadhouse that my wife and I frequented. My partner and I would run in for a Blue Ribbon or two and listen to the band play. Occasionally we'd check the two-way radio in the ambulance to see if we had a call. Those were my drinking days." Tim wiped a fine line of sweat from his upper lip. "One night I drove by the bar and it looked like my car parked in the lot, a '52 Ford hardtop, robin-egg blue and white; Continental kit on the back; damn, I loved that car. The agreement was that Dee Dee, that's my ex-wife, wouldn't go to the roadhouse without me, but it looked like the rule was being broken. Not too many cars around like that Ford. That night I stopped back just before closing and talked to Freddie, the bass player in the band. Freddie and I were buddies. He said she was there earlier, and although he didn't want to tell me, he finally made it clear that she was there regular-like, usually with the same guy.

"When I asked her about it the next day, she said she was at her sister's and went directly home after. I knew she was lying and was pissed inside, but just dropped it. I didn't know it then, but I see now, she was an alcoholic just like I was, and when she had a few drinks, she liked a good time, just like I did. Well, I kept my eye on the place, and for the next week every time I drove by that roadhouse I got madder and madder, even though the car was never there.

"About ten days later we picked up a heart attack victim and were heading to the hospital. Unfortunately for him I had to drive past the roadhouse. I was zippin' about 85 mph down that road. Just as we were passin' the place, I saw it, my fuckin' Ford. Man, I hit the brakes and did one of those U-turns they do on TV, and spun into the parking lot. As I opened the door and started for the entrance, I could hear my partner crying out, 'TIM, Timmmm, we need to get this guy to the hospital! What the hell are you doing?' I yelled back, 'Fuck that motherfucker. Should have taken better care of himself.' I was furious and I was going after Dee Dee.

"I burst through the swingin' bar doors of that honky-tonk, just like in a Western movie—thought I was John Wayne. I spotted her at the end of the bar with the jerk. I walked over, looked him up and down, and then looked her in the eye. With my left hand I grabbed her half-full glass of beer from the bar and with my right hand I unzipped my pants, wangled out my willy and pissed in her glass."

Tim was bent over in the chair, face buried in his lap trying to muffle his loud laughing. "Shit, Falcon, you should have seen the look on her face. You should have seen the look on the dude's face. You should have seen the look on the faces of the folks in that shit-hole. The band stopped playing. Silence. All eyes were on me, standing with my dick in one hand and the piss cocktail in the other, just waitin' to see what I was gonna do." Tim paused, waiting for my reaction.

"Damn, Tim, what DID you DO?"

"I drank it."

"You did WHAT?"

"You know, down the hatch, cheers, bottoms up, chug-a-lug."

I stared at him. "Why the fuck did you drink it?"

"Well, between me and you, I just couldn't think of anything else to do. When I held the glass up, my hand was trembling from anger; I wanted to put on my tap shoes and dance like Peg Leg Bates across her face. I needed to strike out somehow. Did ya ever see those TV shows or movies where a bright ray of light shines on one of the actors, kind of like a portent of something special, like a miracle? Well, just then I had a spiritual revelation. When I held up that glass of lager-piss, I looked at Dee Dee and she had this amber hue cast across her face, making her look a pale yellow, like she was, what's the word, a,b,c,d,e,f,g,h,i,j, j, ja, jaun, jaundiced, that's it. Always go through the alphabet when I forget a word or a name—helps me remember.

"Anyway, her complexion was yellow, like she was sick with that liver disease alcoholics get. Lookin at her I felt nothing but pity. Now, look at this situation; all eyes were on me. I had to do something bold, something that would make a statement. But DAMN, Falcon, the fury was gone. Everyone was speculatin' and anticipatin' about what was about to happen. Was Johnson gonna belt her boyfriend, beat his wife? What was he gonna do? SHIT, I was a dancer, not a fighter. I wasn't gonna attack her fancy man, and I don't hit ladies, even bitches, so I wasn't gonna get physical with her. I had to do something no one expected, but I felt no anger anymore —so I drank the beerpiss."

"Christ, Tim, I didn't believe it the first time you said it."

"Fuck that shit, it was just my piss mixed with beer, didn't taste too bad. But it wasn't over yet. I looked her in the eye and said real loud so everyone could hear, 'A man's gotta do what a man's gotta do. I'd rather drink piss than have you in my bed.' Fuckin' place went wild. People were clapping, cheering, 'Duke! Duke! Duke!' I lifted my head, turned a 360 to gaze everyone in the eye, puffed my chest out like a robin, and walked out the door. I left with my pride and a new nickname. Looking back at it now, I guess you could say it was a kind of urine therapy."

Tim and I were both laughing now. He stood up and walked to a chair at the conference table and straddled it like a saddle with the back-support in front. He bent forward and rested his arms on the chair back and then set his chin on his arms and gazed at the floor.

"Now, let me tell ya, Falc, you know that spiritual experience? When I got in the ambulance I went through the whole scene over and over. It finally hit me. That light didn't come from God; it came from the spotlights on the mirror behind the bar. When I held up the beer glass, the light reflected from the mirror behind me through the glass and onto Dee Dee's face. Now I was disappointed at first that I didn't have a real supernatural encounter, but think about it. It calmed me down, made me do what I did. Maybe it was Jesus, Buddha, Allah or one of them guys. She works in strange ways, even shining light through piss." Tim laughed. "Ya know God is a woman who speaks Spanish and is a single parent, don't you?"

Wiping the tears from my eyes with my sleeve I looked at the Duke. "Bullshit, Tim, this is bullshit. Tell me the truth, this is bullshit, right?"

"Nope, all true. Shit, Falcon, I'm a fuckin' legend at the Topanga Roadhouse. You go there and ask about the Duke and they'll tell you the story, even show you the mug sitting in a glass case."

"What about that poor innocent bastard with the heart attack?"

"Fucker died! And I lost my job, but it was worth it."

I shook my head. "Don't you feel bad about that?"

"Sure, but the way I figure, the fat fucker was full of cholesterol, nothing was gonna save him. If he didn't die today he was gonna die tomorrow."

"How long before you got divorced?"

"I filed the next day and went over and told her. All she wanted to do was argue about who was gonna get what. She wanted half of this table, half of that chair, half of the car, half of the bed. I guess I still had a lot of anger built up from the night before. The reaction of the crowd made me feel good then, but now she didn't even talk about us and the year we spent together, only about getting half of the money, half of the furniture, half of everything. I erupted like Mount Vesuvius; no miracles that day.

"I walked into the pantry, grabbed a hammer, a prying bar and a saw. I started by cutting the living room coffee table in two. 'One piece for Dee Dee, one for me,' I said as I separated the debris. I broke the radio in pieces and carefully sorted her half and my half. The TV was next and ended up like the radio. I was just starting on the bedroom when the cops arrived and arrested me. Thank God they came before I went after the dog. Dee Dee ran out with the first blow to the coffee table. That was the last I saw her. After getting out of the pokey, I went back to the house to get a few things, went to the lawyer's office, signed the divorce papers and gave all of our possessions to her but the car. Bitch wasn't gonna get that car. I headed north to the oilfields to look for work. Never saw Dee Dee again."

Tim stretched and looked toward the door. "Falconi, I talk too much. I gotta go, and by the sound of all the noise in your secretary's office, so do you. Look, we play poker every Monday night. It's at Leroy's place tomorrow. Come and join us, about 7:30. Yo ho, teacher-o."

Five Card Stud and Stud Camels

"I call your fifty dirhams and raise fifty more," said Leroy. Leroy Houston could cook the best chili and barbeque ribs in Dubai and it was a culinary treat when it was his turn to host the regular poker game.

"You're the barbeque king in this town, Leroy, but I am the stud of five stud poker," challenged Josh. "I can tell when you're lying."

"Ja-Ja-Josh, now you know I'm the king of many things. Cookin' barbeque is hard, but not winnin' when you got the cards. Ha ha, Cassius Clay, oops, I mean brother Mohammed Ali, needs to hire me to write for him, I'm good. What about you, Frankie?" asked Leroy.

Frankie threw his cards face down on the table. "Shit, I know you got it. You're too dumb to bluff, I'm out."

"Frankie, you just a ch-ch-chickin' sh-shit, you honkey redneck."

Just then the doorbell rang continuously. Tim Johnson, no doubt, late as usual.

After two months of playing substitute I had now become a regular in the weekly game. Players come and go but one constant was that Tim Johnson was always late. I hadn't played at Tim's house, but the fellas told me that even at his place they'd be thirty minutes into the game before he came down from the bedroom, freshly showered and laid.

Leroy set his cards down and shook his head. "Je-Je-Jesus, Ashok, answer the door before Johnson breaks the fuckin' bell. Christ, he does that all the fuckin' time and he knows the goddamn door's open. Da-da-damn houseboy, Ashok, don't have enough sense to answer the door when the bell rings."

"Now, Leroy, be gentle with Ashok," said Lenz. "It hasn't been all that long since you were singing 'Let My People Go,' and now you own one of your own."

"Na-na-now don't go talkin' like that, Matt. He ain't no slave. He's my houseboy and I'm his boss, that's all. Black men don't own black men—well, except in Saudi Arabia, I guess. But I have to admit my people musta trained these Indians good, 'cause Ashok knows every excuse in the book to get outta doing work."

Enter Tim Johnson, making enough noise to wake the dead,

followed by a handsome Arab youth about Frankie's age. Tim's guest had a regal face and strong straight body, definitely an outdoorsman. If he were dressed in ornate robes and sitting on a camel, you'd find his photo on the cover of National Geographic.

"Yo ho, you bunch of desert dykes," greeted Tim. "Man, it's hotter than two rats fuckin' in a wool sock out there and it's only March. Hey, this here's Mohammed." Looking toward his visitor, Tim said. "Mo, let me introduce you to this group of Fookie Wookies. This here is Leroy Houston. This is his place. That old fart there is Matt Lenz, a snake oil salesman. Over there's Josh Sampson, works for Oilfield Services. Baby face there, is Steve Jeffery, a Lafayette Voodoo child, another oilfield products peddler, and this here's Frankie Focaccia, he's a biga shota, workin' with NN at MOMS."

"Nice to see you again, Mohammed," said Frankie.

Mohammed reached for Frankie's outstretched hand. "Hi, Frankie. Nice to see you too."

"That kid standing by the food is our new mark, Frickin' Falconi, boss of the American School."

Something about the young Arab's demeanor and Frankie's acquaintance with him led me to respond with the formal, "Pleased to meet you."

As Tim sauntered over to his seat he passed the buffet table, grabbed a paper plate and threw a few pieces of ham on it. He took his seat, setting the plate on the table next to his poker chips. "Relax, Mohammed, and watch me teach these oilfield delinquents how to play poker."

Leroy pushed a pile of poker chips Tim's way. "Ti-Ti-Tim, give me 1,000 dirhams for the chips and fifty for the house to cover the refreshments and food,"

"Would you like a ham sandwich or something to drink, Mohammed?" I asked.

"Something to drink would be fine, non-alcoholic thank you. I'll pass on the sandwich."

Of course, he wasn't gonna touch the ham. It just struck me that according to Islam, ham is *Haraam*, forbidden. It goes back fourteen hundred years to the days of the Muslim Prophet Mohammed (Peace be upon him) when, due to lack of refrigeration, eating pork, which became disease prone because of the heat, was forbidden. Even today it's still part of the Muslim religion, just like it is a part of Judaism, one of the many common denominators between Arabs and Jews.

"Now don't go telling Daddy about us pig eatin' gamblers," Tim said with a big smile. "He might not think it's all that funny and kick me out of Dubai."

"You know my father better than that," Mohammed said. "He'll laugh about it. Besides, he knows you were one of the oilmen who came to Dubai on the first offshore drilling rig in 1965 and stayed here to help build the country."

"Hell, I was just a snot-nosed kid, not much older than Lou there," Tim said.

"Well, you certainly knew the drilling business. Discovered oil for Dubai. My dad will never forget that. I enjoyed the entertainment, gents. Sorry I can't stay to watch the game but I have to go. I just wanted to come in and say hello. Take care and have a fun evening."

With that, Mohammed proceeded around the table, shook hands with all of us and headed for the door. Tim hurriedly moved forward to escort him to the entrance. As he closed the door I heard him say, "Good night, Shaikh Mohammed."

As soon as door closed, I yelled out. "God damn you, Tim Johnson. You just brought Shaikh Mohammed here, the son of the Ruler of Dubai, and didn't even tell us who he was. You shit ass. We could've really said something to make fools of ourselves."

"Well, we didn't," said Frankie. "Hell, I've known Mohammed for awhile. He's a cool guy. We've been diving and riding together. He's still got the *Bedouin* spirit in him, but he can be as Western as we are, and he's a real gentleman. Loves the ladies. Have you ever seen that helicopter flying low over the houses and beach in Jumairah? It's Mohammed checking out the girls sunbathing. He's been known to fly under the electrical wires to look at something special. The girls love him. When they see him coming they stand up, take off their tops and wave them at him."

Tim cut everyone off. "I wasn't gonna make a big fuss over him. He'd feel uncomfortable. Frankie's right. He doesn't want any special treatment. He's a good guy; just don't piss him off."

"You can say that again," chimed in Lenz. "Did you hear what he did at the airport last week? You know those gates that the guard has to lift up to let you in? Seems like the guard was gone, probably takin' a piss, when Mo pulls up. After blowing the horn for five minutes, he gets pissed, kicks the big Mercedes into first, hits the gas and busts the gates to shit. Doesn't like to be kept waitin'."

Once the excitement and storytelling calmed, we resumed our fifty-two card ritual, watching the chips move from one player to the next and then congregate in front of Tim and Steve.

"Hey, fookie fookie. Ashok, come here and get me a soda water," Tim called out to the houseboy.

Josh stood up and stretched. "Let's take a break for a bite and a piss."

It obviously sounded good, as we all got up from the card table and moved to the food table or the toilets.

"Why did you bring Mohammed here tonight?" I asked Tim as I stood next to him.

"Well it wasn't planned," Tim said, and I could tell he was leading into one of his stories. "When I got here I cased the windows of the house next door to see if I could catch a look at one of J. R. Dumont's beautiful secretaries. Fuck, I don't know who hires them honeys but they only bring in the best-looking British girls. Four of them share the house next door. I didn't see any broads through the windows, but I did see a fine new 1974 Pontiac Grand Am convertible in the drive. It was red and had white leather seats. The top was down and I wanted a closer look at the inside of that car. I'd never seen one in Dubai before.

"As I walked over and got nearer to the trunk, a long female leg slid up from the back seat and draped itself over the covering that hides the convertible top when it's down. Naturally, I was curious; it's a nice car and I wanted a better look. I was a couple feet from the back of the red beauty when it started shaking like there's one of those California earthquakes. First we got the jumpin', then we got this awful hullabaloo, squealing and grunting, like there was a pig farm in the back of that car. Of course I had to investigate. Shit, one of those pigs sounded like it was in pain and may have needed my help, *ha, ha.* Just as I reached the trunk of the car and started to peer into the back seat, the noise stopped, the vibrating slowed and up popped this good lookin' young stud with his dark hair and beard all wild."

"Don't tell me it was Shaikh Mohammed, Tim," I said.

"Fuck no, Falconi. It was Dodi Bin Din, Mohammed's best buddy. When it comes to women, those two guys always have the best. Anyway, Dodi, smilin' like a happy goat herder, looked around and spotted me. He stood up on the back seat, both hands holding his *dishdashah* up above his knees, and yells out, 'Hi ya, Tim. How ya doing?'

"Well, he obviously looked like he had just eaten something, but you can bet it wasn't bacon. There wasn't a porker in the back of that car; she was a beauty. 'Hey, how ya doin, Dodi?' I replied.

"'I'm great. Hot and sweaty, but great. Where you going?'

"'I'm just going next door to play a little poker.'

"'I just finished a little poker myself,' Dodi said with a big smile.

"As we're talking, I looked up at the front door of the house and there stood Shaikh Mohammed with his arm around a good looking blond.

"'Hello, Tim. Did I hear you say that you're playing poker? Mind if come and watch a bit?'

"'Hell no, come on over,' I said. In the back of the car, up popped Flick Marrin, secretary to the president of J.R. Dumont. A Flick and a dick, *ha, ha,* get it? Flick, Dodi and I chatted while Mohammed went in and freshened up and then I brought him here. All of the foreign girls seem to go for Mohammed. He's one good-looking dude. Most of all he's rich and will probably be the Shaikh who will eventually run this place. He may seem a bit wild now but once he matures a bit and realizes that his brothers don't have the ability to take care of business in Dubai, he'll settle down. He's still young."

"Will he ever become ruler? Isn't he third in line for succession?" I said.

"You watch, he'll work his way in to become Crown Prince, and when the time is right he'll take over."

"You mean he'll stage a coup and overthrow his brothers?" I asked.

"Naw, the Maktoum boys are shrewd and they have thick blood. They'll never use force against each other. They'll just horse bargain, cut some kind of deal. You know, like I'll give you all of this for that. You just wait. It'll happen."

Leroy called to us. "Let's get this game on the road," he said.

It was Tim's deal and he was energized, ready to play. The visit by Mohammed really got him hyper.

"Hey, Leroy," said Tim.

Oh, oh, I could see something coming. Tim's tone of voice told me he had a deep thought on his mind. That could mean he was conjuring up one of his jokes, or trouble.

"Now what do you want old man?" responded Leroy.

"Now, you're a black American and your wife is from Thailand right?"

"You know that's right, Duke."

"Well, does that make your kids American ty-coons?"

Even before the coon in tycoon came all the way out of Tim's mouth, he stood up laughing, hitting his hands together, and slapping his thigh. The rest of the poker players were holding in their laughs and watching Leroy, who threw his hands in the air along with a couple of poker chips that flew across the room. The stomach of Leroy's big 300-pound body pushed the poker table back three feet, and then with a crash of human meat and chips clashing together, he prostrated the top half of his body on the table. With his head cradled in his arms he laughed as hard as the Duke did. God bless Leroy. A lesser man would have taken offense. But this was the Duke, we were all friends, we knew one another's personalities. It was like calling Frankie or me a Dago or Wop, the kind of cut down that only friends could do to friends. Race, creed or color meant nothing to us. In Dubai, we were all equal.

Once we settled down and Leroy had a chance to get a few digs into Tim, we got back to playing poker.

"All right, Steve Bin Bitch, let's see if you can win this one," taunted the Duke. He was still on a roll.

"What the hell does Steve Bin Bitch mean?" I asked.

"It's just the Duke's way of being cute," explained Lenz. "The Arabs use the term *Bin* meaning 'son of.' For example Majid Bin Jabir really means Majid, son of Jabir. Tim is just calling Steve a 'son of a bitch' in his cute way."

Steve threw a fifty-dirham chip on the table. "I open *Abou* Smoky."

"Sorry, I'm slow, but now what's that mean?" Again Lenz obliged.

"*Abou* means father. When Steve said *Abou* Smoky, he's really calling Tim 'father of Smoky,' who in this case is Tim's dog."

"That's right," chimed in Steve. "I opened, you father of a dog. Do you call or not, Fido?"

The *Abou* and *Bin* banter continued until it wasn't funny anymore, but at least I learned that Arab names usually have three parts. The first name is the given name of the person. Shaikh Mohammed's first name is Mohammed. Shaikh is his title of royalty. The second name is the father's name. In this case it is Rashid, the Ruler of Dubai, but *Bin* is placed before the name Rashid to designate "son of." The third name is the family or tribal name. Shaikh Mohammed Bin Rashid Al Maktoum is literally Mohammed, son of Rashid of the Maktoum family or tribe. So I was Luigi, son of Giovanni, of the Falconi family or tribe. Luigi Bin Giovanni Al Falconi. Neat, huh?

It was close to midnight, our agreed quitting time, and Steve Jeffery was making a big deal over the fact that most of the chips were stacked in front of him. It wasn't enough that he was lucky; he had to keep rubbing it in as to what a great poker player he was. I could tell Frankie was tired of the banter when he interrupted Steve and said to Tim, "Hey, congratulations. I understand that you landed the camp contract for the drilling in the new onshore oilfield. Who'd you pay for that contract?"

Tim looked up from his cards, and with a child-like look of dejection stared at Frankie for a moment, as if offended. "Shit, all of the big boys were going after that one. You know how I won it? Not because I'm buddies with Rick Roberts, drillin' boss of Kuwait/American Drilling Company, but because I had the lowest bid."

Tim set his cards on the table. I could tell he was getting ready for more than an answer to a question. He looked at all of us, one by one, and then continued. "Abdulla Catering, MIS, DUMAK were all bidding on it. You were too, Frankie, at MOMS, but I got it. Mine was the lowest bid, no hanky panky, just good business. I don't kiss ass to those guys at Continent or the other oil companies like most of those service company leaches. Shit, they latch on to a COC manager and do anything for a contract. Those guys are Dubai oilfield COC suckers, but not me, I just offer the best job at the lowest price— no ass kissin'."

Tim stood up, puckered his lips, shook his ass, clasped his hands together and giggled. "Really pissed off some of them, especially, what's his name at Abdulla Catering? You know, the Lebanese prick? Hader, Hoder, Haider, ya, that's it Halib Haider. Fuck, he's upset that I'm gonna prepare the well location. He doesn't even know what the hell a well location is. He doesn't have the slightest idea. He's a caterer, but the greedy son of a bitch wants to get into my business. Fucker should stick with serving lunches."

Walking over to the desk, Tim picked up the phone for visual effect and continued his tale. "This God damn Lebanese shit calls Roberts, and here I am in the office talking to Rick. You guys know Rick. Like all drilling hands, he likes to drink once in a while. That morning Rick tells my girlfriend Evie, his secretary, that he's going to the drilling site. But he never went there because I drove by Poncho Villa's restaurant and seen his car, your car, and Steve's. You and some of the other oilfield bandits were sittin' in Poncho's at ten in the morning playing liar's poker and doin' shooters with Jose Cuervo. Anyway, I'm sittin' there in his office waiting to take Evie home when Rick walks in half sloshed, drunker than a piss pot, no drunker than usual."

Tim set the phone down and with a clomp, clomp, clomp, walked across the floor, mimicking a drunken Rick. "'Hi ya, Tim, how ya doing?' Rick says to me. Then Evie says to Rick, 'Halib Haider called and wants to talk to you.' Well, when Rick gets drunk he's a real obnoxious motherfucker. The first thing he says, right in front of Evie, and if it was your mother, or even Jesus Christ's mother he'd still say it. 'What's that fucker want?'

"Ya see, this is just the way Rick talks. Don't bother me none, I don't care if he jerks off in front of the whole world, that's his fuckin' business, okay. Just then the phone rings and Evie answers it."

Tim walked back and picked up the phone again, cupping his hand over the receiver. "She's holding her hand over the mouth piece like this, and tells Rick that it's Halib. Rick takes the phone from Evie and listens to this Lebanese dumb fuck say, 'Rick.' Then Rick cups his hand over the phone and says to me, 'Tim, listen to this asshole, Lebanese motherfucker, listen to him, huh.' That fuckin' Rick takes the phone, and holds it out so I can hear Halib when he says. 'Are we ever gonna get any work in that oilfield or is that asshole Johnson gonna get it all? What can he do that we can't do better?' Now I'm listening to all of this shit, see, and you know I have never said anything bad about Halib in all of my life; I've known him for years. I've never tried to make sandwiches and get into his business, yet this bastard is saying this about me. Now you know what that fuckin' Rick did, sorry drunk son of a bitch, he says to Halib? 'Well, I don't know, Halib, but why don't you ask Tim? He's sittin' right here. *Ha, ha.*' Fucker hands me the phone."

Tim is clapping the phone on his upturned palm, laughing like hell. "Can you believe that motherfucker, Rick? My eyes are buggin' out. I just look at the phone, look at Rick. I ain't gonna get cross-threaded with nobody. I could give a fuck about that job out there. Stick it in your ear. Bid on it, you asshole. I only got the job because I was the lowest bid. Take the job if you want it. I grabbed the phone and slammed it down. Can you believe that damn Rick? He sits there laughing like hell. I called him a fuckin' asshole and left his fuckin' office."

"With all the business being doled out, there's plenty for everyone," Steve said. "What we need is an in with Majid Bin Jabir, the Director of the Energy Office."

"Hell, that ol' Bin Jabir is sharp," Tim said. "He comes down to Dubai from Bahrain, and gets close to the ruler by saving his ass when Dubai was broke. After a few years making a few million here and there, he sees the big money is in oil. So he convinces Rashid that he, a raghead from some little shit sandbox island up the Gulf, knows everything there is to know about the oil business. Fuck, Bin Jabir thinks that drilling is something you do to a vagina. He doesn't know piss from oil, but that's all right. You know why? Because the ruler knows fuckin' less!"

Tim took his seat at the table and leaned back in his chair. "Shit, Bin Jabir's made lots of money for the ruler and the ruler loves Bin Jabir; and Bin Jabir loves the ruler. Bin Jabir's a swingin' dick. He's got hotels in London, apartments in Monte Carlo, buys his clothes from that Iranian wet-back on Rodeo Drive in Los Angeles, uh, what's his name, bees-ass or some shit like that?"

"Bijan," I said.

"Ya, that's it. Well, Bin Jabir thinks he's a smart motherfucker. Hell, I think he's smart too. So he takes on the oil business for Dubai. Good for him, and he does a fuck of a good job too. And I bet he and the ruler make a fuck of a lot of money. This Bin Jabir is in tight with Rashid now, but only if Rashid is around. As soon as the ruler heads for paradise, Bin Jabir's out. Bin Jabir knows he has to get as much as he can now. But for now he's the 'in man,' and he's rich. The richer he gets, the more credibility he'll have. One day, ten years from now, he'll be so wealthy that nobody will know where he came from or, if they do, they won't say shit. Do ya think people care that John Kennedy's daddy was a bootlegger, or the chairman of Occidental Oil, ol' Arm and Hammer, worked for the Russian commies? Fuck, no! Hell, in a couple of years they'll probably make Bin Jabir ambassador to Fuckywuckyland. All of the Fuckywuckians will call him 'your extraordinary,' 'your excellency,' 'your ex-lax' or some shit like that. And you know what, so will we. Why? Because the son of a bitch is richer than hell. He's got more money than we'll ever have. That's why, and that's just the way it is. When I see him alone in his garden, I'll still say, 'Hi, Majid,' cause he knows I know, and it will be all right, just between the two of us. But when I see him in public, it will be 'Your Excellency,' 'cause he knows I know, and if I tell, I'm on the next boat outta here. This guy ain't afraid of anything now. He drives a fuckin' Lincoln Continental—the only one in the Middle East since the Israeli boycott law banned Ford. Does he give a damn about some boycott law? Fuck no! If he's beyond the law now, wait 'til he's filthy rich. Shit, to him the Arab and Jews are both 'wanky whackers;' they're brothers. Probably why they're always fighting. Shit, he says let them kill each other, ain't no skin off his weenie. Shit his banana peel is already gone, just like his brother Hymie."

"Well," Steve said. "before he becomes untouchable, we got to figure how to get Bin Jabir to influence some business our way. You're in good with him through Iskar, ain't you, Tim?"

As Tim turned toward Steve, I could see the furrows of skin grow on his forehead and the eyebrows draw up to join them. "Fuck no! Sure, I know him, see him and even shop for him. Shit, one day Iskar has me run out to buy underwear for the rich fucker. As much money as he's got, he still wears Jockeys just like you and me. We may wear the same underpants, but we are not in the same league as Bin Jabir. Hell no! He'll say hello to us when we see him, let you paint his pool, right, Lenz? And buy him Jockey's, but he does business with the big boys, guys like Scrudds, at Continent and Brandon Davidson, the Chairman of Dumont. He's not gonna deal with little piss ants like us."

"Maybe we need to get closer to him and the royal family," Matt said. "We could pitch in and buy one of those racing camels so we can be with the locals at the Friday camel races. You know, rub shoulders with Rashid and his sons where Bin Jabir can see us."

"Camel races? Where do they have camel races?" I asked, swaying from the topic of conversation. Having lived in Dubai for less than a year, I was still learning about the local culture, and racing camels sounded interesting. I could just picture a racetrack with viewing stands and satin-clad camel-jockeys riding on the humps of these gangly creatures.

Tim's eyes glanced in my direction as if acknowledging my comment, and then honed in on Steve. "Forget that shit. You have no chance in hell of getting any business at that level."

As if that comment closed the subject, Tim turned to me. "Falcon, you never seen a camel race? Next Friday morning I'll come to the house and we'll take the family. The kids will love it. You have a four-wheel drive, don't you?"

"Sure, we just traded the Daihatsu for a new Toyota Land Cruiser."

"Good, we'll use your car."

"Last hand," called out Leroy. "It's midnight."

Frankie thought it was unlucky to sit in the same seat every week, so tonight fate had him sitting next to me. Throughout the night we borrowed chips from each other or made change from each other's kitty. There was a sense of trust that had developed between us. Even so, I was surprised when, during the last hand, he bent over and said, "My brother Rocco will be in town in a few weeks. He wants to go diving in the Musandam. You want to go?"

"You bet." I was thrilled for the opportunity to dive with Frankie, especially since we would be using the *Puss and Hoots*, a 120-foot yacht owned by Frankie's godfather NN. But I was even more honored that he would allow me to meet the "famous" Rocco Focaccia. Frankie was a bit secretive about the family, and usually only close friends, shit, there's that word again, were introduced to them. I couldn't wait for this last hand to finish so I could get home to tell Marie that I was going diving with Frankie and his revered brother from New Orleans.

I lost a few hundred dirhams that night but I was up two invitations, one to the camel races and one to dive.

I'd Walk a Mile for a Camel

The following Friday, the Duke pulled up to my house at 8:00 a.m. sharp. The Land Cruiser was packed with my family and a cool box of soft drinks and water. Even in April the midday heat could dehydrate a watermelon.

A few minutes later a yellow Suzuki with three carrot-topped kids pulled up. It was Josh Sampson and his family. I had asked Josh to join us for the races. After trading my daughter for the redhead Sampson boy to allow friends with friends, Tim and Evie hopped in our car and we were off.

"Which way to the camel racetrack?" I asked as we drove away.

"Racetrack? Racetrack?" Tim laughed. "There ain't no fuckin' racetrack; it's just desert, you'll see. Head straight on the Awir Road until it ends and follow the dirt path. I'll direct you when we get close."

Once we left the macadam, the dirt roadway became a carnival ride for the kids, up and down small sand dunes like a mini-roller coaster. Occasionally we'd hit a big dune, propelling the kids in back off their seats, almost hitting their heads on the roof of the car. Marie held our two-year old tightly in her lap. No seat belts in Dubai cars in those days.

After twenty minutes of bouncing we reached a baffling crisscrossing of several routes etched in the sand heading in every direction.

"Take the sand track to the left that leads up that big dune," commanded our navigator.

Onward we went, up the sand hill to the summit. From our elevated perch we could see a large flat area below filled with four-wheel drive vehicles, herds of camels and groups of Arab men and small children.

Tim pointed to the gathering below. "That's it. Drive down and stop anywhere so we can get out to take a closer look at the camels."

Josh Sampson's son with the Ruler of Dubai, His Royal Highness Shaikh Rashid Bin Saeed Al Maktoum, at the camel races in 1975.

"Where do they race? I asked.

"Right here; this is it," Tim replied, holding in a laugh.

Once out of the cars we roamed about the area, looking at the beasts and listening to the verbal exchange between groups of men, obviously making camel talk and wagering on the morning's races. The Sampson kids with their red hair made quite an impression on the locals. A couple of the Arabs offered to buy their son and his sisters for camels and money. Just in jest we thought. Or hoped.

I had read about the single hump Arabian dromedary, but this was my first opportunity to examine one of the gangly beasts, even if it was from a safe distance. Looking at the fur-covered mound rising like a small hill on the top of its back, I remembered reading that this hump was not for storing water, as most people think, but was a mound of fat. However it is true that the dromedary only needs water every three or four days, but that's because they can drink up to a third of their body weight.

Slowly I walked around to face the sandy-colored animal. Sticking out my top lip, I tried to mimic the deeply-cleft upper lip. All I could think of was Robert Mitchum's chin. Seeing a flutter of the long, sophisticated-looking eye lashes, I looked to see if I could detect the third eyelid that moves from side to side, much like a windshield wiper, to keep sand out of their eyes.

All of the racing camels had a small peg with a string attached inserted in their noses. In my elementary Arabic I asked the trainer what it was.

"*Khezaam,*" he replied.

I was able to ascertain that unlike a horse, which has a bit in its mouth attached to the reins to steer it, the reins, or *rassan,* of the racing camels are connected to the string of the *Khezaam.* A gentle pull on the reins guided the camel's direction.

All of a sudden the Arabs headed for the cars, except the little Arab boys. I couldn't believe my eyes when I saw their small bodies, not much bigger than our two-year-old son, being hoisted just behind the hump of the camels on a saddle called a *khorj* and tied on with rope so that they wouldn't fall off. There were no stirrups so their tiny feet just dangled or were crossed on the saddle.

Tim half-jogged back toward the car. "Come on, let's go."

I gathered the kids and we ran behind Tim and hopped in the car. Our engine started in unison with the others, just like Indy race drivers.

"Just follow the cars," said the Duke. "When they move, we move."

Once the child jockeys were on their camels, the old *Bedouin* trainers slapped the camel's hindquarters and they were off. At the same instant the pack of jeeps took off. Soon the cars were driving alongside the racing camels. The driver of each packed vehicle tooted his horn while the occupants leaned out of the windows, cheering, screaming and banging on the sides of the cars to encourage their favorite. All of our kids in both cars, as well as we adults, followed the example of our hosts. Straight across the hard salt flats the camels ran, and we drove, a cacophony of voices, camel grunts, horns and metal beats. What a trip!

From a distance the small *dishdashah*-wearing jockeys looked like little stuffed teddy bears on top of their camels, using their short sticks to strike the tough hide of their steeds. The tiny torsos of the mini-jockeys were shaking up and down while they held on to the camel's hairy hide for dear life. Pulling alongside one of the racers we noticed that he was sliding off the camel to the left and then disappeared.

Fearing that the little rider fell off and would get trampled, we slowed down until the herd passed to see if we could help. Once the camels went past us we looked on the ground, expecting to see the battered body, but could find nothing. We sped up to catch the mob, and as we closed in on the rear of the pack of running animals, we spotted the riderless camel, except that it wasn't riderless. The wee jockey had slid off to the side of the hump and was riding at a 45-degree angle from his steed on our blind side. The ropes held him on but he had to be hurting.

He wasn't in too much danger from speed; even the fastest racing camels can only run about ten miles per hour, but they have endurance and are able to cover up to a hundred miles a day. Unlike a horse, which lifts both front and then hind legs, the camel raises both legs on one side and then the other, giving it a rocking, shuffling gait. This rocking motion is why the camel inherited the term "ship of the desert."

Finally the camels started to slow to a gallop and then to a walk, indicating that the race was over. Vehicles stopped and passengers disembarked to congratulate their riders and trainers and to help untie the boys from the camels. The little fellow that we saw doing the trick riding was released and helped down to the ground, apparently unharmed.

What a gas! It wasn't at all what we expected, but it was really great fun. The morning continued with several more races. We followed a couple more events in the car but spent most of the time walking through the camps of trainers, jockeys and their camels, taking photos, drinking tea and learning about camels.

"Come on, Falcon, they won't hurt you," encouraged the Duke. "Follow me. I'll take you to pet that big one over there."

The Duke led me to the largest camel I had ever seen. Just as we came face to face with the desert beast, Tim quickly stepped away, leaving me alone to confront the camel. In a quick gesture, the animal pulled back his long neck and made a sound as if he were sucking air into his nose. With a downward motion his head came forward and out flew a camel-size gob of greenish brown and yellow mucus, smack onto my shirt. Stunned, I jumped back to where an amused Duke was doubled over in laughter.

"Ya got to watch those camels, Falcon. They have a bad habit of spitting on people if they get too close. *Haw haw*."

V
Sam and Abdul

The Arabian Blackbeard

Two weeks after my first exposure to camel races, Frankie's brother Rocco, or Rocky, as he was known to his close friends, arrived from New Orleans. Rocky, as the chosen heir of Flatface, took care of the family business as well as operated a number of well-known enterprises throughout Louisiana. The most familiar to the folks in New Orleans was a bar on Bourbon Street called "Rocky's Place." It was a favorite nightspot for the natives and the tourists who came to experience an alcoholic concoction made with a secret recipe called the "Climax." If you didn't have one while you were drinking it, you were guaranteed to have one later; however, there was no guarantee that you could remember it. Selling souvenir gift items to the tourists who were eager to celebrate their experience of having a "Climax" at Rocky's was bigger business than selling the drinks.

Rocky arrived early in the week, and after catching up with his jet lag by lying around the beach and sightseeing in Dubai, he was ready to head toward the Arabian Sea coast of Fujairah for some scuba diving.

It was mid April, and although the weather was still hot during the day, the cool breezes and temperate water made for great diving. My only diving experiences at this point in my diving career were in the waters of the Arabian Gulf and the fiords of the Musandam Peninsula. It wasn't until I had the chance to experience diving in Hawaii, the Caribbean, and the Red Sea that I realized how lucky I was to do my novice diving in the Musandam fiords, some of the most beautiful underwater venues in the world. The waters of the Oman are laden with colorful coral and provide a habitat for an abundance of underwater sea life.

A new two-lane highway had recently been completed, linking Dubai through Sharjah to the mountains of Fujairah. Anyone familiar with the Rockies or Alps would scoff at calling 3,000-foot barren rocky hills mountains, but after the flat desert terrain, these were mountains. Six months earlier the only routes through the mountains were via riverbeds called *wadis*, which carried rushing waters from the mountains to the sea during the rainy season. Local Arabs dug wells, made primitive cisterns and built aqueducts to carry water from the *wadis* to their date palm groves. These canyons were a green belt, with their rocky riverbeds lined with palm trees and little fertile gardens. Ten months of the year, dry rocky canyons formed a maze through the mountains, creating roadways. During the other two months rain made them impassable. Flash floods washed away cars and drowned campers in their rushing waters.

With the new route, travelers no longer had to drive all-terrain vehicles through the *wadis* to get to the coast. The road cut hours off the trip and made it quite comfortable, although less scenic.

The *Puss and Hoots*, NN's yacht, was offshore Khor Fakkan, a beautiful little half-moon bay located on the coast just south of the Musandam. Because Rocky had only a few days before heading back to the States, we decided to drive across to Khor Fakkan rather than take the extra time to travel to and from Dubai on the boat.

When Frankie pulled up to my house at 6:30 a.m. on that Thursday morning, I was patiently waiting in front with my dive bag packed. I was ready to go. WOW, a trip on NN's yacht.

As I started to pick up my gear, I was surprised to hear the familiar voice of the Duke coming from the back seat.

"Let's get your school-teaching ass going, Falconi."

"What are you doing here, Tim?" I said. "You don't dive. From what I hear, you've never even been in a swimming pool, much less the sea."

"Diving, water, shit, no! Do you know what fish do in that water besides piss and crap? They fuck! I definitely don't swim where fish fornicate. Nah, I'm just going along for the ride. I need to get away from Dubai for a couple of days and relax."

Frankie moved from the driver's seat to the rear of the car and opened the tailgate so I could load my gear. "Relax, my ass, Johnson," he said. "You're coming with us because you've got big bad guys in Dubai trying to collect money from you and you want to get lost."

"Shit, no!" Tim glided his long fingers through his snowy hair. "Well, yeah, in a way, sort of, but just for a couple of days until my bankers work out the problem."

I threw my gear in the back of the Land Cruiser, hopped in the rear seat with Tim, and off we drove. Thirty minutes down the road, Johnson grabbed the sleeve of my shirt and tugged.

"Looky here." Like a child showing his closest friend his most prized possession, Tim slowly opened a leather portfolio and pulled out several neatly packaged documents. With a big smile on his face, he carefully removed one of the papers from its plastic sheath, unfolded it, and laid it on the seat area between us. It appeared to be an old nautical chart showing the delineation of the Oman Mountains and the Musandam Peninsula with its fiords and coastlines. The outlines of the coast and mountains seemed to be hand drawn with Arabic and English writing to identify geographical areas, villages and coves, probably safe ports. It clearly showed that the Musandam Peninsula was created by the tops of the Hajar Mountains of Oman before they dipped into the sea at the Straight of Hormuz.

"What a beautiful old chart," I said, touching the parchment-like paper.

At the bottom right hand corner a red wax seal, with two short ribbons bound by the wax, adorned the document. The words written above the seal identified it as a product of *Admiral Heratio F. Scott O.B.E., Hydrographer for His Majesty King Edward III, Royal Navy*, and the year 1768.

"Damn, Tim, this is over two hundred years old. Where'd you get it? How much is it worth?" The Duke just looked at me with a shit-eatin' grin on his face and opened the second document.

"None of your fuckin' business, Falcon. Now look at this one."

I caught Rocky and Frankie glancing over the seat at the charts and then smiling at each other while Tim played "tease the Falcon."

Tim laid out a modern, nautical chart on top of the old one.

Flipping between both charts, Tim said, "See how similar both of these are, Falc? Amazing how accurate an old chart like this can be. Now look closely at this area here, this little inlet near the village of Khasab. See, in the old chart, it's drawn in clearly. Now, look at the new chart. Gone! Where did it go? Two hundred years difference between both maps. During that period, how did this little bay disappear?"

"It looks like a squiggly line to me. Almost like a corkscrew. Maybe it's not an inlet."

"Well, why would it have a name on it then," asked the Duke. "It was here 200 years ago. Now it's not."

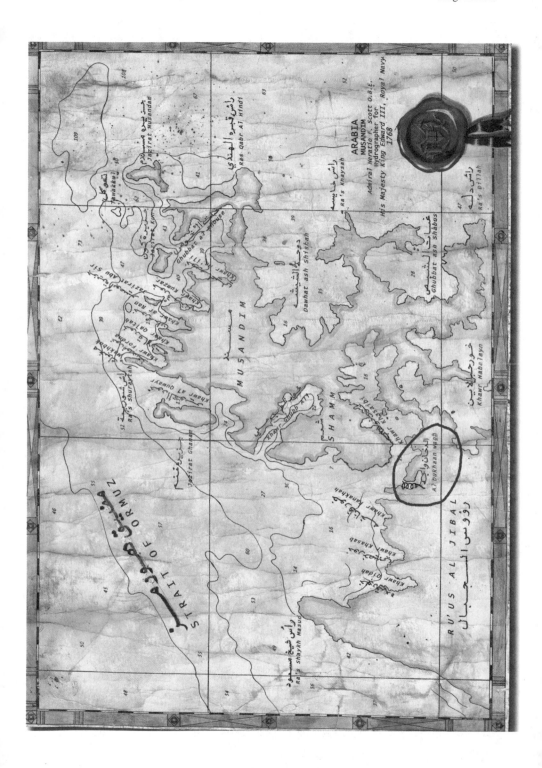

"You sound just like a fuckin' schoolteacher, Falcon. No, there is more to this than nature." Tim's long, thin finger traced a route on the old chart. "Pirates have used these little hidden bays and waterways that cut through the Musandam as a place to hide from the British or whoever they robbed. They had fast ships with low draft so they could come into the shallow waters and hide in these little waterways. Like this one right here." Tim pointed to one of the many coves shown on the map. "The British or Dutch ships were big and couldn't follow. Hit and run was the way the pirates of this area played the game. Look at the name written above the inlet. Can you read it?"

"Let me see, (ال دخان وجه) aaal, al, du, du, duk." I shook my head. "Sorry, the Arabic letters are small and I haven't learned them all very well."

"You dumb shit, Falconi! Look right above the Arabic writing."

Readjusting my eyes, I saw the words written in old English script above the Arabic. "Oh! Uh, it says *Al Dukhaan Wag*." I felt like a real dummy.

Tim took his long-fingered hand and raked his white hair toward the back of his head in frustration. "Now ya got it, Falc. Al Duke-on, OooooEeeee, The Duke, Falcon, Al Duke, me, I'm the Duke. Don't you see, it's fate? It was my destiny to come to Dubai, to find this map. I was meant to be here."

"I think you're distorting the pronunciation a bit and taking it too literally," I said. "The word has a more guttural sound than the way we pronounce Duke."

"Who gives a shit about guttural, literal, clitoral? I know what it sounds like. Now tell me, what does *Al Dukhaan Wag* mean in English?"

"Well, '*Dukhaan*' means 'smoky or black' and '*Al*' is the article 'the.' And '*Wag*' means face. It says 'the smoky face.'"

"Right on, that's what it means all right, Smoky Face! Huuumm. Ya see, Falcon, I've been studying this for some time, and you know who I figure Smoky Face is? That's Black Beard the pirate. Yep, that's who it is. See how it translates. A gray-black beard covering a white man's face becomes a Smoky Face. I believe ol' Smoky Face, or rather Black Beard, used this inlet as a hiding place to get away from the British Navy." He sat back and gave me a minute to digest his theory.

Unable to wait any longer, he nodded. "You know what that means. Treasure!"

"Jesus, Tim, don't you think you're stretching it a bit? It could mean Smoky Robinson. I don't think Black Beard was ever in the Gulf. I think he was in the Caribbean."

"Falcon, those pirates were all over the five seas, and this map was made just after Black Beard's pirate days."

"Seven seas, Tim."

"Five, seven, nine, who gives a fuck. They went anywhere they could find a gold doubloon, piece of eight, or piece of ass. It's no coincidence that Black Beard's name got on this map."

"Smoky Face," I corrected.

"Smoky, black, whatever, it's all in the translation," Tim said as he stretched out his long index finger and pointed to the words on the map. "It's there because he was here, right at this spot, and we'll be there tomorrow."

Peering over the back seat, Frankie smiled. "So that's why you came, to find treasure."

Tim became silent—deep-thought silence, making the rest of the drive a peaceful respite. There was no changing Tim's mind when he got an idea up his ass. If he believed in something, he'd go to the end of the earth to prove it.

Reaching Khor Fakkan, we shuttled out to the yacht in the bay. It was perfect timing to enjoy a sunset dinner on the aft deck, an epicurean delight. As soon as the meal was finished and the galley was squared away, the captain lifted anchor and set sail for the bay at Khasab, a little coastal village in the Musandam Peninsula of Oman. We headed for our bunks. Well, really double beds in our own rooms. Tim and I lost the toss, so we had to sleep in the cabins that shared a bath, while Frankie and Rocky had private baths. Tough job, but someone had to do it.

As I lay in bed swaying gently with the movements of the sea, I looked out the porthole toward the starlight night, thinking about tomorrow's dives and my good fortune to be a friend of Frankie Focaccia. What a way to dive. No sixteen-foot dive boats, no lugging heavy tanks from the car to the boat, no messy clean up of equipment after the dive, no hauling tanks to the dive shop for air. Frankie could use his godfather's yacht whenever he felt the urge, which was often.

Appropriately named the *Puss and Hoots,* it was a luxurious way to get away from life in the oil patch or the classroom. The boat had an eight-man crew plus the best nautical chef in the Middle East. It had cabins for ten people, a lounge with two chesterfields, lounge chairs, card tables and a dining room that would seat ten formally. Communications were via satellite so faxes and telephone calls were easily received.

We usually cast off from Dubai early evening and woke up the next morning at Khasab. Or we anchored off one of the many islands that dot the coast of the Emirates. Since we drove to the east coast, our trip to Khasab tonight would be short.

Anxious to get to sleep, I hoped morning would come even sooner. Just before I dozed off, I thanked God for my family—and for my rich friends.

When we awoke, the yacht was anchored off the coast near the little village of Khasab, just as planned. Rocky, Frankie and I, eager to get the most out of our one full day of diving, were up at first light and joined each other on the stern for a light breakfast and to watch a brilliant sunrise over the mountains.

As we planned our dives for the day, a scraggly faced, untamed-haired Tim Johnson, wrapped in a pink *Puss & Hoots* monogrammed bathrobe and mid-heel furry pink slippers left by some past female guest, shuffled out on the deck from the lounge and joined us.

Frankie looked at the morning spectacle of the Duke and shook his head. "My, don't you look stunning this morning, Timmy."

"Good fuckin' morning to you too," replied the Duke.

Rocky and I giggled at the spectacle but thought better of saying anything.

"Where are you Hookie Fookie's headed today?" Tim asked.

Frankie stood up and looked toward the coastline, pointing north. "I thought we'd take one of the small tenders and run up the fiord to Ras Al Lema, then out to perforated rock and back here for lunch. In the afternoon, we'll go towards Buka and dive the walls along the coast,"

"What about you, Tim?" I asked. "Just plan to lounge around here on the boat?"

"Shit, no! I'm gonna follow my map to *Al Dukhaan,* explore the shore, and maybe climb up to the plateau to see if I can figure out what happened to that inlet."

"Well, be careful," I said. "This area is inhabited by the *Shihuh* tribe. The desert tribes consider them to be wild men. I've met some of the *Shihuh* who live on the fringes down near the village of Shams in Ras Al Khaimah. They were hospitable because I was with an Arab from Dubai who they knew and trusted, but even they say the mountain dwellers can be a bit untamed, to put it mildly. I guess living in caves or houses made of stones with no roofs can make you a bit hostile."

I walked to the railing. Pointing toward shore, I continued. "Can you see those stone houses in the village of Khasab and on the cliffs up the side of the mountains? Those are penthouses compared to what the *Shihuh* in the hills live in. They speak no recorded language. If it weren't for learning some crude Arabic to read the Koran, they probably wouldn't be able to speak to outsiders."

Rocky joined me at the deck rail and studied the village buildings. "How in the hell do they live?" he asked.

"See the small boats at the shoreline near the base of the cliff? They're basically fishermen. At the end of a day fishing they carry their catch to their families in the mountains. They walk like mountain goats on these rocky cliffs and raise crops up on the plateaus in the winter. The climate at their altitude is milder than the desert and there are some flat plains on the mountaintops, which allow them to grow oranges, bananas, and all kinds of vegetables. They also hunt. Believe it or not, there are leopard, rabbits and other game in those hills."

"Hear that, Johnson?" Rocky said. "They see that wild white hair of yours and they're either gonna shoot you as wild game or welcome you home as a long lost brother." He grinned, surveying Tim's fuzzy pink outfit. "Or maybe a lover."

"Only if he wore a loincloth and wrapped himself in bandoleers like they do," I said. "Oh, and you have to carry a hatchet like American Indians. It's not really a hatchet but an axe with a small head, about four inches across, and a two-foot handle. They use it as a tool and as a weapon. They've been known to split a few heads with those axes, but lucky for you, Tim, they don't take scalps. But they might take yours if they catch your ass climbing around in their back yard. Just last year a German was surveying for electrical power lines and he accidentally killed one of the mountain tribesmen's sheep.

They shot the kraut."

Tim looked up with a smile. "Sure that *Shihuh*-guy shot him. That was the old dude's favorite sheep; he loved that wooly little fucker. Now he has to sleep alone until he trains another one. That's really baaaaaaaad." Tim broke into a cackled laugh. "Fuck, don't worry about me; I lived in San Francisco. I know how to treat another man's sheep." On the word "sheep," Tim's hand hit his thigh and he reverted to his donkey laugh. "*Haw, haw, haw.*"

Frankie stood. "Let's gear up and go."

Rocky and I headed toward our pile of equipment, leaving Tim to study his maps and charts.

As our small Boston Whaler pulled away from the mother craft, I yelled up to the deck. "Be careful of the sheep, Tim."

The first dive of the morning was nothing short of spectacular. We started in the protected inlet and swam along the rocks around the head or *ras* that extended into the open water and around into another cove. Rocky and Frankie collected lunch of a large grouper and a smaller red snapper, plentiful in the waters of the Emirates and Oman. Yes, we spear fish, but only to eat. Whatever we brought aboard would be turned into a gastronomical experience by the chef. I followed behind the two fishermen with the catch-bag. We kept to reasonable depths, no more than sixty feet.

When we surfaced, Alberto, one of the Filipino crewmen, had the Whaler positioned right next to us. After a break to ice down our catch, change tanks and to re-hydrate our bodies, we headed to Perforated Rock, an outcrop literally in the Strait of Hormuz. Millions of years of wind and seas had eroded the large rock to the shape of a giant donut sitting on end.

The currents in the straits are treacherous. It's like the force of water flushing down a toilet, only multiplied a million times. When tides change, water from the Indian Ocean runs into the Gulf, or the Gulf waters run into the Indian Ocean. Either way, until you get below sixty or seventy feet, you could get caught in the current and float the 35 miles across to Iran in no time.

Descending with the anchor line in hand, we reached the bottom and then swam out to where the shelf of rocks drop off, step by step, like a stairway leading down to the ocean floor. Reaching the edge of the first step, we followed the wall of the ledge to the second shelf at about sixty feet where we could comfortably control our movements.

Frankie liked to see the big fish and this dive was to show them to Rocky. We sat and watched a six-foot barracuda, nurse sharks, stingrays, coral grouper, lion-fish, angelfish and so many others that I couldn't identify. I felt like I was inside the tank at an aquarium. Frankie had his shotgun shell powered spear gun loaded and ready for the big one, but we were all so mesmerized with the variety and quantity, and their close proximity, that I figured he decided not to hunt.

Once back on the tender, I said, "I'm proud of you, Frankie. All of those easy shots and you didn't attempt to make a kill. No challenge, no hunt, you're a true sportsman."

"Sportsman, my ass," Frankie said. Then he and Rocky broke out laughing.

"What's so funny?"

Frankie looked at me, and between laughs, said, "If I shot one fish and you put it in that catch bag you're dragging around, do you think the sharks we saw are gonna let you get it to the surface? They can smell blood a mile away, and even though nurse sharks don't usually kill people, they could easily mix up your arm for that bag." Frankie gnarled his fingers, imitating shark teeth, and grabbed my arm. "Now you know why we made you the bagman, Lou boy, *ha, ha ha*."

That wasn't the end of my toting the catch bag, but you can bet your life I was always looking over my shoulder, ready to drop that bag if demanded by some sub-sea predator.

Back at the *Puss and Hoots,* we pulled alongside the dive platform on the stern and handed our catch bags, spears, tanks and fins to one of the crewman who was on the landing. He passed them to a crewmember standing at the top of the four-rung ladder on the stern that accessed the back deck. Because of the solid rear railing and the crewman standing at the top of the stairway, we couldn't see the deck. As we passed up the first load we heard a loud, "Baaaaaa." Frankie, Rocky and I looked at each other just as another "Baaaaa" traveled over the side to our ears.

"What the fuck," Frankie said as he dropped his tank back into the small boat and did a basketball player's leap from the boat, to the ladder, to the deck. "Johnson, what the fuck is this?"

When Rocky and I reached the deck, we were confronted by a smiling Tim Johnson, four laughing crewmen, an awe-struck Frankie, a dirty, curly-coated sheep, and, of course, lots of round little sheep turds on the deck.

"This is a present from my buddy *Shihuh* Sam over there on the hills of *Al Dukhaan*," Tim said.

"How in the hell did you communicate with him, yet entice him to give you what, for him, is an expensive present?" I asked.

"You know, it's amazing, but I never have trouble talking to anyone. Once you get going it's easy. I'm not sure his name is Sam, but it sounded close," Tim said. "By the way, Frankie, remember that little boat I used this morning? Well, it had two engines, and I couldn't see any need for both of em, so I left one with Sam."

"You traded a four hundred dollar, forty horse Evenrude outboard engine for a FUCKING SHEEP?" screamed Frankie.

"Nah, that sheep's not for fuckin', he's for eatin'," Tim said without the hint of a smile.

Rocky and I laughed so hard that I almost pissed in my bathing trunks, and Rocky held his side. It must have been infectious, because then Frankie started laughing, as did the Duke.

"Okay," Frankie said, "what do we do with the sheep? No way are we gonna slaughter a sheep on the *Puss and Hoots*.

"Don't get the hair on your ass up," Tim said. "I'll take him back in the morning. I've got to take your mechanic back to Sam's place tomorrow to hook up the motor. I've got some more exploring to do. I'll trade the sheep for something else."

"You gonna put the motor on his fishing boat," I asked Tim.

"You ever seen one of them boats up close?" Tim said. "They're made of reeds, date palms, grass, all kinds of growing shit. Haw, haw, I can just see that little bastard now. He starts that motor and it's gonna cut that fuckin' grass boat in half, just like a lawn mower. That engine will take off through the boat and leave Sam sittin' on his little brown ass treading water." Tim giggled. "Naw, it's not for the boat. He's got a well up there with a system of channels. He pumps the water by hand from the well into a cistern and then opens a floodgate to let the water flow throughout his fields. I figured the ship's mechanic could gear down that motor and rig it so it will turn the hand pump. Save that sorry sumbitch a lot of hard work. We'll leave him some fuel, but he can get more petrol in Khasab when he runs out."

"What a great humanitarian gesture, Tim. I'm seeing another side of you, a caring, helpful side of you."

"Humanitarian gesture my ass," piped in Frankie. "Tim's been in the Arab world too long. A favor earned is a favor owed. Tim will collect from *Shihuh* Sam in some way, right, Tim?"

Tim looked at Frankie with that same shit-eatin' grin.

We all had a good laugh over lunch about Samira, as we named our short-term pet sheep, and listened while Tim told us about his foray into the *Shihuh's* rugged homelands.

Later that afternoon we dived along the walls of the mountains as they plunged into the sea near the village of Buka. It was a relaxing drift dive that didn't take much energy. We picked up a few lobsters from their hiding places under the rocks along the mountain wall for dinner, and explored some of the caves that cut into the cliffs.

Returning to the boat, we cleaned up and met on the deck for after dive drinks and hors d'oeuvres of fried hammour, a white meat gulf grouper. After three dives and a light lunch we were ready for the grilled lobster, caught just a few hours earlier.

If NN was onboard, dinner dress was smart casual, or sometimes formal, and always in the main dining room. With no NN and just Rocky, Tim and me as guests, Frankie took the casual route, avoiding use of the formal dining room for the table on the back deck, where we all dressed for the occasion in shorts and t-shirts.

After a day of diving and a full belly I was ready to hit the hay early and headed for my cabin. Tim followed, while Frankie and Rocky stayed up to watch videos.

In the morning we took the small tender and explored some of the fiords that were too small for the yacht to enter. Instead of diving, we stopped occasionally along our route to snorkel along the rocky walls of the inlets. The plan for the day was to have lunch onboard the *Puss and Hoots* and then drive back to Dubai.

When we returned to the yacht, Tim was already onboard, sitting at the table on the back deck sticking his fingers in a clay pot filled with a light brown liquid.

"What ya got in there, Tim," Rocky asked first.

"Oil, light crude. It's the damnedest thing."

Tim held out a greasy finger so we could see the residue covering the tip.

"When I was up on the mountain yesterday with *Shihuh* Sam, I noticed clay lamps in his hut that had smoke residue on them. I didn't think much of it until I lay in bed last night and started thinking about where he'd get fuel for them lamps."

Tim wiped his oily finger on his handkerchief and looked intently at the oil pot. He finally looked up and continued.

"I'm sure he could get oil in the village of Khasab, but these people are dirt poor. They're not gonna spend money or barter for something to burn when they can use wood. When I went back today to take Samira the sheep home, I asked Sam where he got the fuel, and he motioned for me to follow him. We headed to the far side of the mountain where there was a deep crater, almost like an open pit mine."

While he continued talking, Tim used his hand to designate his route down in a corkscrew direction.

"Sam led me down a path that had been cut into the rock. It was well worn, like it had been used for generations. At the end of the path was a cave. We went in about twenty feet and there was a fire burning on the ground. The fire was a small pool of oil that had been ignited. About ten feet farther back was a larger pool of oil with an occasional bubble burping up in it. It was a fuckin' oil seep."

"How could you get a seep at that altitude?" asked Frankie.

"By the time we reached the bottom of that bowl we were at sea level and the oil was bubbling up from the earth's belly" Tim said. "This pool of oil must have been here for millions of years. I remember one of the geologists in the old days tell me that there were gas chimneys off the coast of the Musandam."

"What's a gas chimney, Tim?" I asked.

"It's a seepage of gas up through a fault from below the surface of the earth. If it's in the ocean, the gas will come up from the ocean floor and bubble to the surface of the water."

"Wow, if they know there's gas, there must be oil. It could be one hell of a discovery. Why don't they explore off the coast near the gas seeps?"

"There's not always oil where there's gas," Frankie said. "Besides, the oil companies don't want to discover gas because there's no market here. Most of the gas they produce with oil production is burned. If you ever fly over this area or Saudi Arabia at night, you'll see bright orange balls of light. Those are gas flares. Millions of dollars up in smoke because there's no industry to use it."

"The real reason," Tim said, "is that the oil companies don't want to make the investment for the infrastructure needed to produce gas. We're talking millions to build a processing plant, pipelines and all that shit. The Seven Sisters, the world's major oil companies, are whores who only want the quick profits from oil. Some day the countries in the Middle East will regret that they let the oil companies waste that energy. The day will come when they regain control of their own natural resources and the Western countries will suffer."

Turning our attention back to the burning oil, I recalled some information I had come across not long before. "I remember reading about the Zoroastrians, a religious sect that worshipped fire. They were quite prevalent in what are now Iran, Iraq, Azerbaijan and even India. Just outside Baku in Azerbaijan, there were temples that had continually burning flames. Even high winds couldn't blow them out. They later determined that they were gas seeps, just like your chimneys."

"You got it, Falcon. That's what we have here, only it's oil." Tim got up from the table, walked into the lounge and returned with his charts. Unfolding the old one, he set it on the table and pointed to *Al Dukhaan Wag*. "I think you were right, Falc. This isn't an inlet."

We all stood around and looked down at the chart.

"How about rising smoke?" I offered.

"Or a corkscrew stairway," Frankie said.

Leaning down, I placed my forearms on the table and studied the wavy lines. "Let's say that the oil seep burned constantly for hundreds of years or even a shorter period," I said. "The smoke would rise." I swirled my hand in the air to replicate the rising smoke. "This could be designated by the squiggly line you thought was an inlet. The rising smoke would eventually darken the face of the mountain; *Al Dukhaan Wag,* or the smoky face. This is what the mapmaker may have been trying to represent. Rising smoke."

"So much for my Black Beard theory," Tim said in a disappointed tone.

"And your hopes of treasure," Frankie teased.

Tim's disappointment was short lived. With a big grin, he said, "Treasure, like beauty, is in the eye of the beholder. How about black gold, gentlemen?" The Duke laughed. "I told you it was my fate to find that oil. I'll bet only a few people know about that seep. We need to get the oil exploration concession for this area. Not hard to explore when you already know where to look. They may not be able to drill offshore, but you sure as hell can drill onshore." Tim raised his thick eyebrow. "Frankie, don't you know someone from the Oman royal family?"

"Yeah, I went to college in London for a couple of years with one of the Shaikhs from the Omani royal family, Shaikh Raisee Boutie. He's the first cousin of Sultan Boutie. As a matter of fact, I introduced him to NN a couple of years ago and they're now business partners in a couple of ventures. We can work with NN on this. He knows how to go about getting an oil concession."

"Sultan Boutie." Tim said the name in a slow precise manner. "That's an appropriate name. Rumor is that he doesn't have any children because he likes it in the ol' booty."

"Christ, you're crude," Rocky said, laughing.

"Frankie, as soon as we get back, you talk to NN and contact your Shaikh friend to set up a meeting. We're all partners in this one, gang."

"Wow, thanks, Tim." Not even one year in Dubai, and I was gonna be in the oil business. My mind was already transporting me to my Walter Mitty fantasy world. This time I was an oil magnate, a Middle East oil tycoon. Like counting chickens before the eggs hatch, I was counting barrels when Frankie brought me back to schoolteacher reality.

"Hey, fellas, we have to get a move on if we want to drive through the mountains before dark. I'll have the cook get something ready for us to eat while we shit, shower, shave, and pack. I'd like to take the route along the coast to Dibba and then the back track through the mountains to Masafi so Rocky can see the beauty of the coast from the shore. Let's be ready to have lunch in forty-five minutes. Then we're off."

Having a Climax at Rocky's Place

The road from Khor Fakkan to Dibba, mostly a hard rocky track, was being converted to a modern asphalt road. We'd drive for a few miles bouncing on the washboard surface of the old trail, and then get a respite with a few miles of smooth ride on a new blacktop surface. The view of the coast was spectacular. Various shades of blue water lapped at the sandy beach or broke against rocky outcrops. At one point we had the choice of driving over a small mountain or take the chance of driving around the outcrop on the beach. The tide was out, so we voted to save the extra thirty minutes it would take to go through the mountain pass and headed for the beach. Drive fast and never stop; this was the rule for soft sand beach driving, and Frankie followed the rules. We must have been going 70 mph. At that speed it took about ten minutes to skirt the rocks and get back on terra firma.

At Dibba we turned left from the village and headed along a mountain track toward Masafi, where we would be able to join up with the new road back through Sharjah to Dubai.

We had traveled about an hour and were passing through the highest part of the mountains, close to the village of Masafi, when we saw a large convoy of military vehicles ahead. Jeeps, armored personnel carriers and even a tank were positioned along the side and across the road. We cautiously approached the checkpoint and stopped our vehicle.

A British officer and a UAE officer greeted us pleasantly. The British provided military advisors to the Emirates and also engaged in fighting communist insurgents in the Dhofar region of Oman, which bordered South Yemen. We were a long distance from that fight, so we knew it couldn't be the communist rebels.

"Good afternoon, gentlemen," greeted the Brit. "Please get out of your vehicle."

We all obliged, welcoming the chance for a stretch. Tim walked over to a lone acacia tree, put a handkerchief on his head to protect his brain from the sun, and sat under the partial shade of the disarrayed branches while Frankie, Rocky and I stood by the side of the road.

"Do you have any weapons with you?" asked the British Colonel.

Frankie responded that all we had is some diving gear, which included a couple of dive knives and spear guns. While he was talking, several of the Arab soldiers rummaged through the car and our bags. Jabbering excitedly, one of the inspectors ran up to the Arab officer and held out a box of shot gun shells, the ones that Frankie used in the spear gun. The Arab officer and the Brit colonel walked away from us, stopped at the side of the road, and spoke together quietly.

When they finished, the Brit came back and asked why we had these. Frankie walked toward the car and went around to the back storage area, which had already been opened. He grabbed his spear gun and pulled it out, holding it point upward. He had previously removed the deadly tip so that it was just an unarmed gun with a blunt spear. As soon as he pulled out the spear gun, twenty soldiers reacted in unison and pointed their rifles and AK 47's toward him.

Seeing his little brother being confronted, Rocky placed himself between the soldiers and Frankie. "Whoa, whoa, now fellas, it's just a spear gun and it's not armed," he said in a soothing and calm voice, while slowly moving his hands, palm down, in an up and down motion.

The British officer understood the words, but more importantly the soldiers understood Rocky's calming tone and hand motions, and pointed their guns at the ground. The Brit spoke in Arabic to the soldiers, and then he and the Arab officer walked over to Frankie. Joined by Rocky in the four-man huddle, Frankie showed how the shotgun shells were used to power the spear in the gun. They talked for what seemed a long time, but was only a few minutes. Soon they were laughing and walking back in a group toward us. The soldiers, seeing the relaxed mood of their bosses, also mellowed, re-shouldered their arms and smiled at us.

Frankie turned toward us. "It seems that we've been caught in the middle of a small tribal disagreement between some of the *Shihuh* who live on the fringes of the mountains of the Musandam and the Arab tribes who have farms at the base of the mountains and into the Masafi area. Someone has been riling up the natives, so to speak, smuggling arms and causing unrest. They think it may be religious radicals from Iran or infiltrators sent by the Dhofar rebels trying to open a second front for the Omani's in the Musandam, and to get the UAE involved to complicate the situation. We can't continue on this route to Masafi. It's back to Dibba and Khor Fakkan and to Dubai the way we came."

I threw up my hands and lowered them to my waist. "Shit, that will take hours."

"Nothing we can do about it unless you want to run the gauntlet and see if we can maneuver through the tank and armored carrier, as well as twenty armed soldiers." Frankie smiled at me. "We'll even stay here while you drive through," he said.

Tim, who had been sitting calmly under the tree and listening to the verbal exchange during this ordeal, walked up to us and said, "I've got an idea. Get into the car and I'll explain."

Once reseated in the Land Cruiser, Tim ordered Frankie to head back to Dibba. We waved to the officers and soldiers with big smiles, turned the car around and retreated.

"Have any of you ever driven the *wadi* route from Dibba across the mountains to Ras Al Khaimah?" Tim asked.

"Oh, you mean *Wadi Al Bih?*" said our driver Frankie. "Sure, we all have. Great idea! It will be quicker to go that way rather than drive all the way back to Fujairah. If we can move quickly, before it gets dark, it will be a neat scenic ride for Rocky. I just have to remember where we join up with the track that leads to the *wadi.*"

"I know," I said. "Just go back to the outskirts of the village of Dibba where the track roadways converge. There's one road to Masafi, one back to Khor Fakkan, and one leading to the village. We take the road to Dibba village, and at Al Hisn, don't turn right toward the village, but head north, straight on the track toward the mountains."

"Yeah, now I remember, Falc. I've driven it before so I'm game. Let's try it."

Frankie drove like lightning. Going fast actually lessened the vibration and the shaking caused by the rough rocky roads, making it a more comfortable, but also more dangerous, ride. We covered the route back to the rendezvous point in about half the time as our outbound journey. At this point the track leading to the *wadi* consisted of *subkah*, which was mixture of salt from the shallow sea water table, and mud. In the summer, it was dry and hard as a rock, but when it was wet it was like mushy clay that could swallow a car. Thirty minutes later it evolved into a gravel roadway, the result of small rocks that had washed into the mini delta area where the water from the *wadi* spread out and flowed to the sea.

Driving along we passed familiar sights, which confirmed that we were on the right route. After about ten miles the road became dangerously narrow and steep as we climbed up the first mountain. At the lower level of the *wadi* we could look up and see stone dwellings built against the walls of the mountain, much like those at Khasab.

Frankie maneuvered much slower through the *wadi* as large boulders, dislocated by flash flooding, had to be skirted. Slow speed was also essential in order to navigate the frequent zigzag curves climbing the mountain. I felt comfortable as long as I was on the side of the car that was toward the mountain, but I was extremely uneasy when I was on the outside and could look straight down into the deep ravines adjacent to the crude roadway—especially when we came upon the occasional rusted carcass of a vehicle, lying on its side or roof, on the bottom of one of the gorges.

We'd traversed the first two smaller mountains and were descending to the deep narrow valley, which separated them from the last, and largest, mountain. This was the final climb that would take us into Ras Al Khaimah.

Reaching the bottom, we followed the flow of a small stream traveling along the bed of the *wadi*. I remembered the stories about flash floods and became eager to get to higher ground. But nature called and I had to take a leak. It was the middle of April and the rains were over, so I thought it would be safe to suggest that we make a pit stop.

Tim dozed in the car while Frankie and Rocky relieved themselves on the front tires of our trusty transport. I'm one of those guys who can't urinate when there are other people around, especially in a public john if someone is using the urinal next to me, so I walked thirty yards ahead around a bend, out of sight of my companions. I had just finished emptying my bladder and was shakin' my own hooded wanky, when I heard the distinctive grunt of a camel and the giggle of a man. I abruptly turned around with my penis still in my right hand, and was confronted by an Arab and two camels. Although my prick was pointed directly at the intruder, it was no match for the long rifle pointed at me. The Arab might not have beaten me to the draw, but I was sure he could shoot first. With nervous hands I holstered my limp weapon and zipped up my pants.

My opponent was a rough-looking gentleman, unusually large for an Arab tribesman. Bandoleers filled with long, wicked-looking bullets formed an "X" across his chest and back. His *dishdashah*, once white, was stained gray and brown with dirt and yellow from sweat. It had been a long time since he had washed his clothes, or, from the pungent odor filling the air around me, his body. The bottom of his *dishdashah* was shorter than normal, reaching only to the top of the naked ankles, well above his blackened bare feet. His thick, white/gray beard, dirty and disheveled, fit in well with the rest of his appearance. On his head was a *ghutra* that hung down without being secured by the *hegaal*.

Except for the fact that he was unusually grimy, probably from living in the mountains, he fit the stereotype of the extremely religious fundamentalist Arabs I had seen in Saudi, Qatar and Kuwait: the long beard, the short *dishdashah*, the loose head cover. I thought he might be one of the rebel rousers that the military was looking for. When I glanced over at the camels, I was convinced. Strapped across the back of one of the beasts was a large long bundle covered in brown burlap. Protruding from the end of the bundle were several obvious rifle barrels. The other camel carried his personal effects, cooking pots, tenting, blankets and other survival gear. In his left hand he held the rope reins from the two camels while using the right to hold the rifle, which was still pointed at me.

I decided it was time to break the standoff and tried to dazzle him with my recently learned Arabic. *"As-salaamu aleekum* (Peace be with you), *Ahlan wa sahlan* (welcome)," I greeted the uninvited visitor.

"Aleekum is-salaam, (and peace be upon you)," said our visitor.

Now this was a good sign, I thought. We had communications. But not for long. He pushed the muzzle of his gun in my stomach, removed it, and then motioned with the gun for me to move, at the same time speaking rapidly. Between my fear and rudimentary knowledge of Arabic, I never understood one word he said, but I understood gun-sign language, and I started walking back toward my companions as directed. I was scared. So much for my dreams of being a rich oilman. And I was confused. Why did he return my greeting and then make me feel like a hostage? Arab friends told me later that it would not have been polite for him not to respond to my greeting. Yeah, mountain Arab rules of etiquette, Rule #5. Only after greeting your opponents may you take them prisoners.

As I approached the car I could see that Tim was awake, standing by Frankie and Rocky, drinking a Pepsi. They heard us coming and looked our way. I don't think any of them could see that my new mate had a gun pointed at my back, because they all broke out in big grins. As I got closer, I heard Rocky say, "Wow, this is great. I need to get my camera out of the car and take some pictures. This is really somethin', seeing this Arab guy and camels up so close."

There was only ten feet between my new Arab friend and my American friends when they finally noticed that my Arab friend was probably not a friend.

"Holy shit!" exclaimed Frankie. "Now what the fuck?"

"Look at that old gun. Looks like it's from the civil war. I need my camera." Rocky excitedly turned and headed for the car.

Just then Tim stepped in front of Frankie, and with his right hand, gently moved me to the side so that he was face to face with our guest.

Remember, Tim had just awakened from sleeping in the car, and according to his code of personal appearance, he had not shaved for several days while we were on the yacht. Some of his long, white hair stuck straight up, some out to each side of his head like wings and some down over his eyes. This, coupled with the rough stubble protruding from his face, made for a frightening vision. He stood in front of the man and raked his hair back with his fingers like he always does, revealing his pale blue eyes. He stared at him for what seemed an eternity, and then spread his face into a big "Duke" smile. At the same time he held out his right hand in a welcoming manner. In his left hand Tim held an opened can of Pepsi. Slowly shifting the cold can to his right hand, he offered the drink to our visitor.

The Arab immediately relaxed, dropped his gun-laden arm and smiled back at Tim. Taking the drink, he put it up to his mouth and took a big gulp.

Paaatooeeee! He immediately spit out the liquid onto the ground. "*La, la.*"

We all knew that meant "no, no."

Looking at us with a scowl, he threw the can into the bushes. "Beer, beer!"

We all knew what that meant too. So much for my theory about this guy being a religious fundamentalist radical. He liked beer and he had a load of guns. This guy was just an opportunist making a buck by selling arms.

Frankie walked to the back of the Land Cruiser, opened the back tailgate, pulled out a can of beer from the cooler and brought it to Tim.

Using the beer as bait, like the pied piper, Tim walked toward a trio of date palms as the man and his camels followed. When they reached the Palm trees, Tim sat down on the ground with the beer still in his hand. The arms dealer removed the bundles from his camels and hobbled them by tying a black rope around the two front feet of each beast. The black rope was the *hegaal* that was missing from his headgear. The loose bondage allowed the camels to dodder slowly towards the vegetation and water to get nourishment, but kept them from wandering too far away from their master. He then squatted, laid his rifle on the ground and took a position facing Tim.

The Duke popped the top on the can and handed it to our visitor, all the while looking directly at the Arab and speaking to him in English. At first the visitor paid little attention to Tim and concentrated on drinking his Bud, but Tim persisted and soon he was responding in Arabic.

What an unusual sight, the sun descending over the tops of the mountains, sending the last rays of the day down on a grubby looking, beer guzzling *Bedou*, sitting with a wild-haired white man under palm trees in a mountain gorge with camels nibbling on the bushes behind them. Oh, and Rocky the Tourist, sneaking around like a paparazzi, taking candid photos. What a great Budweiser commercial, I thought.

I looked at Rocky. "Good thing you have photos, 'cause no one will ever believe this."

Rocky needed to reload his instamatic and headed for the car with me following.

"Looks like we're not gonna get outta here tonight," Frankie called out to us. "It will be dark soon, and there is no way I'm gonna try to drive at night through the mountains on these roads. Why don't you unload the cooler, our duffel bags, and anything else we can use to set up a camp where Tim is sitting? It looks like as good as place as any to start a fire and spread out our towels on the ground for the night."

We soon had the semblance of a camp with a small fire to throw some light on our party. I say party, not in the definition of a group of people, but party as in: let's party, because that's just what Tim and the Budweiser *Bedouin* seemed to be doing. While we organized for the night, Tim kept dipping for cans in the cooler to keep our guest supplied. For a man who didn't drink, the Duke sure knew how to enable others to drink. Of course, it didn't take too much encouragement for our Arab beer lover.

The gun on the ground wasn't a big deterrent; we probably could have overpowered him and just left. But knowing this gent had friends and family along the route led us to play out the script that Tim was masterfully creating.

I didn't know if the full moon was a good or a bad omen, but watching Tim carry on convinced me that the lunar energy cast by that planet was magical. As they sat near the small campfire, Tim spoke to Abdul, as he now called him in his native tongue, and Abdul would answer in Arabic, just as if they really understood each other. I grant you there were a lot of hand motions, body language and facial expressions to help, but tonight Tim was speaking in tongues, and the boozy *Bedouin* understood. They were actually communicating.

I had seen this type of communication between people speaking different languages before, but only in children. At the Dubai Oil Company School, we took on students who did not speak any English and mainstreamed them into regular classes, augmented by English language tutoring. I was always astounded at how the non-English-speaking child could work and play with the English-speaking child as if they understood every word. After completing three months in school, students were almost fluent in English. Children were amazing. I always thought that the world would be peaceful and loving if adults could exchange thoughts and words as easily as kids. Now, here I was watching adults communicate. Perhaps in the Arab's case, it was the child brought out by the beer, and for the Duke, perhaps it was because he had the heart of a child. I now understood how he was able to get along so well with *Shihuh* Sam.

Later on that night, Tim reached into one of the nylon bags that carried our gear and pulled out a T-shirt belonging to Rocky. He handed it to Abdul. Abdul took the gift, held it up in the light of the fire and looked at the words printed on it like he was reading them. Turning the shirt around, he saw the picture of a frog sitting on top of a large glass with green liquid in it, and laughed. Abdul rose from his squatting position, walked over to one of his bundles and opened it. He removed something, and then rejoined us at the fire. After sitting, he handed Tim an old knife as a return gesture. Tim reached in Rocky's bag again and this time pulled out a baseball cap and handed it to Abdul. Again Abdul went to his goods stash, and came back with a small bag, which he handed to Tim. Opening it, Tim poured some of the contents in the palm of his hand; small wood chips. Tim looked at the chips.

"What the fuck's this?"

Abdul caught the drift of what Tim had said. He took one of the chips and placed it on the fire. Immediately the area was filled with the aromatic smell of incense.

"*Oudh*," said Abdul.

Shit, *oudh*. "Tim, do you know what that little bag of wood chips is?" I asked. "It's one of the Christmas gifts from the Magi to the newborn King. Frankincense." I knew that it was precious, rare, and came from the roots of a tree that only grows in Oman.

"Looks like unfinished toothpicks to me, but it does smell wonderful. Looks like I'm getting the better end of this deal."

This gift for gift exchange continued on into the night. Drink a beer, exchange goods for goods. Rocky and Frankie had already tired of this scene and dozed off. I soon followed.

A fly, buzzing around my nose, and the grunts of camels, woke me. Rubbing my eyes, I saw the light of morning coming up over the hills. Using the towel that I had slept on, I wiped the morning dew from my face, and then looking around, I saw Tim, Rocky and Frankie fast asleep around the embers of an almost dead fire.

Abdul was gone, but not far. He had rounded up his grazing camels and was in the process of roping his possessions to the hump on one of the beasts. In the gray light of early morning, I watched his silhouette and misty features while he continued his chore. By the time he had completed the task, the sun was sufficiently high to cast warm rays through the palm trees and morning haze, illuminating the figure of Abdul. What I saw was the most extraordinary spectacle. This was definitely a KODAK moment. I reached over and grabbed Rocky's camera, which was lying on a rock next to his prone body.

As I looked through the aperture and focused on Abdul, the image in the frame was priceless. Abdul stood next to his camels facing me. A shaft of light from the morning fireball above beamed through the branches of the tall palms, giving Abdul a saintly countenance. In the background was the open ravine of the *wadi*, clustered with date palms and bordered by high mountain cliffs. From the waist down Abdul's *dishdashah* flowed like a skirt to his ankles. Tightly stretched over the top half of his torso concealing the upper part of his *dishdashah*, was the red T-shirt gift from Tim, emblazoned with big white letters:

I HAD A CLIMAX AT ROCKY'S PLACE
New Orleans, Louisiana

After 30 years the faded instamatic photo of Abdul still sits on my desk

Abdul's bandoleer was sheathed across his right shoulder. On the crown of his head, sitting on top of his headscarf, he wore a black baseball cap flaunting the logo of the New Orleans Saints. The drapes of the scarf rested on his bulky shoulders and then flowed down his back like an extra long French Foreign Legion hat. Covering his eyes were the Duke's aviator sunglasses. God, what a sight!

Seeing me with the camera in front of my face, Abdul gave me a big, blackened and broken-toothed smile, and then soberly waved goodbye with his rifle bearing hand. I snapped the photo. Abdul turned and led his animal companions down the *wadi* toward wherever.

I was relieved to see him go, but elated by the experience. With his departure I realized I wasn't going to end up as ant food in *Wadi Bih*. My physical future as an oil baron was secure.

I woke Rocky and Frankie. We loaded our gear, including Tim's new knife, frankincense wood, camel blanket and other items bartered from Abdul and headed for home. We reached Dubai just in time to drop off the film before the shops closed at 1:00 p.m. for the afternoon siesta.

VI
Jinn and Gin

The Spirits of Dubai Past

One of the greatest benefits of being an educator is the two-month summer vacation. Believe it or not, eight weeks back in the U.S.A. was not enough time to make up for ten months' worth of visits to family and friends. We had to shop for a year's worth of clothes for three small children, and, of course, we had to stuff ourselves with ten months' worth of Big Macs, Whoppers, pizzas and other junk foods that we couldn't get in Dubai.

As an administrator, I had to return to Dubai earlier than the teachers to prepare for the '75 school year by unpacking and distributing books and supplies, making schedules, and seeing that the building was in shape. When the staff arrived I concentrated on working with them to plan the year. Greeting and orientating the new teachers to the school and to life in Dubai was another important task. Of all of these assignments, orientation was the most fun. The previous spring I'd made a three-week recruiting trip across the U.S.A. to find teachers who could fill the vacancies left by departing personnel and to fill new positions created by increased enrollment.

It takes a special person to live as an expatriate. No matter how deeply I tried to delve into their psyche during the interview to determine if they had the right stuff, final selection boiled down to a gut feeling. We sent literature to prepare the new recruits for life in the Emirates. But writing won't prepare people for the two-inch cockroaches, for living with bare necessities, for the 120-degree summer heat and ninety-nine percent humidity. The only answer was to develop an in-depth orientation program when they arrived which covered as much as possible, especially culture shock, and hope for the best. One year I had to repatriate a teacher after only three weeks because he couldn't live without Jif peanut butter and Ritz crackers—or his mother. I think it was really the mother. The orientation was important but no matter how good it was, if you weren't cut out for expatriate life you were not going to be happy, and an unhappy teacher was not an effective teacher.

I was lucky enough to have a staff psychologist, Dr. Reid Thornton, to help prepare the orientation program. Reid was a hummer and strummer, and during the previous school year he had made friends with another guitarist, Sal Rains, one of the pilots for

J.R Dumont, the offshore construction company. Together this twelve-string duo developed quite a repertoire of tunes to liven up our weekend house parties. They even played a bit professionally at one of the local clubs.

Reid and the orientation-planning committee decided that rather than sit and lecture to the new recruits, we would put on a series of skits to show the difficulties of adjusting to life in Dubai. There were various scenarios to mimic living in the heat and humidity, shopping in the *souk*, communicating with people who spoke no known language and driving in Dubai. Of course, I was recruited to be in the skits. In one I was the crazy taxi driver. In another I peed on a wall. Let me explain. For family privacy, a high wall surrounds each house in Dubai. It was not uncommon, but shocking the first time, to find a laborer from the building site next door squatting and peeing next to your wall. That was my job in the skit; act like I was a worker peeing on the wall of a teacher's villa. Of course it was all done in humor accompanied by music and singing. The grand finale was the boisterous singing by the veteran staff of a song written for the occasion by Reid and sung by him and Sal called, *Dubai Home*. The lyrics told it all:

> *Life here in ol' Dubai just ain't like it was back home*
> *The suns too hot to walk around, we got no telephone*
> *And I have caught me Dubai tummy, it ain't no fun to see*
> *The only thing that's green here now is me*
>
> CHORUS
> *Oh Dubai Home, Dubai friends*
> *Hello to sands that never end*
> *There ain't no need to sit and wonder why*
> *The folks here don't say "hello" they say "Dubai"*
>
> *Oh, those bugs here in ol' Dubai*
> *Oh, Lord, I wish that I had known*
> *The cockroaches so plentiful are bigger than a toad*
> *The lizards are getting bigger daily*
> *The spiders they are too*
> *I just hope they don't eat me or you.*

CHORUS

The water here in Dubai they say is fit to drink
But water from the cold tap can burn the kitchen sink
And when you try to take a shower it'll dribble on you by the hour
It's enough to make your body stink.

CHORUS

The shopping in ol' Dubai brings you nothing but despair
Prices are exorbitant, selection is quite rare
You open up the things you buy and watch the critters fly
It's enough to make you want to cry

CHORUS

Well, the Dixie neighbors that abound must think the war's still on
Cause every time I go outside they all seem to be gone
They whisper low in Southern drawl
Write YANKS GO HOME upon my wall
What's a poor ol' Dubai Yank to do

CHORUS

When a lady goes outside she must find lots to wear
'Cause the local gentlemen will all take time to stare
Some men stare at knees and toes
While others take off all their clothes
But I guess that's just the way it goes.

I'm sure the picture's clear regarding what we tried to prepare those novice teachers for and how we tried to do it. They were entering a new life in Dubai in the early seventies, and without humor to get through some of the tough parts, I would end up sending them home to their moms.

The start of the new school year would have been uneventful but for the phone call from the chairman of the school board, Earl Scrudds, informing me that His Highness Shaikh Rashid Bin Saeed

Al Maktoum, Ruler of Dubai, was scheduled to visit the school the following Monday. We had just opened a new junior high wing, and he was coming to tour the school and officially inaugurate the new building. It was a great honor but a real headache trying to organize a formal ceremony in just three days. Thanks to Maggie, when His Highness and Earl arrived we were ready.

Maggie, several selected staff and I waited at the entrance as the motorcade drove up to the front of the school. As His Highness exited his car, he was immediately attended by Majid Bin Jabir, who always acted as his guide, and in this case, translator. Security seemed low-key, as there were more television cameras and newspaper journalists than guards. Although it seemed unconscionable that someone would want to harm a ruler as loved as Shaikh Rashid, his security only appeared to be minimal. I learned after the visit that many of the plain-clothes spectators were actually police. It seemed that Rashid hated to be surrounded by guards so his security detail tried to blend with the crowd.

As rehearsed, I greeted him at the door. After the introduction and a few words in Arabic by Bin Jabir explaining that I was the school headmaster, Shaikh Rashid looked at me in a most peculiar way and in an excited manner spoke to Bin Jabir. A smile broke over Bin Jabir's face as he translated.

"It seems that His Highness does not believe that you are the head of the school. He says that in the Arab tradition a man must have gray hair and preferably a beard with at least some gray in it to show that he has gained his knowledge through years of experience. You have neither gray, nor a beard, and are much too young to be a *Mudeer Al Madrassah*, the head of the School."

"Please explain to His Highness," I replied, "that when he was my age he was assisting his father to govern an entire Emirate. Since I have only a small school, I only need a small portion of his wisdom. I am young enough to understand the needs of the students, yet old enough to know what is required by the parents."

As Bin Jabir translated, the ruler's lips parted showing his white teeth surrounded by a big grin. In what I perceived as a sign of approval, the most respected leader in the Middle East made a comment to Bin Jabir and then patted me on the shoulder and moved on with Mr. Scrudds for the tour and ceremony.

Monkey Business

With school back in session, the Duke resumed his regular visits. He kept me up on the gossip of which wife was sleeping with her husband's best friend when her husband was offshore. He told me which of the locals was getting the best contracts from COC. And he kept me informed of NN's wheeling and dealing to secure the oil concession in the Musandam. His tales of how the money was going to change my life kept me pumped, at least for the half an hour that he was around. It had been almost six months since the dive trip. Summer vacation had come and gone, and I was already well into the new academic year. The oil deal was just another one of my Walter Mitty daydreams. When I received the summons to attend a meeting at the Duke's house to meet Shaikh Raisee from Oman about the oil concession, I couldn't believe it was truly happening.

As I stood in front of the ten-foot steel gates of the Duke's humble abode, I realized that in the year that I had known Tim this was the first time that I had been to his villa. Waving in the wind at the top of a flagpole inside the gate was a white pennant with what looked like two eyes and a smiling mouth. I made a mental note to ask the Duke about it, and then rang the bell.

Waiting for the servant to allow me entry, I heard animals and birds chattering behind the high walls. Cut into the large steel gate was a small man-door four feet high. Servants and children in the family used these mini-gates. The large gates of a villa were only opened for the master of the house and guests. Hearing the flip-flop of rubber sandals approaching, I stepped back to allow the portal to be opened. As I moved away, only the small door swung outward and a hand motioned for me to crawl through. Slightly offended that I was not allowed entry through the large gates, I justified the incident as my now being a friend rather than a guest.

In the courtyard, two chimps with furless red bottoms played on ropes and tire-swings in a large cage. Next to their monkey house was an aviary with numerous varieties of parrots, parakeets, and other small singing birds. And next to the birdhouse was another cage with several smaller long-tailed monkeys like the ones you see holding a tin cup collecting alms for their organ-grinder master. As I walked past the red-butted monkey house, the two primates lunged toward the front of the cage, loudly conversing with each other in their native tongue. Since they had my attention, I stopped to look at them. As I watched, they simultaneously stroked each other's primate-penises. Using an awkward cross-armed maneuver they were soon masturbating each other at full speed. I jumped back just as the white liquid globule shot toward me. Having avoided the first sexual advance, I decided to go into the house before the second shot was fired.

As I entered the foyer I saw several pairs of shoes neatly placed on a small Persian carpet. It looked like Tim had gone native, at least regarding the tradition of removing one's shoes before entering the house. Peeking through the doorway to the living room, the snow-white thick pile carpeting caught my eye. Of course, it wasn't just Arab tradition; it was the white carpet that meant so much to the Duke's perception of success. He just wanted to keep his white shag clean. Casing the room I saw Iskar sitting at the grand piano keying a Dean Martin tune and singing softly. NN sat in a wingback chair that was directly in front of the Yamaha and standing beside him was Frankie.

The other guest, I presumed to be Shaikh Raisee. He was dressed in an elegant gold robe made of silk with black velvet piping. His head was covered with a black silk turban wrapped in the distinctive Omani style. The Shaikh had a perfectly trimmed black beard with flecks of gray, giving him an air of sophistication.

"Hey, Falcon, I see you found the place OK. Now you know where to come for Wednesday's poker game. Did Frick and Frack put on their show for you outside?"

"If you mean the masturbating monkeys, yes," I replied.

"Ole Iskar here taught them how to do that, didn't you, Iskar?"

"Actually, it was the Narian twins who taught them. When you had that monkey cage in the den they liked to watch the girls work on me in the living room. Little voyeurs they were. What can I say—monkey see monkey do."

Just then, an African Gray parrot in a white Moroccan cage hanging behind the piano screeched, "Fuck Iskar."

"Now that was one of your training successes, Tim," Iskar said. "Tim thinks it's cute to transfer his linguistic knowledge to other equally intelligent creatures."

"Tell me what the flag in front represents," I asked Tim.

"Hell, Falc, I thought you're studying Arabic. That's the Arabic letter 'T' for my name, Tim. Looks like a smiling face, don't it? That's why I had it made. The Duke's home is a happy home."

It would be many years before the movie Forrest Gump came out, giving Forrest credit for the happy face. I remember sitting in the theater and wanting to yell out, "No, Forrest, no, it wasn't your idea; it was the Duke's."

"Gentlemen," interrupted NN, "we're all here, so let's adjourn to the dining room table where we can spread out the maps and chat."

As we walked toward the large, highly polished table, Frankie held back and took a minute to introduce me to Shaikh Raisee.

"Shaikh Raisee, this is Lou Falconi. He's the headmaster of the American school and a good friend of ours. He was with us on the diving trip."

I shook the Shaikh's hand, and in my best Arabic I greeted him with a "*Fursa Saeeda*," which literally means "happy opportunity," but is the same as "pleased to meet you."

Since Tim's oil discovery, Frankie followed up on his part of the deal and spoke to NN. According to the game of status played in this part of the world, you go to the Shaikh; he doesn't come to you. There was no doubt that NN was a smooth talker and getting Raisee to travel to Dubai was a coup in itself. Things move slowly in the Gulf. Only after months of discussions did NN finally convince him of the spoils that could come from meeting with us. Shaikh Raisee was savvy and knew NN well enough to realize that any invitation by him could mean serious business with great rewards.

NN sat at the head of the table with Iskar and Tim on one side, Frankie and me on the other, and the Shaikh at the end. Tim spread out the maps and briefed Shaikh Raisee on the chance discovery of the oil pool in the Al Hajar Mountains of the Musandam.

"I've had the oil analyzed and this is high quality light crude, equal to the best on the market. It's a top dollar product," NN explained.

As the discussion continued I daydreamed about the wealth this little venture would bring. Frankie had earlier explained to me that NN would get one of the major oil companies to finance the development of the oilfield. NN would be paid a ten-percent overriding royalty from them. This meant that our little group would receive ten-percent of the gross income off the top. In my mind I calculated production scenarios while the others talked. If we produced 50,000 barrels of oil at $15.00 per barrel, that's $750,000 per day, I thought. We would get $75,000 of that. I roughly estimated that that was over $26 million per year. WOW! Even if I only received one half of one percent, I would be earning $130,000 per year. I was set for life.

I became aware that Shaikh Raisee had taken over the discussion and was talking seriously to us.

"Gentlemen, I have spoken to my cousin, His Highness the Sultan, about this matter and he is exceedingly supportive of your request for a concession. The terms, of course, will have to be formally negotiated with our Ministry of Petroleum, but they have been advised to treat you favorably. However, there is one small request that His Highness has asked me to discuss."

At this point the Shaikh reached for a long cardboard tube on the table. He opened the end and removed a rolled up document. As he smoothed it out on the table he continued talking. "As you are aware the Oman is experiencing political difficulties in the Dhofar region of our country." With his finger he placed it on what we could now clearly see was a map of the UAE, Oman and Yemen. Pointing toward the bottom of the map he continued. "This is the area that borders Yemen. Since the British left Aden in 1967 the communists have dominated the political and military situation in Yemen. They are sending insurgents across the border into Oman to incite the tribes in the area to secede from Oman and join communist Yemen."

Moving his finger to the Emirate of Ras Al Khaimah, Shaikh Raisee explained that the communists were also smuggling guerilla fighters into the UAE mixed in with the hundreds of Pakistani and Indian immigrant laborers who enter illegally through the Northern Emirates.

The Shaikh looked at us with serious eyes and continued. "These guerillas are heading for camps in the Musandam where they will join dissident *Shihuh* tribesmen and other Marxist rebels. If properly armed they could split the area in two, attacking the UAE and Oman from the Musandam, as well as Oman from Yemen. If they succeed, all of Oman, including the Musandam will be communist. This would give the Russians, Chinese, Cubans and their ideological friends control of the Straight of Hormuz. Forty percent of the oil from the Middle East travels to the West through this water gateway. The Western democracies and the Gulf countries cannot let that happen. If Oman falls to communism, the UAE will be next. If we are to prevent a world war over Middle East oil, we must stop them now."

"The U.S. will never fight a war for oil in the Middle East. They have other resources," said NN.

The Duke surprised me by giving his opinion on world affairs, a subject I didn't realize he followed, or even had any interest. His comment was another of the uncanny prophecies that I later chalked up to his unconscious ability to tell the future. "Shaikh Raisee is right," said Tim. "The next war will be over oil and it will be right in our backyard, in Saudi or Kuwait. Before the end of this century we'll see it happen. Water will be another cause for nations to battle one another, but right now oil is the flavor of the month."

"I agree with you," said the Shaikh. "The West will not let control of oil fall into the hands of the communists or an anti-West dictator. We will see what the future holds. Let me continue.

"These rebels have lived in their rugged terrain for centuries and they use it to their advantage by crossing and re-crossing the 288-kilometer border between Oman and Yemen to ambush our Omani forces from caves along the *wadis*. They support the DLF, Dhofar Liberation Front, who are aligned with the Yemen NLF, National Liberation Front. Together they have proven to be a persistent thorn in our government's side. Our Omani troops have been doing a valiant job of keeping these rabble-rousers from causing a full-scale revolution. The British have unofficially sent in advisors to help and the Shah of Iran has also covertly given financial and military aid, but more assistance is needed. Many of the mountain tribes in the highlands oppose communism as a godless scourge that is trying to drive their people from Islam. We have the support inside Yemen of these *Jebalis,* as we Omani's call the mountain people. They are willing to give up their *djambia,* their traditional curved knives, for AK-47s and Kalashnikovs and fight the communists. Many of the Omani *Jebalis* are already fighting alongside of the British and Omani troops. They say that these men are excellent fighters. With the backing of the *Jebalis* who live on the Yemen side of the border, this would give Oman support from behind the lines."

"Shaikh Raisee, you talk as if these people are different from the rest of the people of Oman and Yemen," I said.

"They are different. They are ruthless warriors with an obsessive sense of honor and loyalty. They are respected and feared by people outside of the mountains. No one knows for certain where the *Jebalis* first came from. Some say northern Arabia and some even whisper that they descended from the Jews. From wherever they have evolved, they still have very old traditions and beliefs. Even today they practice the ancient *Raboul*—the medicine chant to drive out the evil spirit from the body of a sick person. And they believe in the spirit of the *Jinn*."

"Shit, I believed in the spirit of Gin for many years. If I drank enough I even became invisible, just like a spirit," Tim said and laughed.

"*Jinn,* Tim, not Gin," Shaikh Raisee corrected with a smile."A *Jinn* is like your leprechauns. There are good *Jinns* as well as some cantankerous ones, but mostly they are just mischievous. They are not harmful in a physical sense. Many people believe that the mountain people can call upon these spirits to help protect them and keep outsiders away from their remote villages."

"Do all of these mountain tribesmen see the *Jinns*?" I asked.

"I have been told by one of these tribesmen that only certain members of the clan can see the *Jinns* —those whose hearts are pure. The *Jinns* appear to them as small men wearing traditional robes and headscarf. Instead of the *djambia*, they wear a magic belt around their waist. They rub the belt to make them appear and disappear. There have been many stories of townspeople who have had experiences with the deeds of the *Jinns*."

"If you ask me, those Yemeni mountain men have been chewing too much of that green leaf narcotic *Qaat* for their daily high," Tim said.

"Have you had any experiences with *Jinns,* Shaikh Raisee?" I asked.

A small grin passed across the Shaikh's face. "Not directly, but I was told a story by a reformed thief who claims that he was caught by a *Jinn*. He said it was the episode with the *Jinn* that made him leave his criminal ways. It happened in the market in Sanaa', when he was looking for an unsuspecting visitor to ply his pickpocket skills on. Because of their peculiar dress and unkempt beards, he easily spotted several South Yemen mountain men in a group bargaining with a merchant. As he walked past them he staged a stumble. Simultaneously with the action of falling into the crowd, he grabbed the money pouch from the oldest looking gentlemen and ran.

"The victim realized he had been robbed and yelled, 'Stop, Thief,' and pointed at the running scoundrel. A crowd pursued him, but he disappeared in the maze of alleys in the *souk*. While the tribesmen huddled together, the old man was observed by the merchant and others to be carrying on a one-way conversation while looking down toward the ground at nothing. In the meantime, the thief had taken refuge in one of the public bathhouses. Shedding his clothes and hiding the money, he entered the water with three other bathers. Within a few minutes numerous bubbles from around his body floated to the surface, giving off an appalling odor. The other bathers and the attendant scolded the man about his inconsiderate and repulsive behavior in a public bath. He argued that the smell did not emanate from him but they did not believe him."

"Yep, it was the *Jinn*. Gin always made me fart too." After a few chuckles around the table, Tim apologized for his interruption and Shaikh Raisee continued.

"Soon after the bubbles, the other bathers' backsides were pinched and prodded. Although the thief was on the far side of the bath, his now angry fellow bathers again blamed him. Deciding that it would be best to leave, he stepped from the large pool, and while doing so he tripped. He said that unseen hands pushed him. He fell back into the bath, landing on the largest of the bathers, who started to pummel him. The thief broke away from the thrashing bather, climbed from the water and ran into the privacy of a toilet stall. Closing and locking the door, he rested, and then squatted in the traditional manner to relieve himself over the hole in the floor.

"As the story goes, while he was urinating, something grabbed his privates and pulled him down so that he lay prone on his belly, face to the floor, with his genitals sucked down into the unsanitary abyss. He screamed and cried for help. The attendant, the bathers, as well as many pedestrians who were walking outside of the bathhouse ran to the stall and forced open the door.

"One of the passersby was the tribesman from whom the thief had stolen the money. Recognizing the crook, and seeing the predicament that he was in, the old man laughed and spoke to the ground, saying something in a language the townspeople didn't understand, but from his tone they said it was definitely a command, probably something like 'let him go.' At this point the thief's penis was released, and the police, who had arrived on the scene, took him away.

"At the police station, the thief returned the money to the old man and asked him to whom he spoke to gain the release of his family jewels. 'It was the *Jinn*,' replied the tribesman. 'He had pursued you after you stole my money, and he stayed with you until he could arrange your capture.' The incident so frightened the thief that while serving his time in jail he became a, I guess you could call it, newborn Muslim. He has led an honest life ever since and is a true believer in the *Jinns*."

"Do you believe this really happened?" Frankie asked.

"Oh, yes," replied Shaikh Raisee. "This story is typical of those passed on by eyewitnesses of other events involving these spirit people. The *Jinns* support good and fight evil. They never do great bodily harm, but they can be quite a nuisance and invoke fear in people with evil intent."

Silence enveloped the room as Tim's houseboy entered. "Would any of you gentlemen like more coffee or another drink?" Tim inquired. Orders were placed and business resumed.

"Enough time telling stories; let's get back to business," the Shaikh said. "We have been trying to send some special goods to these small mountain enclaves, but the overland routes from Oman have been blocked. Sea shipments directly into Yemen have also been intercepted. His Highness asks your support. NN, your yacht enjoys uninhibited navigation all over the Gulf and Indian Ocean. We would like you to take some goods from Muscat and deliver them in Yemen. As a luxury vessel, it offers excellent cover. It would be a nice vacation for your wives and friends, and perhaps some children onboard would be extremely helpful.

"Excuse me, Mr. Tandoody, telephone for you," Tim's houseboy, Alfie, announced.

Iskar rose from his chair and stood at the table. "Gentlemen, carry on: I'll just be a minute."

"We would be pleased to help His Highness," NN said as Iskar departed, "but I must have some guarantee that should my yacht be confiscated or something more disastrous happen, that I will be compensated."

"The oil concession will be granted even if the mission fails. It will more than compensate for any loss that may occur," the Shaikh responded.

I squirmed in my seat. I had been pretty naïve the previous year when we went on the salvage trip, but I had learned a lot since. It seemed quite apparent that we were being asked to run guns and other arms to the tribes. Since meeting the Duke and Iskar, I thought I would do almost anything to make my million, except sell drugs, sell arms, or murder. Now here I was, considering narrowing the list to two. After a brief thought, I took one step down on the morality ladder and accepted that I would go along with the assignment. However, no matter how desperate I was, I would not put the lives of my wife and children at risk by taking them along on the floating bomb.

Frankie, seeing my discomfort, said, "What's the problem, Falcon? You seem uneasy."

"I don't object to running arms to help fight communism. But I can't put my family in physical danger."

"Wait a minute, young man." Shaikh Raisee's body grew rigid in his seat and he glared at me. "Who said anything about arms? We have plenty of ways to get military assistance to the tribesmen. This cargo is something special, which must be sent through a guaranteed route with no trace of where it came from. I cannot tell you what it is until you arrive, but I can guarantee it is not any type of weapon and that in its physical form it cannot cause bodily harm."

I was relieved to hear that I wasn't going to be an arms dealer, but it was too late to climb back up the morality ladder. Once you take a step down, you have to earn your way back up. At the rapid rate I was descending, it would be a long hard climb back to the top.

A mumbled discussion broke out between Frankie, NN and Tim. Addressing the Shaikh, NN said, "Tell His Highness that we will do as he requests. When should we expect to make the journey?"

"Thank you, NN. His Highness will be deeply appreciative and will repay this favor ten-fold. The goods will not be received from England until mid-October. As we will need to work out the details at the arriving end, I estimate that we should be prepared to make the voyage at the beginning of November. The *Eid* festival, which celebrates the end of fasting during the holy month of *Ramadaan,* comes at that time. This will mean a long holiday in the Emirates. It will be a good reason to take a cruise for a few days."

The Shaikh rose, shook hands with us and took his leave.

As Tim accompanied Shaikh Raisee to the door, I confronted NN. "Shouldn't we have an agreement between us regarding how we share our interest?"

An indignant NN looked at me with a half scowl-half smile twisted across his face.

"We don't do business that way here, Lou. Signatures on paper can only cause problems later. We are all friends and—"

I cut him off before he could finish. "Friends take care of friends. Right, I know."

Just then Iskar re-entered the room with a look of excitement on his face.

Flying Naked

"That was Shaikh Mohammed on the telephone," Iskar informed us. "It seems that some extreme political Palestinian group hijacked a British Airways 747 and ordered it to head for Dubai. In the interests of the safety of the passengers and crew, the government gave them permission to land. We must keep that telephone line open in case His Highness wishes to contact me for advice."

From the corner of my eye, I saw the Duke snicker at this last comment and then say, "Shit, this is the second time in a year that a hijacked plane landed in Dubai." Tim leaned his chair back on two legs, put his arms in the air and then cradled his head with cupped hands. "There was that Lufthansa jet, now this one. This hijacking shit has got to stop. It ain't safe to fly anymore."

Sliding back his chair, Frankie stood and stretched his arms. "I read where a lot of airlines have hired sky marshals to travel on the plane to prevent hijacking. They are armed and unknown to the passengers. I think that we should have at least five or six on every international flight."

The Duke was now on his feet and ready to deliver his opinion. "Shit, Frankie, do you know how much that will cost? Airlines and the government won't pay for it. The passengers will. Hell, I've got a simple way to solve this problem, and cheap too. What the airlines do is issue each passenger a loaded gun as they board the plane." Tim giggled as he explained his solution. "With each passenger on the plane having a gun, do you think those hooky kooky skyjackers are gonna be brave enough to try to take it over? Even if they get guns and bombs onboard, it will be a suicide mission because one of those 200 people will be crazy enough to shoot the sons-a-bitches. Poof, no more hijackings. When the plane lands, they collect the guns from the passengers. Simple and cheap, like I said. Better yet, let's make everyone travel 'butt nek-ed'. Shit, how ya gonna smuggle on bombs and guns, except up your ass. Any fucker walks funny while they're boarding, ya pull 'im out of line and do the ol' cavity search."

"Christ, Tim, you're as crazy as those hijackers."

I was surprised to hear Iskar call Tim crazy. Maybe eccentric, maybe bizarre, but definitely not crazy. Just then the phone rang and we all jumped. Iskar grabbed it on the second ring and talked in

Arabic at a hyper pace. When he finished the conversation he solemnly looked at us.

"These boys are serious. They just shot one of the passengers and threw his body on the tarmac. The plane has been refueled and they are now taking off."

Iskar's comment resulted in silence. The hijacking crisis brought back the reality of just how volatile the situation in the Middle East was. Any one of our family or us could have been on that plane. And just next door in the Oman, people were fighting and dying. Living in the last oil boomtown of the Gulf had its risks.

Stone Doctors or Stoned Doctors

School was running smoothly, and Marie and the kids were excited about the trip on the *Puss and Hoots*. The cover story was that we had been invited to accompany NN and Frankie and their wives, along with Tim and Evie, on an eight-day cruise during the coming holidays. Showing Marie a map of the area, I traced the route with my finger, explaining that we would travel along the coast of the Northern Emirates and around the Musandam, then down the coast of Oman to Yemen. We'd stop at ports along the route to do some tourist things, and, of course, dive.

NN received word that the goods had arrived in Oman and set a date for our rendezvous. Shaikh Raisee would meet us in Muscat and two Omani *Jebalis* would join us to assist on the Yemeni end. Should we be boarded and checked by the Yemeni's, the mountain men would pose as crew. They would be carrying seaman's cards to document their status. According to NN, our instructions were to anchor offshore Nishtun, about seventy nautical miles from inside the Yemen border, where we would be met by friends who would take possession of the goods. The two *Jebalis* would leave the yacht and accompany the goods until they reached their destination. They would then make their way back to Oman through the mountains. Once the goods were off the ship we were free to steam back to Oman waters.

The cruise to Muscat took a leisurely two days. We stopped in Khasab to register with authorities and to get the proper holiday cruise documentation. The next day we docked at Muscat, where all of us, with the exception of NN, disembarked and were given a grand tour of the old and new city by one of Shaikh Raisee's retainers. When we reboarded, the loading of the mysterious cargo was complete and the two new deck hands were ensconced on the yacht. I greeted both of them with my *Khaleeji* Arabic, only to be ignored. I assumed that the Arabic of the Dhofari was much different or that they did not wish to socialize. From their unkempt appearance, I deduced that they were just two uneducated mountain men in the service of their Sultan.

Frankie and I were curious about the goods so we opened the deck hatch to look at what had been brought aboard. As we glimpsed into the poorly lit hold we were surprised to see that there were only two galvanized metal trunks about three feet long, two feet wide and no more than two feet in depth. With our curiosity aroused, we made guesses about what they could contain. Suddenly one of the new shipmates abruptly closed the hatch and motioned for us to move away, which we promptly did. Very protective, I thought.

After dinner in port we weighed anchor and headed toward Yemen. I had done some reading about its history, especially the name. It was known to the Romans as Arabia Felix, meaning happy or fortunate Arabia. I found that Yemen is green and mountainous in some places and hot and desolate in others, with a variety of terrain and climate. In the Old Testament Yemen is referred to as "the South." It is said that the Arabic word *Al-Yaman* derives from the name of the ancient Ruler Ayman Ibin Ya'Rub Ben Qathan; however, old Arabic legends and even the Yemenis say that *Al Yaman* derives from the word *Al Yumm* meaning blessing and prosperity. Others say the classification Al Yaman derives from *yumna*, which means right from the *Kaabah*, which is the holy stone of Islam in the holy city of Mecca. Whatever the etymology of the name, it sounded like an exciting place to visit, even if it was just for a port call.

I had not anticipated the distance between Muscat and the Yemen border until NN mentioned during dinner that we would have to cruise continually for the next two days in order to reach the port of Salalah. From there it would only be another eight hours to our destination of Nishtun. With three bored and seasick kids to entertain, the two-day voyage became dreadfully long. I loved being

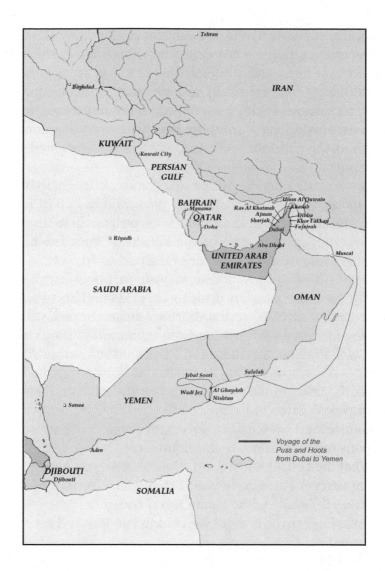

on the yacht for short trips, but when you're constantly moving and shut inside, it was like being in jail. Marie and I kept the kids in the lounge, afraid if they went on deck, one of them would fall over the railing into the Gulf of Oman or Arabian Sea. Tim, Evie, Frankie and Joanne had no children to contend with, so they were able to enjoy some time outside. NN's wife couldn't come on the trip so he invited a "business associate," as he called her. They were quite busy with NN's corporate affairs and spent most of the time in his large master cabin probably reading faxes from the mirrors on the ceiling.

NN had his own harem of beautiful companions made up of young secretaries, bored housewives whose husbands were offshore for weeks at a time, and professionals flown in from London. It definitely wasn't his personality or looks that attracted the bikini-clad, or sometimes bikini-less, ladies who volunteered to come onboard to provide the puss in the *Puss and Hoots*. Everyone else knew it was the 120-foot yacht, but NN was too conceited to ever figure it out.

I was ecstatic when we awoke after the second night to find that we had moored in the Salalah harbor. We would be in port for most of the day to take on diesel and supplies. I was thankful for the chance to get my land legs back and let the kids loose for a few hours on terra firma while we did a day tour of the port town.

That night we steamed directly to Nishtun. It was just after dawn when I joined the men on deck for breakfast. The two Omani deckhands had already gone ashore to make contact with their associates and obtain permission from immigration for us to enter Yemen. NN, Frankie, the Duke and I had finished eating and were enjoying a second cup of coffee when our scouts returned. Once onboard, the taller of the two approached the table and addressed us in crisp clear British English.

"Gentlemen, according to my orders, three of you will accompany me to deliver our consignment."

"What the hell," I blurted out. "What's going on here?"

"I'm sorry for the deception. Let me introduce myself. I am Colonel Saeed Yayahe of the Oman Royal Guard."

"Great English; no wonder you couldn't understand my Arabic," I said sarcastically.

"Royal Military Academy Sandhurst, class of 70," replied the colonel. "I didn't mean to offend you, but in port in Muscat it was important that my identity be kept secret. Please only refer to me as Saeed."

Sandhurst was the British equivalent of our West Point. This Omani *Jebali* was college-educated, a trained warrior who spoke at least two languages and probably more. He continued to explain the program. While he was doing so, his assistant, probably another colonel, had the crew retrieve the two metal trunks from the hold and bring them on deck.

"We have obtained special passes for three of you to go ashore on an archeological excursion," the colonel said. "Identification papers had been prepared in Muscat attesting that Frankie Focaccia, Lou Falconi and Tim Johnson are all university professors, trained professionals in the field of archeology and anthropology." Pointing to his aide, he continued, "You will be given a special permit to travel in the company of Mustafa and me to the interior. We will proceed from Nishtun through Wadi Jez, then into the mountains to Jebal Soori, where we will deliver our goods. From there we will backtrack overland to the port city of Al Ghaydah, where NN will meet us the next day with the Yacht. Is everything arranged from your end?" he asked NN.

"Yes, the Al Ghaydah port authorities have given us permission to dock, and immigration knows that we will be picking up passengers," replied NN.

"Jesus Christ," I blurted out. "You mothers have done it to me again, just like the dive trip to recover the lost cargo. Damn all of you." I was angry, and for the second time in front of my friends I was feeling really stupid.

"Now calm down, Falcon," the Duke said with a smile. "We needed you and the family to help with our cover, and we were afraid that you wouldn't bring them if you knew we'd have to spend some time onshore." The Duke was doing his best to placate me but I wasn't in the mood to be pacified. "There is absolutely no danger to your family. They'll be safe onboard and ready to meet us tomorrow. Our little excursion will only take twenty-four hours, and then you'll be back on the *Puss and Hoots* having a nice pleasant trip back to Dubai."

Seeing that I still wasn't happy, Tim gently grabbed my arm and guided me from my chair toward the stern railing. Speaking in a soft tone, he said, "I know you pretty well, Falc. I'll bet you figured how much you'll make on that oil deal. Now you have to earn it. For the next twenty-four hours, just keep thinking about how much money you'll make."

He had me—the money. I returned to my seat at the table. "I want to know what the goods are. And one more thing: I won't carry weapons." I hoped that my statement might have earned me half a step up the morality ladder as I felt the need to regain some self-respect.

On the colonel's command, Mustafa opened one of the trunks to reveal brown paper-wrapped bundles. He picked up one of the packages and tore off the cover, revealing a thick pile of currency notes.

"This is the material we are transporting. Fifty million dollars in Yemeni riyals and twenty-five million in U.S. dollars—all counterfeit. Made with the assistance of friendly governments. We hope that distribution of the counterfeit riyals throughout the country will destabilize the Yemeni economy. The paper that the riyals are printed on has been chemically treated. It will last about six months, after which it disintegrates. That should piss off some of those commie capitalists," Colonel Saeed said with a grin. "Can you imagine the chaos as thousands of Yemeni's converge on the banks with crumbling currency notes?"

"Shit," said Tim. "Sounds like you were trained at the Sands Hotel in Las Vegas, not Sandhurst."

Obviously pleased with the plan, the colonel smiled and continued explaining the plot. "The US dollars are specially marked. The intent is to use them to pay some of the unsavory arms salesmen. Banks around the world have been tipped off to watch for them. When these scums deposit their hard-earned cash they'll find out that it's worthless. They'll seek revenge on the buyers for cheating them. Unfortunately, this will only stop a small part of the weapons into the Yemen. Most of the arms are coming from China and the Soviets as military assistance."

Accepting my fate, I asked to excuse myself so that I could talk to Marie and explain that she and the kids would be without me for one day. The Duke, being the master of deception, stopped me and called Frankie to join us. "We need a common story to tell the girls. How about us good Samaritans delivering some medical supplies to one of the villages in the interior?"

Frankie and I agreed that Tim's idea sounded as good as anything and unanimously voted that the Duke would be the one to dazzle the girls with our sense of humanitarian spirit and desire to help people in distress. By now they were awake and taking breakfast in the main dining salon. When Tim finished telling them his story, I actually think they were proud of us. Back down the morality ladder again.

Qaat, Rhymes with Pot

It had been pre-arranged that the trunks would be taken by one of the local fishing boats to a small village down the coast. Frankie, the Duke, the two phony crewmen and I went ashore on the yacht's tender. We immediately checked in with immigration and customs to present the letter of invitation from the Yemen Government to visit the area and to show our credentials. The Customs and Immigration office was a small dilapidated building made of crumbling concrete blocks. The roll-down shutters on the front gave it the appearance of a large garage. Entering the musty-smelling headquarters, we were greeted by two uniformed men sitting behind a small battered table. Facing the table were several straight-back wooden chairs, each in some form of disrepair.

As we took a seat, Colonel Saeed handed them the letter and our passports while explaining the purpose of our visit. While the formalities of checking the documents was undertaken by the immigration officers, I began joking with my archeologist associates and addressing them as Dr. Johnson and Dr. Focaccia. Trying to lead Tim into taking on his role of an anthropologist, I rubbed my chin with my hand and said, "Tell me, Dr. Johnson, do you think we will discover the ruins of the ancient city of Yemonite?"

The Duke enjoyed the role-playing. He raised his right hand, brushed back the hair from the front of his face and looked at the ceiling as if in deep thought. And then in slow, articulated English, he looked at the head of Customs and explained what we were going to do in the mountain villages.

"Well, ah ya, ah, we're looking for the lost tribe of Yemonite who are supposed to live in these here mountains. We really believe that they are asshole descendants of the biblical sodomites from Sodom and Gomorrah."

I twisted my face to keep from laughing as the customs officer kept nodding his head up and down, listening to Tim's dissertation as if he understood every word. I whispered, "Tim, what if they understand what you're saying?"

In full tone he replied, "Fuck, Falcon, they don't understand shit. Look at what he's doing with our passports. The motherfucker is opening them backwards. *Ha, ha*, look at the fool."

"Remember, Tim, Arab writing is from right to left. For them the beginning of a book is what we know as the end. It's just his normal way of opening a passport."

"Well, it sure as shit ain't normal to hold it upside down. Look at that dumb fuck. He's pretending to read my passport information, and I can see my photo is head down. Shit, he can't even read Arabic, yet read or understand English. Hell, we can say whatever we want to these guys."

Without ever looking at the visa, the officer attacked an empty passport page with a large rubber stamp, leaving a big red square with squiggle writing in the middle. He stamped the other two passports and then handed them back to the colonel. With big smiles all around, hands were shaken and riyals were slipped to the officials. *Baksheesh,* the Arab art of the payoff. It was the only way to get anything done in a country like Yemen.

Parked in front of the customs house were two antique Land Rovers. This was our transportation to the small coastal village where we would reunite with our cash. The trunks of funny-money had already been taken from the *Puss and Hoots,* and clandestinely moved by a small fishing boat to our meeting point in the village.

After a two-hour ride along the rocky coast, we entered a small village consisting of a few huts, made of a reed called *barasti,* and one stone house. Fishing nets were spread out on the sandy beach while several men sat at various spots along the net repairing torn cord. We were led into the small stone house where we were handed local Arab clothes and ordered to change.

I had no trouble with the long shirt, but it took Mustafa's assistance to wrap the embroidered skirt, called a *futah,* around my hips. A rope belt held the skirt securely in place. I was then given a sheath and strap holding a *djambia* to wear over the belt. I protested that I wouldn't carry a weapon.

With a look combining frustration and puzzlement, Colonel Saeed explained to me that this was the most important article of "clothing" for the men of the highlands, and I must wear it. However, it was more for show than a weapon. He said that there were two kinds of daggers: the J-shaped *asib*, which most Yemeni men carry, and the less curved *thuma*, which is only carried by the religious upper classes. The daggers can be very expensive, especially if they have an ivory or rhinoceros horn handle. Convinced that it was just another item of clothing, I put it on.

To complete my ensemble, I was given a scarf. Unlike the *ghutra* in the Emirates, the scarf was not held in place by a *hegaal* but just draped loosely over the head and sometimes just worn on the shoulders like a shawl. I looked like a *Jebali* nerd with my white docksiders. Mustafa noticed the mismatch and soon a pair of well-worn sandals was placed at my feet.

Abdullah Duke, as I now called him, looked quite impressive in his skirt and jacket, while Frankie looked like a Yemen Mafia hit man. While we dressed, several men, associates of the Colonel, packed wads of riyal and dollar notes in woven carpetbags that I later learned were actually saddlebags for camels or donkeys. Once we were dressed and the bags packed and loaded into the vehicles, we departed down a dusty dirt road.

My sinuses ached from the fine sand sucked into my nostrils until I followed the example set by the natives and wrapped the scarf around my nose and mouth. The hard seats of the old vehicle strained my back. When we stopped three hours later at the entrance to *Wadi Jez*, I could barely stand. Two men and four donkeys greeted us, and the bags were hastily transferred onto the backs of the beasts. Looking at the large boulders and steep rocky inclines surrounding us, I realized that this was the end of the road for the Rovers. With the donkeys fully burdened and no other means of transport in sight, I assumed correctly that we would be walking. As we hiked into the depths of the *wadi*, I thought that the terrain appeared similar to the Musandam and Northern Emirate of Ras Al Khaimah. That is until we climbed to the first plateau. Appearing before me and climbing toward the sky, like steps for Goliath, were magnificent terraced gardens cut into the side of the next level of mountain. The alternating stripes of green agriculture and brown rock reached up to another plateau. "What type of crops are grown here?" I asked Saeed.

"Lemons, vegetables, and cereals. Coffee was once a major crop, but unfortunately, the growing of the green leaf narcotic *Qaat* has become more lucrative, so the farmers no longer plant mocha. Did you know that Yemen invented the drink, coffee, in the eleventh century, and that Mocha is named for the Red Sea port, Al Mukha?"

Saeed explained with pride. "I guess you can't blame the farmers," he said. "They make five times as much for *Qaat* as for other crops, including coffee. I have read that in Yemen, one-half to two-thirds of arable land is now cultivated for *Qaat*. The only positive thing that the communists have tried to do is ban the tradition of chewing this tranquilizing plant in the afternoons. They will fail."

After walking the jagged path to the top of the next flat mountain, my feet were scraped and bleeding. I stopped to check my wounds and to look down from my perch to trace our progress. As I gazed up the steep slope of the next mountain, I was awestruck at the sight crowning the crest. Placed precariously atop the peak was a city with multi-level, stone-tower houses. Each house was square, connected to the next house by a tall wall. Growing like hair from the head of the mountain was a fortress, strikingly similar to a European castle. The slope of the mountain and the exterior walls of the buildings merged into one continuous surface, all a part of the high mountain. Windows of the buildings faced out into the open sky as if cut into the side of the rock. There was no chance of sneaking out at night in these houses; it was at least two hundred-feet from the window to the base of the next tier of the mountain. This isolated village with its arable gardens on the lower levels was definitely built for defensive purposes and had probably been there for hundreds of years. It was impregnable, at least from the ground.

The zigzag walkway, hand-cut into the rock, followed the path of the terraces and adjacent *falaj*, the aqueduct system that gravity fed water from cisterns on the mountaintop to the crops on the ledges below. I thought that I was in shape, but the steep incline had my heart beating and my lungs gasping in the cool, thin air. The Duke was dragging well behind. When I saw him rub his left arm several times, I became concerned and waited while he caught up with me.

"Are you all right, Tim?"

"Ya, I'm fine. I just hate high places and have a little chest pain and a stiff arm. I'll get it checked out when we get home."

As we continued the hike I realized that this was the only route to the fortress village unless there was another trail on the backside that wasn't visible from our starting point below. Approaching the city, I could see that only one entrance was cut into the wall and adjoining houses that formed the battlements which surrounded whatever was inside. At last we entered the gates and were greeted by what appeared to be the whole male contingent of the tribe, all wearing ammunition packed bandoleers and carrying automatic weapons. They were friendly, I hoped.

An enormous tribesman approached me, his eyes looking curiously effeminate due to the ritual kohl make-up. His long hair flowed over massive shoulders. With his rifle and deadly looking *djambia* dagger tucked into his indigo cloth waistband, he definitely wasn't a cross-dresser. The colonel, seeing my surprised expression, explained that long hair and dark eye makeup was common for men in the mountainous highlands.

We followed our hosts through town to the small central square where the donkeys were unburdened and sent back down the mountain. The colonel selectively handed out the currency-filled saddlebags to Frankie, some of the tribesmen and me. As I followed the crowd through the narrow, winding streets, the lofty tower houses looming into the blue sky mesmerized me. As most of the windows were on the higher levels, it was confusing to determine just how many stories the tallest of these dwelling were, but I guessed that some were eight or nine floors. I soon confirmed my calculations as we were ushered into the biggest of these skyscrapers and I counted floors as we climbed. The stone foundation walls appeared to be at least three feet thick. But as we were led up the low narrow stairways the walls gently tapered and appeared to be mud brick or another type of lighter construction materials.

As we climbed I could hear the heavy breathing of the Duke behind me.

Looking down at the floors I could see that they were rows of heavy tree trunks topped with bundles of small, coarse wooden mats. Not only was the village a citadel, but each house was an individual stronghold.

Reaching the highest and most pleasant room of the house, known as the *mafraj*, we were greeted by the village leader, Shaikh Hamed Tarid. In perfect English he invited us to sit on the cushioned and carpeted floor where we were served water, fruit juices and tea. I hadn't realized how famished I was until I was comfortably seated and drank the refreshing mint tea and several glasses of cool water. It had been almost eight hours since we left Nishtun, and fatigue

Jebel Soori - A Mythical Magical Mountain City

and hunger was starting to set in. Around the opposite perimeter of the room, the wild-looking village men sat cheek to cheek with their legs crossed, curiously watching us masquerading *Jebalis*. A servant entered and laid a small plate in front of each of us. It looked like we were going to eat—at least we wouldn't starve. Another man entered the room with an armload of what looked like tree branches. He proceeded to distribute them to all of the guests in the room.

Picking up some of the small leafy branches, Frankie sniffed them. "*Qaat*! Looks like this isn't lunch. It's the afternoon *Qaat* session."

Hearing Frankie, Shaikh Hamed smiled. "Have you tried this before?"

"No, Shaikh, I have only seen others chew it in Somalia," replied Frankie.

Shaikh Hamed proceeded to tear off the tender leaves from the branch. "Just put the leaves in your mouth and chew lightly, holding them between the molars and the cheek. Try not to swallow the saliva." He demonstrated with the first leaves and then continually stuffed more of the vegetation into his mouth until his left cheek stuck out like a tumor.

Yemeni friends who live in Dubai had told me about chewing *Qaat*. Until twenty years ago, it was a weekend habit for the rich. Now, it is chewed everyday by a large percentage of Yemen's population. After work ends in the early afternoon, groups of ten to fifty people convene in a house or a coffee shop, to chew for three or four hours. It's a social gathering where people relax, talk business, recite poetry, or, as in this session, deal in politics.

I knew that *Qaat* is a stimulant, and as a child of the sixties who enjoyed a toke or two, I was willing to try anything once. I eagerly stuffed my mouth and ground the green leaves like a cow chewing her cud. I couldn't help but swallow some of the juices produced. The combination of an empty stomach and the bitter saliva made me a bit queasy. Shaikh Hamed must have noticed that my face matched the color of the leaves and ordered some tea with milk to be brought to me.

Leaning over to me on his right, the Duke whispered into my ear, "Falcon, if I put this Yemeni bubble gum in my mouth, I know I'll want to start drinking again. Grab me a handful of those tissues."

I reached for the box, pulled out a few sheets of the course paper, and handed them to Tim. With a smile on his face, the Duke held the paper in both hands and lowered them between his legs where no one could see him rolling the paper into a ball. He cupped the wad in his right hand. Then, faking a coughing spell he raised the hand to his mouth and pushed it into his cheek. The resulting chubby cheek looked just like the other *Qaat* filled faces in the room.

Nudging Tim, I discretely pointed across the room. "Hey, Tim, look at that little kid across the room sitting between the guy with the vest and the man with the old sport jacket."

Tim looked up and down the opposite perimeter of the room. " I don't see any kid."

"Over there. He's standing by the door now."

"Oh ya, there he is. Looks like a little league baseball pitcher with a chaw of tabaccee in his mouth. Seems awfully young to be doing drugs. Shit, now where did that little desert dwarf go?"

He was now back where I first spotted him, sitting with legs crossed on the cushions opposite me. The miniature tribesman looked at us as if he knew we were talking about him. He smiled and bowed his head in greeting. It was a happy, friendly and welcoming smile coming from the face, not of a young boy, but a man with undersized features and physique. I smiled back and then returned my attention to the *Qaat*.

Either the tea settled my stomach or I was getting high, because I felt no pain. The sensation was almost like smoking grass. I felt alert, re-energized and a bit euphoric. Unlike the eating binges that followed smoking marijuana, I actually lost my appetite. After three hours of masticating and drinking water and tea, I think I reached my peak. Sounds in the room ran together. Objects were blurred but the colors bright. Across the room some of the tribesmen lay on the floor, sound asleep. My little friend wasn't among them. He was gone. I laid my head back against the wall, looking up at the designs the tree trunk beams made on the ceiling. "Holy fuck! How'd that little shit get up there?" My elbow poked the Duke's side, jerking him to attention. "Hey, Tim, look up at that window across the room. Do you see him, that little guy?

"Falc, you've been chewing too much. All I see is a window."

With half opened eyes I slowly scanned the length of the rows of wooden ceiling shafts, following them to where they entered the adjoining wall, and then dropped my sight to the high window. As I gazed out into the blue sky, the miniature face of the man-child tribesmen peered back at me and then quickly vanished. I rubbed my eyes, closed them, and then looked again. From the side of the window, the face of the mountain midget slowly entered the frame. "Look, he's just standing outside the window and playing peek-a-boo with us, Tim."

"Standing, standing! What the fuck do you mean, standing, Falc? That's the outside wall. Unless whoever you're seeing is two hundred feet tall or on stilts, he ain't standing."

The Duke and I looked at each other. I grabbed his hand and squeezed hard. "Tim, you really see him, don't you? It's not just the *Qaat*? I know I'm not hallucinating. You haven't done anything but chew on a tissue and you saw him by the door."

Tim looked me in the eye and squeezed back. "Falcon, all I can say is that I saw a little tribesman earlier. Maybe it's the elevation? The thin air is getting to you. Sorry Falc, I'm not high like you. People get high on second-hand smoke but never second-hand chew. If it will make you feel better, I'll ask Frankie."

Tim rose to his feet and walked past several dozing Arabs until he reached our companion. They carried on a brief conversation and then Tim returned to his seat on the floor. "You're fucked, Falcon. Frankie didn't see a little person in the room since we've been here. When I asked him if he saw anyone outside the window, he looked at me like I was nuts. Let's just keep this to ourselves and forget you even thought you saw the little guy."

"*Yella! Yella!*" was all that I understood of the speech leaving the mouth of the Arab who burst into the room. Besides saying, "Let's go," he was excitedly informing Shaikh Hamed that something was going on. Before I could determine what was happening, Colonel Saeed took charge and started giving orders in Arabic. He then directed the Duke, Frankie and me to be calm. I walked to the outside wall and looked out the window.

Coming up the same path that we had traveled a few hours earlier were a half-dozen well-armed pseudo military men. They had fatigue-type jackets with military ammunition belts, but they wore the tribal skirts under them. Their appearance didn't instill much fear in the enemy, whom I assumed was us. They looked pretty rag-tag and the chance of them ever getting into the walled fortress was next to nil. I wasn't too alarmed as I addressed the Colonel. "Saeed, shouldn't we be heading out the back door?" I spotted the bags. "Should we just leave the money? I assume we've made delivery."

"Yes, we've completed our job. Shaikh Hamed will take over as banker. There is no need to be concerned about that government patrol coming toward the fortress. This is a common occurrence. They cannot get in, and will eventually leave. Sometimes the Shaikh will placate them by allowing one or two of them to enter and conduct a search of the village for arms. Today there will be no search, but they will stay outside the gates for a day or two just to harass the villagers. I'm afraid there is no back door. We must wait until they leave."

"Wait a day or two! We can't wait. My family expects me to meet them in the morning. We have to leave today." I walked back over to the window and looked down on the ascending troops.

Joining me at the window, the Duke patted me on the back.

"Don't worry, Falcon. We'll just be a day or two late."

As Tim consoled me, I felt a tug on my *futah*. Looking down, I saw two little hands hanging onto the skirt. Sitting on a low coffee table next to my leg was our diminutive friend. He raised his sad-looking face. Placing his small chin in his hand, he rested his elbow on his knee and gazed straight ahead, as if in deep thought, as if he were a mini-model for Rodin's "The Thinker."

Suddenly he jumped from his seat and ran to the nearest saddlebag. He untied the leather strap and retrieved several packets of money. Appearing at the window, he tore open the packets one by one and threw the money into open space.

I lunged for the little guy, only to see him exit the window with the last package of currency. Some of the notes spun like the blade of a whirly-bird as they descended to earth. Others floated like leaves falling from an autumn tree. Many of the bills, caught by the updrafts along the mountain, were carried far away from the soldiers below.

Looking up toward the window, the rag tag army watched the November money shower. Once the first riyal note was captured and identified, the soldiers broke ranks and pursued their new prey, the money. Scrambling from the footpath, they ran along the cultivated tiers of fruits and vegetables, lunging at green and red slips of paper. Leaping from one landscaped step down to another they snatched the money, piece by piece, determined to capture these symbols of capitalism before they could corrupt the populace. Within minutes they were far enough away from the trail that it would require a lengthy and rigorous climb up or down in order to reach the walkway.

"Quickly, now's our chance. Follow me." As he gave his orders, Colonel Saeed picked up his rifle and small traveling bag. "Mr. Lou, what a brilliant idea. I only wish you had told me about your plan so I could have been ready to move out."

What plan, I thought. "I didn't do anything, Colonel. It was that little tribesman." At least I think it was. After all that chewing I wasn't too sure of anything anymore.

Frankie was the first to fall in behind the colonel. Tim and I followed closely and Mustafa was the tail man.

We double-timed out the fortress gates and started down the mountain track. In front of me I could see Tim's head shaking back and forth. When he again looked back at me, I yelled, "What fuckin' plan? Didn't you guys see that weeble wobble out the window with the money?" Over my own babbling, I could hear the Duke drawing deep breaths and frog-like sounds emanated from his chest.

"Tim, are you all right?"

"Yeah, just don't like heights—gives me vertigo and makes it hard to breathe," he gasped.

"Look, Tim," I said as we continued our trek, "it's obvious that no one could see the miniature man outside the window but me. I agree; just forget I said I saw him. My mind is still messed up enough with that *Qaat*. I don't need to try to figure this out now. Just leave it."

Going down was a lot quicker, but one hour seemed like one day. Just before reaching the base of the mountain, Mustafa unlatched the two-way radio from his belt. I hoped that he was sending for a helicopter to pick us up. When we reached the entrance to the mountain trail, there was no helicopter—just the donkeys and their two masters. By the looks of their dilated pupils, the mule drivers had spent the last few hours waiting for us by enjoying their daily ration of *Qaat*.

Colonel Saeed gripped the rope reins of two of the largest animals and led them to us. Handing one of the ropes to Tim, he looked at both of us. "You two can ride double on this one. Here, Mr. Frankie," he said as he handed him the rope. You are a very big man and need one donkey by yourself."

"One big ass deserves another big ass, right Frankie?" laughed Tim.

Looking up at the Duke, Frankie smiled. Even after our experience with the soldiers and our rush down the mountain, the Duke was still able to make light of the situation.

Alternating between a few hours of riding, walking, and resting, we finally reached Al Ghaydah at dawn the following morning. All I could think about was a shower, a big breakfast and my bunk. Thank God the trip back to Dubai would be a leisurely four-day cruise. Our last stop in Yemen would be to obtain an exit stamp in our passport and board the *Puss and Hoots*. Before entering the town, we stopped to change back into our Western dress, which Mustafa produced from a dirty saddlebag.

The office of Customs and Immigration was much larger than the one room garage in Nishtun. It was old and dirty, but a proper building. Posted at the entrance and in the halls were a number of soldiers, more formally attired than those we saw at Jebal Soori. We followed the colonel into the immigration office, greeted the officer in charge and took a seat while Saeed produced our documents.

As I sat down, I reached into my pant pocket to pull out my handkerchief. With it came my money clip. It was a big heavy gold clasp, a gift from Tim. It landed on the floor with a loud bang. The intensity of the reverberation of the metal on the wooden floor startled the guards and customs officials. Still nervous from our little escapade, I wanted to placate our gun-toting hosts, so I excitedly called out in a loud voice, "FLOSY! FLOSY!"

All hell broke loose. The Yemeni screamed, Colonel Saeed yelled and three soldiers rushed into the room. They grabbed me by the arms, pulled me from my chair and started to roughly drag me from the room. As I was being physically removed from the office, I called, "Saeed, Saeed."

Before we reached the end of the hall, Saeed, my savior, appeared with the immigration officer and they calmly spoke to the soldiers, who released me. As we slowly walked back to the office, I asked Saeed, "What the hell was that all about? All I said was flosy, flosy, which in Arabic means my money, my money."

Saeed smiled. "Your pronunciation needs some work, Mr. Lou. The word for 'my money' is *faloosi*. You said *flosy*. In Yemen, FLOSY, is the acronym for a Nasserite political organization known as the Front for the Liberation of Occupied South Yemen. FLOSY fought the British occupation of South Yemen but the National Liberation Front, a Marxist organization from which the present government evolved, eventually eradicated the organization. Many FLOSY members live in exile in neighboring Arab countries. The Yemen government is still concerned about those FLOSY members in exile and considers them to be enemies of the State. They thought you were a foreign radical supporter of FLOSY. They have all calmed down, but I suggest that we get our documents and get back on the yacht, which is waiting for us in port."

Chickens Can't Dance

The trip back to Dubai was a relaxing comedown from the climatic experience of the Yemen escapade. The leisurely cruise allowed us to again stop in the Oman port of Salalah, as well as to do some more diving in the Musandam.

Throughout the journey I became increasingly concerned about the Duke. Since returning to the *Puss and Hoots*, he wasn't himself. His skin took on a gray pallor, his hair seemed even whiter, and his lethargic behavior wasn't typical of the energized personality that we were all used to. There were no jokes, stories or even four-letter expletives uttered on the return trip. When I asked about his quiet demeanor, he just said that he was tired from the mountain walk and was in one of his thinking modes.

The day we reached port in Dubai, I cornered Evie in the lounge before disembarking. "Evie, I don't think Tim is feeling well. We need to get him to a doctor."

"I agree," said Evie. "I've tried to talk to him about it, but he either avoids the subject or tells me that I'm being paranoid and he feels fine."

"Let's get together this week and come up with a plan to convince him his body needs a little maintenance. I'll give you a call tomorrow."

"Thanks, Lou," said Evie. "I appreciate all of the help I can get when it comes to influencing Tim on any decision."

A week after our adventure with the mountain men of Yemen, we received word that the terms of the oil concession had been finalized and that a formal signing ceremony would be held in early December. This was a cause for a celebration. It also became the venue for Evie and me to stage our little plan to get Tim to see a doctor.

The Duke, Evie, Marie and I, along with the Focaccia's and Iskar and a friend, decided to head for the Safari Nightclub for an evening of dancing. In cahoots with Evie, I invited Dr. Shabibi and his wife. The doctor was the only cardiologist in Dubai in those days. He was a personable man with great social graces and competent in his profession. I thought that if the Duke could see what a nice guy the doctor was, we might get him agree to go for a checkup. As it turned out, a little birdie must have told the Big Man upstairs, because He made the decision for the Duke.

It was a great Thursday night bash. If Tim wasn't feeling well, you'd never know it by the way he was cutting the rug with the ladies in the club. Dubai was a small community socially and everyone knew of the Duke's skill as a dancer. He was the first to introduce a new dance step, a new dance tune or a new dance craze. If it was good enough for the Duke, it was good enough for everyone else in Dubai. In Dubai, the Duke was the king of dance.

We all loved to watch Tim swing with the fifties and sixties tunes, or steam up the room with a sexy tango. For a man who could execute the most complicated of dance moves, the Duke was surprisingly simplistic when it came to his favorite dances. For some strange reason he was fond of the group dances that everyone's drunk uncle loved to lead at weddings, graduation parties or christenings, such as the conga, the bunny hop, and Tim's favorite, the chicken dance. It's the dance that goes with the "Chicken Song," the one with the "dede dede dede dee, dede dede dede dee." When doing the chicken dance you bend your arms at the elbow and flap them like chicken wings while you crook at the knees and kinda hop around like a chicken.

It was about 1:00 a.m. and the Duke was out on the dance floor doing the chicken dance for at least the third time that evening. Marie and I were a bit tuckered, so we sat at the table keeping the doctor and his wife company. While chatting, we watched Evie and Tim pecking on each other's cheeks while they flapped their wings. Flickering rays of light from the Disco ball that hung over the polished floor danced on their faces, almost in tune with the music. The Duke was in his usual chicken dance position, knees bent and thumbs tucked into his armpits to make his elbows look like the tips of his man-wings. All of a sudden his right wing began flapping erratically, going faster and faster and faster, like a hand held fan moving rapidly. Then the left wing started a similar movement. Following the example of their leader, the dancers on the floor began to imitate the rapid wing motions. They were all running around thrashing madly like someone let a fox into the chicken coup.

"Look, you guys, Tim's teaching a new move to the chicken dance," I said.

The wings flayed wildly on the dance floor when abruptly, on the up motion of the flap, Tim's right wing froze with the thumb under the armpit and the elbow lifted higher than the shoulder. Sure enough, the rest of the imprinted chick dancers immobilized their right wing in the same position as Big Bird. After continuing to dance like a bunch of broken wing poultry, Tim's left arm shot up and became immobilized in the same position as the right wing.

"What the hell is he doing?" I said out loud to my tablemates. Here was the Duke and forty other hens and roosters hopping around with their thumbs jammed in their armpits and elbows in the air.

Now it really got interesting. Tim's head started moving back and forth from left to right as if he was trying to smell his armpits. Sure enough, all the dancers on the floor followed the new move and soon the whole place was full of fowl-armpit smellers.

Just as the song was ending, the Duke fell to the floor, landing on his back and moving in a circular motion, propelled by his still hopping chicken feet. Break dancing didn't come out until the eighties, but I saw ol' Tim Johnson doing it ten years earlier. Within a minute the floor was full of copycat break-dancing chickadees.

Once the music stopped, the laughing crowd slowly rose from the floor and returned to their tables—everyone except the Duke. Through the dispersing crowd, I saw Evie kneeling down next to Tim, patting his hand and stroking his forehead. Her eyes circled the room looking for a familiar face; they settled on me and silently cried for help.

Jumping from my chair, I ran toward her, closely followed by Dr. Shabibi, who also saw Evie's silent plea. Reaching Tim, I pulled my handkerchief from my jacket and wiped the sweat from his face. His head was still shaking with spasms, his skin a spectral pallor. Tim appeared to be unconscious, and to my untrained eye, closer to a dead duck than a chirpy chick. Shaken by the sight of my helpless companion, I moved back to make room for the doctor.

As Dr. Shabibi examined Tim's eyes, the inside of his mouth and any place else decency and proper medical practice would allow in the middle of a dance floor, I noticed that the Duke's wings were starting to loosen and fall back into their normal position.

Dr. Shabibi leaned toward me, and in a whisper to shield Evie from the urgency in his voice, said, "Lou, we need to get Tim to the hospital. Please call an ambulance."

I rushed to the Maître d' stand and grabbed the phone. In those days there was no such thing as a "911" number, so I dialed the operator and in broken Arabic and excited English explained that we had an emergency and needed an ambulance. I must have been successful, as within minutes two attendants in white jackets appeared in the club pulling one of those ambulance gurneys. Moving the cot into position next to Tim, they lowered it to ground level and gently lifted his body onto the white-sheeted bed.

Like the phoenix rising from the ashes, Tim abruptly rose from the birdie bunk. Now sitting on the rolling bed, he looked at the attendants, looked at Evie and then looked at me. "What the fuck is going on? Can't ya see that I'm in the middle of a dance here?"

"Just calm down now, Tim," I said. "You passed out, and Dr. Shabibi here recommends that we take you to the hospital in an ambulance."

"Ambulance, my ass. Bullshit! I ain't getting into one of those fucking things. I used to drive one of them mobile morgues. I know where they're gonna take me."

At this point Evie took over and calmed Tim down. It was finally agreed that he and Evie would ride to the hospital in my car and that I would follow the ambulance to the hospital. Tim was finally gonna get his check up.

We soon learned that the Duke had experienced a heart attack. According to Dr Shabibi, it was most unusual as to how it affected Tim physically during the actual attack. When I visited him in his hospital the next day, Tim was ranting about getting the fuck out of this place. After two more days of tests it was determined that no major heart damage had occurred. Tim was given an ultimatum to either head back to the states for a proper examination and treatment, or risk a more serious attack. With Evie's urging he agreed to let Dr. Shabibi set up an appointment for him at the Houston Heart Clinic, but not until after the signing of the concession agreement. The Duke was determined to be there—and he was.

Luigi Falconi

Praise Be To God

The concession-signing ceremony took place on December 2, 1975, the fourth anniversary of the formation of the United Arab Emirates. In Oman, it wasn't a holiday, but the date still had significance as the Emirates was home to most of those present. NN, Frankie, the Duke and I sat and watched while the Sultan of Oman and Duffy La Rouche signed the documents. Duffy was the son of Scotty La Rouche, a legendary Australian oilman known as one of the blue-eyed Shaikhs. He made a fortune in North Sea and Middle East oil. Scotty was making an effort to introduce his sons Duffy and Maccie into the business.

After the signing, we were to be introduced to His Highness the Sultan. While I waited for my turn to meet the Omani ruler, I cornered NN and asked why he chose Scotty's company.

"Let me explain the facts of life, Lou," said NN. "First of all, I like the idea of having a Australian company join us. Australia is a politically neutral country and is accepted by the Arabs. Second, Scotty's sons had no objection to giving us the ten-percent royalty. And third, they paid a finder's fee of three million dollars to my company."

Frankie walked up and joined our conversation just as NN completed point number three. NN then turned away, leaving me alone with Frankie. Facing my friend, I said, "Do we get any of the bonus money?"

"Only in your dreams, Falcon. That money will be used to pay for favors that helped our group get the concession and the favorable government terms. Shaikh Raisee and the oil Minister will receive one million. Another million is kicked back to Duffy La Rouche and his brother Maccie, for convincing their dad Scotty to commit Scarab Petroleum to take over the financial obligations and grant the royalty. NN's company will keep a million to cover development costs, past, present and future."

I was confused. "Why would you give the La Rouche boys money that came from their own company?"

"Falcon, my boy, it's not their money. It came from shareholders and their dad."

"You mean that they are actually stealing money from investors and their own father?" I couldn't believe what Frankie had just told me. "That makes them thieves. How can we trust them?"

"We can't," Frankie said. "But once you know the character of the people you do business with, you deal with them according to that character. In this case, we just have to steal more from them than they steal from us."

I already knew that NN had questionable business ethics, but in this part of the world crooks only stole from crooks, just like Frankie said. Crooks never stole from friends. I was really glad to be a friend of NN.

It was my turn to meet Sultan Boutie. As Shaikh Raisee presented me he explained to him that I was the gentleman who arranged for the money shower over the Yemen Mountains. By this time I was beginning to believe that perhaps it *was* me and not some little Yemeni.

The Sultan smiled, "I understand from my good friend Shaikh Hamed Tarid that you had some help. He was quite impressed. It is highly unusual for an outsider to see the mountain *Jinns*. It is even more unusual that the little people would assist a foreigner. You must be good men with true faith in God."

I turned toward the Duke, who was within earshot. A feeling of liberation transcended my body. Looking at Tim, I watched his face take on an angelic tranquility. With his pale blue eyes raised heavenward and his curling white hair falling over his forehead, I saw the embodiment of an adult version of one of those little cherub faces you see in a Michelangelo or DaVinci painting. It was like looking at the ceiling of the Sistine Chapel. Any minute now, I thought, he would reach out with the forefinger of his right hand to touch the foot of God. Instead, he used it to nudge my shoulder, making me aware that my audience with the Sultan was over. The gracious Sovereign shook our hands and turned to greet other guests.

As we walked away, I whispered to the Duke. "See, I wasn't seeing things. It wasn't the *Qaat*. Shaikh Hamed saw our little friend too. *Al Hamdu Lillaah*, PRAISE BE TO GOD," I cried out, turning everyone's attention toward me.

"You're fuckin' nuts, Falcon. Keep that praise-to-God shit down.

The next thing you know you'll be a convert, down on your knees on a little carpet, waving your arms up and down."

"Timbo, if it helps explain things like the *Jinns*, I'll gladly convert. I'm beginning to think that this quest for the Holy Grail ain't all I thought it would be. Maybe there are a lot more important things than money."

"Like what?"

"Like you've always told me, Tim: family and friends."

VII
The Focaccia Letters

Drilling Holes — Geology or Gynecology

The more time I spent with Tim, Frankie and the friends, the more intense was my desire to hit the big one. It was bad enough that the Duke so easily influenced me that I began using much of his colorful vocabulary. I even started to covet the material possessions that were so important to Iskar and the Duke.

Being a school administrator was the pits when it came to money in the bank. Even the best days in the classroom and having a great staff didn't make up for the thin paychecks. Working overseas was more lucrative than in the States, but still the remuneration was middle class. I knew that I wanted more for my family and myself, and I was going to get it, and fast.

In February of 1976, Scarab Oil began their seismic program in the Musandam. Shooting seismic over the mountain terrain was more difficult than anticipated. Weeks of delays and poor quality seismic led to cost overruns that ate up the funds that were to be used for drilling the first well. Covering up the disappointing results of the seismic, the La Rouche family hyped the concession potential and issued more stock to raise $30 million to drill two wells. Without good seismic, the well locations were picked with the scientific support of a divining rod rather than geology and geophysics. The first well was located directly next to the seep that the Duke had discovered. The only oil that was found by the drilling crew was the oil that dribbled from the seep pool into the well hole. It was pretty obvious that the oil Tim discovered had migrated from a source that was nowhere near our concession area. At the end of September, Scarab Oil issued a press release claiming that they drilled a second dry hole about one mile from the first.

After the concession was signed the previous December, Tim headed to the heart clinic in Houston. His Christmas present that year was an angioplasty and replacement of neck arteries. Heart problem or not, this Musandam oil was his treasure and he made sure that he was back in Dubai by the end of February tracking the seismic and drilling program.

Soon after news of the second dry hole, I visited Tim in his office to have him educate me about drilling and explain what went wrong.

He was an oilman and knew the drilling business. In the meeting room, I found him studying long sheets of paper covered in squiggly lines, spread over his large conference table.

"What are you looking at?" I asked.

"Seismic print outs."

Tim reached into a box on the floor and pulled out a roll of paper. Weighting one end with an ashtray, he rolled it down the length of the table. He anchored the far end with a book and studied the colored patterns from end to end. "Drilling logs," he said as he scrutinized the paper.

"Haw, haw, haw." Slapping his thigh, Tim danced around the room. "Them sumbitches really did it, they pulled it off. I thought somethin' was fishy"

"Jesus, Tim, pulled what off? Let me in on the joke."

"Well, rumors around the oil patch insinuated that the second well was never drilled. According to what I just looked at, it's true. Based on this seismic, they couldn't have possibly drilled the well represented by these logs. They are most likely from some ol' dry well that was drilled elsewhere. The $15 million that they claimed it cost to drill the well went into the pockets of the La Rouche clan and the drilling company, and probably NN and his partners."

"What about us? We're partners too," I protested, not considering the fraud that was perpetrated. Two years in Dubai and I was now willing to make money by deception. I really had slipped down the ladder.

"Naw, these are big boys. We're not in their club. Screw the little partners and the shareholders."

Pulling out a chair, I sat down and stared dolefully at the logs.

"Don't look so glum, Lou. There's always a way to make money. When you have a setback, you don't sit around feeling sorry for yourself, you move on to the next plan. Hell, the La Rouche family saw the writing on the wall. By the looks of that seismic, after the results of the first well, there wasn't a chance in hell that the second would be any good so they took advantage of a bad situation and made it good. For them, anyway.

"Making a buck is easy. Just come up with an idea and follow up. Ya know, Lou, most people don't get rich because they're too lazy or insecure to follow up on their ideas. I made some big bucks with simple plans, not always totally legal, but not illegal either. I remember once making five grand by putting a one-line classified in several popular business and skin magazines. The advertisement simply read,

Send $1.00 to PO Box 1234
Los Angeles, California

"Now, Falcon, I wasn't using the mail to defraud," Tim explained. "The ad never promised anything in return. But Americans are curious and stupid. Hell, after paying for the advertising I made 5K on the deal.

"Now, stop feeling sorry for yourself and get your ass out of here and go think of an idea."

Caro Mio Fabio

I wasn't the only one who was ready to accept Tim's challenge. Over the last two years, Frankie and I had developed a confidant relationship. We talked about finances and smoked grass. We talked about women and drank. We spent a lot of time scuba diving and blowing bubbles. Like episodes of a daytime soap opera, the secrets of the Focaccia family were slowly revealed to me. Frankie knew that he could return to New Orleans at any time and would be welcomed into the family business. Any job would bring instant financial success, but Frankie wanted to make it on his own and become independent. He didn't want to owe the family anything. He had great money-making ideas, all legitimate, but all needed a million or two of seed money. I figured that I only needed a few hundred grand to make me comfortable.

We talked, drank, smoked and brainstormed a thousand ideas. But it wasn't until New Year's Eve that we received inspiration from two old friends, Jack Daniel's and Mara Juana.

Several families decided that we'd avoid the usual hotel or house party and usher in 1977 with family and special friends by camping out in the desert. We drove to our favorite spot in Mesriff, about thirty minutes from Dubai. It was close to the city, yet far enough away to allow us to become one with nature in the vast and desolate landscape. It was also far enough from town that we could play loud music, drink, smoke grass and raise hell without bothering anyone but the camels.

We arrived in the late afternoon to allow the kids time to ride three-wheel motorcycles and play in the sand. Camp was set up at the base of a large dune. After a hot dog dinner and some usual campfire songs and stories, we relegated the kids to the tents and broke out the dry refreshments. It was just over an hour until midnight. The fire was burning and the kids were fast asleep in the tents. Frankie and I sat around the fire with our ladies. Our friends Josh, Del, Kevin, Steve and their wives climbed the big sand dune to look at the star-filled sky and contemplate the meaning of life with a few beers and a joint or two.

Frankie, Joanne, Marie and I passed a reefer around and talked, while Frankie and I sipped bourbon from plastic cups between drags. Booze and marijuana-induced conversations have no logic as to topic. Soon we were talking about Clifford Irving's attempt to forge a biography of Howard Hughes and what a great scam it was. Too bad he got caught and went to jail.

"You know what the problem was, why he got caught?" Frankie asked. "It's because he tried to produce too much. Why forge a whole fuckin' book when you could get the same result with a one or two page document? Those few pages would have still been worth millions. The forger thought he was an artist, not a con man. He became obsessed with his artistic ability and forgot about the con. He let his creative side take over from the business side. A book has too much history to cover. He got carried away, and he got caught. Plus he based it on a living person. Ya gotta do it to someone who's dead so they can't check it out as easy."

I took a drag and passed the joint on. "You're right," I agreed. "He should have something a lot simpler like a few letters from Hitler to the Pope or his made-up male lover."

"You guys also missed one point," Joanne said. "Howard Hughes, Hitler and those others are too high profile, too famous in history. You need a minor figure who was involved in a major event. It would be harder to trace facts."

"Ya, right," I said. I was really mellow now. "Better yet, someone who likes to keep his privacy, like your uncle Flatface." Fabio had died a year earlier and Frankie didn't seem to be too broken up about it. After all, he may have been the Godfather to most people, but he was only an uncle to Frankie.

"What about the event?" Marie asked. "Wouldn't it have to be something well known, like having an affair with the president or a secret deal between heads of state?"

"How about the assassination of a president?" I offered. Looking at the reflection of the fire in Frankie's glazed eyes, I could almost hear the gears in his brain turning and I knew what he was thinking. There were dollar signs in those pupils. When he spoke, I wasn't surprised.

"What if we forged a letter or two indicating that Flatface was behind the Kennedy assassination? He's always getting blamed, so we might as well capitalize on it."

"How will your family, especially your uncles, react?" I asked.

"Shit, after all the crap the government has put my uncles and our families through, it will be like poetic justice for them. Screw up history and make a few million dollars."

"Sounds good to me," I said. "Let's do it."

As Frankie looked into the fire I could see his white teeth getting bigger behind the slit in his mouth until a huge smile spread across his face.

"I know just the modus operandi," he said. "Fabio was a renowned Lothario. He was a skirt chaser and always had at least one girl on the line, especially after he became angry with my Aunt Rosa for slamming the kitchen door in his face. But none of them meant anything, except for one—Stella. My father said that Uncle Fabio really loved her, and when he was jailed and deported temporarily by Bobby Kennedy, it was Stella that he contacted more often than anyone else."

Standing up, I started to head for my Land Cruiser. "Hold up; let me get a pencil and paper. I need to start writing this down." When I returned, the campsite-cons were abuzz in discussion. Throughout the next hour we threw out ideas and wrote drafts. Frankie had contacts with a top-notch forger in India who provides passports, university degrees, birth certificates, anything you want.

All he needed was a sample of Uncle Fabio's handwriting and the words we wanted written. Frankie said that this guy was the best and would even make sure the paper was produced in the right year. We worked on the letters, ending up with the three we thought were the ones we'd use.

July 28, 1962

Mia Cara Stella,

I'ma miss you so much mia amore.

That'a pig, Kennedy let his brother lock me up and kick a me outa the country for what! Justa so he can say that he'sa fighting the Mafia. What'sa he crazy. There is a no thing as Mafia. He see a bunch of old friend get together and he says it'sa organisa crime club. Shit'a, it'sa a social club. We play bocchi, shuffle the board, that card game breisca, and listen to Frankie sing. Is'a this against the law of this great country.

That sum of a bitch he ain'ta gonna get'a way with it. He can fucka that movie star but he no gonna fucka me. I talk to Fidel and he says he agree. The man gotta be teach'a lesson.

I be'a great patriot for America. I helpa Lucky organize the resistance in Sicily during the biga war, and I help the Allied forces when they occupy Italy. Looka how they treata me now.

I'm a see you soon my love. My breciola grows big thinka of you.

Amore,
Fabio

August 3, 1962

Mia Cara Stella,

I miss you like the birds missa the worm. Do you missa my worm mia amore?

I tell you that Irish potata gonna get his. It'sa shame that a nice catholic boy has to act like a WASP. My friend 'Che' the Cubano he telefona me from Sout America last week. He say that we gonna shuta up Mr. Presedente for good. I no think his plan work. I'ma thinka the only way to shut him up is cut off his meatballs. But I say 'Che,' OK. If'a no work then we do my way. 'Che' say OK.

I'ma miss you my little linguine.

Amore,
Fabio

August 7, 1962

Mia Cara Stella,

You reada the paper about the movie queen. Looka like Che plan no work. Che tell me that blondie die in the bed with the firsta prick inside her but that faga Hoover help JFK and his lawyer generale brother to cover it up. Che say his people supposed to put poison on the inaside of the condom but they maka mistaka and put ona outside. The movie star lady has a brute' climax. They try to say ita was pills. But it'a was the poison, bong, she gone. Too Bad buta serva her right for fuckin that Mick.

Now I do it my way. My friend Jack Ruby call me from Houston today and I tell him to go ahead with my plan.

Oh my Stella, I missa you so much. My Sisceelian sauseech and my heart ache for you.

Amore,
Fabio

After finishing our masterpieces, the four of us sat back, toked another joint and contemplated our next move while the rest of our friends climbed the large sand dune next to our camp site.

"We need some time to think this out, Falcon," Frankie said. "I'm taking the *Puss and Hoots* to the Red Sea off the port of Hurgada for several weeks at Easter to entertain a business associate, Ed Stroller, a VP of J. R. Dumont. Why don't you join me during your school vacation? I've already invited Josh and Steve to come along and help me entertain. Majid Bin Jabir may join us but with his new posting as Ambassador to Switzerland, I doubt if he'll make it."

Even in the desert darkness, I just know my eyes lit up. It was business entertainment for Frankie, but for me it was the chance of a lifetime, diving in the Red Sea. And from NN's yacht. God is definitely good. My ecstasy instantly abated when I remembered there were already plans in place for the holidays.

"Gee, Frankie, that would be swell, but Marie and I have been talking about taking a trip with the kids for spring break." Bless Marie, she could read me like a book, even back then. I looked at her and before I could say another word she was talking.

"Lou, you'll never get another chance like this. I want you to go."

"It's settled then. Count me in, Frankie." I gave Marie a big hug and a kiss.

The Dune Moon

"Hey, you guys, come on up," howled Kevin from his sandy mountain perch. "It's beautiful up here. The sky is almost as clear as Montana."

"Na, it's almost midnight. Why don't you guys come down so we can ring in the New Year and sing 'Auld Lang Syne'," I yelled back.

"Okay, we're coming down'"

I jumped up from my position as the fireside scribe and laid the letters aside. "Quick, Marie, Joanne, Frankie, let's moon them," I said to my fellow forgers. "The light from the fire will illuminate our bums so they'll see them just as they reach the bottom of the dune."

We all pulled down our Levi's and took our position, rear ends pointing north toward their entry and our faces toward the fire. We rested on our forearms and knees with our asses in the air waiting to hear the surprised campers.

"Aiiiiiiii Eiiiiii Oooooo!" The screams became deafening. The dune sitters decided to surprise us also, and they ran down the steep sand slope spraying beer, throwing water and any other liquids handy. Unfortunately, in their inebriated condition they couldn't quite calculate what it would take to stop their downhill momentum. What it took were our butts. Steve hit first, then his wife Lulu. Next came Del and Karen. Finally Kevin and his wife Ann hit the group. It was like a game of twister, except that instead of legs and arms there was bare bottoms and noses, some close enough to get a whiff of the smelly parts.

"Oh, oh," cried a laughing Kevin as he noticed that the smooth skin next to his cheek was Marie's rear.

"What the fuck," yelled Steve as I pushed up my backside, trying to get him off me.

"Oh my God." Ann laughed, as she patted Frankie on his bottom cheeks.

Joanne was doing everything possible to get those blue jeans back up. What would the girls at Bryn Mawr think?

I looked at my watch. It was 1977, so I started to sing, "May old acquaintance be forgot," and soon the whole gang joined in while we untangled our bodies, pulled up our pants and kissed each other.

Little voices began to cry out from inside the tents, so we woke up the few kids who were still asleep and brought all of them out to join the celebrations. It was a great way to welcome the New Year.

Looking at the star-filled sky, I made a silent toast to the Duke, who was in Houston recovering from his second heart surgery. "To '77, Tim," I said to myself. "This is the year we strike it rich."

Have You Seen Pierre?

Because of the Muslim and government holidays, the school calendar was a bit different from those in the States. Spring vacation didn't coincide with Easter but came early during the first half of March. Frankie and I ended up jetting to Cairo alone, as Josh and Steve had to back out of the dive trip.

We flew the two hundred miles to Hurgada in a small Egyptian, vintage prop plane—vintage meaning circa 1950. Disembarking, we vowed to drive back to Cairo rather than get back on that flying coffin.

The Sheraton Hotel Guest Relation's Manager met us at the airport, took our meager belongings, and scooted us off to the hotel in their limo, a thirty-year-old Mercedes. There wasn't a lot of baggage to handle, as all that I packed for the ten-day adventure was a bathing suit, underwear, Levis and T-shirts. The boat had all of the diving gear and anything else we needed. The hotel was pleased to have the luxury yacht floating offshore from its beach, as it was the largest boat around and added a bit of prestige for them.

When we boarded the yacht, Captain John gave Frankie a fax telling him that Ed would try to arrive later in the week. He never did. This meant that Frankie and I had the whole ship for the entire ten days.

After unpacking, we went ashore to explore the hotel grounds, and then strolled next door to the Club Mediterranean, where we met the dive staff, which consisted of a group of friendly young French men and women on a working holiday—more holiday than work. Also on staff was a young and newly trained doctor who handled all hotel accidents, including operation of the decompression chamber used to treat the bends, a malady that scuba divers get when they absorb too much nitrogen. Once this lively group found out we were the occupants of the *Puss and Hoots,* they became our best friends and offered to take us to the finest dive sites. We declined the guided tour but did take their advice on site locations. As thanks, we invited them to come aboard for dinner when we returned to port in a couple of days.

The following morning, before the sun was on the horizon, Captain John had his crew at work guiding the yacht up the coast to Abu Ramada Island, a dive site recommended by our new French friends. Being bold and foolish young men, we were looking for white tip sharks that were common in certain areas of the Red Sea.

About 10:00 a.m. we anchored at the dive site. While we were suiting up, Frankie looked at me with a wry smile. "Falcon, what's the deepest dive you've ever made?"

Knowing that Frankie had something on his mind, I was cautious. "About 120 feet. Why?"

"Before this trip is over, you're gonna pass the 200 foot mark."

I shook my head. "Nah, Frankie, I don't need to go that deep; it's just a waste of air and there's nothing to see at that depth that you can't see at 60 or 70 feet. The coral, the sea life, everything I want to see is right in the 60 to 80 foot zone, and it's safe."

Frankie handed me a yellow net bag. "We'll see, my man, but right now we need some groceries. I'll take a spear gun and we'll get some fish for lunch."

We checked out each other's equipment, and then did a giant stride into the cool water. Bobbing on the surface, we did one last safety-check, set our watches, checked our dive computer and headed down the anchor chain. The clear blue water was amazing; even more amazing was the abundance of sea life under, over and around us.

At about 120 feet, Frankie gave me a sign to stop. He continued on to what, in the crystal clear water, looked about ten feet deeper than where I was. He ascended back to my depth and, in diver's sign language, signaled for me to follow him. We headed up toward an outcrop of rocks and multicolored coral in about 60 feet of water. Hanging on the rocks, we watched the various varieties of fish and other sea animals pass by on their way to whatever it was they do all day. All of a sudden Frankie looked at me, or rather past me, and stared. Slowly I turned and was face to face with the most gigantic napoleon fish I had ever seen. It had this large hump protruding forward from its head just above the eyes, which is probably why they're also called a humphead wrasse. Underwater, it looked so big I thought that the story of Jonah and the whale could have been Jonah and the napoleon fish. A bit freaked, I swam away, but it pursued me. I turned, it followed. I went up, it followed. I went down but it stayed with me. It was like leading an underwater wrasse-rumba line.

Frankie sat on a rock watching, and judging from the amount of bubbles coming from his regulator, he was laughing like hell.

Finally, a bit bored with the pursuit, Frankie waited until there was a bit of distance between Napoleon and me and let go with his high power spear gun. It was a quick kill, and the fish floated limply while we tied a rope through his mouth and gills. Swimming to the surface we found that, even in the buoyancy of the water, the weight of the fish was more than we expected. At the surface, we called for help from the crew. Two of them took the rope with our lunch attached but were unable to pull it from the water.

Frankie and I took off our gear and got onto the dive platform while they held the fish. By the time we climbed onboard the captain and two more crewmen were on the stern uncovering the winch. While Captain John prepared a cable attached to a loading net, two men jumped into the water to help keep the fish afloat. Once it was properly rigged, the captain threw the net to the swimming helpers and they enclosed the catch. It was now an easy task to winch the fish from the water and lay it on the deck. Water magnifies, but this was still one huge fish, at least 100 pounds. We'd eat well for the next few days.

That evening, I was stretched out on the couch in the lounge watching a video when Frankie, sitting across from me said, "How deep do you think I was when I had you hold at 120 today?"

"Only about 10 or 20 feet deeper than I was."

"No, Falc, I was at 203 feet. See, not much different. Tomorrow, you break 200."

"No, thanks." I turned to watch the film.

The next morning we made two dives and each time, coaxed on by Frankie, I went deeper and deeper, reaching 180 feet, while Frankie continued that extra 20 feet waving for me to come and join. The clarity of the water was amazing. The 200-foot level 20 feet below was like looking through a clean glass, just an arm's length away. I didn't quite have the nerve, yet I wanted to stay close to Frankie. If I had a problem, I needed to be able to reach him to buddy-breathe.

He finally made me do it. On the afternoon dive I followed him through the crystal water to 205 feet. I felt so calm and happy. Hell, what was I afraid of? This was easy. Then I recalled what I had been taught about deep diving and why you had to be careful. At a depth of about 100 feet, excess nitrogen affects divers. It can induce a false sense of security and loss of judgment, which are not always noticed.

It's compared to the effects of too much alcohol. This is what's called nitrogen narcosis. Yep, I was definitely a drunk diver. In diving lingo, I was narc'd. I'd follow anyone anywhere. Maybe Frankie's tolerance level was high since he did a lot of deep diving, but I knew I was well beyond my limit. I slowly ascended back to the 60-foot level and waited for Frankie to join me. We continued our dive at a reasonable level and then headed to the surface.

On deck we celebrated my false machismo and senseless deep-water excursion with a bottle of champagne while the boat headed back to Hurgada.

That evening, our new French friends joined us aboard for dinner. Sitting at the round table on the back deck, we talked diving and ate deep-fried fish. It was delicious.

"Where did you dive, Mr. Frankie?" asked Jacques. "Did you go to Abu Ramada Island where I suggested?"

"We sure did, and it was beautiful diving, just as you said it would be."

Colette, an attractive dive instructor at the club, chimed in with her broken English, "Deed you zee Pierre?"

Colette already had my attention with her good looks, but that cute accent made me eager to get in on the conversation. "No, we didn't see any other boats or divers in the area," I said.

"No, no, Pierre iz not a divair, he iz a beeg beeg napol-eon fish. He is very genteel. For the last two years we have been feeding heem zee eggs, boiled. He now let us feed him by zee hand. You can even touch heem on zee head. He will follow you in zee water unteal you give heem zum food. Zee tourists love to zee him."

By instinct Frankie and I looked at each other and simultaneously paled. My stomach felt like it was ready to erupt. The last piece of Pierre that I had swallowed was just about back on the plate. I promptly excused myself from the table, jumped up and headed for the privacy of the ship bow. Leaning over the rail I regurgitated pieces of Pierre, back to the deep where he belonged.

Walking up behind me, Frankie blurted out, "Jesus, Falc, we killed their tourist attraction."

"Not we, Kimosabi, you're the Pierre perpetrator. I had nothing to do with the murder."

"Fuck. What do we tell them?"

Regaining my composure and my stomach, I grabbed Frankie's shoulders, looked him in the eye, and burst out laughing. I couldn't help it. Soon Frankie caught the laugh bug and we both laughed until we had tears in our eyes. The black humor of our terrible deed finally broke through the serious side of our crime.

"We killed Pierre, we ate Pierre, so there is no *corpus delecti*," I said to Frankie. "Therefore we have committed the perfect crime. We have eaten the evidence. There is no trace of Pierre, except for the few pieces left on the plate and they may be gone when we return to the table, so we shall go back to our guests and continue as if nothing unusual has happened." And we did.

Frankie and I drank more than usual that evening, but it was a grand party. We avoided our French acquaintances for the rest of the trip until the last day, when we needed their assistance.

The Chamber Pot

We were at Ras Mohammed, the tip of the Sinai Peninsula, making our final dive before heading back to Hurgada for the night. Ras Mohammed is reportedly a favorite shark habitat and we were hyped up to experience swimming with the beasts. The next morning we would head back to the airport in Cairo via a local taxi, avoiding the decrepit Egypt Air commuter aircraft.

My deep dive profile for the last few days of our trip was foolishly impressive, to me at least: Abu Ramada Island, 120 feet; Giftun El Saghir Island, 140 feet; Umm Gammar Island, 205 feet; Abu Ramada Island, 180 feet; Ras Mohammed, 195 feet. It was dumb, but it seemed okay at the time.

We did our dive calculations with our PADI dive tables and we also had one of those new electronic dive computers to back us up. With the confidence of Jacques Cousteau I headed into the water for that last excursion. The dive was much like the others but we limited our maximum depth to 160 feet, as Frankie wanted to save air so he could do an inspection of the hull at the end of the dive. Since Barnacles growing on the bottom could slow the ship's speed and lessen fuel efficiency, he'd have the crew do a scraping after we left, if necessary. As an executive of the company that owned the yacht, he could have the crew do the inspection, but he was a hands-on marine man and liked to do things himself.

We finished the underwater excursion and hung off at about ten feet, blowing off nitrogen. Frankie motioned for me to remain where I was, holding on to the anchor rope. He then disappeared under the bow of the *Puss and Hoots*. I waited for what seemed like ten minutes, then checked the digital read-out on the dive calculator to see an "all clear" reading. Just then Frankie returned, and I motioned to him that I was going up and darted to the surface. I didn't make a nice slow ascent for the last ten feet. Instead, I literally popped up. I thought nothing of it at the time, as our calculations—and the computer—told me I was clear of nitrogen.

I was already aboard when Frankie came up ten minutes later. A few minutes after that, a mild pain tingled the joint of my right shoulder and my arm numbed. Frankie knew exactly what was wrong. I had an air embolism, a bubble of air in my shoulder joint, or more likely, the bends. As the professionals like Frankie would say, I took a hit.

"Lie on the couch," Frankie commanded. He made me lie on my left side with my head lower than the rest of my body. Frankie lit a joint and handed it to me. "Take a few drags. It'll relax you."

Frankie turned to Saju, the cabin boy. "Call Captain John," he said.

The captain instantly appeared, and Frankie ordered him to find out where the nearest decompression chamber was and how long it would take to get there.

Captain John soon returned. "Sir," said the captain, "the nearest chamber is located at the Club Med in Hurgada. I can make it in two hours if we travel at twenty knots, or about three hours at fifteen knots."

Frankie started to say something, but then hesitated. "No need to rush and blow the engines. Lou will be fine. Let's cruise at fifteen knots."

Frankie had me sit up briefly to drink some Gatorade and orange juice, and told me to stay awake. To keep me from falling asleep, he told me stories about his experiences with professional divers who got the bends on the job. It was his way of trying to take my mind off the fact that I had little bubbles in my shoulder joint looking for a way to get out and float up to my brain, like bubbles in a shaken soda pop bottle.

In my mind, I had a vision of the bubbles going down my arm and reaching my fingers. And then, like hitting a dead end in a maze, they turned around and floated back up my arm, through my shoulder, up my neck into my head and then to my brain. I interrupted Frankie's storytelling, and asked him if this could really happen.

"Shit, Falcon, one time we came up from working on the leg of a semi-submersible drilling platform and my partner took a hit. Before we could get him out of the water, a big bubble started to form in his chest. I could see it protruding under the skin, moving up and getting bigger. By the time it got to his neck, it was the size of a baseball. Then it disappeared. I guess it was going through his neck into his head. A couple of minutes later his head started swelling until it was as big as a basketball. "I was panicked. What do I do? It was like his body was possessed by some type of alien sea creature."

"Jesus, Frankie, did he die? What happened?"

"Well, I grabbed my dive knife and stuck the tip right here." Frankie pointed to the space between the bridge of his nose and his forehead. "As soon as I penetrated the skin, air rushed from his head with a loud swissssssssh and his body popped out of the water like a deflating balloon. He actually landed on the deck of the workboat. When I finally got out of the water and reached him, he was lying on the deck with a big smile on his face and a few drops of blood dripping down his nose. Hell, he was fine.

"I'm gonna go to my cabin, Lou-boy, and take a quick shower and change. I'll be right back. Try not to fall asleep."

One of the symptoms of the bends, similar to my *Qaat* chewing experience, is that it can cause hallucinations. This, and a few inhales of marijuana, made a perfect cocktail that even Timothy Leary would have liked to try.

Even though Frankie had me laughing, I was a bit dizzy and must have hallucinated. Turning my face to the ceiling, I saw my body. It had become a giant helium-inflated balloon, like those in the Macy's Thanksgiving Day parade. My head was huge, as were my arms, legs and torso. I was spread eagle, back against the ceiling, facing my real body lying on the sofa below. My butt would bounce on the ceiling while my head dropped down. Then my head would rise and the back of it would bang on the ceiling, while my butt dipped down. After bouncing like a teeter-totter, a beautiful girl balloon, with nothing on but a nurse's cap, glided into the room and positioned herself next to my flying blimpy body. In her right hand she held an enema syringe with a red bulb on the end of it. With her left hand she grabbed the back of my bathing suit and pulled it down over my air-inflated fat ass and shoved the syringe into the enlarged anus. The red bulb immediately began getting bigger and bigger, while my dirigible body began to get smaller. In just a minute the red bulb was enormous and my body was back to normal size and floated down to reunite with me on the couch. It was then I knew everything was going to be OK.

I must have dozed a minute, because I was jolted by what sounded like a big fart.

Just at that moment, Frankie appeared. "Christ, Falconi, who in the hell broke wind in here? Smells like someone shit their pants."

"Not me." But I knew what it was. It was the big red ball on the enema syringe. It was so big it exploded, like a big fart. Besides sucking out the nitrogen bubbles, it must have picked up a little bowel gas. I don't know if it's biologically possible, but I think that I farted out some of that embolism. My arm still hurt, so I didn't get it all, but I did feel relief. How do you spell relief: F-A-R-T.

It was an apprehensive three-hour trip for me, but we finally floated in to Hurgada and rushed to the Club Med. The doctor and staff who would operate the chamber were on standby and waiting for us when we arrived. The chamber was a frightening sight, one that I associated with those little iron lung-shaped containers that I used to put my extra pennies in as a kid to help fight polio.

It hit me with a jolt. I was gonna get into this round tomb, this mini waterless submarine, for the next several hours. Oh God, claustrophobia!

While I was viewing the cure vessel, I listened to Frankie talking—no, he was arguing—with the doctor.

"You don't use that valve. You turn this one."

"No, no," the doctor said. "It is this valve. See, it controls this gauge."

"Yeah, and if you open that valve, my friend will blow up like a cheese soufflé. Listen, Frenchie, that valve is for the gauge on the end."

"No, I am sure that it is this one," Frenchie said.

"Well, doc, if you turn that, it will put so much pressure in the chamber that my friend will be flatter than a crepe suzette."

Shit, flatter than a crepe, blown up like a soufflé, it sounded like a French cooking class, and I was the main course.

"Monsieur Frankie, I am a diving doctor and I know what I am doing."

"Okay, do it the way you want," answered a frustrated Frankie.

The chamber had a small anti-chamber with a bench, and an attached larger internal chamber with a cot. Two round windows dotted the large section and one small window interrupted the door of the entry area.

After listening to the exchange between Frankie and the doctor, I was more than a bit concerned, I was scared. When I heard the doctor's say, "Please get into the entry chamber," that was it, I was shit scared.

Beads of sweat covered my forehead. Breathing heavily, I reluctantly walked toward the metal cylinder and climbed in. Looking through the round door, I yelled, "Now let's think this over, gang. Maybe we should go on to Cairo." My last word was cut off when someone closed the door. CLANG! What a terrifying sound. I now knew what our cat felt when I banged shut the door to his carry-cage after shoving him inside. He only had the veterinary doctor to contend with. I had a mad French doctor.

I looked out the window and saw Frankie and the doctor again bantering back and forth. It looked like the disagreement was still on, but I couldn't hear a sound. Just then the doctor's voice came through the speaker above my head, loud and clear.

"Monsieur, push the intercom button to the 'on' position and then open the door into the inner chamber and lie down, please."

I turned on the intercom and grabbed the handle to the door, giving it a hard push, but it wouldn't budge. I pushed and pulled, and pushed and pulled some more, but nothing. "I can't get the door open," I said to the microphone.

From the speaker I again heard Frankie and the doctor arguing about which valve, which gauge, what to turn, what to do. Becoming even more frightened, I thought of the James Bond movie, "License to Kill," where Bond shoves the bad guy into the decompression chamber and drops the pressure quickly so that the villain's body pressure rapidly expands and he bursts like a balloon. Remember the blood and guts splattering on the round window of the chamber? I did.

Finally, the doctor conceded and Frankie took over the operation.

"Just be cool, Falc. I've operated these many times onboard our dive work boats. First I'm gonna increase the pressure in the outer chamber."

I heard the "swish" of air enter, and then the sound of the door to the large chamber snapping open, allowing me into the larger compartment.

"We let the pressure get that stuck door open," Frankie said.

I was now convinced that my man Frankie knew what he was doing.

"OK, Falc, I calculated our dive depth. I estimate that we need to do a level five decompression and take you back to 200 feet. I'll slowly bring the pressure back up to normal, but it will take four to five hours, so get comfortable."

"Thanks, Frankie, but how do you get comfortable in a tomb?" I tried to sleep, but only had nightmares. I finally reached for a magazine and grabbed the closest one at hand, *Penthouse*. Christ, why would anyone want to read porn in a decompression chamber, unless, yep, that was it, the staff had kinky sex in here. Thinking about the hallucination of my inflated body, I figured that maybe you could inflate the pressure and get a giant erection. Just a thought.

Apparently I must have drifted off to sleep, as the next thing I remembered was Colette knocking on the window to wake me up. "It iz time to come out," she said.

The doors burst open and I was outta there like a shot. The pain was gone and I felt great. However, even to this day my shoulder occasionally aches, especially in cold weather or after lifting weights.

How lucky I was to have had Frankie and to be so close to a decompression chamber. It could have been my brain that pained me, not my shoulder. I learned a valuable diving lesson. Each person's body is different. Frankie had no problem, yet I did. There was no fault with the electronic dive calculator or our dive calculations, it was just popping up that last ten feet. My interest in diving was stimulated by this experience and I wanted to learn more. This was the reason I went on to become a certified PADI diving instructor.

The next day we made the kamikaze cab ride to Cairo. I thought that it would be better than the flying coffin. After the Egyptian driver tried to make mummies out of us by passing lines of cars on the two lane road and playing chicken with the oncoming ten-ton trucks, I highly recommend a poorly maintained vintage aircraft rather than an Egyptian taxi.

Frankie flew on to London and I went to the Heliopolis Sheraton for a couple of days rather than heading back to Dubai. It's recommended that a diver avoid flying immediately after diving. With my recent experience, I wanted to make sure it was safe, so I delayed my departure for two days. It gave me a chance to look up friends I had met in Cairo when I lived there before moving to Dubai, and to wind down before heading back to Dubai.

Less than a week after our trip, I was told the *Puss and Hoots* was being moved to a new berth in the south of France when distress signals coming from the yacht were picked up on marine radio frequencies. One ship close by established radio communications and was told by the captain of the yacht that the engine room was on fire and out of control. Following the law of the sea, the closest ships turned course and headed toward the blazing boat. Upon arrival, they reported finding the crew ensconced in the tender, but there was no sight of the *Puss and Hoots*. It had already sunk. Thank God the crew escaped safely on the tenders.

Never Burn Your Bridges—or Your Boats

The *Puss and Hoots* wasn't the first boat from Dubai to burn and sink. Sitting in my hotel room back in Cairo, I remembered another boat burning story. It happened in the winter of '75 just outside of the Dubai port.

Terry Desjardin was in charge of offshore contracting for COC and had the final say on which company got contracts for fuel and material supply as well as crew changes. It wasn't hard to figure out why Terry got a lot of gifts and favors from the service company executives. The great thing about Terry was that he always shared the benefits with friends, so of course I made sure I was a friend.

The Duke and I were sitting in Poncho's restaurant when Terry walked in. His face was cut and bruised and he shuffled his feet in a slow gate as if walking were painful.

"Hey, Terry, looks like one of your lady friends did more then just sit on your face," yelled the Duke in a greeting way. "Come on over here with the Falc and me and tell us about her."

"Hi, Tim. Hi, Lue. Shit, I wish it was whips and chains. At least the climax would have been worth it." Terry, in obvious agony, bent his torso and slowly slid onto the booth bench seat. As he reached for the Margarita the Duke had poured for him from my pitcher, we saw that the palms of both hands were cut up like raw sushi.

"Damn, Terry," said the Duke. "Looks like you been jacking off a razor-blade dick. What the fuck you do?"

Shaking his head, Terry slowly unbuttoned his shirt and pulled it apart to reveal a web of red swelling scratches and cuts across his chest. Then, lifting his left leg that was hanging over the edge of the bench, he pulled up the bell bottom trouser. The appendage looked like a piece of mutton hanging from the hooks in the Dubai meat souk, much worse than his chest and hands. "Shit, you should have seen it a couple of days ago."

"Who did this?" I asked. "I'll get some of the guys and we'll go get them. Nobody does that to our friend."

"Forget it, Lue, it was just from a party, the one on the boat Thursday night, the one you couldn't come to. Man, what a party. The President of MOMS, ole NN, arranged for me to use their 40-foot Riva party boat to—well, PARTY. They had it stocked with food, booze and a few stewardesses on layover. When some of the guys and I arrived, the party was already going."

Terry twisted in his seat, took a chug of the cold drink, and continued the story. "The wind was up that night and the seas were too rough to take the boat out to open water, so I asked the captain to head outside the port and anchor about 100 feet from the sea-break wall."

"Yeah, I remember watching them build those walls during the port expansion. They used a combination of tetrapods, three-legged concrete blocks, and large jagged boulders cut from a quarry in Ras Al Khaimah. They built that wall about fifteen feet above the water level at high tide," I commented.

"Damn, Falc, shut the fuck up so we can hear the story," the Duke said.

Jerry looked at the Duke and then at me while rolling the cold drink glass between the palm of his hands, probably relieving his pain.

"The music was blaring, guys and girls in skimpy bathing suits danced with the rocking of the boat and the drinks flowed, Dom Pérignon, Courvoisier, Jose Cuervo; something for everyone and everyone drank and drank.

"As the party went on, bathing tops came off and a little playful groping started to take place, a pinch here, a cupped breast there, and most enjoyable, a rear testicle tickle from one of the stewardesses.

"Shit, we were having such a great time that we didn't even notice the flickering lights and broken lyrics of the music, but the captain and crew did. I saw them move toward the rear of the boat and lift the engine compartment cover. I was having such a good time and didn't think much about it until I saw several crew running past me with tools and flashlights. I told Fifi, an Air France stewardess I was dazzling with my best lines—damn what a set she had—to wait for me, that I'd me right back"

"Ooo ii, I do love French pussy."

"The word is *oui*, Tim," I corrected.

"We, me, us, who gives a fuck, everyone loves French pussy, haw, haw, haw," roared the Duke.

Terry's sad eyes stared at me until the Duke's laughter faded, and then he continued. "Brandy snifter in hand, I walked back and saw the captain bent over looking into the hatch with a flashlight. When I got there, the mechanic had exited the engine compartment and was standing next to the captain speaking in strange tongues and waving his flashlight into the black abyss below.

"I asked the captain what was wrong and was told that the wires were shorting and giving off sparks. Hell, I knew something about boats, so I bent over to take a look. Just as I did, Fifi came up from behind and reached between my legs for a testicle tickle. Well, that can be quite a surprise if you're not expecting it."

"It's quite a surprise even when you are," I said.

"Shit, I let out a shriek, jumped up, hit my head on the open engine hatch and dropped my glass of Courvoisier. The sound of glass breaking as it hit the engine below couldn't be heard by anyone on the boat. It was drowned out by the sound of the explosion as the brandy came into contact with a random spark and ignited the engine compartment and then the fuel fumes coming from an adjoining compartment. The blaze was instantaneous. I yelled for everyone to jump overboard, no time for a lifeboat to be sent over the side. The captain, crew and I used the few seconds we had and went through each cabin to make sure everyone was off the boat.

"I was just thankful we were not in open water but close enough to the sea-break wall for everyone to easily swim to safety. It was a lot closer than shore. When we reached the jagged stone and interlocked tetrapods, the twenty or so skimpily clad swimmers and I realized that it was low tide and the fifteen foot wall of rocks was now twenty feet high and covered with barnacles, clams and other flesh-cutting shell creatures. We had no choice. We were drunk, cold and half nude. Swimming to the sandy beach wasn't an option. We had no choice but to climb."

Terry looked up and stared at the murals of Mexico on the wall behind Tim and me and continued talking. "Ah, it was a gallant rescue. Everyone helped each other—up, up, up, until all reached the dirt road at the top of the sea break. Damn the barnacles, get to the top, and we did.

"The cold water and colder air numbed our bodies so none of us had an idea about the extent of our injuries. It was only when we turned toward the blazing boat that I could see from the reflected light blood running down flesh cuts on bare legs, arms and chests.

"Reality finally set in when I heard the sirens and saw the flashing lights of the police and fire engines coming from the port. The problem was just starting. Here was a group of half naked and fully drunk men and women and a burning boat. Too much for me to explain to the police, let alone my wife. I did the only thing I could do. I abandoned my friends and quietly slinked back toward the rocks."

Tears welled up in the corner or Terry's eyes. He turned his face to the side, trying to avoid showing his shame. "The climb down was just as bloody as the one up. Once back in the water, the sea salt burned my entire body as I swam to shore."

I could see the smile on the Duke's face and knew he was seeing nothing but humor in Terry's saga. I kicked him under the table. When he looked at me, I shook my head. He knew what I meant and held back on his comments.

"What happened when you go to the beach?" I said.

"Well, I live not far from the port and just one road back, so I walked home. Damn, it was the most painful experience I ever had—and fuckin' cold with just a bathing suit on. I could see the port fireboats arrive and spray water on the burning boat. I also saw the mass of police and fire truck lights on the port wall road, just where I left the rest of the party. What I couldn't see, and only found out later, was what happened just before the police arrived. The captain had friends all over the port. One of them had a boat moored just next to where we exited the water and he quickly ushered everyone onboard. When the police arrived the boat was slowly leaving its dock with the half-nude aquanauts. NN's office was informed of the situation and few minutes later the boat pulled up to MOMS dock where it was met by company medics who tended their wounds and gave everyone a pair of coveralls to wear. They were then put in a company bus and delivered to their homes.

"Only the captain and crew were left on the sea-wall road to greet the police when they arrived. The explanation of an explosion caused by a spark from a shorted electrical fire satisfied everyone."

"Did you get home OK?" I asked.

"Oh yeah, but that was just the start of my bad luck. Lori, my wife, thought I'd be gone for most of the night. I told her it would be a very late poker game with the boys. I had lost my keys when the boat sank, so I decided to sneak in through the sliding glass windows in the dressing room just outside of our bedroom. I got in without making much noise. I guess it didn't matter, as the moaning and groaning coming from my bedroom would drown out the roar of a freight train. I'm no brain surgeon, but I knew what was going on. Bursting into the room, I attacked the jumble of bodies in the bed with a vengeance. Soon the tide turned and I found that I was the one being attacked by my wife and her lover. They kicked, gouged and dug long fingernails into my already battered body. I thought there were a lot of long fingernails. When I finally was able to switch on a light, I saw why. I was fighting off two women. My wife's lover was the wife of one of my best friends. One of the guys I left at the port—"

"Come on, Falc," the Duke said, "We got to go. See ya later, Terry." Throwing a few bills on the table, he got up and headed for the door with me in pursuit.

As we exited Poncho's, I asked, "What's the rush?"

Tim turned and bellowed, "Haw, haw, Haw. He cut his ass up two times, swam all the way to shore, and then walked home to find out that his wife is a dyke. That's good, that's fuckin'good. Teach the sumbitch to abandon his friends."

I stared at my friend.

Tim turned and looked me almost as if he were angry. "Ya never abandon your friends Falc. Never."

VIII
Decisions, Decisions, Decisions

Dr. Falconi's Traveling Maintenance Company

My little escapade with the decompression chamber during the spring break kept Frankie and me from discussing Uncle Fabio's letters. It was May, and the final year of my contract at the school would soon be finished. I still hadn't made my fortune. Ever since I'd moved to Dubai and met the Duke I had become obsessed with making money, quick money. There was something about the atmosphere. It was pure electricity and I wanted my share of the charge. I was in the middle of the biggest oil boom of all time, surrounded by some of the most colorful, eccentric and successful wheeler-dealers in the world. Seeing people like Iskar, Majid Bin Jabir, NN and others making millions had the effect of hypnotizing me into believing that I could do it too. Sure, I could save my money in three-percent interest CD's or invest in small gain stocks, and in twenty-five years I might have enough saved for a comfortable retirement or to start my dive shop. But I didn't want that. I wanted to make profits like the gold smugglers made, and I wanted to make it NOW, while I was young.

I was coming close to selling my soul to achieve my goal, thinking that maybe I just had to go a little further down the morality ladder to keep success from slipping through my fingers. There was still the Focaccia letters.

Without other options to keep me here, my plan was to return to Boston University and finish my Ph.D., becoming Dr. Falconi, and then go out and get a job doing the same thing I do now. A frustrating outlook, knowing that by the time I finished my doctorate the boom in Dubai would be over and so would my chance to make my millions. I needed some advice. I needed to talk to the Gentleman Rogue.

It had been several months since I had seen the Duke. Soon after uncovering the Scarab Oil scam, Tim began having heart problems again. His second surgery, a triple by-pass, went well, but his recuperation wasn't as speedy as the previous year after the angioplasty. For six months after the operation he remained at his homes in Texas and California building up his strength. We had been in touch by phone and letters, but it wasn't the same as being with him in Dubai. When Tim was around there was never a dull moment. I began to recognize that his companionship meant more than having a good time or an adventure. When I had a problem I would go to Tim. When I needed money I would go to Tim. I finally realized that he was my best friend, and I missed having him around.

As I anxiously walked up his front steps, a smiling Duke, book tucked under his arm, was standing at the door to greet me.

"Damn, it's good to see you," I said as I grabbed his thin hand in an emotional handshake, and then gave his emaciated body a gentle bear hug. "You look great, Tim. Better than after your first operation," I lied.

"Yeah, uh, those guys in Houston really are the best. Shit, that Pillsbury doughboy, Doctor-the-bakery,"

"DeBakey," I corrected.

"Bakery, Bakey, whatever, he and his team fixed me right up. I'll tell you, Falcon, watch what you eat. All the years I worked on the rigs I ate bacon and eggs for breakfast, bacon and eggs for lunch, and shit on a shingle for dinner. That pig grease just clogged up the old tubes. No wonder the Arabs don't eat that crap. The only healthy thing I ever ate, well except for the sugar in it, was angel food cake."

"Sorry, Tim, I'm a bit naive, what's shit on a shingle?"

"You know, that dried chip beef cooked in a cream sauce and spread on toast. We called it 'shit on a shingle' on the rigs. They did that roto-rooter job last year and replaced a couple of neck arteries. Now they replaced all of my heart arteries and did a change out of these two here."

With a raised right hand Tim made a "Victory" sign with two fingers. Bringing them toward his neck he followed the jugular vein and carotid arteries from the base of his chin to his chest.

"I was feeling great," continued the Duke. "Went fishin' the day after the first operation. Shit, you know how good I was when I came back last year. You were with me when we went out dancing at the Gold Tola and the Safari Club."

As if trying to convince me that he was as healthy as he was after the last operation, Tim raised his hands, holding the book as if holding a dance partner and slowly waltzed his way from the foyer across the white shag carpet into the living room. He dipped the invisible damsel toward the blue satin couch, and with a gentle twirl sat her down, sliding the book face down on the coffee table. He then took a seat on the adjacent cushion and continued his discourse.

"Like I said, I was feeling great after the first surgery. That was up until I started having these strange fainting spells. At first I didn't realize what caused them. I eventually figured it out. Whenever I turned my fuckin' head to the left I'd black out. Hell, once I knew how to do it I'd do it on purpose. Whenever Evie would start talkin' about getting married, I'd just twist my head and pass out. End of discussion."

"I remember one night at Iskar's when you did that. I thought you were just putting us on," I said.

"Shit, no! Evie begged me to get it checked but I didn't think it was a big deal—until that storm we had at the end of last year. It was rainin' harder than a cow pissin' on a flat stone. I was driving on the Deira side and I couldn't see cause of the rain so I rolled down my window to look for traffic. I turned my head and BANG! I'm out. My fuckin' head is layin' outside on the window frame getting pissed on by the gods. That was it. That's when I headed back to Houston."

"Well, you look great."

"Wait a minute; I'm not finished. These bakery guys opened my neck up and found that one of the plastic tubes they put in the first time to replace my old neck artery was twisting."

Tim let out that special laugh of his. "*Haw, haw haw*. Twistin' just like a fuckin' garden hose. The son of a bitch was faulty. When I turned my head to the left it would bend and shut off the blood flow to the brain. Boom! I'm on my ass. I told them witch doctors that for the hundred grand I paid for the first fuckin' operation you'd think they could afford to use good industrial plastic hoses instead of the goddamn garden variety."

"I'm just glad you're feeling better now. What's that book your reading?'

As if being ashamed of being caught in the act of doing something intellectual, Tim stammered. "Uh nothin, just some shit I picked up in the States."

"Let me see. I'm always looking for something good." Still standing, I reached down, picked up the hardback and turned it to look at the cover. "*The Prospect of Immortality* by Robert C. W. Ettinger," I read out loud. "Sounds interesting. What's it about?"

Apparently the subject had some interest for Tim as he jumped right in to explain. "Da ya remember a while back when I showed ya that article about them scientists saying that they froze a hamster and brought him back to life? Wouldn't that be somethin'? Die and then come back to life."

"Yes, I remember. We had a good laugh, talking about all the possibilities of pulling scams and scaring the hell out of friends, and enemies, by dying and then coming back to life."

Tim took the book from my hands and opened the cover to the inside jacket. "Well, this guy," he said and turned the open book so I could see the author's photograph. "He started studying this way back in the sixties, ya see, and he formed a group called the Cryonics Association; I think now it's called The Immortalist Society. Anyway, they believe in this shit." Laying the book back on the table, he adjusted his position until he felt comfortable.

"Well, I had a lot of time the last few months, so I started lookin' into this. Cryonics is freezing people in liquid nitrogen so they can be brought back to life in the future. Not much diffcrent from them Egipshuns. You saw them mummies and daddies in that big museum they have in Cairo. Instead of bringing dead people into the afterlife, cryonics is gonna bring us back to real life."

Still standing, I looked down at the seated Duke. "Never do it, Tim. When you're dead, you're dead; that's it. You can believe in heaven or paradise, and hopefully there will be one; if not, it's just over, just energy dissipating and joining the earth's energy."

"Don't be such a skeptic. Look at all the medical advancements we've made, transplanting organs and everything. Throughout history we have proof of people living one hundred and fifty years or more. Even the bible tells stories of long-life saints. Hell, Falc, diseases in the 1940s and '50s that used to be fatal can now be cured. In thirty or forty years, we'll cure all kind of disease and regenerate organs, like my fucked-up heart here. The only problem I see that's holding us back is the bureaucratic government trying to control everything. The law says you can only be frozen after you've been declared legally dead." Tim sat forward in his chair, leaned toward me, and in a hushed voice whispered, "They got to freeze you before you're dead, like them hamsters, before it will work."

"Now that's a chilling thought," I said, not intending the pun. "No one will do it, and if they did, it would cost a bundle to keep you frozen. Plus, they could go to jail."

"Hell, it's cheap, about thirty-five grand. And that includes your capsule, kinda like that decompression chamber you spent time in. Price includes blood replacement with some type of coolant. Probably the same shit they put in the radiator of our car, *haw, haw*. I figure I'll just do it myself in my garage in California. Just before I croak, Evie puts me in the tube and quick-freezes me into a Dukesicle, haw, haw."

Tim shoved the book toward me. "Here, take it and read it. I've finished. Ya might broaden your outlook on life—or rather death."

Taking on his paternal look, Tim folded his hands on his lap and directed a piercing blue gaze at me. "So what's on your mind, Falcon?"

"I just came over to see how you were doing since you got back."

"Bullshit! I know you and something's bugg'n you."

I couldn't fool Tim. "You're right. School will be over in two weeks and I finished my contract. I've been given a grant to go back to get my doctorate, but I'm not sure if I want to go. I'm not sure if I want to stay in education."

Tim looked at me with those pale blue eyes. "Can't make no fucking money runnin' schools, kin ya? You're in a hole, Falcon. You know the 'Rule of the Hole,' don't you? If you find yourself in a hole, stop diggin'. You got to do what you want to do. Follow your dream, Falconi."

"It's not that easy. I'd like to stay here, but with a wife, three kids and no money in the bank, I can't stay unless I have some way to pay the bills while I chase my dream."

"Hummm. Since these operations, I've slowed down a bit. Iskar tells me that we should take on a new partner, one that I can give all the shit work to. How about it, Falc? Fifteen percent of the company after the first year and another eighteen percent after the second. That will make you an equal partner in two years."

"That sounds generous, but what about a salary? I have to have a regular income."

"Okay. I'll pay a grand a month, you can live on that. What do you say, Falcon? I don't have time to fuck around with people who can't make decisions."

I continued to stall, needing time to think. I had almost finished three years in Dubai and thought I would be leaving. Now I had a chance to stay, earn interest in a business and work with the Duke. There was no doubt in my mind, but this was a big decision, too big to make alone. I really needed to talk to Marie.

"Tim, I know you like fast decision makers but I really need to think about this."

"Fine, ya got until school's out, then the offer's gone." Tim stood up, walked over to me and grabbed my hand. "Do what you gotta do."

During the following week, Frankie and I met several times to refine the letters and talk to our man in Bombay. School was out and my contract completed. The day before I was to give my decision to Tim, I received a call from Frankie.

"Hey, Falcon! Look, something's come up on the letters. It was a great idea, but just not the right time. Veepee, the Bombay artist we were going to use, went to prison for forging Indian ten-rupee notes. Christ, with his talent, why he was wasting it printing paper worth about three cents each is beyond me."

"Can't we find someone else?" I asked.

"We could, but there are other considerations—the family. My brother Rocco feels that it's too sensitive. Uncle Fabio hasn't been gone long enough. Maybe in ten or twenty years it will be okay, but not now."

Frankie's revelation was more frustrating than disappointing. But like the Duke always said, don't sit and feel sorry for yourself, just move on to the next scheme, and I knew what the next scheme was.

Marie and I had already talked it over. She was always supportive, and the change in plans didn't seem to faze her a bit. As long as we were together as a family she was willing to encourage me in whatever I wanted to do. But it was the realization that there would be no forgery fortune that really made up my mind.

When I visited the Duke to inform him of my choice, he calmly shook my hand. "Welcome to the club," he said.

Little did I realize that when I shook hands with the Duke that day, my decision would keep me in Dubai for another thirty years.

Unfortunately, I wasn't quick at math. When I finally calculated housing costs, school tuitions and airfares home, I realized that $1,000 a month wouldn't even come close to covering my expenses.

Marie headed back to the States to put the kids in a tuition-free public school for a few months while I got my feet on the ground. We weren't happy about the arrangements, but again, she stood by me, knowing I had to do this. To save overhead on rent, Tim had me move into one of his guest bedrooms.

The King is Dead—Long Live the King

"Tim, Tim, come here! Listen to this."

"Presley's body was discovered at 2:30 p.m., yesterday, August 16, 1977, Memphis time, by his road manager, Jerry Esposito, in a bathroom in the singer's multimillion-dollar Graceland Mansion. He was rushed to Baptist Memorial, where he was pronounced dead. Elvis was forty-two years old." As the announcer on Dubai 92 FM continued his eulogy on the sad demise of the greatest singer of all time, the Duke and I just stood in stunned silence, staring at the radio.

Finally, Tim interrupted the peaceful calm. "I remember seeing him on Ed Sullivan in 1956. Shit, they wouldn't even show him from the waist down, afraid his swaying, thrusting hips would get the young girls too horny. The bands at the old roadhouse used to play his music all the time. Loved that guy, still do, always will. The good and the great die young, Falc." The Duke turned off the radio and slowly walked to his collection of 78-RPM albums. He began fingering through them and pulled one of his favorites from the rack. Gently, as if the black vinyl disc contained the spirit of the King, he placed it on the turntable, turned the knob and watched as the phonograph arm dropped the needle on to the album.

With the King singing softly in the background, the Duke began to sway around the room in a one-man dance routine. "Come on, Falc, no time to be sad, we should be celebratin' the greatest singer ever, Elvis." Grabbing my hand, he pulled me into the middle of the living room. Two grown men, dancing together in stocking feet on white shag carpet, our tribute to the King.

The Odd Couple

The Duke's big house soon became small as Iskar decided to join us while his place was being redecorated. What a trinity we made: Iskar, god the godfather; me, god the son; and Tim, god the wholly eccentric. Life was a constant party; poker on Wednesdays, dinner parties on Thursday's and barbeques on Friday. Even during the workweek we had lunches at the villa for business associates. I soon found myself becoming Tim and Iskar's social secretary rather than a partner in T & J Maintenance Services.

Much of our entertaining was with a bunch of Australians, ironically led by Scotty La Rouche, of the Musandam drilling fame. They were going to build a gas plant in the new port and industrial area south of Dubai called Jebel Ali. The Duke didn't make a penny on the drilling deal and had no love for Scotty, but he definitely planned to make money on this project. He covertly referred to Scotty and his sons as the La Douche family. Scotty's silent partner in the deal was none other than Majid bin Jabir. With our own partner Iskar being so close to the Ambassador, we would have to screw up royally not to get some work.

Aquarium of Erotica

"Falc, Iskar wants to have a pool party at Bin Jabir's Thursday night. Get Alex and arrange the food, booze and whatever. Iskar and I will take care of the guests and the pussy."

Wow! Ever since seeing Bin Jabir's pool a couple of years ago, I'd dreamed of attending one of the notorious pool parties; now I was organizing one.

"Put that case of Black Label over there, and ice down all of that Dom Pérignon," I ordered. Looking up over the bar at the glass wall, I could see a blue-suited T & J maintenance man directing the metal arm of a pool skimmer, cleaning the water for tonight.

"We all set?" came the question from behind me. I turned to face the Duke.

"Man, do you look sharp." With the white flowing locks and tall slim stature, the man in front of me looked like a Mediterranean playboy: dark blue silk sports jacket, white silk shirt opened at the neck, and white trousers with a small flare at the bottom. "You even shaved."

"It's Thursday. I always shave on Thursdays. How do you like the duds? Armani. Even have a belt from Bijan in Los Angeles," he said pointing to the white leather strap. "Evie and I went in there when we were home for the operation. Hell, you need an appointment to even get in the fuckin' store. NN is a regular so he arranged it up for me."

I could tell it was story time.

"Shit, Falc, I walk up to the front of this place, and before I could even press the entry bell, they had the door open. A guy in a long-tail tux says, 'Welcome, Mr. Johnson, we've been expecting you,' like he knows who I am. Then he hands Evie a glass of champagne and me a sparkling water. Now, how the fuck does he know I don't drink? Can you believe it, they were expecting me, like I was some big movie star or some rich dude like Bin Jabir or NN. I walk around like I was a rich dude and pick up a nice looking shirt, nothing special." Clapping his hands loudly, the Duke burst out in his signature, "*Ha, ha,*" while continuing with, "That motherfucker was $1,200. The cheapest suit was $4,000 and the shoes a grand. I finally picked up this belt. When the personal shopper guy says $500, I almost shit, but I had to buy something."

"This must be going to be one helluva bash for you to get here so early," I said.

"Just thought I could make sure the little details are being taken care of while you head home to get ready." Tim reached into his jacket pocket and withdrew several small gold puzzle rings. "Here, put these in your pocket. They might come in handy for you tonight. I call 'em 'leg spreaders'. Just when she wants to but she doesn't, pull out one of these, slip it on her finger, and she will. *Haw ,haw.*"

"Thanks, Tim," I said as I took the gifts and hurried to the exit. Looking over my shoulder I saw Tim place several rolls of film on the bar, obviously getting ready for the little details.

Borrowing Tim's big Cadillac, I sat back in the big leather seats, turned on the radio and headed home to get ready for a wild night.

Welcome to the Hotel California, such a lovely place.

Living at the Hotel California, that's what I'm doing, I thought as I drove and sang with the Eagles. Living in Dubai and living with the Duke was just like *"livin' it up in the Hotel California,"* a wild ride. *"You can check out any time you like, But you can never leave!"* Suddenly a cold chill ran up my spine.

I arrived back at Tim's house, had a few drinks, and moped around for a couple of hours in a feeling-sorry-for-myself state of mind. Like a broken record, those damn lyrics, *You can check out any time you like, but you can never leave*, kept running through my head. Guilt at having fun without my family, fear of being trapped in the sensualities of Dubai. Whatever it was, I quickly cooled to the idea of attending my first real booze, drug and sex orgy. I finally picked up the phone and called the one person who understood me. Talking to Marie raised my spirits enough to motivate me to get dressed and return to Bin Jabir's to carry out my social duties.

As soon as Abdul opened the gates I could hear the sound of Jimmy Buffett's *Margaritaville* blaring throughout the usually peaceful neighborhood. It was not yet midnight, early according to Dubai's nightlife time zone, and the party was going strong. I expected nothing else.

Stepping into the enclosed pool area was like walking into a Scheherazade story. I was a character in a modern "Arabian Nights" tale, looking at beautiful women in minimal two piece bathing suits frolicking with beautiful men in skimpy, front-bulging Speedo's in the pool, in surrounding lounge chairs, on blankets on the lawn, in the garden, everywhere. Tim and his VIP guests were in the underground grotto bar having their own party while watching the action through the glass wall.

Through the sobs and muffled screams of a distressed lady, a thick Arab accent could be heard yelling, "You're coming with me, you pig." Diverting from my route to join the Duke, I moved toward the ruckus. Standing at the opposite exit to the pool area was a large Arab man wearing a disheveled *dishdashah*. In the flickering light of the tiki torches, the glassy eyes, full black mustache and long wild hair conveyed a sense of pure evil. His headdress, hanging on his shoulders, moved with the motion of his waving arms. The flaying right hand held a small black pistol while his left thrashed at the frightened young woman's head with a black rope, his *hegaal*.

Turning in my tracks, I left the pig-screaming Arab and cries of the damsel in distress behind and made a beeline to the grotto door. "Duke, Duke," I yelled while descending two steps at a time. As I hit the floor, Tim was heading toward me. "Come quick, some guy has a gun!"

"I know. That fuckin' Abdullah Dhabi is at it again. Every time the fucker gets a few drinks, he goes crazy. Looks like he's trying to take another blond home to add to his trophy case. This one must have heard the stories and wants no part of it. For some of these girls, a gold Rolex isn't worth a bloody asshole. Iskar says for us to do something."

"What do you mean us?"

"Just part of the job, Falc. Follow me."

The angry Arab and the blonde eye-candy were still in their stalemate as Tim unabashedly walked up to the gun toting Abdullah Dhabi.

"Hey, Abdullah, why you want to take this bitch home. You already said she was a pig. Now, you know you can't eat pig, much less fuck one. *Ha, ha, ha.*"

Abdullah stopped shaking the gun at the girl and pointed it at Tim. It looked like the Duke's crass humor wasn't going to work this time. Dhabi leisurely turned, moving closer and closer, the tip of the gun's barrel finally resting on Tim's Bijan belt buckle. Abdullah's eyes slowly surveyed Tim: shoes, trousers, shirt. Arriving at Tim's face, a spark of recognition flashed in his blank eyes.

"Tim, Tim, my good American friend." Dropping the gun on the ground, he grabbed the Duke with both hands and planted big wet kisses on both cheeks while hugging closely. "Where have you been, my friend? You never come to visit."

While the two were reminiscing, I snatched the gun from the ground and grabbed the hand of the fair maiden. We fled together out the gate, leaving Tim in the affectionate clutches of the inebriated pig-man.

In the outer garden, I led the shaking beauty to the steps of Bin Jabir's villa where we sat quietly, my arm around her shoulder, fraternally hugging while she de-stressed. Throughout the next hour we talked about her, Dubai and me. Even though the hug transformed from fraternal to romantic, she was vulnerable, and I still hadn't sunk far enough down the ladder to take advantage. Anyway, Linda, as I now knew her, wasn't what I thought all the young stewardesses and secretaries in Dubai were.

I learned a lot about the beautiful young girls who came to Dubai during those days. They were just working kids trying to save a buck to buy that flat in London or go back to school and, like the rest of us, they enjoyed a good party. Not all of them were willing to ingratiate themselves into the grasp of people like Iskar and Abdullah Dhabi for gold jewelry or money. A few did, but more actually fell in love with local men. Those who went as far as marriage, usually against his family's wishes, found that their exciting life with the suave, good looking Arab who swept them off their feet, sometimes became a nightmare. After a couple of children and a few extra pounds, the second wife, a local chosen by the family, arrived on the scene, relegating the foreigner and her children to a limbo existence, no longer belonging to their European or North American family, and not accepted by their Arab family. Yes, I concede there were some that did work, but not many.

Linda and I eventually returned to the party and I released her to the safety of her airline friends.

Joining Tim in the grotto I saw Abdullah Dhabi sleeping soundly on the billiard table, covered in one of the exotic animal skins that had been hanging on the wall.

"Come on. Relax and watch the show," invited Tim.

I pulled the bar stool close to him and ordered a double scotch. "Geeze, Tim, does this type of thing always happen at these parties?"

"Naw, we've had a lot of sick people from too much booze, but ol' asshole Dhabi is the exception. He has some stroke with the royal family and is in charge of dealing with the foreign diplomats in Dubai. Thinks he can do whatever he wants. His wings will get clipped eventually. Everyone usually just has a good time, like that there."

I followed Tim's pointing finger to the window on the pool to see a couple in the final act of removing bathing suit bottoms. As her shapely legs wrapped around her aquarium partner, the young man eagerly grabbed his erect shaft and guided it into her. Their back and forth rhythm resulted in gentle currents through the water, causing rubber lounge rafts at the far end of the pool to bounce their riders up and down on small waves.

If the chaos theory is correct, I wondered how many couples screwing in the ocean it would take to cause a tidal wave.

Most of the men and women in the grotto were enjoying the show. The amorous attitude was spreading. For those still dressed, zippers unzipped, and skirts and dresses rose, as Iskar's fornicating friends took over empty chesterfields and dark corners.

I felt like a voyeur as I walked through the mangled bodies toward the door. Tim followed behind, taking photos of the oblivious copulating couples.

The Duke soon joined me by the buffet table as I picked a shrimp from a large ice carving of a skyscraper that was being built in Dubai. The Trade Center, at thirty-five floors, was to be the tallest building in the Arabian Gulf.

"What do you think of this, Falc? Dubai is really moving forward. Whoever thought we'd ever see a building like this in the middle of the desert? Guys like that property developer, Zacharia Sooria over there, are gonna make big changes here. He's the Arab in the blue swim trunks holding the briefcase and talking to those two ladies."

"I noticed him earlier. Couldn't very well miss him. Not too many people in swimsuits carry a briefcase. What's in it?"

"Dunno," Tim said as he grabbed my arm and led me toward our subject. "Let's go find out.

"Hi ya, Zack. Hope you're having a good time?"

Turning away from the ladies Zacharia looked up and smiled. "Tim Johnson, how are you my friend?"

"Great, Zack. I want you to meet my new partner, Lou Falconi— Zacharia Sooria, a good friend of Mr. Bin Jabir and Iskar."

"And you also, Tim. Delighted, Mr. Falconi. I'm sure we will see much of each other."

"Zack, Lou here wants to know why you're carrying the briefcase at a pool party."

"Oh, it is rather out of place, isn't it? I came directly from a business meeting and didn't go back to the office. Dubai has almost no crime, but I didn't want to leave it the car." Fumbling with the locks, Zack finally snapped one, then the second latch open. Sitting down on the end of the lounge, occupied by a lovely lady, he proceeded to place the case on his knees and then slowly raised the top.

"Oh, Zack!"

I felt the orgasmic exclamation from the young beauty was quite appropriate as I looked at bundles of U.S. $100 dollar bills. "My god, there is one hell of a lot of dollars here."

"Almost one million," replied Zack with a big grin as the lounging lady slithered closer, placing her arm around his shoulder. "It was a very good meeting."

"Here, give me that." Tim took the case, closed the top and pushed the latches shut, while randomly rolling the combination dials. "Let me put this some place safe for you, so you can enjoy the party, and," Tim looked at Zack's eager companion, "the company of this stunning woman."

As Tim and I walked away, Zack made his move, or rather, she made her move.

"I've had enough for one night, Tim. Mind if I head home? The boys are all organized for clean up."

"I know how you're feeling. Inputting all of this activity and information can be draining for a beginner. See you tomorrow. Hell, by the looks of that sun on the horizon, it is tomorrow."

Walking toward the car, the Eagles lyrics again played over and over in my head.

"You can check out any time you like, but you can never leave!"

A new day was dawning, but feelings from the past day had to be dealt with. Was this the life I really wanted? I had a few internal conflicts to work out, and I needed to find out—if it wasn't too late to check out.

Days of Reckoning

The concept of time in Dubai isn't real. It's like time travel: it goes so fast that the past becomes the future and days replay like a stuck phonograph record. Add the screwy one-day Friday business weekend to the formula and time gets completely lost. I was in one of these warps for almost six months before I attempted to face the reality of life. I wasn't cut out for this type of business or this lifestyle. Yes, I still wanted to make the quick bucks, but not this way. I was a family man and didn't function well on my own.

The Duke knew I wasn't happy and sensed that I didn't belong. Believe it or not, he was even protective. Ever since the pool party, he made an effort to keep me away from Iskar's twisted world. Business was good. The gas project was going ahead and the new company president from Australia was thoroughly enthralled with the Duke and his entertaining.

The day after one of his poker parties for the top management, Tim approached me. "Ya know, Falc, this gas thing is gonna be big, and them boys behind the project like you. They're putting together a management team and need an Administration Manager. You'd be great in that type of job, eight to five, paid housing, school fees, airfares. The type of security you need in your life right now and I can't offer. Why don't you talk to them?"

Like always, the Duke was reading me like a book, and like always, I took his advice. I was soon to be in the gas business. Only an employee, but I would get what I wanted, my family back with me. I still had bigger plans.

I guess that I never really checked out of the Hotel; I was still in Dubai. I just changed rooms.

IX
As Time
Goes By

Mr. President's Ass

"Mr. Falconi, there's a Mr. Wanker, Mr. Yankami Wanker who is insisting that you'll take his call. May I put him through? He said it's about an oil deal in the Musandam."

I tried to regain the composure of the senior executive that I was, and told my dignified secretary that I would take the call.

"Katy Christ, elevator music on the telephone, you can tell the king is dead," the Duke said."

"I only know one wanker around here. It must be the Duke I'm talking to," I answered with a spirited welcoming tone."

"Falconi, what's this president shit? You were nothin' but a babysitting school teacher when I got you a job in that gas company ten years ago, now you're trying to pass yourself off as the president of an oil company?"

"A lot has happened in the last decade. If you'd stick around here more and not spend so much time in California, you'd keep up on things." I loved this banter with Tim; it was like the old school visits.

"Don't worry about me. I know everything that goes on in this place. Remember those microphones in the ol' Ten Tola Bar? Have ya checked under your bed lately? *Ha, ha.* I need to see you today. Come by my place about seven."

"Everything okay? You need money or anything?"

"Shit no, Falc, just get your presidential ass over here tonight."

CMFM Shoes

"Take those fuckin' Gucci's off before you come in here," the Duke yelled from the living room.

"I know the drill," I responded as I kicked off my shoes and proceeded to join Tim. "Damn, did you get new carpeting?"

Tim, always the perfect host, stood and walked over to greet me. "Nah, almost twenty years old. See, them Arabs are smart. This no-shoe culture thing can save a lot of money."

I grabbed Tim and gave him a big bear-hug. "It's sure good to see you. You don't know how much I miss the old days when we saw each other all of the time. Life's not as exciting as then."

"Know what you mean. These last ten years during the Ruler's illness have been a bit slow, both business and partying. That's why I haven't been here much." Tim stopped talking while his houseboy set gold-rimmed coffee cups on the small table in front of us and served the black brew. "Business has been up and down for years. See what happened while I was gone this time? Another rash of warehouse fires. Remember what I told you, the 'Warehouse Fire Index'?"

"Yep, an insurance lesson from the old days," I said. Tim's "Warehouse Fire Index" was like the Big Mac Index of economics, where you can get an idea of a country's economy by comparing the price of a Big Mac in that country's currency with the U.S. price. The "Warehouse Fire Index" was a predictor of coming hard economic times, a recession gauge, so to speak. He hit it right on the nose again.

"I remember that we had a lot of big fires in Dubai and in the surrounding Emirates during the last years of the seventies, and in the mid eighties. Looks like the index is up again, the fires are starting. If the merchants are having difficulties, then we must be heading into another economic slump.

"When are things going to get better?" I asked.

Tim looked me with his soothsayer stare. "Rumors are that the Ruler is bad. He's been sick for a few years now. Once he leaves for paradise, things will change here. Remember what I told you about Shaikh Mohammed. Keep your eye on him. Better yet, get close to him and ride his *dishdashah* all the way to the top, cause that's where he's going. He'll be running this place soon."

I drank the last of my coffee, set the cup back on the saucer and confronted Tim. "What's on your mind? You could always tell when something was bothering me. Well, now I can tell you have something you want to talk about."

"You're getting good, Falc. Intuition can't be learned; it's instinctive, but it needs conscious effort to be able to pull it up from the depths of the mind. Maybe I taught you something after all." Tim stood and walked over to the flower vase on the table at the end of the sofa and began plucking dead leaves and petals. "Ticker's not tickin' right. This time it's a transplant. I'm not gonna make this one, Falc. I've had a good ride, and I can deal with heading off into the sunset, but I want to leave something. I don't have kids, so no grandkids will remember me, but I got stories. Stories about this place that will make Belinda Van Helt's book, *Shaikhs and their Oil*, look tame.

"*Ha ha*, did I ever tell you about how she tried to get Iskar to open up and tell his secrets for that book of hers?"

Tale time. Damn, it was a good feeling to have my private storyteller back. I poured another coffee and settled back in my chair.

Tim turned from the flowers, a long stem rose in his hand. "Roses, wine, caviar. She used all the bait she could—including her pussy. Iskar's in London and agrees for this bitch to interview him for this book. Invites him to her hotel room for dinner. When she opened the door she's wearing this short black dress, cut down to her belly-button. You could see the top of the black nylons that ran from her thighs down to her CMFM shoes."

I waved my hand like a child in a classroom eager to be called on. "What are CMFM shoes? A brand like Jimmy Choo's?"

"Catch me, fuck me shoes, now stop interruptin' me. Anyway, Iskar walks in and sees the set up, dinner for two. The table was three foot in diameter, the flowers on the table were seven foot high, and they had nineteen mics in them, *ha, ha*. It was so fucking out of proportion."

Tim claps his hands, then passes them, palm up and down against palm, using the gesture for "having enough." "Iskar smiles and says, 'Thank you, ma'am. Mr. Bin Jabir just called. I gotta go.' He never says a fuckin' word, *ha, ha*. Iskar says it wouldn't have been so bad but she didn't even have the table cloth long enough to hide the wires going back underneath to this flowerpot. See, she was just gonna go have a nice soft candlelight dinner in her room with Iskar, and she was just gonna pull all the corks out during this whole two hour dinner conversation. And then, the bedroom naturally had a flowerpot too, ya see, and-a, she woulda had about a four-hour session there with that fucker. Iskar may have elected to stay all night, or maybe he would have elected to go home, but after four hours with Iskar, she'd be ready to throw him out. Cause she wants to review her tapes and take notes."

Tim stops. "Gotta pee, be right back."

Walking back into the living room while zipping up his trousers, Tim was already talking. "And Iskar says he could smell the mics burning as soon as the door opened. But ya know, he did eventually throw a dick into her."

"So you want to save these stories; I guess you mean in a book. Is that what you're saying?"

"You got it, Falc, and you're gonna write it."

"Tim, I'm not a writer. You need a professional."

"Nope, you can do it. You got a lot of book learning and you told me you even taught English Literature. Shit, Falc, this is easy. We sit and I tell you stories with a tape recorder. Then you write the book, same as this Van Helt bitch. You're the only one I can trust." Piercing blue eyes stared as Tim's right hand slowly raised, and a protruding index finger touched his right temple. "What I got in here could bring down half the VIPs in Dubai. Can't trust it with anybody but you."

"Christ, Duke, it's been years since I've been in a classroom."

"Don't need to be good, or even published. Look at that Rushie guy."

"Rushdie," I corrected.

Tim peered at me with scolding eyes for breaking in. "Look at how much money that sumbitch must have made just by pissin' off people. If people think that someone is gonna spill the beans on them, don't you think they would want to stop it before it was in print? We don't ever need to publish it; we just need to let it leak out to some of the big people who are in it that this book has been written and is sittin' in a London safe deposit box ready to be published. Now, don't you think Colonel Harcross might be sent by his boss to stop this? And, Falc, how do you stop it? You pay."

Confused by what I'd just heard, I looked up from my chair at the still standing Tim. "But I thought you wanted to leave something for the future, to be remembered by, no grandkids, no family, that shit—remember?"

"Yeah, I want to be remembered, by Evie. I want to buy her a big house in California and leave her enough so she can have a good life. I never really loved anyone, but I know now that I do love Evie. Shit, I don't care if after I'm gone she screws some dickhead in the bedroom of the house I give her. *Ha, ha,* can't ya just see this. She's on the bed lookin' up at the ceiling while this guy is throwing one to her. She starts to cum and begins yellin', 'thank you, thank you'. This guy's chest is pumped out like a rooster, thinkin' he just gave her the best shot she ever had, when she finishes up with, 'thank you, Tim, for giving me this nice bedroom in this nice house that I can use to screw some nice guys'. *Ha, ha.* Fuck, when I'm gone, I'm gone. And the stories, hell Lou, after you give the original to the colonel or whoever, you can keep a copy and read them to your kids."

I stood up, laughing so hard that I began to cough. "Tim, just like the old days—another scam to make millions. Blackmail, I love it. Okay, I'll do the writing, but once it's done, you're on your own to pull off the scam."

"Deal, Falc. But this is no scam, not blackmail. We're just selling information, most of which was public but has been hushed up."

Tim and I latched hands, another shake, a binding agreement, another deal, just like the old days.

"And I'll make sure you get a nice check after it's sold. We start this week. I don't have time to waste; leaving for the U.S. in June to wait for my new heart."

He's a Pig-Hearted Man

I watched the small spokes of the tape rotate in the cassette player on the coffee table as the Duke conveyed yet another delicious story.

"How much we got now, Lou? Turn that fuckin' thing off. Gives me the creeps to know my voice is on that tape."

"We've got almost six hours."

"You'll have to work with that. Evie and I are off at the end of the week. We plan to make the pilgrimage on our way back to L.A."

"Wow, you're going to Mecca. You're not even a Muslim"

"Fuck no, we're going to Graceland. Need to pay homage to the King. It's been eleven years since he joined Buddy Holly and the boys." Tim got up, grasped his hands together and lifted them up behind his head. "Ahhh, that feels good. Damn limbs fall asleep, not enough circulation," he said as he stretched

"I'll get this transcribed next week. I'm just too busy now, and I can't trust my secretary to do this. Blood secrecy oath between friends, remember?"

"Fine, but when can you get into the real writing? I want to do something with it by the first of next year."

I sat quietly for a moment. "That's a tall order. Remember, I do have an oil company to run, and I'm traveling a lot now."

"Best time to work, when you're all alone in those lonely hotel rooms. Now, ya are all alone, aren't ya, Lou *ha, ha?*"

"I'll do my best to get something on paper by the end of the year." I collected the recorder and stood. "Good luck, Tim. I'll see you when you get back in a few months. Hope they give you a human heart and not some pig heart. Have you read where they're experimenting with pig hearts for human transplants? Can't you just see all of your Muslim friends here, not wanting to shake hands with you anymore?"

Without making his usual humorous rebuttal, Tim slowly walked over and put his arms around me. I thought I detected a small bit of dew seeping from his eyes.

"Don't worry about me. Just remember, this is for Evie."

The Day the Music Died

October seventh, nineteen ninety, was the first day in my office since returning from a three-week-trip to southern Africa. My site supervisor and I had just smuggled $50,000 into the northern jungle areas of Mozambique to build roads and bridges, and to hire equipment and men for our upcoming seismic program. Having just finished a civil war, there was little infrastructure left, and more AK47's available for sale than picks and shovels. We needed to get things moving or we would lose the concession. I decided to take a rule from the business philosophy of the Duke: "If you need something done that can't be done, throw cash at it." We bought the support of the tribal and government leaders in the area and soon permits were issued, materials became available and workers lined up for jobs. Cash, not the lion, was king of the jungle.

The medical tape that we used to hold the packets of bills in place under our shirts and coats caused a nasty rash. I was multitasking, reading the morning paper while rubbing my itching back against my desk chair when my secretary, Macy, walked in.

"Sorry to interrupt you, but something is going on," she said apologetically. "The radio just switched from rock to classical music. You know what that means."

"Thanks, Macy. I'll call one of our friends in the government to see what it is." In the past, when the radio switched to classical music, it meant a royal family member had died. The Ruler had been ill for almost ten years, but he always seemed to hang on.

"Yes, it's true," said my friend Ebrihim. "The Ruler's Court has just announced that His Highness Shaikh Rashid died this morning."

"Thanks." I slowly placed the receiver in the cradle, thinking about the great loss to Dubai.

My mind shot back to the day the tall lanky man visited the Dubai Oil Company School so many years ago. When he was introduced to me, I noted that he wasn't at all handsome, like I thought a ruling Shaikh should be, but he had a look that projected royalty. His long patrician nose and his tall, thin physique gave him a regal aura. Trying to think about what made him different, I recalled childhood stories of the wise and judicious kings in days of old, mostly biblical kings, such as Solomon. It seemed that these kings had a special intelligence and sensitivity to be benevolent monarchs, the difference between authentic royalty and a man who was a king by title only. Shaikh Rashid was a modern Solomon.

I believe that for the *Bedou*, born into desert hardship, planning for the future was a sixth sense that seemed to be coupled with the ability to trade and barter. It was this rare extra sense that gave Rashid an edge when deciding on major projects for Dubai's future. He knew that the source of the country's wealth, oil, was a commodity that would not last forever and could not be depended upon to support future generations. His goal was to make Dubai self-sufficient once the petroleum resources had dried up. With the assistance of his trusted aides, Rashid thrust his country into the 21st century, making it a modern business and commercial center. I silently gave thanks that Shaikh Mohammed would be around to carry on his father's task. Of all of Rashid's sons, I believed that only Mohammed inherited that rare extra *Bedou* sense

Picking up the phone, I punched in Macy's extension. "Please notify everyone that the office is closing."

Like everyone else in Dubai, I headed home to mourn.

The Islamic tradition of burying the dead before sunset, and the concept that the death was God's will, is mentally and emotionally comforting. It brings immediate closure so that life can go on. In death all men are equals, and even in the case of a beloved royal like Rashid, this mandate of mourning, accepting God's will, and getting on with life, was followed. I watched the television as his son, Mohammed, used his bare hands to dig the hard sandy soil, making a fitting resting place for his father.

"Marie, the phone's ringing, can you get it?" I yelled through the door of my study.

"It's for you. It's Evie and she doesn't sound good."

I walked to the hall and took the phone. "Evie, is everything all right?"

"Tim just passed away. He was next in line on the donor's list, but he just couldn't hold on," she blurted incoherently between sobs. "Lou, he told me that if anything should happen to him I was to call you immediately and tell you that you were on your own, and that you were to continue with the project. He said you'd understand."

My stomach felt like a heavyweight boxer had hit me. I was speechless as the mild nausea passed. "Thanks, Evie, I understand. Do you need anything, money, help? Is there anything I can do?"

"Thanks, but I have my folks here; we'll manage. I'll let you know when the burial will take place."

"Once I know when, I'll fly over."

"No, Lou, Tim asked that no one attend. He said that he came in this world alone and wanted to leave the same way."

Two of the most dominant figures in my life, both gone on the same day. Such an absurdity.

Beyond the grave, Tim Johnson was holding me to my handshake. I walked back to my study and opened the file cabinet drawer. Removing the transcripts and the shoebox of tapes, I thought of my last meeting with the Duke almost two years before. My promised draft was already a year overdue. I knew what I had to do, no matter how long it took.

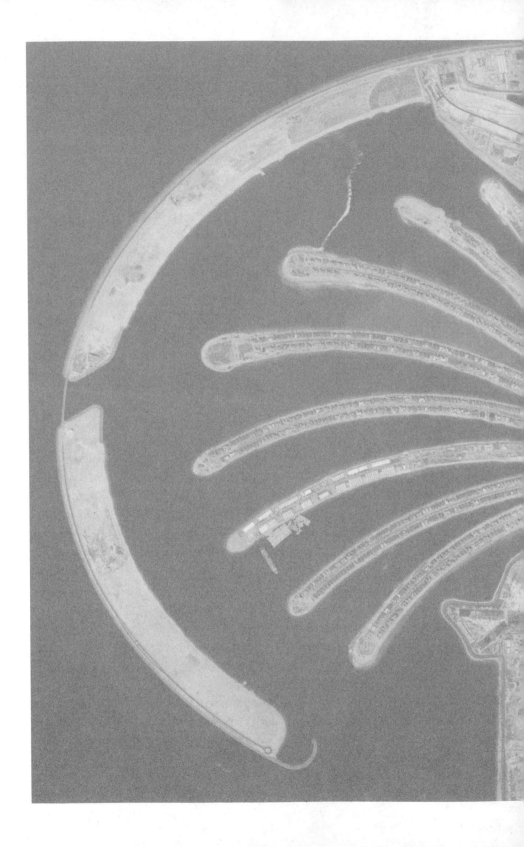

Part Two

Dubai Delight

X

The Last Con

The Art of the Deal

"Silence on the set please. Lights, camera, action," came the internationally recognized phrase from the director.

John Peregrino stood back in the shadows, away from the actors, extras and camera crew, watching the scene in front of him unfold. An intense wind blew across the helicopter deck of the Burj Al Arab Hotel, carrying with it the hushed tones of a conversation between the two gentlemen to the left. John turned his head to try to eavesdrop, but the muffled sounds were indecipherable.

Turning to observe the activity between the leading men, Christopher Lloyd, the Dr. Emmit Brown character in the "Back to the Future" movies, and Matt Damon, John felt a sense of pride, wondering what the Duke would think if he were here to see his life and stories being made into a major motion picture.

"Cut. Let's break." The order from Academy Award-winning director Clint Eastwood released a cacophony of banging chairs, equipment, and rising decibel levels of voices, as almost everyone headed for the single door and the refreshment table inside.

As the two men moved toward the front of the deck, John followed, script in hand, pretending to read. He settled into one of the blue canvas director's chairs, covertly viewing what was probably the more interesting scene of the day.

His Royal Highness Shaikh Mohammed Bin Rashid Al Maktoum, Ruler of Dubai and U.A.E. Vice President and Prime Minister, took the hand of Theodore T. Thompson and guided him to the edge of the heli-deck. Teddy, as the press called him, didn't balk at the un-Western handholding like most foreigners would, but he did seem uncomfortable and stayed well behind the low safety barrier, leaving Mohammed standing a few feet in front.

The awkward positions proved to be to John's advantage as their distance forced the voice level of their discussion to be raised high enough to be easily heard.

"No disrespect, Your Highness, but my project will put Dubai on the map, even more than this movie we're producing. Do you think I agreed to fund a two hundred million dollar motion picture about some eccentric oilman in an obscure desert Disneyland just

A 2006 Aerial view of one of the three man-made islands off the coast of Dubai

because I liked the script? Hell, no. I believe Dubai has the perfect geographical position, the perfect government, and the safest, most progressive atmosphere of any country in the world." Teddy hung back, taking steps forward but always retreating after he delivered his spiel.

Shaikh Mohammed's teeth clenched and his jaw took on the stubborn set that said he wasn't impressed. "Mr. Thompson, I've met numerous large investors, Bill Gates, George Soros, Donald Trump, who all had great ideas, but none better than the ones we ourselves have already carried out and plan to do in the future. Look along the coastline below to my right and left. Three man-made islands in the shape of palm trees, each with hundreds of luxury villas, hotels, amusement facilities and marinas. Dubai is becoming known as the newest wonder of the modern world." The Shaikh lifted his hand

and pointed south, in the direction of Jebel Ali. "Look this way towards that second large palm. Almost thirty-five kilometers further up the coast near the border with Abu Dhabi, we have begun construction on the new gateway of Dubai, a modernistic waterfront development. During the next ten years, two hundred and fifty master-planned communities will be built there at a cost of over twenty billion dollars."

His Highness stopped, but only for a moment to collect his thoughts. "This is only the start. From this will evolve the Arabian Canal, a seventy-five kilometer inland waterway, much like those I've seen in Florida, in your country, but on a much grander scale. Cost: ten billion dollars."

Mohammed lifted both arms forward with upturned palms, then spread them apart and held the pose. "Look across that road to the southwest. Internet City, Media City, Knowledge Village, all thriving economic clusters, and we have many more of these cities evolving. Cost: several billion.

"Desert Disneyland? Yes, we will have an Arabian Theme Park with Universal Studios as only one of the anchor projects in Dubailand. But believe me, your Mr. Walt Disney could never imagine something like our Desert Delight, another five billion dollars. Should I continue on about the one-point-six billion dollar Dubai Festival City, or eleven golf courses, or—"

"You've made your point, your Highness." Teddy shook his head. "We've done our research. What you have done in the years you were Crown Prince is amazing. And since 2006, when you became the Ruler, your developments stagger even the most creative imagination. You have every conceivable type of city within your city: Healthcare City, Industrial City, Biotech City. Hell, I was around one of the main hotel districts in Deira last night, and with all the hookers, I thought I was in Titty City."

"*Haw, haw, haw.*"

The hairs on the nape of John's neck rose. He flipped through the pages of the script until he found what he was looking for, a scene where Lloyd, as the Duke, makes one of his humorous remarks followed by his classic *haw, haw, haw.* John quickly dismissed the déjà vu experience as coincidence and continued to listen to Teddy's sales pitch.

"But is it enough to carry you and your people economically fifty, one hundred, years into the future? What I'm proposing will bring in ten thousand more families than Halliburton brought to Dubai when it moved its corporate headquarters here. Just imagine what type of job market will be created for all of your young college graduates

Shaikh Mohammed turned away from Teddy. Reaching up he adjusted his wind-blown *ghutra* then returned to his original position. "Please explain your proposal once more, Mr. Thompson."

A large smile spread across Theodore Thompson's face and his eyes sparkled—a look I'd seen before on the face of an old friend when he knew he had the sale made.

"United Nations City will be for future generations of Dubai's citizens. The UN has been in existence for sixty years, and it will be for another hundred. The money you're generating now will be nothing compared to what will happen during that time. You think that you have a hot real estate market now; wait until it's announced that the United Nations is moving their Headquarters from New York to Dubai." Again retreating from his forward motion, Teddy waited for the rebuttal.

"But look at the cost, not just for construction: operations, security, and the land area you said was needed is almost one hundred square miles. Most important, how do you know for sure that we can get all of the member nations to agree to move to Dubai?"

John peered over the top of his script as Theodore Thompson moved in for the kill. Overcoming whatever it was that kept him from moving toward Mohammed and the edge of the helideck, he walked forward and faced the Ruler, eye to eye.

"The land? Hell, if you don't want to use any more of that sandy waste out there, we'll build another island. Land and the cost of building and operations can be dealt with. Our figures show that the two hundred billion dollars of investment needed to build a Free Zone and independent UN city, complete with offices, housing, schools, hospital and all other infrastructure, including a private airport, would be recovered in rental and other fees within twelve years. From then on, it's pure profit for Dubai, and this doesn't take into consideration the billions of dollars of peripheral income that will start immediately with construction. You think you're booming now, just wait. Once the UN agrees and gives New York City their ten-year notice, investment will flow like you've never seen." Teddy took a deep breath and continued to stare intently at the Shaikh, almost as if challenging him to reply.

"You didn't answer the most important question. Can you guarantee that you can get them to agree to move to Dubai?"

"Your Highness, that is the one point that I can't guarantee, but I'm prepared to spend one hundred million dollars to try. We've put together a two-year promotion using the best public relations firms in the world. President Bill Clinton, Nelson Mandela, Donald Trump and a number of Hollywood stars, famous musicians and professional athletes, all of who have been to Dubai and love the place, have been retained as consultants, actively campaigning with us. We'll talk to every UN Ambassador and every one of the 191 member states personally, and at the highest levels. Most Americans want to see the UN leave New York as much as New York City does. Even the U.S.A. government wouldn't shed a tear. America is on our side on this one." The master salesman fell silent.

Just as John thought that it was over, Theodore Thompson went in with the coup de grâce.

"If we fail, we still win. A high profile, two-year campaign promoting Dubai in almost all the countries in the world, will guarantee that every man, woman and child on this earth will learn what a magnificent place Dubai is. The new investments will still flow in greater than before, my film will become a blockbuster, and your real estate boom just gets bigger. Remember, you didn't have to invest a penny." Teddy shuffled backwards toward the comfort of the larger deck area and bumped into John Peregrino's chair.

Looking up from the script, for the first time John saw the intense blue eyes that just a moment ago had been staring down one of the most powerful people in the world. John thought he detected a twinkle, a glint of recognition.

"Excuse me, I didn't see you there." Mr. Thompson nodded toward John.

John stood and extended his hand. "Not a problem. I'm John Peregrino, historical and cultural advisor on the movie."

Teddy took the outstretched offering. "And the author of the *Duke of Dubai*. I'm—"

"I know who you are," John said. "Mr. Theodore T. Thompson; everyone does. But I'm afraid that you're mistaken. Lou Falconi wrote the book."

"Sure, Falcon, I understand."

John, stunned into silence, looked down at the firm, yet aged and spotted hand he still held, a stark contrast to Teddy's youthful face. It had been more than fifteen years since anyone had called him that and no one still living in Dubai ever referred to him by that name. "Why'd you call me Falcon?"

Before Teddy Thompson could reply, Shaikh Mohammed cut in on the duo.

Teddy put his arm on John's shoulder and turned to the Shaikh. "Your Highness, this is John Peregrino, uh hum, historical and cultural advisor on the film."

"Yes, Mr. Peregrino and I have crossed paths before. We need to move, Mr. Thompson. Lunch will be waiting."

"Before you leave, may I ask a question, your Highness?'

"Of course, Mr. Peregrino."

"Did you like Lou Falconi's book? You weren't offended by anything in it, were you?"

His Highness looked intently at John. "I didn't personally read it, but it doesn't matter what I think as long as it's good for Dubai." With that he turned and walked away, leaving John's question unanswered.

Teddy started to follow, and then paused. Turning back toward the confused film advisor, he said, "I'll get my people to set up lunch or for us tomorrow. We need to talk."

John watched as the familiar looking body exited through the door. It couldn't be him; he's sixteen years dead. That man wasn't a day over forty-five. Could it?

Surf City

What did we ever do before hi-tech, John thought as he furiously tapped the keyboard. He was determined to read everything ever printed about the man called Theodore Timothy Thompson. Hours passed as he downloaded, printed and searched again. Leaning his head back, John reached up and massaged his aching temples. The strained vision and throbbing skull forced him to throw the switch, blackening the bright screen. After assembling the documents chronologically, he rose from the desk and ambled to the comfort of his favorite reading chair.

John took a drink of his green tea and contemplated what he had read. How could anyone rise from obscurity to one of the wealthiest and most powerful financial people in the world in less than two decades? Little could be found on Theodore Thompson prior to 1990, and the early years of the '90s were sketchy.

"This guy is as reclusive as Howard Hughes," John commented aloud.

John learned from the material found in the public domain that Mr. Thompson was able to nurture a small bankroll from some property he sold into major real estate investments in the Los Angeles area. After 1990, Theodore Thompson took on a low public profile and his wife Evie ran the day-to-day affairs of the business. Yet by the end of the 1990s, he was recognized as one of the shrewdest, yet ethical, dealmakers on the West Coast, and owned a large part of the city.

The low profile disappeared at the start of the new millennium when Teddy's photograph and lifestyle became a hot subject in the tabloids. A favorite of the paparazzi, he seemed to enjoy flaunting famous movie divas and young heiresses in front of the press. It was said that his marvelous sense of humor and story-telling techniques made him a favored guest at parties and clubs. His purchase of MGM Studios, RCA Recording Company, and the World News Group in 2001 made him more than a guest in Hollywood.

Big contributions in the elections of 2000 and 2004 brought him into the inner sanctum of political power. Only a master could manipulate the conservative Christians of middle America into accepting support from a media tycoon, the type of businessman they seemed to despise.

Shit! How the hell could someone just evolve from nothing? The official biography issued by his press seemed believable, but they gave no birth date and mentioned nothing about his age.

Public medical records were almost non-existent, but one investigative reporter was able to get into the emergency room of the hospital when Mr. Thompson collapsed while helping the President campaign during the last election. Dressed in a doctor's gown, the scandal sheet journalist was able to see the shirtless entrepreneur as he was being examined. He reported the surprise of the real doctors when they saw the chest scars, indicating that their patient had previously had some type of heart surgery. The slimy sleuth was never able to uncover what kind of heart surgery or when and where.

John made a note to hire one of those search companies to find out more, then put the research aside and picked up the movie script to review the next day's shoot.

Jumpin' Jinn Flash

John was startled from his sleep by Attaturk's cold, wet nose and long whiskers brushing against his cheek. The Turkish Angora cat was like an alarm clock, and for once John was thankful for the 6:00 a.m. wakeup call. Lifting his limp body from the recliner that unintentionally became his bed last night, he stretched and turned his torso, loosening the stiff back. "Damn, I hate getting old," he said to himself as he headed off to get ready for work.

The five-mile commute from John's home in the Emirates Lakes community to the Burj Al Arab hotel took an excruciating thirty minutes of bumper to bumper driving. Arriving at the entrance to the hotel John handed the keys to the valet and walked toward the glass elevators. As he rode to the helicopter deck level, John gazed at the palm-shaped island below, and the numerous buildings along the trunk of the tree-shaped island, and the villas on the fronds jutting into the sea. A soft computer generated voice told him that he was at his destination.

As advisor, John had full access to all areas of the film set, and took advantage of every opportunity to be present during the shooting of the movie. Observing intently as the special effects crew prepared the small stuntman for his leap of faith, John was interrupted by a hotel messenger.

"Excuse me, Mr. Peregrino. Mr. Thompson would like to inform you that lunch will be served in his suite, 2750, at one p.m."

Before John could offer a thank you and a tip, Director Eastwood ordered quiet and the actors took position.

Looking at the script, John read the scene:

The Duke of Dubai

Screenplay by

Michael Samuels and Nicholas Alexander
in collaboration with John Peregrino

Based on the Book by

Luigi Falconi

SHOOTING SCRIPT

EXT: HELICOPTER DECK ON BURJ AL ARAB HOTEL.
THE DUKE AND LOU FALCONI HAVE CHASED THE JINN TO
THE HELIDECK WHERE THEY HAVE HIM CORNERED AT THE
EDGE OF THE PLATFORM.

INT: Quick pan below. Camera fades to door of deck. Lou
and The Duke burst through door, run toward Jinn, who is now at
edge of deck.

DUKE
(Out of breath from running)
Gotcha now, ya, little fuckin' fairy.

LOU
(Out of breath from running)
We've got to catch him. This is the
only way to vindicate me for all those
years of shit I've been taking since Yemen.

CAMERA ANGLES IN CLOSE
LOU
Now!

(Tim and the Duke leap for the Jinn just as the Jinn jumps from
the helicopter deck)

John thought about the *Qaat*-induced Jinn episode that he, or rather Lou Falconi, experienced all those years before. Was it really that green leaf, or could it have happened the way it was written in the book? He was looking forward to the filming in Oman when that scene would be recreated. Maybe the modern replay would help to settle the doubt that still lingered.

The adding of the present day twist, a deviation from the book, also troubled the author. He had hoped that the film makers would keep close to the original story, but he understood that in order to bring the past into the future and to showcase modern Dubai, the scriptwriters needed to take poetic license to give their audience what they wanted, action and humor, and this was both.

John's heart fluttered and a gasp escaped from his throat as the small stunt-*Jinn* hurled himself from the deck toward the cerulean sea below. Cameras, stationed on several of the floors beneath, caught the action as the actor drifted slowly to the ground under the canopy of his mini-chute. The editors and technical magicians would remove any vision of the chute and the audience would eventually see only a small *Jinn* float mystically to the ground.

With the scene wrapped, John headed for the next production, lunch with Theodore Thompson.

The Burj Al Arab—A Dynamic Dubai Landmark

A Matter of Life after Death

As the room butler answered the door to Theodore Thompson's suite at the Burj Al Arab Hotel, John Peregrino reviewed his mental plan to find out more about his host and any knowledge that he may have about the illusory Duke.

"Please come in and be seated," requested the gentleman's gentleman. "Mr. Thompson will be with you in a moment. May I get you a drink while you're waiting?"

"Just water with no ice, please." John had been in suites of the Burj Al Arab before, but the opulence of each room was unique and exciting. At the entrance of this one, a white marble staircase snaked in a circular pattern to the level above. The inlaid marble and tile floor of the foyer was a stark contrast to the adjacent luxurious sitting area where deep blue cushions on low sofas seemed to contradict the blue, green, gold and black stripes of opposing lounge sets, all set off by gold-covered wood trim.

Theodore Thompson made a Duke-like entrance into the room. "What do you think of this floor, Falc? Makes my white shag look like pussy hair," he said as his shoeless body rhythmically swayed into the room, keeping time to the Elvis tune in the background.

He's a good con artist, John thought. He's playing with my head, acting the Duke imposter, trying to get me to doubt. "What do you think of the entire hotel, Mr. Thompson?"

"Call me Teddy. Everyone does. Shit, when Shaikh Mohammed started to build this one billion dollar hotel at a time when oil revenues were dropping, I thought it was foolish. I was a skeptic; just like people twenty-five years ago thought some of his father's projects were follies. Reading about it then, I referred to it as Shaikh's erection. Men tend to think with the wrong head sometimes, and I felt this was one of those times. I have to give him credit; it's one hell of an impressive building. The elevators are so fast they almost make you cum, rather than go, *haw, haw, haw.*"

John smiled, rose from his seat, and walked to the wall of glass overlooking the blue Arabian Gulf water. As he gazed towards the direction of Iran, he remained silent.

"Hey, John, how many inches does a ruler have?"

"Twelve, of course," John replied.

"Nope. Mohammed's got about 1,000 feet here. *Haw, haw.*"

Teddy Thompson turned to the room butler who stood on duty next to the bar. Raising his right hand, palm downward, Teddy waved his closed fingers rapidly back and forth toward the floor. "Hey, Bubba, go do something somewhere else."

When the obedient servant left the room, Teddy looked at John. "Let's cut the small talk, Falcon. I know who you are, and you know who I am. That pseudonym you used to write the book, Lou Falconi, was pretty good. You've been able to hide it for these last few years, thanks to a publisher who saw the monetary benefit of it. But it's time to come out of the closet, both of us. By the way, it took ya fuckin' long enough to write it, and it isn't even what we agreed on. Where are all of the juicy stories about the scams, the sex and deals I told you? I guess this will just have to do—for now." Teddy walked to the flower vase on the table and plucked dead leaves and petals.

"What's your game, Mr. Thompson? You're no more than forty-five years old. Tim Johnson would be almost seventy-five. You have coal black hair, greased back like a Spanish flamenco dancer, dark complexion like a fake suntan, and you dress like a dork. The Duke wouldn't be caught dead in an expensive Italian suit." John hesitated, realizing the unintended witticism, then continued. "He hated suits; only sport jackets and casual clothes for him. And my god, that pencil-thin moustache, how corny. Who are you emulating, David Niven? Don't you believe in the old platitude, 'let the dead rest in peace'?"

Teddy turned from his plucking task and raised his arms in the air like an evangelist preacher. "Cosmetic surgery, the elixir of life, the fountain of external youth, a lot of it and often." He dropped his arms and plopped on a large chair. Resting his feet across the arm of the overstuffed lounger, he reached up with his right hand and stroked the smooth skin on his cheek. "Only the best doctors. Not only a new heart but also a new face. *Ha, ha.* Remember how I hated to shave?"

Teddy moved toward John, grabbed his hand and rubbed the palm against his face. "Had my face exfoliated—everything except the upper lip. No hair, no shaving. The hair's a different story. When Evie and I went back to the States, we didn't have much money, so we settled for black hair dye, Vitalis, a moustache and a change in wardrobe. The look grew on me so I kept it."

John stayed close to Teddy, examining his young face, his aging hands, his entire exposed anatomy. Deep inside a feeling kept niggling at John. *This guy can talk the talk and walk the walk, but something's just not right.* "I have to admit you do sound like him, but your enunciation and vocabulary is nothing like the Duke."

"Let me tell you, Falcon, the hardest part was trying to stop swearing and learning to talk like a proper English country squire. Hell, I took diction class and everything. Once we sold the houses and property in Santa Barbara, we changed our identities and started to amass our fortune. Evie was actually the brains behind the money. I was low profile, always in the background. She played the property and stock markets while I played poker. We both won big. Eventually we changed our names and developed the business into the TTT Group."

"And what about Evie? Where is she now?" *A trick question,* John thought. John and Evie had occasionally corresponded since Tim's death, and John's accountant sent regular checks with Tim's share of the royalty after the book was published, but neither of them had any great desire to see each other, and had not done so for almost twenty years. *Perhaps too many memories,* he reasoned. Even so, they had the occasional telephone conversation, like the one last evening.

"Back to her roots in the little village she owns near Madras. Actually, it's a city. She's a good lady and still as beautiful as ever. We've done well, and now she spends time giving something back to her people, building hospitals, schools, setting up small businesses for abused women. I believe that you just talked with her."

No bite, but he does know Evie and where she is, John thought. "And she approves of all of your womanizing?"

"Hard for a leopard to change its spots, John. But I'm not as young as we were in the old days. Most of that was for show, trophy-friends, good for my reputation."

"Look," John said. "We're getting nowhere here. So you know Evie, you know some of the history of Dubai, and you act like the Duke, but there is no way to convince me that you are."

"Relax, Falcon, and let's eat."

Teddy walked up to John and guided him to the table. "You'll like lunch, my favorite, chipped beef on toast and angel food cake for dessert."

As the couple entered the lavish dining room, the butler reappeared and guided John to the chair at one end of the table, while Teddy sat at the opposite end. A small intimate table with a low flower arrangement in the middle replaced the usual large table in the Burj suites.

"Don't worry, Lou, there are no microphones in that flower pot. Bon appétit," Teddy said.

"Bon appétit to you, Mr. Thompson."

Both men ate silently, looking only at each other.

Finally John broke the stalemate. "Okay, let's say I believe you are Tim Johnson, alias Theodore T. Thompson, which I don't, but humor me for a moment. How'd you do it? Or better yet, why?"

Laying his napkin on the table, Teddy bent his body forward, his head crossing the imaginary line separating each half of the game table. Once in John's territory, he said. "Remember what I told you about getting in a hole, don't cha? Well, I got in a hole and needed to get out. This heart thing was the perfect way. I'd had enough of Iskar and the deception. One piece of advice I tried to drive into you, Lou, was that there is nothing more important than family and friends, real friends. I was an orphan, but always wanted family. Evie is the love of my life. I thought that we might be able to still start one."

"So you decided to disappear by faking your death."

"Naw, wasn't like that at all. Dubai's a hard habit to break, so I thought I'd withdraw gradually. For almost ten years between surgeries, I spent time living between Dubai and California while getting something going business-wise in California. Remember how much I was away during the '80s? Once I had money coming in, I could pull up and quit the ol' boys club. It was on a trip with Iskar that I realized it was time to tender my resignation."

Teddy's facial features relaxed and he pulled back, tipping his chair on the back legs. Rearranging his body position, much like John remembered the Duke doing just before "story time," he smiled and said, "Let me tell ya about it."

The face was Teddy, but the voice, facial and body features were definitely the Duke, and that was enough to make John really feel like it was story time.

"Remember that blond secretary Iskar had? You know, Falc, the one whose husband managed one of the big banks, ah, what was it, ah?"

"American Trust."

"Yeah, that's the one. They were both Italians, right?"

John looked at Teddy suspiciously before answering. "I know he was, but I'm not sure about her."

"The thing I didn't like about her, number one, uh, the hair on her legs. Evidently, where she came from, they don't believe in shaving hair on their legs."

"Then she must have been Italian too," John said with a smile.

"The fuckin' hair on her legs was about an inch and a half long; looked like a fuckin' gorilla to me," Teddy said.

"But Iskar liked that too." Without thinking, John, was becoming a willing participant in the conversation.

"I think he did. Yeah, he used to say he didn't like curly pussy hair, only the straight smooth silky kind. Anyway, this Itai girl goes to work for Iskar. I'd go over to his house and here's Iskar sittin' there with his *dishdashah* on in the livin' room, and here's ol' floozy, the secretary, with her bathrobe on, ya know. It's about three or four o'clock in the afternoon, and I thought boy, this is a damn good relationship, boss and secretary sitting here, and she's only been a secretary to this fuckin' Iskar, shit, two or three weeks, but a helluva a good relationship here. But I could still see these fuckin' hairy legs stickin' out, see."

Stopping the story, Teddy repositioned his body several times in the chair. Finally finding a comfortable spot, he continued. "So anyway, to make a long story short, what I'm getting at is that he throws a fuck into her and she goes home to, to, uh, her husband, what's his name?"

"Mario." John closed his eyes and imagined the Duke's face across from him. As the sound of the familiar voice again resumed, John was back in old Dubai with the Duke.

"Now, this girl goes home and tells Mario what an intelligent man she's workin' for. 'My god, you wouldn't believe. He's got dignitaries coming out his ass in there. He's got bankers, he's got this, he's got Mr. Bin Jabir calling him ten times a day, he has to go to the Ruler's office every day.' 'Well why don't we take him out for dinner?' the ol' man says. 'My bank would like some of that. That's what we're here for, some of that electric light business, the bonds, whatever work is going on here in Dubai where they need money. I'd like to loan them money from my bank.'"

Teddy crossed his arms in front of him. "See, ah, this banker has done his homework, his office briefed him; he knows who the big players are in Dubai, and he knows Bin Jabir and the Ruler are the ones he needs to meet. So she comes back to Iskar, invites him to dinner, and he says, 'Yes, I think that's a good idea.'

"So we go to dinner, Iskar, this girl and her husband, and myself; we all went to the new Intercontinental Hotel on the Creek. So Iskar spends all of the time selling himself and combing his hair and saying everything that the banker wanted to hear. Whatever the banker says Iskar agrees to. 'I can do that, I can do this, I can fix that up, I can do everything for you, that's no problem.' Iskar flips out that gold lighter to light the banker's wife's cigarettes, stands and pulls out her chair as she gets up to go to the john, and ah, if he had to, he would have wiped her ass if it would impress her husband. Of course Iskar orders champagne and caviar all evening, and insists on paying the very large bill. And the banker was quite impressed with this fuckin' Iskar.

"So the next day Iskar calls up this young banker, Mario, and says, 'Ah, I got just a tiny problem. Mr. Bin Jabir is out of town, and we got this impress or out-press or express account, whatever, anyway, well, right now it's kinda low on funds and could you give me a temporary loan until Mr. Bin Jabir gets back to town?'

"'Oh, oh, Mr. Tandoody, anything for you, anything. How much do you need?'

"Iskar says, 'Oh, let's say two hundred and fifty thousand dollars?'

"'Of course. I'll send my man over with it right now. Cash or check, or . . .' What do you call those things we used in those days, Falc?"

"Cash draft or traveler's check."

"Iskar says, 'Just give me a draft made out to Iskar Tandoody. It's cashable here, isn't it?'

"Banker says, 'Of course. Take it to the National Bank and cash it right this minute, Mr. Tandoody, or I'll cash it right here and bring it to you.'

"'No, I'll send my man over to pick it up.' The check comes, and it's now ten minutes before twelve, just before the National Bank closes. He calls this bank and says, 'I got this big check and I want special clearance on it,' and shazam, he's got all this money in his personal account.

Dubai Creek 2006

"Now a week or two goes by and uh, the secretary, the wife, happens to hint every once in a while, 'Say, my husband asked me to mention that two hundred and fifty thousand dollars, that temporary loan that you needed for His Excellency's account. My husband didn't want to disturb you or nothing, Mr. Tandoody.'

"'Oh yes, you tell him I got it in hand, and as soon as His Excellency, his extra extraordinary, Majid Bin Jabir gets back, we will square everything up,' all in these big fuckin' words.

"Anyway the next day this fuckin' Italian gets a telex from his boss in Bahrain, saying, 'Who gave you the authority to loan an Indian boy who makes five thousand dirhams a month, without any collateral or security, two hundred and fifty thousand dollars? Please be advised that Shams Al Shams will be down tomorrow to replace you.' I read the fuckin' thing so I know it says this. Now, that's the end of the fuckin' banker."

Eyes still closed so as not to see the Duke-pretender's face and break the spell, John said, "I remember that whole thing now. Iskar cultivated that for a few months before pulling his con. His secretary had a birthday and he called me to go buy her a little Suzuki jeep as a present. I went crazy getting it done in one day so he could give it to her that night. Hell, he spends twenty-five hundred on her to get two hundred and fifty from her ol' man. What a sleaze."

"Yeah, I was gonna mention that Suzuki shit," Teddy said as he slapped his thigh and broke out in that "*haw, haw, haw*" laugh.

The smacking noise broke the spell and John's eyes opened to see Theodore Thompson, not Tim Johnson, across from him. Disappointed, he withdrew from the conversation and let Teddy continue alone.

"Two or three weeks later, Iskar and I are on a KLM flight to London. So I say, 'What about our little Italian boy, the banker? What ya gonna do to help him out?' Iskar says, 'Fuck him, fuck him, it's his fuckin' fault he loaned me two hundred and fifty thousand fuckin' dollars. It's not my fuckin' fault. He could have said no. Why do we give a shit about that wop?'"

"I said, 'Goddammit, Iskar, that's not the way to do business. You bring his ol' lady in, ya throw a fuck to her, and then you talk her into throwing a fuck into the ole man and get her to make him believe that you're like God in this town. His whole career is down the drain.'

"Iskar looks at me and says, 'Fuck 'em.'

"Now here's when I realized that I was in a hole and still diggin'. I already knew he was screwing me on my invoices for work I did with Bin Jabir. He'd collect the money from Bin Jabir for a job and then tell me, 'Oh, we can't ask his lordship to pay for that.' Shit, I'd say what the fuck you tell me to do the job for? Why didn't you just tell me we had to do a job for Mr. Bin Jabir, but we're not gonna get any money for it? Then I woulda put rocks where I put silver, sand from the beach in the cement, plastic instead of marble. But Iskar says to me, 'No, no we got to do it first class.'

"Sumbitch is conning me too. Real friends don't screw friends, Falc. I always knew what he was, but now it was crystal clear. I had to get the fuck out. And I did, the only way I could—by dying."

XI

That's A Wrap

Up the Creek

The final day of shooting in Dubai was to take place on the "Creek," the famous estuary that divided the two parts of the city, Deira and Dubai. John stood at the boat dock watching the fleet of *Abra's*, rented by the production company, as they were loaded with cameras and other equipment. The gaily-painted craft, normally used as taxis joining the divided town, ferrying shoppers and businessmen from one side to the other, were movie-crew boats today.

The natural tidal inlet from the sea was called a *Khor*, but for some reason it became known as the Creek. No one can explain how this metamorphous occurred. The Duke had always speculated that it had something to do with the Texas and Oklahoma oil workers who came in the '60s and referred to it as the "crik," later gentrifying it into "Creek." The Dubai Creek was a tidal basin snaking about six miles through the heart of the city. The commercial areas of the city were originally located close to the mouth and midway up the inlet where the water was deep enough to allow the dhows to dock during high tide and unload goods for transshipment overland. Further up the Creek it became shallower and the water spread out into a lake, which had no commercial use, but was a rest and feed stop for flocks of migratory birds as they traveled north or south.

With a smile, John recalled the polluted state of the inlet when he first arrived in the city. Crews of the dhows would dump their trash and garbage into the water as well as using it for other purposes. On the back of each dhow is a half-circle shaped appendage called a "cat box." This was the ship's head. The plumbing was simple: a hole cut in the floor just like an outhouse. This was fine in the high seas, but when docked in the Creek it meant raw sewage in the water. In addition, uneducated laborers could be seen squatting down with their baggy pants spread out to cover their dignity, using the Creek as a big toilet, paying no heed to the signs posted that stated in big black English, Arabic and Urdu letters **NO URINATION OR DEFAECATION**. Fortunately, the daily tides continually brought in fresh water and carried away the refuse, keeping the Creek decently clean. The Creek that John looked at now was clean enough to swim in, thanks to the strict enforcement of Dubai's environmental laws. John could never understand why the signs in the old days were in

English as the people the message targeted couldn't even read their own languages—tribal versions of Hindi, Farsi or Urdu, yet alone English.

1974 warning sign

Scanning the rows of high-rise buildings along both shores, John's mind tried to recall the skyline of the early '70s, with the single bridge built in 1962, the government buildings and the tall wind-towers attached to the remaining houses of the Shaikhs and merchants, but it wasn't possible to comprehend the changes that had taken place. He would have to leave it to the ingenuity of the filmmakers, who would digitally transpose this modern link of skyscrapers back into the Creek of the Duke's day. There was no doubt in John's mind that this waterway was Dubai's umbilical, the lifeline that made the city what it is today.

Once the filming in Dubai was complete the crew would move to Oman and then back to Los Angeles for the final sequences.

John was aware that Theodore Thompson had left Dubai on his Lear jet just after their storybook luncheon, first to India to pick up Evie, and then back to Los Angeles via Hong Kong. Still uncertain if the pretender was really Tim Johnson or a charlatan with evil intentions, John decided that a face-to-face with Evie was the only way to solve the matter. He was now determined to see her when he was in Los Angeles for the final shooting

L.A., City of Angels

Sitting on the wharf in Santa Barbara, John and the other two scriptwriters discussed the filming.

"I'd really like Clint to re-shoot the roadhouse scene. Something about the piss drinking wasn't quite how I imagined it," Michael Samuels said.

"I agree," said Nick Alexander, "but unless we have a specific idea that will convince Clint, he won't be willing to spend the extra money or take the time for a re-shoot."

"I think I can help on that one," John Peregrino said, thinking of Evie. "I have a friend who knows a man who was actually there. I'll see if I can get her to look at the rough cut."

With that settled, the three scribes broke company, each going his own way. John's route was back to Los Angeles for a reunion with an old friend.

The midday traffic allowed for a leisurely ride, time for John to collect his thoughts and strategize how to approach Evie about Theodore Thompson.

A long whistle emanated from John's puckered lips as he arrived at the exclusive gated neighborhood.

"Wow, looks like Evie won the lottery," John said out loud. After giving his name to security, the large metal gates slowly parted. Following the directions given by the guard, the compact rental car found its way through the elaborate estate. After another security check, John was allowed to proceed up the oak tree-lined brick driveway to the front entrance.

Except for the graying hair and a few lines around her eyes, the lovely lady who opened the door was unmistakable.

"Evie, Evie," was all that John could say as they embraced.

"It's been a long time, John. Please come into the den. I've arranged for some refreshments."

John took a seat on the large overstuffed sofa as Evie faced him in a stylishly upholstered wing chair.

"It looks as if you've done well since Tim's been gone" John hoped she would hear it as a question and not a statement.

"Yes, Tim invested well," she said, not elaborating further.

After the chitchat, John went right to the matter at hand, Theodore Thompson.

Before responding to John's questions, Evie digressed and told him of her philanthropic projects in India and how much money she still needed to carry on her work. Listening to Evie, John realized there was at least one angel in this City of Angels.

Finishing her narrative, Evie finally revealed to John what he'd come to hear. During the next four hours John listened to a tale of love, deception, enormous financial gains and a plan for one more sting. Four cups of coffee later John entered into one of the most bizarre pacts he had ever made.

XII

I Did It My Way

Walking the Red Carpet

It was a beautiful star-studded evening, not just in the Dubai desert sky but also on the grounds of the Madinat Jumairah. The premier of the *Duke of Dubai* was a triple crown for the now renowned Emirate. The first premiere of a major Hollywood motion picture, the first about Dubai, and location of one of the biggest entertainment news stories of all time.

TTT Studio (formerly MGM), World News Group, and Arabian Authors Publishing, the publishers of the novel from which the movie was adapted, had undertaken a coordinated media blitz that rivaled a U.S.A. presidential campaign. Theodore Thompson wasn't afraid to spend money. Television and radio spots, promotion by talk shows in the U.S.A. and Europe, newspaper articles and advertising, every conceivable medium, was used by the high profile public relations firms contracted by Thompson. The message was that after three years of anonymity, the "Deep Throat" of Dubai would be exposed at the worldwide premier of the film. And, that a second, more startling revelation about the fictional lead character, Tim Johnson, would be made.

Even before the movie was finished, John Peregrino knew it was only a matter of time before he was revealed as the author of *The Duke*. That revelation was not as important to him as his loyalty to Tim's memory—his only reason for reluctantly agreeing to Evie's plan.

He enjoyed watching the talk shows and the debate on "Hard Talk" about who really authored the novel. Late Show host David Letterman's number one on his list of the ten most likely people to have written the book was none other than Bill Clinton, citing his previous White House experience with Monica and his frequent visits to Dubai as the inspiration. Most of the flurry was centered on speculation of authorship. The fictional aspect of the book's character seemed secondary at this point.

The film was screened in the Madinat cinema, but the after-viewing cocktails and media opportunity were taking place in the Amphitheater. The simulated Creek with the almost full-size dhow made a fitting backdrop. Throngs of press, photographers and interviewers were already mixing and talking with the movie's stars when John and Theodore Thompson entered.

Everyone's attention immediately shifted to the duo. Like rugby players trying to break through a scrum, the two gentlemen forced their way through the crowd to the stage. Walking up the two steps of the platform, John was greeted by his publisher, Alistair Hastings, while Teddy took a seat with the VIP's behind the microphone stand.

"Ladies, gentlemen, please, may I have your attention," announced the publisher. "As you know, there has been a lot of media hype about the book this movie is based upon and some of its characters. We, the publishers, have never hidden the fact that the author, Lou Falconi, was a pseudonym. This evening, I would like to introduce the man behind that name, Mr. John Peregrino."

As John nervously took his position, the mumble of hundreds of voices tested the acoustics of the outdoor theater. Well-designed, John thought as the amplified noise prevented him from speaking. Finding a break in the conversation level, he cut in. "I would like to thank you, all of you, for the interest you found in the story of old Dubai and the interest created for the new Dubai. Like all authors, I may have taken some literary liberty in creating my characters. The facts in this story about the history and development of the city-state of Dubai and its illustrious royal family can be found through researching other literature on the United Arab Emirates. With no intention to mislead the reader, I admit that the stories about life in the 1970s oil boom days of Dubai and the adventures of the "The Duke" as conveyed by me in the book are, like Lou Falconi, not totally factual. But they could have been true. Most of the exploits involving the Duke really happened, maybe not quite like I've written them, but in some form or another with a bit of literary freedom. The events don't follow the proper chronology of occurrence but take place as they fit in my mind and in my story, but the photographs used are all originals, and as we know, photos don't lie.

"Although the characters were conceived in my psyche and birthed through *The Duke*, there were many eccentric personalities that lived in Dubai during the early 1970s. Some people may imagine that they recognize themselves or a friend in the book. If I have offended anyone who thinks he was a model for any of these characters, again my apologies, but my book-people are not real. Remember—this is fiction.

"The Royal family and the nationals of Dubai are a benevolent and dedicated people who have done marvelous things for their country. In thirty-five years they have propelled Dubai into a model city for the new millennium. If I have offended any of these great tribesmen, please forgive me and accept this in the spirit of fun, as is the intention of this book."

John fidgeted, playing with his notes and then asked for attention again. "Now about the characters in *The Duke*. Remember that great poem by Robert Frost that begins, 'Two roads diverged in the woods'? Fate plays strange games with each of us. We set out on our journey through life following one road, only to have it diverge many times during our travels. As creatures with a free will, we make the decisions on which way to turn, but circumstance or divine intervention, or perhaps just mischievous meddling from a *Jinn*, influence those decisions. During the thirty-some years since I first made my acquaintance with the many colorful Dubai residents who evolved into the composite characters of Iskar, Frankie, Josh and others, I have tried to imagine the passages that these fictional friends might have gone through. Observing how time has transformed myself, makes me realize that there are no constants in life, only diverging roads. Let me tell you what I envision as the road these story-bound friends may have taken."

John looked up at the audience and adjusted his reading glasses. "After the Duke's death in America was reported in Dubai in 1990, Iskar continued to run T&J Contracting Company. He also kept his prestigious position as assistant to Mr. Bin Jabir for a few more years until the new generation of royalty no longer sought advice from their father's counselors, such as Iskar's boss Bin Jabir, but surrounded themselves with their own trusted advisors. Iskar saw the writing on the wall and decided to prepare for his retirement. He was caught trying to pull off another bank scam, but this time he was held accountable and placed under house arrest for almost five years.

"Poor Iskar had more than financial problems. He was also going through his own internal identity crisis. During his house incarceration, he apparently worked out his conflicts. When he was finally allowed to leave the country, he immediately went to Sweden.

Two years later Iskar Tandoody returned as Sister Tandoody. Not only did he undergo a sex operation, he also found Jesus. After leaving Sweden he/she became a member of the order of the Sisters of Charity. She returned to her native India, where she now works with prostitutes in the slums of Calcutta. Mother Theresa once said Sister Iskarina was a saint on earth.

"As a young man I really admired Iskar's charm and sophistication with the ladies. It seemed like he knew exactly what they wanted and how they wanted to be treated by a man. Now I understand why. He was a real gentleman—and a real lady."

As the crowd roared with laughter, John continued his epilogue. "And what about Iskar's boss Bin Jabir? You won't find his significant contributions to the development of Dubai mentioned in their history books, but I imagine that, if he were real, he would be living a very comfortable life, and as his character epitomized the best in Arabian tradition, he would always have an open door and cup of tea for old friends, even his old enemies.

"In my crystal ball I see that the scuba diver-defecator, Josh Sampson, moved back to his beloved Montana where he is known as Brigadier General Josh Sampson, leader of the CanAm Mountain Militia. They are a group of dedicated Americans and Canadians whose objective is to annex the Canadian Provinces of British Columbia and Alberta to the United States. Josh's Canadian counterparts work from inside the Provinces to stir discontent with the rest of Canada, especially French-speaking Quebec. From the U.S.A. side of the border, Josh and his group convey misinformation through the Internet, magazines, television and other media in an effort to Americanize Canadian youth with U.S. music, fashion and other aspects of our culture. His wife Nellie says that at least it's a job and keeps him out of her hair all day."

Again, raucous laughter broke out. John raised his hand to the audience and gestured for silence. "Remember Matt Lenz the paint salesman? He retired from sales and took up oil painting as a hobby. You may have read in "Paint and Pool" magazine that he coupled his newly discovered talent with his old knowledge of paint coatings and is now the supremo swimming pool artist in California. Matt has decorated the floors of the pools of some of the most famous people in the U.S.A. and other countries. The Virgin Mary in the bottom of

Madonna's pool and the giant pizza in Pavarotti's are just a few of his works. His masterpiece is the one he did for the wife of a well-known politician at her new home in New York. It's the face of an infamous young female government intern with her mouth puckered as if she were blowing a bubble. The drain for the pool is right in the middle of the pucker. No telling what this wronged wife is planning to have sucked down that pool drain.

"And NN, the owner of the *Puss and Hoots,* is broke and living in Texas, rent free as a guest of the state. He should be released sometime before the end of the decade."

"Wait, there's more. With the Russians, Asians and every other immigrant group trying to copy the Italian mafia business plan, Frankie and Rocky decided to put the family business to sleep and try a new direction. They moved to Las Vegas, where they are well-respected, legitimate businessmen. You may have read about their new five hundred million-dollar casino, 'Le Casino Du Climax.' Over the last few years they observed that Vegas was trying to take on an image as a family entertainment destination, much like Disneyland. They decided to take the contrarian view and cater to the mature adult crowd. Rocky said that they wanted to take Vegas back to what it was originally meant to be, 'Sin City.' Their casino has the world's largest collection of original erotic art hanging on the walls of the lobby, the guestrooms, and the hotel's six restaurants. All of the stage shows are live sex performances with an international theme. Carnal professionals have been brought in from Bangkok, Manila, Hong Kong, Moscow, Bombay and many other countries to put on tasteful erotic-art shows. The 'Kama Sutra Son et Lumière'—Kama Sutra Sound and Light Show—is sold out months in advance, as is the Thai show, 'Anna, and the King and all his Friends.' Rocky and Frankie have brought good taste to pornography.

"These two entrepreneurs have thought of every detail of the interior decoration, down to the gold plated penis shaped faucets on the bathroom sinks and tubs. Even the symbols on the slot machines have been changed. Three virgins and you hit the jackpot. They have put the adult back in Las Vegas.

"As for me and my wife Marie, yes, the same name as Lou's wife, we share our time between Dubai and Northern California where we play the role of grandparents and try to grow enough grapes on our Falcon vineyards to make a batch of Falconi wine. Like the Duke said, Dubai's a hard place to leave."

John stopped, turned and looked at Theodore Thompson, leaned in close to him and whispered into his ear. Teddy nodded.

John again addressed the crowd in a soft tone. "As I explained, the fictional characters in *The Duke* are assembled, piece by piece, from characters that have come and gone in Dubai over the years. Except for one. The main character on which *The Duke* was based does exist. Occasionally I pull out my old notes and tapes—yes, I have recorded stories narrated by the Duke himself—and wonder if I should write the book that the Duke really wanted published, the more exotic and erotic experiences of the rich, the famous and the royal folks in Dubai, but then I have second thoughts and believe that it's best left for the ages."

Again, John turned and looked back at Teddy. Their eye-to-eye contact confirmed "it's a go," and John faced his audience. "Yes, the Duke does exist. Ladies and gentlemen, I would like to introduce the real Duke of Dubai, Theo—"

Before John could finish, all hell broke loose. Lights became brighter and questions flew from every angle. Cameramen, news personnel and spectators fought for position and broke through the security barrier, storming the podium stand.

Alistair stepped forward to take control. "Ladies and gentlemen, please, please, can we have your attention." Seeing that the pleas were not working, he called over one of the security guards, who pulled a radio communicator from his belt and spoke into it. A minute later an electric powered *Abra,* part of the Madinat fleet, pulled up and berthed behind the stand.

"Come on, let's go," Alistair ordered as he guided Teddy and John to the boat. Making good their escape, they left the crowd for the secure and quiet trip down the artificial waterway to Teddy's suite at the Umm Qasr Hotel.

After disembarking onto the hotel dock, John turned to Teddy. "Well, we didn't quite do what Evie wanted, but I guess we still pulled off her little con. Even though I wasn't able to make the full disclosure in my announcement, the stir caused by what was said will still make millions for her charity work. I guess I'll have to issue a press release to finish what we started here."

Moving toward Teddy, John grabbed his shoulders and looked directly into his eyes . "There is still something that I need to know from you before I write my revelation for the press. Do you really want to go through with this? We were ready to announce to the world that you are Tim Johnson, alias Theodore T. Thompson, but I need to know for certain, do you really want to live the life of a dead man? Or do you want to be you, the young, smart, loving and educated man who deserves his own life? No matter what we say, the donations and profits will flow in for Evie. I just need to know what you want; which road you want to take. Once that press release is issued it will be tough going back."

"Look at me. I walk like him, I talk like him, I have the same mannerisms. I am him. I loved Tim Johnson more than anyone. He taught me everything I know, and the stories, not just those you know, but many others, enough to fill several books." Teddy turned from John and walked a few paces to the edge of the water. "Evie is like a mother. She could never have children, but she treated me as her own. I want to do whatever she asks, and playing this role is the only thing she has ever asked of me."

John confronted Teddy again. "I can't believe that Evie would ever put you in a position to make such a promise. There must be more to this than you and she told me. I just want you to be sure of who you want to be and why you're doing this."

Teddy took a step back. His blue eyes never wavered, but his voice trembled. "You made a promise to Evie. Just write what you agreed." Like a dejected child Teddy turned and ran.

Jinn and Gin Revisited

Sitting in his bedroom with an old friend, Mr. Gordon, a fine gentleman and gin, John thought about his confrontation with Teddy. With Marie on the West Coast waiting for the birth of a new grandchild, he turned to the clear liquid as his companion and confessor. John had never been a big drinker, but tonight he needed to conjure up an old spirit—the spirit of a Tim Johnson who didn't die in 1990; the spirit of a Tim Johnson who did have the family he always wanted. In the old days a little grass would have done the trick. With none available he would have to rely on the gin to summons the *Jinn*.

Evie's reasoning for going ahead with the ruse was noble. The money generated would all go to her charity foundation in India, hundreds of millions of dollars to help thousands of battered women, abandoned children, disabled men. But it just didn't seem like a plan Evie would devise on her own.

John recalled how Teddy explained that owning a film studio had its perks, like the gloved prosthetics that gave his hand that aged look and feel that initially confused John and led him to believe that he was really his friend the Duke. Thirty-five years of age to forty-five was easy—no surgery, just the moustache and greasy hair. But even with the miracle of plastic surgery, convincing people that a seventy-five year old could look forty-five was going to take an Academy Award performance by Teddy, especially as the years roll on.

He felt uneasy. The essence of the Duke seemed to permeate the scheme. But how? He was dead. And, even more puzzling—why?

Filling the tumbler with the clear liquid, John prepared for the alcohol-induced séance by replaying Evie's story just as she had told it.

With closed eyes, John retrieved the memory of that meeting in California with the genteel matriarch sitting across from him in the large wing-chair and the story she told.

"What you were told was correct. In the 1980s we did start to plan our "escape," as Tim laughingly called it, going back and forth between Dubai and Los Angeles. But the medical reason was more of a cover. Tim did have the early surgeries, and later a transplant, but we discovered that he had a better reason to spend time in

America. Do you recall that Tim had a wife whom he divorced in 1952?"

John nodded.

"Of course you did; it was in the book. Tim left California as soon as the divorce was settled. Without family, no one, including his few friends, knew where he had gone. It seems that Dee Dee, his ex, was pregnant. Abortions in those days were not an option, even for a woman of Dee Dee's character. Unable to track down Tim for help, she had the child. Although he carried her last name, she must have had some feelings for Tim as she named her son Timothy Blanchard, her maiden surname.

"It couldn't have been a very nice life for the boy. The detectives that we hired to track her history reported that mother and son had lived in a rundown shanty outside of Bakersfield until Dee Dee died of an overdose in 1968.

"Fighting in Vietnam was at its peak, so it wasn't hard for a lanky sixteen-year old to lie his way into the Marines. Apparently it was just what he needed."

Again, the gin helped John visualize Evie pausing to sip her Earl Grey, then setting down the cup and continuing.

"Tim always thought the boy was probably like him, craving a family. He believed he found the camaraderie of the Marine Corps to be that substitute family. Whatever it was, it was good for young Tim. He finished his high school education and started taking junior college courses until he shipped out on his first Vietnam tour.

"His records show that he quickly rose in rank. During his second and final tour in Vietnam he had been nominated to Officer Candidate School. His tour was cut to six months to allow him to catch the summer term in college, and that's where he was headed. Very impressive for a twenty-year-old soldier. The officer in charge wrote in his report that it was Tim's last day at the inland base before flying to Saigon and then on to Los Angeles. Sandbags were piled along walkways between buildings, but only about five feet high. It was explained to us that this was more for protection from mortars and bomb shrapnel. Most of the men wore their helmets when walking between buildings, but knowing he was going home, young Tim had other things on his mind and carelessly left his helmet on his bunk. As he walked to the shower he was hit in the back of the head by a sniper's bullet. The doctor who reviewed that part of the report for us said that the injuries were similar to those of President John F. Kennedy's, except that young Tim's was fatal instantly. It was March 28, 1972."

John, in a semi gin stupor, recalled how Evie pulled the lace hankie from the sleeve of her dress and wiped her eyes.

"Just before young Tim had shipped out that second time in October of '71 . . ." She again wiped an eye and then continued, "he married a lovely young lady named Anna Rollings, who he had met the year before in junior college. She, like Tim, had no family, and like Tim, was trying to get an education to better her life. It was to be a homecoming surprise for Tim, but Anna never got a chance to spring the surprise, to tell him that he was going to be a father, something he wanted so badly.

Anna was a strong girl. She took the money from the military death benefits and went back to finish school as a medical laboratory technician. She named her son after his father, Timothy Blanchard II. Anna and Timmy were the epitome of a happy single-parent home.

"Anna was testing vials of blood in a centrifuge. She removed her protective goggles to more easily read what she was writing when something happened to the spinning machine and several vials shattered, throwing blood-covered glass shards around the room. One landed in Anna's eye. The damage from the glass wasn't bad, but she developed what we now know as Human Immunodeficiency Virus (HIV). In 1980, they had no real name for what her symptoms developed into, but now it's called Acquired Immune Deficiency Syndrome (AIDS).

"As I said, she was a smart girl who loved that little boy more than anything else. Her husband's letters from Vietnam contained stories about his father that were told to him by his mother. He was a good storyteller, Anna told us. Using what she knew about her husband's father though these stories, and the services of a private detective, Anna was able to track us down. Her son Timothy was ten years old when this emancipated young woman knocked on our door in 1982. It didn't take long to tell us her story. The photos of her husband, Tim Blanchard, were spitting images of Tim Johnson, the Duke. And the boy, well he was definitely Tim's, grandson. Of course, we took them both in. Your friend the Duke finally had his family.

"Anna died in 1990, the same year as Shaikh Rashid and the year your friend Tim Johnson, the Duke, decided to die, at least in Dubai. His heart was giving him problems again and he wanted to spend as much time as possible with his grandson—no more traveling to Dubai, no more covert life. He just dropped out. We had already changed our names to Theodore Timothy and Evie Thompson. Under the pretext of Tim's, or rather Theodore's illness, I took over the business."

John recalled Evie's pride, when she told of Timothy Blanchard II's MBA from Stanford at age twenty-four and law degree from Yale at twenty-six, just as if he were her grandson also. Evie said that it was during his grandson's college days that the Duke became even more obsessed with making sure no one else could ever track down his past or find out that Timothy Blanchard II was his grandson.

Running through the facts of his mental soap opera, John recalled that Evie said Timothy Blanchard II joined the TTT Group in 1998 as her assistant. His identity as the grandson of the co-founder, Theodore Thompson, was never revealed to anyone.

Smiling to himself, John thought about what a great television series this would make. It was a script right out of la-la land. John reached over, grabbed Mr. Gordon by the neck, shook him a few times, and took one last drink, straight from the bottle. Closing his eyes, he transported himself back to that overstuffed sofa and played the next episode. Just like the first time, he was amazed at how easy Evie made it sound.

"In California, everyone has face-lifts, breast implants or some type of cosmetic work. Since Theodore T. Thompson had not been seen in public for over ten years, no one even flinched when, at the beginning of the millennium, a younger-looking, fully-recuperated Theodore T. Thompson resumed his position as a high profile chairman and CEO of TTT Group. Any connection with my assistant Timothy Blanchard II quitting his job and a few months later Theodore Thompson rejoining the company after an absence of ten years went unnoticed. Tim's grandson had become Tim, or rather Theodore T. Thompson

John abruptly returned to reality from his gin-induced memories. "Where are you, my old friend?" The spirits were still working, but it was turning out to be a one-way conversation. "Duke, my friend, what do I do? Do I keep my pledge to Evie and continue to pass off your grandson as you, or do I give young Timothy Blanchard II the freedom to live his life as himself and not you? I know you're involved in this somehow. Tell me what to do." This plea for intercession was the last John made before he lay back on the bed and passed out.

The Ghost of Dubai Past

The gin infusion made for a fitful night's sleep. John tossed, turned, and tossed some more. Whatever spiritual visitors he had must have influenced him, as he seemed determined when he woke. Looking at his watch, John picked up the phone. The twelve-hour time difference for once worked to his advantage as he dialed his home in California.

After the usual caring discourse with Marie, John came to the real point of his call. "Marie, I need you to pull out my Tim Johnson tapes from the safe. I think it's tape IV. About midway in the tape, Tim and I have a conversation about life after death. Can you call me back when you find it? Love you, too."

The hot shower purged the gin cobwebs from his aching head. John's room service breakfast sat on the tray untouched as he reclined on the bed, nursing his self-induced malady. The ringing phone jolted him back to consciousness, and he lunged for the receiver.

"Yes, that's the one. Play it over the phone for me." Listening intently, a smile broke over John's face. "That's enough, Marie. I heard what I needed. Got to go. Love you. Bye."

For the second time that morning John dialed a California number. "Evie, hi. This is John. Oh you saw it on television? Quite a scene, wasn't it? I hope it has the effect you wanted. I plan to issue a press release finishing up my statement. But before I do, I need to clear up some things that bother me about all of this. Look, what year did Tim die? Really die?"

Evie's reply, "2003," was just what John needed to hear.

"The book was published that year. Did he read it before he died?" John grinned at Evie's confirmation that he had. After a few more minutes of conversation, John informed Evie that he needed to see her again

"Emirates Airlines has a direct flight to Los Angeles that leaves at midnight. With the twelve hour time difference, if I leave tonight, I should arrive at your place about 8:00 a.m. tomorrow."

The Preservation of Being

John passed through security and drove up the familiar brick drive to the Johnson mansion. At the front entrance he slowed, stopped and looked at the front door. Deviating from his original plan, he guided his vehicle toward the elaborate eight-car garage and servant's quarters at the rear of the main house. He parked in front of the farthest door, got out of the car, and strolled the length of the building, examining the windows of the apartments along the second floor. As he reached the end he looked around the corner. In a grove of trees at the back of the property stood what appeared to be a windowless stucco chapel.

Curious, he walked up the cobblestone path to the entrance. He pushed the brass handle of the large wooden door and the heavy object moved inward with unexpected ease. As his eyes adjusted from the bright California sun to near darkness, he focused on the myriad of small colored lights on a large panel about halfway up the back wall. A highly polished stainless steel capsule sat on a pedestal about three feet off the ground. A pale green light radiated from the top. Wires, hoses and large cables connected to the pod crisscrossed to electrical connections, pumps and other mechanical devices on the floor and sockets on the lower wall. Stepping over the tangled mess, John walked up to the container. At the top end of the shimmering stainless steel tube was a large transparent window. Slowly, slowly, he inched forward to look through the glass.

Even though he expected the vision before him, it was nonetheless a shock. "Oh my God, you really did it," he said aloud. Prone on a stainless steel bed was the frigid, lifeless body, older and thinner, but definitely his old friend, the Duke.

"You silly son-of-a-bitch, you really did it. Why?"

"You know why!"

Startled, John at first thought it was the frozen Tim answering him, then he realized the familiar voice came from behind. Turning around, he saw young Timothy Blanchard II sitting in a large leather chair.

"I've been expecting you. Evie called just after you talked with her. We knew you had figured out our secret. When the concierge told me you had booked a flight here I quickly followed. The joys of private aviation—I didn't need to wait a whole day for a scheduled flight."

Timothy joined John next to his grandfather's iced coffin. "Sorry about the cable mess. The recent rains caused some shortage in the circuits. The technicians became concerned and wanted to add a few more redundancy safety systems."

Tim stroked his hand over the green glass covering his grandfather's face. "Peaceful, isn't it? I come here often to visit and to think. Sometimes, just like you, I find myself talking to him."

Both men continued to look down at Tim Johnson, a.k.a. Theodore T. Thompson. Finally, John raised his head. "Evie has nothing to do with this crazy scheme. This was your grandfather's idea. Am I right, Timothy? Your grandfather really believed in this cryonics stuff and you were just holding his place in line, so to speak, until he came back."

"Well, as an abbreviated version, yes, but Evie and I went along with it. And yes, he does believe in this; so do I. Just before he was pronounced brain dead, we began the freezing process. He's not really dead. His life has just been temporarily suspended. No death certificate was ever recorded, his income tax has been filed yearly; for all practical and legal purposes he has never left us."

"Legally, you could be charged with murder, and those who helped, accomplices."

"We did it privately, John, just Evie and me. None of the commercial cryonics centers would do as my grandfather willed. She studied nursing to help out in her hospital in India, and I self-trained in the technical aspects. We used full body vitrification, replacing all body fluids with special solutions. It's quite complex but causes less tissue damage and fewer ice crystals. No one else was involved. Both

Evie and I felt that he had reached his physical end, regardless of what the brain monitors said. It was the only way to have a real chance of bringing him back. My grandfather and I believe that with the advances in medical science and the research that TTT is funding, it will only be a few years before he will be revived. When he is, he'll write what you didn't, the real book on Dubai."

"Is this what it's all about? That damn book? Timothy, you saw how Dubai is now, how the Nationals, the government and businessmen, went overboard to help us during the filming and promotion. What is there to gain by printing things that will just embarrass and hurt them?" John shook his head. "Why didn't he just publish those damn stories himself? He had plenty of time before he died, or froze, or whatever."

"He knew you had been working on the book. When it was published, he really enjoyed it, but just felt there was so much more to tell. Perhaps if he had been able to see the interest it received, the film, the notoriety, he may have dropped the idea."

"Look, if ceding to your grandfather's wish is that important to you, there are other ways to deliver on your promise without trading your identity for his. For God's sake, let the man go and get on with your life."

Even in the cool temperature of the chapel, Timothy's brow perspired. "He was everything to me: my father, my grandfather, my mentor. I'll do anything for him." His voice cracked and small droplets emerged from the corners of his eyes.

Like John would have done for his own son if he were distressed, he put his arms around Timothy and hugged him. "You know your grandfather in a paternal sense. I knew him as a friend and confidant. He was the biggest joker, the most colorful speaker, and the greatest conman ever. I know from experience that the last person he would ever want to hurt would be you, someone he loves.

"When I was a young man, he was a willing teacher, until he realized I wasn't cut out to be a part of the life he led. Once he discovered that, he did his best to protect me and keep me away from it. I truly believe that if he were here, he would feel the same about your future."

John took a deep breath. "You, Tim's grandson, and I, his friend, will write the book he wanted. When it comes time for his revival, re-birth, or whatever, we'll have a draft all done and we can work with him to rewrite, edit and publish it."

A smile broke over Timothy's anguished face. "I think my grandfather would like that."

Timothy and John latched hands, another shake, another deal, a binding agreement, just like the old days.

"Come on, let's go tell Evie. You have a life to live and I still have a press release to write."

Emerging into the bright daylight, John released the heavy wooden door. As designed, it slowly moved on its hinges, slamming tight against the doorjamb, sealing the room from the outside world. As Timothy and John walked towards the house, John paused and turned back towards the door. Beads of perspiration shimmered across his forehead. Weak-kneed, John placed both hands on Timothy's shoulders to balance himself.

"Are you all right, John? You look pale."

John raised his head and tilted his right ear toward the door. But the *haw, haw haw* John had heard emanating from the closed room was no longer audible.

Composing himself, John responded, "Yes, I'm fine," and they resumed their walk towards the house.

Just the wind blowing through the trees playing tricks.

Timmy's Release

The press release was simply the facts from Evie's story, checked and confirmed by TTT Group's legal department.

FOR IMMEDIATE RELEASE:
Joint Release by Arabian Authors Publishing Company (AAP) and TTT Group

AAP AND TTT GROUP CLARIFY FACTS REGARDING AUTHOR OF THE NOVEL, "THE DUKE OF DUBAI" AND THE MAIN CHARACTER IN THE NOVEL
Dubai, United Arab Emirates – October 9. 2006

APP and the TTT Group wish to clarify any confusion in the media regarding any statement made by John Peregrino on October 7, 2006 at the premiere party for the film, "The Duke of Dubai."

Mr. Peregrino, who published the book *The Duke of Dubai* under the pseudonym Lou Falconi, wished to reveal that the character of the Duke was based upon the actual life of Mr. Tim Johnson, who is now deceased. Mr. Peregrino collaborated with Tim Johnson on the stories told in the novel. However, Mr. Peregrino maintains that the stories are fictional.

Mr. Tim Johnson lived as a full-time expatriate in Dubai, United Arab Emirates from 1965 - 1980. Between the years 1980 – 1990, he was a partial resident traveling between his home in California and Dubai.

In 1990, Mr. Johnson's friends and associates in Dubai were falsely notified of his death. Simultaneously, Mr. Johnson and his life-long companion Evie DeSouza were married in California and legally changed their names to Theodore Timothy and Evie Thompson, and conducted business in California using their new names. The business they started became known as the TTT Group.

For medical and personal reasons, from 1990 until his death in 2003, Mr. Thompson (Tim Johnson) became a recluse, never leaving his estate in California. During the period of 1990 – 2000, Mrs. Thompson

---

(Evie DeSouza) acted as chairperson and CEO of the TTT Group on behalf of her husband.

In 2000, executing a complex ruse, Mr. Timothy Blanchard II, posing as Theodore Thompson, assumed the role of Chairman and CEO of the TTT Group and took on a very high public profile. The reasons for this deception are known only to the family, and all legal irregularities in relations to TTT Group to this date have been remedied.

Timothy Blanchard II is the grandson of Theodore T. Thompson (Tim Johnson). He was born on May 12, 1972, the son of Timothy Blanchard Sr. and Anna Rollings Blanchard. Timothy Blanchard Sr. was born in Bakersfield, California, September 3, 1952, and was the son of Dee Dee Blanchard, now deceased, and Mr. Theodore T. Thompson (Tim Johnson). Timothy Blanchard Sr. was killed in Vietnam on March 28, 1972.

Mr. Timothy Blanchard II remains the Chairman and CEO of the TTT Group under his own identity as grandson of Mr. Theodore Thompson (Tim Johnson).

– END –

DISCLAIMER AND FURTHER INFORMATION
Facts contained in this press release have been based upon public documents and verified by third parties. This does not preclude the chance that errors may occur. In such instances where information may be proven not to be as released in this document, neither Arabian Authors Publishing Company nor the TTT Group can be held liable.

Details of the particulars in this Press Release may be obtained by written requst to the contact person listed at the end of this release.

CONTACT:
Mr. Alistair Hastings
Arabian Authors Publishing Company
Voice Phone Number: +971-4-9683512
FAX Number: +971-4-9683510
Email Address: AH@Arabianauthors.com
Website URL   www.Arabianauthors.com

Epilogue

Tim Johnson still rests in his frozen sarcophagus, waiting for his return to humanity. His grandson's schedule as Chairman and CEO of TTT Group doesn't allow him to visit as often as he would like, but when he does, he sits for hours with his grandfather, just as if he were alive. When Evie is not in India, she makes a daily pilgrimage to see her husband. She says that she finds comfort in knowing he is there.

After my first encounter with my frozen friend I've visited only once. When leaving, I again had the same eerie audio experience and have never returned. I'm still not a believer, but I wouldn't be totally surprised when one day I answer the phone and the party on the other end says, "Hey, Falc, I've thawed. Let's play some poker, haw, haw, haw."

Luigi Falconi

Appendix I
A Brief History of Dubai and Bibliography

A Brief History
of Dubai

Research Paper for Lesson Plans with
Bibliography for Ninth Grade Students
Dubai Oil Company School — 1974
(revised 2006)

Prepared by
Luigi Falconi

The Arabian Peninsula

If you're like most Americans, you probably have no idea where the United Arab Emirates is, let alone Dubai. As a matter of fact, most people in Detroit don't know where Cleveland is, and people in Cleveland have no idea where Cleveland is. For some reason, Americans have developed some nationalistic excuse for geography ignorance.

War never seems to accomplish anything, but the First Gulf War and the US intervention in Iraq were a big help in teaching Americans about the geography of the Middle East. When I was in the US soon after the Gulf War and had to explain to someone where Dubai was, I'd ask people if they heard of Kuwait. CNN educated, as Americans are, they would inevitably say yes. I'd then explain that if you went south to Saudi Arabia, which was another familiar name, and made a left, you'd end up in the United Arab Emirates (UAE). That seemed to satisfy everyone.

Most of my friends and other people I talked to when I was home in the States had the traditional Western view of Arabs as a tribe of people who traveled around the desert on camels, lived in tents, and were always fighting one another. And they were all named Ab-Dul, or referred to in derogatory terms such as towel-heads, rag-heads or camel jockeys. This unfortunate stereotype isn't true. The majority of the men are named Mohammed, Hamed or Abdullah and they drive automobiles, like you and me, and live in very nice homes.

However, this wasn't always the case. The first Arabs were farmers and herders who, in the course of time, domesticated the camel and became masters of the desert, traveling, grazing and trading throughout the Arabian Peninsula with other *Bedouin*, as these nomads were called. They were not only respected by the settled peoples on the fringes of the desert, but were also regarded as superior for their sense of pride, dignity and above all, their freedom. They traveled on foot or by camel and they lived in camel hair tents, which were woven on primitive looms by the women of the tribes. Camels made life possible for these desert travelers. Camel milk offered nourishment; camel dung mixed with herbs was used to dress wounds. In a barren land where wood was scarce, dung was also dried and used as fuel for cooking fires. The camel could go days without water and at times of desperation, a thirsty *Bedou* would put his walking stick down his camel's throat and drink the water that was regurgitated. GROSS! Not if you're really thirsty it isn't. Most of all, the camel was a beast of burden, carrying loads of personal effects or goods for trade.

Each tribe was usually made up of an extended family, but other, non-blood members were assimilated for numerous reasons, and some tribes became quite large. Each had their *dirah,* which was the geographical area over which the tribe claimed water and grazing rights. Borders didn't exist until the twentieth century, when the awarding of oil concessions required the fixing of boundaries.

These *Bedouin* were concentrated in the Arabian Peninsula, which is an area between Europe/Asia (Eurasia) and Africa. The Arabian Peninsula is separated from these two surrounding land masses by two offshoots of the Indian Ocean—the Arabian Gulf, or Persian Gulf, depending on the map used, and the Red Sea. The Arabian Peninsula has always been a land bridge between the Indian Ocean and Mediterranean, and between the Far East and Europe.

Located about three-quarters of the way down the Western coast of the Arabian Gulf is a cluster of seven city-states comprised of Abu Dhabi, Dubai, Sharjah, Ajman, Umm Al Qaiwain, Ras Al Khaimah and Fujairah, now collectively called the United Arab Emirates. Their eastern border is the waters of the Gulf and the Western border is contiguous with the Rub' Al Khali desert, known as the "Empty Quarter."

Long before the UAE Federation was formed, the lands making up the country were tribally governed. Coastal areas from Sharjah north to Ras Al Khaimah and over the mountains to Fujairah on the Arabian Sea were controlled by the *Qawasim* tribe, while the vicinity inland was controlled by the *Bani Yas* and other tribes.

In the early 1600s, the Portuguese were the first Europeans to use the coast near Ras Al Khaimah as a base for protecting their trade routes to the riches of the East. They were never well tolerated by the coastal tribes who constantly harassed the Portuguese and made it difficult for them to control the area. By the end of that century the Portuguese had left the Gulf.

No sooner had one colonial power left than another, the British, arrived, looking for a safe passage for trade to India. In 1809 the British, concerned about the interruption of trade by what they considered as pirate attacks on ships belonging to the East India Company, attacked Ras Al Khaimah, destroying many of their vessels. This led to eventual British dominance over the area that became known as the Trucial States, a term derived from the British treaties in the area.

Understandably, views of history are in the mind of the historian. The present Ruler of the Emirate of Sharjah, Dr. Shaikh Sultan al Qassami, in his 1986 Ph.D. thesis titled *The Myth of Arab Piracy in the Gulf*, refutes the British version of history. He claims that the naval attacks were carried out by the British to control the Gulf and monopolize the trade routes from the East to Europe.

In 1820, peace treaties between the British and nine ruling Shaikhs of the Gulf tribes were signed. Later, in 1853, the Treaty of Perpetual Peace was penned with Great Britain, thus guaranteeing British influence in the future of the region. But it was the 1892 Treaty of Exclusivity, which prohibited the Arabs of the area from selling, ceding, or allowing any other country to occupy their territory, which gave the British colonial control of the Gulf's tribal shaikhdoms.

Between WWI and WWII, the British established a cable and wireless base in the area as a link in the communications route to India, and in 1932 the first British establishment was set up in what was known as Trucial Oman.

In 1937, Dubai Creek became a flying boat runway and a landing base was established. By this time, the presence of oil in the area became well known. England, concerned that other countries would seek interests in the petroleum wealth in the area, signed the first oil concession with Dubai in 1937.

The British influence in the area was predominant until the United Arab Emirates was formed in 1971. Even now, the UAE relies heavily on the British. It's quite intriguing how experience influences a person's preferences. Older generations of UAE Nationals who grew up with the British influence and the young UAE Nationals educated in England seem to have strong business and cultural ties to the United Kingdom. Within the last forty years, however, there have been a large number of nationals educated in the US. Because of this influence, and I believe that of television and the Internet, the new generations of UAE Nationals seem to prefer American culture. Just look at all the American fast food restaurants in the city.

Arabs of the Desert

The desert wanderers who migrated to the easier life by the sea and settled in the coastal areas of the Arabian Peninsula usually did so to escape their harsh existence in the desert. The Arabs of Dubai, as progeny of these desert tribes, were a tough and hearty people.

In the West, when we think of Arabs, we tend to consider anyone who is a native speaker of the Arabic language. This is like saying everyone who speaks English is British or American. Most foreigners who speak English as a second language have difficulty understanding the dialect of a US Southerner, and even more difficult are some of the dialects from the United Kingdom, home of the Queen's English. Arabic also varies in diction, enunciation and grammar throughout the countries of the Middle East. Although an Egyptian speaks Arabic, he will privately tell you he is a descendent of the Pharaohs. Like the Egyptian, the Lebanese may say his heritage is Phoenician or Mediterranean. Both deny any direct genealogy with the desert Arab whom many look down upon as the backward brother of the Arab race. Just as Arabic speakers from different Middle East countries cannot be stereotyped, the *Arabi Khaleeji* or Gulf Arabs also vary.

The tribal legacy of the Kuwaiti, the Qatari, the Saudi and the Emirati all differ. Of all the *Bedouin* Arabs who settled in the Gulf countries, the tribes from whom the national population of the Emirates descended seems to stand apart. The tribal Arab of the Emirates, and especially Dubai, has a special inbred charisma that envelops their personality. Perhaps it is because of the difficulty of life before oil, or maybe just a genetic trait bestowed upon them by their god, Allah, for relegating them to their difficult environment. Before settling in Abu Dhabi and later Dubai, these desert tribes lived the typical *Bedouin* life.

Religious faith to the *Bedou* was absolute, giving them a code for daily living as well as spiritual solace. In Islam, prayers were said five times a day, and Friday was always observed as the Muslim Sabbath. Time was a concept that had little significance. The only divisions of the day which mattered were the times for prayer, as determined by the position of the sun. During the holy month of Ramadaan—the Muslim month of fasting—no food or water was allowed to touch one's lips from sunup to sunset. Imagine doing this in the 120° summer sun.

There were no frontiers, no roads, no electricity, and no telephones. Forts and watchtowers dominated the skyline of the small towns and villages that did exist away from the coast.

Creature comforts were few. The date palm provided a staple food and also building material for homes. The palm-frond thatch was used for the sake of coolness and the rectangular homes were built on the dunes above the palm groves, with two or three lodges being enclosed by a high fence and inhabited by one family. Unlike the houses of the cities that had wind towers to supply natural air-conditioning for the Shaikhs and merchants, in the desert only the cool breezes gave relief. The palms were carefully spaced and well tended. They were planted along the salt-flats, close to steep-sided dunes, and in hollows in the sands. The groves were fenced in, and other fences were built along the dune-tops, to try to control the movement of the sands that could easily bury the trees. There was no other cultivation, probably because of the salt on the surface of the ground. Water was available, but it had to be hauled up from man-dug wells. The *Bedouin* owned some camels and a few donkeys and goats, and in the summer many of them went to Abu Dhabi to join the pearling fleet as divers.

Prior to the automobile, and even for a few years after they had been imported into the area, the camel was the major means of transport. Camels didn't get stuck, have flat tires, or have mechanical problems.

The only type of police or security force was the retinue of armed tribesmen maintained by each of the Shaikhs. Desert dwellers were usually always armed with a dagger, a rifle and bandoleer of ammunition. When visiting a town, men of tribal origin felt insecure without their weapons. Freud would probably try to say it was a male thing but for people living in the isolation of the Empty Quarter, town people were really outsiders, not to be trusted. However, the

Bedouin attitude to strangers was different when they were in their own environment.

Members of a tribe were always helpful to another. It was almost considered a crime not to aid one's brother. This Arab hospitality was a byword not only for fellow tribesmen but also for any desert traveler. Even the poor desert dweller practiced it. Today, this hospitality is still shown by the Nationals when you visit their home or hunting camps. Foreigners are treated with kindness and esteem. It would be unheard of to treat a guest with disrespect.

In the desert camps of the *Bedouin*, arrival of a newcomer would always be welcomed by an elaborate verbal greeting, then by a physical exchange. Sometimes it was the touching of the right hand which were held in contact during the salutations but without the pumping action of a Western handshake. Or it took the form of a "nose kiss," three brushing movements of the nose. This probably evolved into the cheek to cheek greeting that is commonly used now.

Food, water and milk were always offered to a visitor, even if it meant that the host or his family would go without. The guest was not expected to pay, but he did have to perform a service.

"*Shu Akbar*," what is the news, was the standard greeting to a visitor to a *Bedou's* camp. Without newspapers, radios or telephones, the remote desert relied upon news to be transmitted verbally, inevitably with embellishments and distortions. It was this visitor who was the bearer of news, and for the hospitality he received, he was expected to pass it on.

One topic of Arab culture that always draws attention is the discussion about homosexuality among the Arab men. Western expatriate kids, like adult expatriates, are not used to seeing hand-holding and cheek-kissing men in the streets and public places.

From the books I have read, it appears to be true that homosexuality is common among Arabs, especially in the towns, but no more so then in Western cultures. However it was very rare among the *Bedouin*, even though they, of all Arabs, have the most excuse for indulging in this practice, since they spend long months away from their women.

One of the most famous travelers Wilfred Thesiger, who knows more about the *Bedouin* than any other European, claimed that active homosexuality among the *Bedouin* was almost unknown. In his book

Arabian Sands, Thesiger says that only twice in five years did he ever hear his *Bedou* companions mention the subject. Once when staying in a town on the Trucial Coast, one of his guides, bin Kabina, pointed out two youths, one of whom was a slave, and said that they were used each night by the Shaikh's retainers. He evidently thought the practice both ridiculous and obscene. On the other occasion, another guide, bin al Kamam, described an execution, which he had watched in Saudi Arabia. The man had been sentenced to death for raping a boy. None of the *Bedou* showed the slightest sympathy for him.

Dubai

Archaeological excavations have established the existence of settlements in Dubai as far back as the third millennium B.C. With the Creek providing shelter, the sea an abundance of fish for consumption, and the availability of fresh water, it is likely that the area was inhabited continuously for well over a thousand years. For several hundred years it existed as a tiny fishing and pearling village of little importance.

During the late 1700s and early 1800s, more and more people were drawn from the difficult life of the interior to the commerce afforded by the pearling and fishing industries on the coast in villages like Dubai.

With the advent of the British seeking to control their trade route to India, the significance of these coastal villages became more meaningful, serving as a supply base, source of goods and safe ports. The first references to Dubai, or "Dubay and Dibai," as it originally appeared in Anglicized print, were in the records of British India in 1799, although it existed well before this date as a fishing village.

The settlement of Dubai assumed some importance with the migration of members of the Al Bu Falasah branch of the Bani Yas tribe from Abu Dhabi between 1818 and 1833. Abu Dhabi was an island city located about 125 miles south of Dubai. The Al Bu Falasah were led by Shaikh Obeid Bin Saeed, who died soon after settling in Dubai. Shaikh Maktoum Bin Butti assumed the leadership until his death from smallpox in 1852 while on a voyage to Oman. The present ruling family in Dubai descended from these rulers.

A veil of mystery surrounded the history of Dubai during the rest of the 19th century, with the most detailed accounts coming from biased records kept by the British administration in the Gulf. There was the natural cycle of competition, intrigue and power struggles between different sections of the ruling family. There was some fighting, although Dubai was spared the agony of violent successions.

One thing Dubai had going for it was a natural tidal inlet from the sea called a *Khor*, which separated the two main parts of the city, Dubai and Deira. For some reason, the *Khor* became known as the Creek. No one can explain how this metamorphous occurred, but I'll gamble that it had something to do with the Texas and Oklahoma oil workers. I'm sure they first called it a "crik" and then later gentrified it into "Creek." There may be some similarity between the word *Khor* and the word Creek, but there is no similarity between the bodies of water that they define. Geographically, the Dubai Creek was a tidal basin snaking about six miles through the heart of the city. The commercial areas of the city were located close to the mouth and midway up the inlet where the water was deep enough to allow the dhows to dock during high tide. Further up the Creek it became shallower and the water spread out into a lake. This lake area had no commercial use but was a rest and feed stop for flocks of migratory birds as they traveled north or south.

The Creek was first used by groups of fishermen who lived in the desert nearby. It later developed into the center of the pearl industry in Dubai. But the Creek's most important role was that a dhow could anchor and unload goods for transshipment overland to the West.

During the 1800s on the Persian side of the Gulf, a city called Lingeh was the dominant port for the east-west trade. It was a successful commercial center for two main reasons:

1. It was located near the Straits of Hormuz, the opening between the Gulf and the Indian Ocean—another location Americans learned from the TV coverage of the Iran-Iraq and Gulf wars—and,

2. Until 1874 it had been a tribally administered area; therefore, it had no taxes.

Dubai's opportunity for commercial prominence came with the decline of Lingeh. The Imperial Iranian Government took over the administration of Lingeh in 1902, and the Imperial Bank of Iran began to collect customs duties on behalf of the government. A law, which introduced very high import and export charges, drove away the prosperous trade from the Iranian coast.

Dubai, with its natural *Khor*, was geographically well placed to benefit from Lingeh's misfortune and also provided a tax-free, liberal commercial climate under Shaikh Maktoum Bin Hasher, who welcomed the merchants, craftsmen, traders and pearl divers. Under his rule, Dubai grew rapidly and was a regular port of call for dhows and steamers, making it the main commercial center on the coast. The population of Dubai doubled between 1908 and 1939 to a peak of twenty-thousand residents.

The city of Dubai continued to grow and became a melting pot with various nationalities and tribes living in different quarters of the city with exotic names usually associated with a tribe, family or geographical area. Shindagah, Al Ras, Bur Dubai, Bur Deira, Jumairah and Um Saqueem housed the Al Bu Falasah, who comprised the ruling family of Al Maktoum, and other families whose names have since become predominant in the local business community.

The *Bahama* quarter in the center of Bur Dubai on the Creek, accommodated the old market, called *Souk*. The Bahama area was named after the very first families that arrived in Dubai from Bahrain and other places in the Gulf, including Lingeh. Arabs from Iran shared this residential area as they spoke the same language and were involved in the same businesses. They were pearl dealers, dhow builders and blacksmiths.

The *Bastakiya* quarter became the home of immigrants from the district of Bastak in Fars near the port of Khamir and other Iranian provinces. They came at about the same time as the Bahama and Arabs from Iran or soon thereafter. Speaking Persian and specializing in trade, they built their houses close to the Creek where boats could be offloaded near the *souk*. They introduced the famous wind-towers or *al barajeel*, a unique architectural characteristic of the quarter, which was a tall square tower, built of coral and mortar like the houses. It was opened on all sides, which allowed cool breezes to be collected from any direction and guided into a downdraft that would enter a house or building to cool the interior.

Al Barajeel or Wind towers found in the old city Bastakiya Quarter of Dubai

Another quarter was named Souk Al Banian, inhabited by Hindus and other Indians who lived and worked next to the Dubai Souk. Until about 1955, Souk Al Banian had a big gate that was shut every evening and reopened the next morning. The Indians traded in perfumes, textiles and other merchandise, imported from India. Many were goldsmiths. Arabs traded their pearls at Indian ports and returned with foodstuffs, commodities and textiles. Dubai rulers and merchants encouraged Indian merchants to invest in the local trade, bringing their experience as businessmen.

The people of Dubai were a mixture of nationalities and religions, yet they lived and worked together and were all treated fairly by the ruling family. Their presence gave Dubai an international character even in those early days.

The Creek was the center of all activity in Dubai, providing port facilities for the variety of businesses located on its shores. The dhows used to anchor as close as possible to the merchants' sheds to unload their cargoes. Small boats carried the goods to the banks of the Creek and directly to the storehouses, located beside the Creek. Customs officers visited the merchants' stores for inspection and duty collection. The dhow building yards and the associated blacksmith workshops were also located near the Creek for the same reason, enabling them to launch their ships directly into the water.

When the pearling industry died out in the 1950s, Dubai's merchants began dealing in the gold trade to India. In those days the people of India were a sponge for gold. Mistrust in banks and the government led the vast population to put their wealth in a commodity that was an inflation hedge, had value in hard times and had liquidity – GOLD.

The country of Kuwait, which was in the upper part of the Gulf, had been the primary exporter of gold to India in the early 1950s. Once Kuwait discovered oil, their interest in gold exporting diminished, and Dubai took over as the main exporter.

The commercial-minded ruler of Dubai, Shaikh Saeed, looked with a blind eye on a trade that, to the Indian government, was illegal, but did not contravene Dubai laws. It was in fact a genuine re-export business.

The profits well outweighed the risk. The demand for gold in India at that time was about $200 million per year. The precious metal could be purchased for $35 per ounce in Dubai and sold for a three hundred percent profit in India.

The British Bank of the Middle East opened branches in Kuwait and in Dubai in 1946 and was a large importer and seller of gold, but on behalf of bankers from Dubai. The National Bank of Dubai and the First National City Bank of New York were also big importers of gold, while some merchants ordered their own gold directly from London.

When I expatriated to Dubai in the summer of 1974, five years after oil production started, the Creek was still the center of commercial activity, including the gold trade. Dubai was becoming even more cosmopolitan with the influx of Americans, British and other Europeans capitalizing on the oil boom, yet it still maintained some of its unique charm. The Creek had been dredged and widened to give it a distinguished hook shape, yet graceful dhows were still gliding in to unload goods from Iran, India and Africa and to take on new cargo for their return trip. With only one bridge, built in 1962, spanning the Creek, gaily painted boats called *Abra's* joined the divided town by ferrying shoppers and businessmen from one side to the other for the fare of seven cents, which, due to inflation, has since gone up to fourteen cents.

Tall wind-towers attached to the houses of the Shaikhs and merchants stood silhouetted against the skyline. In the few years just prior to my arrival, some tall buildings at least eight floors high had been added along the Creek. These buildings were considered very tall in 1973, but nothing compared to the 60 floor mega-skyscrapers in 2000.

The Father of Modern Dubai

Every country has someone who is given the title "Father of the Country." The U.S.A. has George Washington, and Dubai has Shaikh Rashid Bin Saeed Al Maktoum.

In the early days, Dubai had the physical location, the people with the crafts and the trading skills, and a history of economic tolerance and freedom, to make it a successful commercial center. But it wasn't until His Highness Shaikh Rashid succeeded his father,

Shaikh Saeed, as Ruler in 1958, that the real potential of Dubai as a commercial center was realized.

The progeny of a gentle father who relied upon simplicity and diplomacy rather than force to rule, and a strong-willed, business-savvy mother, Rashid would inherit the best qualities of both parents to become a strong ruler—intelligent, fair, resolute, wise and honest. During the twenty years that he served as regent to his father, Shaikh Rashid performed much of the governing.

Rashid's father, Shaikh Saeed, had to deal with militant opposition to his ruling authority, partially brought on by his relationship with the British and partially by the economic troubles of the day. Shaikh Saeed and his Bani Hasher branch of the tribe were often in militant opposition to some of the other families in the tribe who served in his elected *Majlis*, a type of city council. On one occasion in 1934, his opposition resulted in an attempt on his life. His position became exceedingly precarious until 1939, when he arranged a bit of Arab diplomacy, the marriage of his son to Shaikha Latifa Bint Hamdan, Al Nahyan, the daughter of a former Ruler of Abu Dhabi, and one of those groups that were giving him a difficult time. Royalty had been doing this for ages, so it wasn't a unique solution.

The political marriage turned out to be a bit of "shotgun wedding" diplomacy orchestrated by the groom himself, Shaikh Rashid, to consolidate his father's rule. As the story is told, on Shaikh Rashid's wedding day, the men and women of the Bani Hasher group boarded the *Abras* on the Dubai side of the Creek, and singing joyously, crossed to the Deira side of the Creek to celebrate the marriage. The celebrations were to be held near the home of the bride, in an area where many of the *Majlis* trouble makers lived.

Rifles and other weapons were hidden under the long white *dishdashah* of the men and the long black dresses of the women. When the boats landed on the shore, Shaikh Saeed, Shaikh Rashid and their supporters led an attack and captured the Customs House and other vital sites. At the wedding reception, they captured the majority of the opposition. Several leading members of the opposition families were killed and others exiled to Sharjah territory near the Dubai border, but the wedding still took place. This act solidified the position of Shaikh Saeed temporarily, but it would take another two years of fighting between the dissenting tribal members and supporters of Shaikh Saeed and Shaikh Rashid before the dispute ended in a settlement brokered by rulers of the other emirates.

Although this is the account that was told to us foreigners, the real facts are much different. History books on Dubai will tell a much more placid story, but not as much fun to teach.

Rashid was 46 years old when he took over as ruler in 1958. His years as Crown Prince under the guidance of his father, as well as his innate *Bedouin* senses made him a benevolent yet decisive leader, one with the vision to foresee the transition his country was facing, and the ability to meet the challenges of that transformation.

Life in the Arabian Desert was hard and challenging, requiring highly developed senses and skills no longer retained by the younger generations of Arabs living in a modern society. Shaikh Rashid was a part of that rootstock who grew up learning the ways of the *Bedouin*.

Oral history, passed down from generation to generation and so much relied upon by the illiterate *Bedouin*, led to a disciplined memory and Shaikh Rashid's was phenomenal. Pre-modern day Arabs recorded their history and traditions mentally and passed it on verbally. It was said that if you told Shaikh Rashid a fact such as saying that a construction job required 2,000 building blocks, and then five years later say that it took 2,500 blocks, Rashid would correct you and remind you of your previous statement.

Rashid enjoyed telling stories about his father's cunning. One of the favorites involved Dubai's neighbor, Sharjah. The British had a strong political influence as well as an airbase in Sharjah. Because, of this many Western companies shipped goods into the Sharjah Creek, rather than to Dubai. Shaikh Saeed knew that the rulers in the Gulf were concerned that too much Western influence would be bad for his people. Concerned about this loss of commerce, crafty Shaikh Saeed had an idea. Bringing several of his closest confidants in on his plan, he asked them to visit the Ruler of Sharjah. When they met the ruler, they told him how relieved the Ruler of Dubai was that the Western infidels, with their drinking and moral decadence, were no longer coming to Dubai to influence the young people with their bad habits. The Ruler of Sharjah became concerned. If his liberal neighbor Shaikh Saeed felt that way, then the foreigners would surely ruin Sharjah. Thinking that he was smarter than Saeed and concerned about protecting the culture of his people, the old Shaikh prohibited the British trading companies from using the Sharjah Creek, and they were forced to go back to Dubai.

Even before becoming ruler, Rashid, an accomplished equestrian, had a routine of making a morning tour of Dubai on horseback. Later he would make the inspection by automobile. During the building boom of the early 1970s, he was chauffeured around his Emirate every morning at 6:00 a.m., watching the progress of the construction. He could name every plot, the name of the person who owned the piece of land, and what was being built on it. In his *Majlis*, he would tell a guest, "Saleh, I saw your house today. It is going slow; you had better talk to your contractor."

Rashid was a tall lanky man, not handsome, but with a look that projected royalty. His long slim patrician nose and his tall, thin physique gave him a regal aura. I like to compare him to the majestic camel. At first glance it seems to be a rather unattractive creature. Upon closer inspection, you notice that the tall gangling animal walks with a slow royal stride, head held high, fluttering its long eyelashes. Coupled with his pouting and protruding mouth and uplifted nose, the animal's face takes on an almost majestic appearance. Its most important trait is that this creature has the ability to thrive and survive in the harshest conditions. That was Rashid, rough and uncommon at first appearance, but a benevolent Ruler whose people relied upon to survive and thrive.

Reminiscing about Rashid and trying to explain his imperial qualities, I recall childhood stories of the wise and judicious kings of old, mostly biblical kings, such as Solomon. From stories about these kings you learn it took a special intelligence and sensitivity to be a wise and just monarch, and there was a difference between authentic royalty and a man who was just a king by title only. Many men have been kings, but few have had the wisdom of Solomon. In this modern age with few kings in the world to draw from, I believe that Shaikh Rashid is in the same class as Solomon.

One of many examples of his wisdom was exhibited in the early '70s when several of Shaikh Rashid's tribesmen came to complain that he, Rashid, was selling their country to foreigners. This was at a time when it was an unofficial rule not to sell land to non-Dubai Nationals. In this early incident, Rashid had sold a piece of property to a man from Kuwait. Upon hearing of this transaction, a group of tribesmen came to Rashid in his open *Majlis*, a place where all subjects and visitors could come to petition the ruler and listen to his decisions, as well as a social gathering place for residents.

"Why do you sell our land to these foreigners?" they asked.

In his non-condescending manner, the ruler listened intently to their complaints. With all eyes on Rashid, he summoned his Chief of Police. In a loud voice so all present could hear, he said, "Colonel Abdulla, please put out an order to all airports and borders that they are to watch when Mohammed the Kuwaiti leaves the country. If he is carrying the piece of land that I sold him, he is to be stopped and prevented from taking it out of the country."

With that he looked at his petitioners and smiled, while the men in the *Majlis* who were witness to this discussion, burst out laughing. The complaining subjects, realizing their folly, also smiled and took their leave.

Property ownership in the Emirates has since opened up to allow non-Arabs to purchase property. With oil revenues getting smaller every year, the resulting real estate boom has been great for Dubai's economy.

Wilfred Thesiger wrote in *Arabian Sands* that the *Bedouin* had a very fatalistic attitude on life and lived as if there was no future. From examples I've seen, I tend to disagree with this observation. I believe that for the *Bedou*, born into desert hardship, planning for the future was a sixth sense that seemed to be coupled with the ability to trade and barter.

It was this rare extra sense that gave Rashid an edge when deciding on major projects for Dubai's future. He knew that the source of the country's wealth, oil, was a commodity that would not last forever and could not be depended on to support future generations. His goal was to make Dubai self sufficient once the petroleum resources dried up.

With the assistance of his trusted aides, Rashid planned to thrust his country into the 21st century, making it a modern business and commercial center. Rashid would come up with the concept, and then relied upon his assistants to work out the technicalities. One of his most imaginative and energetic projects was building the world's largest manmade port, cut out from the desert coastline of Jebel Ali.

This project cost over three billion dollars and was considered a construction wonder of the world. In 1985, the ruler established the first Duty Free Zone in the Gulf in the new port. The story that circulated at the time was that the port may have become a major naval base for the US Navy had not the UAE Federal Government objected to Shaikh Rashid's plan.

Under Shaikh Rashid's directive, Dubai built an aluminum smelter and gas processing plant. People scoffed and said that these projects would never be successful, but Rashid went forward, only to have them completed in time to reap the economic benefits of changes in the world of supply and demand. The sale price of propane, butane and condensate gas produced by the Dubai Natural Gas Company reached its peak just after the gas plant was finished, allowing its $700 million cost to be paid in three, rather than seven years. When Rashid built the Dubai Dry Dock, it was known as a "White Elephant" or "Rashid's Folly." The year after its completion the Iran-Iraq war broke out and the dry dock boomed. Ships from both countries, damaged as a result of the war, were heading to Dubai for repairs. It was almost as if Shaikh Rashid could predict the future.

Besides the building of many industrial projects, the decade of the '70s saw development of its infrastructure such as roads, utilities and an expanded airport. With this came a boom in civil construction with the building of a large number of office structures and modern housing developments. The 36-floor Dubai World Trade Center and adjacent Hilton Hotel became the center for businesses resident in the country, and for visiting businessmen. In the early days many a deal was cut in that building. Since the building boom of the late 1990s the Trade Center and surrounding area became known to the Nationals as "little Manhattan" and is still the business center for major companies in the Emirate.

Many of the Shaikh Rashid's favored retinue benefited immensely from this boom, especially those people who had proven themselves as honest and trustworthy— "doers," not talkers. Most of the early government and royal family contracts were not put out to tender but awarded by Rashid to his followers. But he was fair and was inclined to spread the opportunity and wealth. In some cases, the wealth never followed the opportunity, as Rashid set the price on a contract, which could prove to be below the actual cost of what it took to complete the project. Many contractors took a loss rather than go back to the ruler to ask for more money, as they knew that there would be bigger and better projects later that would put them in the black. A number of the small contractors of that era have since evolved into family conglomerates that could rival most *Fortune 500* companies.

When oil was discovered in Dubai in 1966, Rashid put his most trusted advisor in charge of the Petroleum Office, a job, and an organization, that would become the most important in Dubai. Dubai's production of 330,000 barrels of oil per day in the early 1970s was small compared to giants like neighbors Saudi Arabia, Kuwait and even the Emirate of Abu Dhabi. Rashid's luck, or fate of the divine, seemed to be on his side, and in 1973 the Egyptian - Israeli War led to the OPEC countries banding together to raise the price of oil seventy percent. At $40 per barrel Dubai had a yearly income of over four billion dollars per year, more than enough for the projects Rashid envisioned and carried out.

The title "Merchant Prince" was an appropriate one for Shaikh Rashid. He not only governed what is called a "City of Merchants," he encouraged financial institutions to locate in Dubai to participate in its development, and by 1971, there were seven major banks. The draw of getting some of that oil revenue as deposits was a big incentive.

Like his wise grandfather and father before him, Shaikh Rashid was tolerant of the differences between races, cultures, religious beliefs and political bearings. He embraced everyone who wished to live in Dubai as long as they contributed to the development of the country as a merchant, an artisan, an engineer or even as a laborer. But he would not tolerate foreign politics or racial discord to be practiced by his guests.

Although he was a good Sunni Muslim, he felt enough confidence in himself and his religion to allow the establishment of Christian churches and places for other religions to pray and practice their rituals. Shaikh Rashid even donated land to different religious sects on which to build their houses of worship. In the case of the Catholic Church, he paid for the construction of the foundation, and his wife, Shaikha Latifa, paid to furnish the church. Shaikh Rashid attended the opening of the Roman Catholic Church in Dubai. A local businessman told me that Rashid had once said that "a man's religion is between him and his God, and a man's finances is between him and his banker, and no one else has any business being involved." This open-mindedness is what has made Dubai into one of the most commercially, religiously and intellectually tolerant and progressive cosmopolitan cities in the world.

Unlike Kuwait, Saudi Arabia and other countries in the Middle East, Dubai is tolerant of the habits of other cultures, and Dubai's hotels have bars, discos, and private clubs that cater to non-Muslim foreigner's taste for alcohol. There is more nightlife in Dubai than most major US cities.

Education was also a priority with Shaikh Rashid. The number of schools and students in Dubai increased dramatically because of his financial support and encouragement to his young subjects to get an education in order to help lead the future of their country. Although Rashid himself had little formal education and was known to own only a few books, he started the first public library in Dubai in 1963.

Also unlike other countries in the area, women are considered to be an important part of society and are encouraged to obtain an education, even at the university level. Women of Dubai hold important positions in the public as well as private sectors. Many people are surprised when they arrive at the Dubai airport and are greeted by female immigration officers. There is no discrimination for local or foreign women, but it is not unusual to pull up at a traffic light next to a car being driven by a local lady wearing a *burka* over her eyes and face. How the hell they can see where they're going is beyond me.

In fifteen short years Shaikh Rashid and his intimate confidants made Dubai into a modern city. The ruler's advisors may have become rich riding on Rashid's dreams, but Rashid's vision would not have materialized into reality without these assistants doing the "hands on" part of the task. Shaikh Rashid knew what the oil wealth could do for his people and had the foresight to plan, but what happened to Dubai after his death in 1990 was even beyond his imagination.

Modern Dubai—1990-2006

The first five years after Shaikh Rashid's death in 1990 appear to have been a period of planning. Shaikh Rashid's oldest son, Shaikh Maktoum was the recognized Ruler, but once Shaikh Mohammed Bin Rashid Al Maktoum was named Crown Prince in 1995 there was no stopping Dubai.

The Maktoum family immediately began to make Dubai one of the most exciting cities in the world. With the introduction of e-commerce and the rapid technological development of recent years, Dubai leads the way in the practice of "cluster economics," by establishing Dubai Internet City in October 2000, Dubai Media City in January 2001 and later Dubai Healthcare City, amongst others. Together with Knowledge Village, they make up the Dubai Technology, E- Commerce and Media Free Zone, a central feature of the plans for Dubai's future. Practicing what they promote, the Dubai's e-government portal opened in October 2001, giving Dubai the world's first fully online government.

With the opening in February 2002 of the Dubai International Financial Center, Dubai has moved into the world of international finance as a bridge between East and West for financial services for all international markets, 24 hours a day, 7 days a week.

Dubai International Airport is one of the fastest growing airports in the world. Emirates Airlines project that they will bring 13 million visitors to Dubai by 2010. In 2001, the state-of-the-art Shaikh Rashid Terminal opened to accommodate the increase in passengers. Construction on another new terminal commenced in 2004.

In 2001, the Dubai Department of Tourism and Commerce Marketing (DTCM) stated that Dubai's tourism growth was the largest in the world. In 2003, there was a 35 % increase in tourists visiting Dubai, for a total of over 5 million. The objective of the Dubai government is to have 15 million tourists per year by 2010.

The Maktoum brothers have introduced many initiatives to attract more visitors to Dubai, the most famous of which is the Shopping Festival. Recent leisure and cultural programs include world class music concerts, theater, cinema, and sporting events.

As the sporting capital of the Middle East, Dubai sponsors major international events such as the Dubai Tennis Open and the Dubai

Desert Classic golf tournament. However the richest horse race in the world, the Dubai World Cup, is the crowning sporting accomplishment.

To cater to business visitors and tourists, Dubai has built some of the most architecturally remarkable office buildings and hotels in the world. "Little Manhattan," the strip of offices buildings on the Shaikh Zayed Road, offers one of the most dynamic skylines imaginable, starting with the Emirates Towers and World Trade Center, south to the man-made island just off the shore of Jumairah, where the world's tallest hotel, the Burj Al Arab, stands. This building, built to resemble the sail of a traditional Arabian dhow, is the centerpiece of Dubai's tourism industry, offering the most luxurious accommodation imaginable.

The architects have gone wild in Dubai: a dhow-shaped building, one shaped like a ship at the Dubai port, the Emirates Airlines training center looks like an airplane. Dubai is one of the few places in the world where architects can be creative. Owners don't care how many feet of rental space they have in their building; they just want exotic designs. There are some monstrosities, but they've also built some beauties, and they did try to save some of the old cultural sites.

Real estate development is at the heart of modern Dubai's post-oil strategy. It appears that it was designed to get expatriate residents committed to Dubai by owning homes and to entice the "beautiful people" who live in warm climates during the cold winters of Europe and North America to invest. Projects such as the three Palm islands, man-made islands in the shape of palm trees, offer additional coastal homes to foreigners and locals. Another islands project called the World is a series of islands shaped like the continents of the world. The U.S.A. is still available, if you have a few million dollars spare cash.

Since Shaikh Rashid's death in 1990, his sons, Shaikhs Maktoum, Hamdan, Mohammed and Ahmed, have carried his dreams forward. Of the four sons, it appears that Mohammed has inherited his father's *Bedouin* skills and vision. Having a penchant for writing poetry, long distance horse racing and many other well-rounded cultural and athletic interests, he is truly an Arabian Renaissance man. As the Crown Prince of Dubai, Shaikh Mohammed was instrumental in directing the country's development. Having already reached his father's goal of making Dubai the commercial center of the Middle East, he has diverted his efforts into another direction to insure the economic future of the country. Dubai has the sun, sand and beautiful blue sea craved by tourists, and Mohammed knows that development of tourism as an alternative income to the country's dwindling oil revenue is not only desirable but also a necessity. Dubai has progressed from a desert fishing village to a small trading town to a world class city and tourist destination in an unbelievably short period of time.

On January 4ᵗʰ 2006, Shaikh Mohammed became the Ruler of Dubai following the untimely death of his brother Shaikh Maktoum bin Rashid Al Maktoum, who succeeded his father, Shaikh Rashid. The day after assuming his role as Ruler, Shaikh Mohammed was elected Vice President of the UAE and appointed Prime Minister.

What Shaikh Mohammed has done for Dubai during his tenure as Crown Prince is only a small part of what he intends to do. His recently published book, *My Vision - Challenges in the Race for Excellence*, gives some wonderful insight into the strategy that he used to go from an Emirate with diminishing oil revenues to a multitude of cluster economic developments. Shaikh Mohammed's plans for the future are even more dynamic

Writer's Note—Reviewing and updating this paper originally researched and written over thirty years ago, I have come to the conclusion that I have been here too long, and I'm not sure I can handle the future Dubai. Change came at a breathtaking pace, not just the technology but the physical changes. New buildings, agricultural projects in the desert, landscaping of the towns and highways, sand dunes leveled and the coastline reshaped, and international airports capable of handling millions of passengers have all come about in just one generation. The Arab has replaced his rifle and bandoleers with the cell phone, his camel for a luxury car, and desert heat with air-conditioning. I have read that people in the West are going through technology-stress syndrome because of the fast pace of the development of electronic technology. Just imagine the stress the citizens and the long-term foreign residents of Dubai are experiencing. Not only must they deal with the anxiety of coping with the changes in technology, but also the stress of seeing their physical surroundings transformed on almost a daily basis. Even more stressful is dealing with the constant challenge to their cultural and religious norms by satellite television, the internet and the foreign tourists who come with little or no concept of Islam and Arab culture. Now, that's stress.

Bibliography

Bibliography for Research Paper for
Lesson Plans for 9th Grade Students
Dubai Oil Company School — 1974 (revised 2006)

**Aesthetics and Rituals in the United Arab Emirates: the
Anthropology of Food and Personal Adornment Among
Arabian Women**
Aida S. Kanafani
Published by the American University of Beirut
Beirut, 1983

Arabian Sands
Wilfred Thesiger
Published by Penguin Books Ltd., 1976
First Edition 1959

Dubai
Robin Moore
Published by Doubleday
First Edition 1976

The Dubai Handbook
Dr. Erhard F. Gabriel, Institute for Applied Economic Geography
Published by the Dubai Petroleum Company, 1987

**The End of Empire in the Middle East: Britain's
Relinquishment of Power in Her Last Three Arab Dependencies**
Glen Balfour-Paul
Published by Cambridge University Press; New Ed 1994

The Father of Dubai
Shaikh Rashid Bin Saeed Al Maktoum
Graeme Wilson
Published by Media Prima
Dubai, 1999

A Hundred Million Dollars a Day
Michael Field
Published by Sidgewick and Jackson
London, 1975

Lonely Planet Dubai Encounter
Lara Dunston and Terry Carter
Published by Lonely Planet Publications; 4th edition 2006

The Making of the Modern Gulf States
Rosemarie Zahlan
Published by Ithaca Press
New York, Rev. 1999

The Myth of Arab Piracy in the Gulf
HRH Shaikh Sultan Al Qassami, Ph.D. Thesis
Published by Croom, Helm
London, First Publication, 1986
Second Edition, Routledge, 1988

The Origins of the UAE
Rosemarie Said Zahlan
Published by St. Martin's Press
New York, 1978

Rashid's Legacy
The Genesis of the Maktoum Family and the History of Dubai
Graeme Wilson
Published by Media Prima
Dubai, 2006

Sand to Silicon: Achieving Rapid Growth Lessons from Dubai
Jeffrey Sampler and Saeb Eigner
Published by Profile Books 2003

The Seven Shaikhdoms
Ronald Codrai,
Published by Stacey International
Dubai, 1990

Shaikhdoms of Eastern Arabia
Peter Lienhardt
Published by Palgrave Macmillan 2001

Tears on the Sand
Maryam Mohammed
Published by Inkwater Press 2006

My Vision - Challenges in the Race for Excellence
Shaikh Mohammed Bin Rashed Al Maktoum
Published Motivate Publishing, Dubai and the Arab Institute for
Research and Publication, Beirut, 2006

The UAE: A Modern History
Mohammed Morsey Abdulla
Published by Croon, Helm
London, 1978

www.sheikhmohammed.co.ae

Appendix II
Glossary of
Arabic Words and Phrases

Glossary of Arabic Words and Phrases
Phonetically Translated to English

Abaayah— A black robe which covers the clothing, worn by an Arab woman when in public.

Abra— Gaily painted boats used as water taxis in Dubai

Abou— The Arabic word meaning "father of"

Al— The Arabic article "the"

Barasti— A reed used to make houses, fences, boats and other constructions

Barajeel— A unique tall square tower built of coral and mortar, designed to catch breezes to cool houses

Baksheesh— The Arabic word which means "gratuity or tip." In some cases it used to describe a bribe or pay off

Bedou— The Arabic word for individual nomads who move around with grazing animals

Bedouin— The Arabic word for groups or tribes of Bedou

Bin— The Arabic word meaning "son of"

Bint— The Arabic word meaning "daughter of"

Burka— A black fabric mask which covers the top half of the face, worn by some Arab women when they are in public.

Dhow— A traditional Arab ship made of wood and powered by motors or sail or both

Dishdashah—A white robe worn by Arab men in the Arabian Gulf and Saudi Arabia

Deerah— The geographical area over which a tribe claimed water and grazing rights

Djambia— The traditional curved knife of the Yemeni. In Oman it is called a Khanjar. The Asib is the J-shaped dagger commonly carried, while the Thuma is only carried by the religious upper classes

Dukhaan— The Arabic word meaning "black" or "smoke"

Eid— Muslim festivals. One follows Ramadaan and another follows the Muslim Pilgrimage to Mecca

Falaj— A system of channels or aqueducts to carry water

Faloos – The Arabic word for "money"

Foutah— The embroidered skirt or body wrap, worn by some Yemen and Omani men

Ghutra— A cloth headdress worn by Arab men in the Arabian Gulf and Saudi Arabia

Haraam— Something that is forbidden under the laws of Islam

Hegaal— The black rope-like lash used to hold the ghutra in place.

Imshii— The Arabic command "to walk or leave"

Jebal— The Arabic word for "mountain"

Jebali—	Term used to describe a mountain person of the Dhofar region of Oman and the Southern border mountain region of Yemen
Jinn—	A spirit or ghost
Kaabah—	The House of God of the Muslims, located in the holy city of Mecca
Kam—	The Arabic word meaning "how much"
Khaleej—	The Arabic word meaning Gulf, referring to the Arabian Gulf
Khezaam—	A small peg with a string attached placed in a camel's nose to steer the animal
Khor—	The Arabic word that refers to a natural inlet from the sea. The word has been Anglicized into Creek
Khorj—	The Arabic word for a camel saddle
Khanjar—	The traditional curved knife of the Oman. In Yemen it is called a djambia
La—	The Arabic word for "no"
Mafraj—	The highest and most pleasant room in the multi-level Yemen house
Majlis—	The Arabic word for a room where Arabs gather socially. Also means a type of city council
Nakhuda—	The captain of a dhow
Oudh—	The Arabic word for "frankincense" or other incense. Also the name of a musical instrument similar to a six-string guitar but with an oval shaped body, much like a lute

Qaat— A green leaf narcotic chewed by the Yemenis

Ramadaan— The Muslim holy month during which everyone must abstain from food and drink from the first light at dawn to sunset

Raas— The Arabic word for "head"

Rassan— The harness which connects the reins to the Khezaam in a camel's nose

Ruboul— The medicine chant used by the Jebalis to drive out the evil spirit from the body of a sick person

Sadeeki— The Arabic word meaning "my friend"

Sheeshah— The Arab water pipe for smoking regular or flavored tobacco called "hubbly bubbly" or "Hooka" in the West

Shihuh— A mountain tribe who live in the Oman's Musandam Peninsula. They are considered to be wild men by the desert tribes

Souk— The Arabic word for "market" or "bazaar"

Taakal— The Arabic verb meaning "to eat"

Tablah— A type of drum much like a bongo drum. The head is usually covered in goat or other animal skin

Taruuh— The Arabic command "to go"

Thamaaniin— The Arabic word for the number 80

Wadi— Mountain passes which carry water from the mountains to the sea during the rainy season, used as passage routes during the dry season

Wagh— The Arabic word for "face"

Wastah— A term to describe assistance and influence

Yella— The Arabic word meaning "Let's go"

Yumn— The Arabic word meaning "blessing" and "prosperity"

Arabic Phrases Used in *The Duke*

Al hamdu lillaah— "Praise be to God"

As-salaamu aleekum— "Peace be upon you"

Wa Aleekum is-salaam— "And peace be upon you." Used as a reply to **As-salaamu aleekum.**

Ahlan wa sahlan— "Welcome"

Fursah saeeda — "Pleased to meet you." The literal translation is "happy opportunity"

Mudeer Al Madrassah— The Arabic word "Mudeer" means "head" or "boss," and "Madrassah" means "school." Together they mean "Head of the School" or "principal"

Shu Akbar— "What is the news?" This is a standard way to begin a conversation, or used as a greeting.

The symbol for the **Arabic letter t or ta**

ت

Arabic *Al Dukhaan Wag*

ال دخان وجه

Admirality chart words meaning "The Smoky Face"

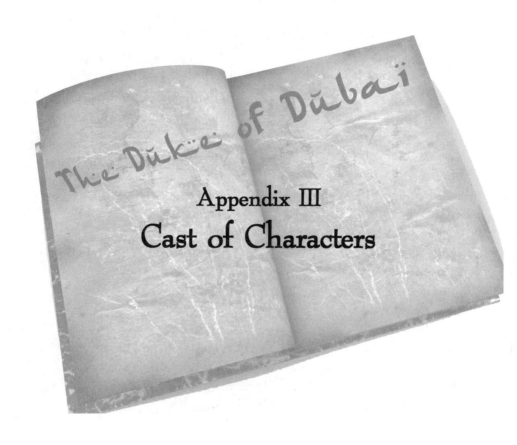

Appendix III
Cast of Characters

Characters

Tim Johnson	**Main character, known as the Duke and later Theodore T. Thompson**
Evie DeSouza	Tim's girlfriend and later wife
Dee Dee Johnson (Blanchard)	Tim's ex-wife
Timothy Blanchard, Sr.	Tim's son
Anna Rollings Blanchard	Tim Blanchard's wife
Timothy Blanchard II	Tim's grandson
Luigi (Lou) Falconi (pseudonym)	**Writer-Character**
John Peregrino	Real author of *The Duke*
Marie Peregrino	John's wife
Marie Falconi	Lou's wife
Josh & Nellie Sampson	Friends of the Falconi's
Billy Sampson	Josh & Nellie's son
Matt Lenz	Friend
Raymundo Ramund	Friend
Leroy Houston	Friend
Ashok	Leroy's houseboy
Steve and Lulu Jefferies	Friends of the Falconi's
Del, Kevin, Karen, Ann	Friends of the Falconi's
Maggie Straight	Secretary to Lou Falconi
Dr. Ried Thornton	School psychologist
Sal Rains	Pilot/guitarist
Alma Fahad	Kindergarten teacher
Alistair Hastings	Publisher
Frankie Focaccia	**Lou's friend**
Joanne	Frankie's wife
Fabio (Flatface)	Frankie's uncle
Rosa	Fabio's (Flatface) wife/ Frankie's aunt

Stella	Flatface's girlfriend
Salvatore	Frankie's dad
Sofia	Frankie's mom
Rocky (Rocco)	Frankie's brother
Nicholas Nicandro (NN)	Frankie's godfather
Young Nicky	NN's son
Iskar Tandoody	Tim's partner/Bin Jabir's assistant
Majid Bin Jabir	Businessman and Director of the Energy Office
Abdul	Majid's Turkish guard
Dodi Bin Din	Young friend of Shaikh Mohammed
Sal Kumoyu	Kenyan Sinatra Singer
Earl Scrudds	President of COC
Pat Riley	COC Government Relations Manager
Brandon Davidson	Chairman of J.R. Dumont
Ed Stroller	VP of J.R. Dumont
Flick Marrin	Secretary at J.R. Dumont
Halib Haider	Manager of Abdulla catering
Rick Roberts	Mgr. Kuwait/American Drilling
May Jamieson	Mom with sweet Southern drawl
Darlene Thompson	Mom who Iskar patted on butt
Deepali	Supermarket Clerk
Gopal	Supermarket Clerk
Pierre	Napoleon fish
Colette	Club Med Dive Instructor
Dr. Frenchie	Club Med Diving Doctor
Abdul	Wadi Arab
Sam	Musandam Shihuh tribesman

Captain John	Captain of "Puss & Hoots"
Antonio	Crewman on "Puss & Hoots"
Saju	Crewman on "Puss & Hoots"
Saleem	Crewman on Bertram boat
Veloo	Crewman on Bertram boat
Scotty La Rouche	Legendary Australian oilman
Duffy La Rouche	Oldest son of Scotty La Rouche
Maccie La Rouche	Youngest son of Scotty La Rouche
Sultan Boutie	Ruler of Oman
Shaikh Raisee Boutie	Oman Shaikh
Shaikh Hamed Tarid	Village leader in Yemen
Colonel Saeed	Oman Military Colonel
Mustafa	Colonel Saeed's associate
Terry Desjardin	Boat Burner

Shaikh Rashid Bin Saeed Al Maktoum
     "Deceased" Ruler of Dubai 1958 - 1990

Shaikh Maktoum Bin Rashid Al Maktoum
     "Deceased" Ruler of Dubai 1990 - 2006

Shaikh Mohammed Bin Rashid Al Maktoum
     Ruler of Dubai 2006 - this printing

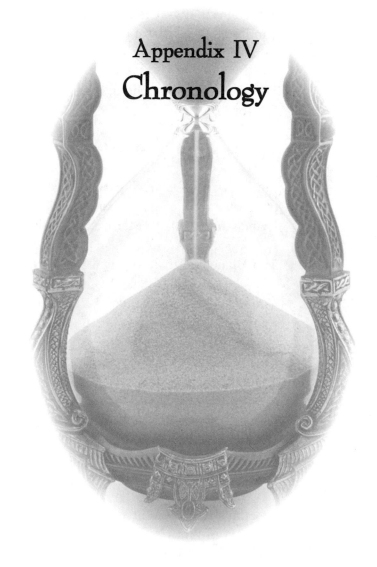

Appendix IV
Chronology

Chronology

August 1931	Tim Johnson (Duke) born in Washington D.C.
June 1951	Tim Johnson marries Dee Dee Blanchard in Los Angeles
February 1952	Tim Johnson divorces Dee Dee Tim heads to Northern California to work in the oilfields
September 1952	Tim's son, Tim Blanchard, born in California
July 1965	Tim Johnson arrives in Dubai
August 1968	Tim's ex-wife Dee Dee Blanchard dies of an overdose. Tim son, Tim Blanchard, enlists in Marines at age 16
June 1971	Tim Blanchard marries Anna Rollings
October 1971	Tim Blanchard starts second Vietnam tour
March 28, 1972	Tim Blanchard killed by sniper in Vietnam
May 12, 1972	Tim's Blanchard son, Tim Blanchard II (Duke's grandson), born in California to Anna Rollings Blanchard
July 1974	Lou Falconi arrives in Dubai
August 1974	Falconi's first encounter with Tim Johnson in Pinky's Supermarket

September 1974	Dinner at Pat Riley's home
September 1974	Falconi meets Tim & Iskar – Bustan Hotel
December 1974	Salvage Operation – just before Christmas vacation
March 1975	Poker at Leroy's
March 1975	Camel races
April 1975	Musandam dive trip & Shihuh Sam
September 1975	School Orientation, visit by Shaikh Rashid Bin Saeed Al Maktoum
September 1975	Meet Shaikh Raisee Boutie
November 1975	Yemen trip
November 1975	Duke's heart attack
December 2, 1975	Signing of Oman Oil concession
December 1975	Duke's first surgery
February 1976	Seismic in Musandam and drilling of the first oil well
February 1976 September 1976	Tim Returns from by-pass surgery Drilling of the second oil well in Musandam
November 1976	Duke's second surgery in the U.S.A.

December 1976	One year after Oil concession signed
December 31, 1976	New Years Eve in the desert— Focaccia letters & invitation to Egypt
April 1977	Egypt Dive Trip
May 1977	Tim returns from U.S.A. after 6 months recovering from surgery
May 1977	Lou leaves education and takes Tim's offer as partner in T&J
August 16, 1977	Elvis Dies
September 1978	Lou takes job with Jebel Ali Gas Company
End of 1980	Duke starts having medical problems and begins spending time between California and Dubai.
Early 1982	The Duke's grandson, Tim Blanchard II, and mother Anna Rollings Blanchard, come to live with Duke and Evie
Throughout 1988	Lou interviews Duke – stories for *Secrets of a Shaikhdom.*
November 1988	Duke has open heart surgery in Los Angeles
January 1990	Anna Rollings Blanchard, mother of Tim's grandson, dies
January 1990	Shaikh Rashid Bin Saeed Al Maktoum, Ruler of Dubai dies

January 1990	Duke stages death and completes identity change to Theodore T. Thompson. Lou starts to write book.
June 1994	Timothy Blanchard II graduates from College
June 1996	Timothy Blanchard II receives MBS from Stanford
June 1998	Timothy Blanchard II awarded Law degree from Yale
July 1998	Timothy Blanchard II joins TTT Group of companies
December 1999	Timothy Blanchard II leaves TTT Group employment
April 2000	Timothy Blanchard II assumes identity of Theodore T. Thompson (Tim Johnson) and resumes positions of Chairman and CEO of TTT Group
March 2003	The novel *The Duke of Dubai* is published
May 2003	The Duke (Tim Johnson) dies
October 2006	Movie *The Duke of Dubai* is made

For More Information visit

www.TheDukeofDubai.com

Credits

Arabic Word Translations: Amir Marcos, Dubai based translator
Pirate Map: Steven Chambers, Dubai Artist
Redhead and Shaikh Photo: Contributed by William Stimpson
Yemen Photo: Jorge Tutor www.jorgetutor.com
Writing in Arabic©David Snyder: United States
Hourglass Halfway© Brent Hathaway: United States
Nubian Village©Franck Camhi: France
Vintage Book©Maksym Yemelyanov, Ukraine
Palm Island Aerial Photo: Rights from MAPS Geosystems, Sharjah, UAE
Dubai 1974 Aerial Photo: Rights from MAPS Geosystems, Sharjah, UAE
Dubai 2006 Aerial Photo: Rights from MAPS Geosystems, Sharjah, UAE